The BloodStone Legacy: Damnation

V.E. Huntley

Published in the United States by V.E. Huntley

The Cataloging-in-Publication Data is on file at the Library of Congress

Paperback ISBN 979-8-9907982-1-2

Hardcover ISBN 979-8-9907982-4-3

ebook ISBN 979-8-9907982-0-5

Book Design by V.E. Huntley

Book Cover Design by 100 Covers

First Edition 2024

Printed in the United States of America

To Chris

For always supporting my sometimes crazy dreams

I'd Like to Thank the Following People

- My husband, Chris: Your love, support, and belief in me and my vampire obsession is why this book is not still sitting unfinished on my computer.

- My Parents: Neither one of you lived long enough to see this day, but your love made me who I am today. Your unwavering belief in me and my dreams, even when you thought I didn't have a real job, meant the world to me. I know you're looking down on me and saying, "It's about freaking time."

- Elle W. Silver: There are no words that can adequately express my gratitude for you coming into my life. You came to me as a beta reader. After getting your feedback, I begged you to be my editor, and you thankfully agreed. This book wouldn't be what it is today without your enthusiasm and guidance. You get Aden and Ellie better than anyone else.

- Jodi Thompson: Even though vampires weren't your thing, you helped me in my early stages of writing with invaluable feedback and ideas, recognizing the broken, complex, and intricate character Aden was. I will always be grateful for your continued support and enthusiasm.

- Bram Stoker: Your story haunted my childhood nights. If it wasn't for you, I would have been able to sleep with my light off. Your Dracula scared the crap out of me but also ignited my fascination with the dark, sensual world of vampires.

- Singin' Judy: You know who I am.

- And finally, My Readers: I'm grateful to be sharing Aden and Ellie's journey with you. I hope you grow to love them as much as I do.

Content Warning

This book contains dark themes and scenes that some readers may find uncomfortable and/or triggering.

- Biting

- Blood

- Graphic Violence

- Non-Consent

- Adult Language - the word "fuck" is used a lot

- Scenes & References of Physical Violence/Abuse/Assault

Healing Properties of BloodStone

- Blood cleanser

- Stimulates the immune system to fight infections

- Detoxifies

- Ancient Egyptians used bloodstone to treat tumors

Prologue

She could barely make out the faint outline of the furniture. Even in the dark, this room was familiar to her, having sneaked into it more times than she could count. But this time was different.

They weren't hurried or rushed, afraid they might get caught by his parents or hers. They were married now.

It was their wedding night, and he was finally going to drink from her, a moment they'd both fantasized about for so long.

His captivating blue eyes, the only things she could see clearly in the dark, bore into hers. They shone with happiness, love, and awe. His eyes were always so intense and full of secrets, but they could never hide his feelings for her.

She moaned, her eyes fluttering closed as they rocked in unison. Every inch of his body covered hers, their synchronized movements sending delicious shivers of pleasure through her body, everywhere their skin touched.

"Look at me, mo ghrá," he whispered, his voice hoarser than she'd ever heard it. "I need to see your eyes."

As she opened them, a radiant smile spread across her face, mirroring the love she saw reflected in his gaze. He loved her eyes as much as she loved his, once telling her they were his true north.

She reached up and traced her fingertips beneath his eyes, which shifted between the intense sapphire blue and the fiery crimson that came out when he was angry or aroused.

"I love you," he said as his body moved over and inside her. He brushed a wisp of stray hair off her face, his touch soft and tender, before lowering his lips to kiss her.

Her hips arched in response, matching his steady thrusts, their kiss leaving her breathless as she lost herself in the feel and taste of him.

He pulled back, his lips brushing hers with every word. "Are you sure you're ready?"

She nodded.

He opened his mouth, and she knew he was breathing her in, letting the scent of her arousal and blood consume him. His fangs lengthened, and his venom trickled over his bottom lip, before landing on her throat.

"I love you, Aden," she whispered, turning her head, to expose her vulnerable throat to him in absolute trust. He pressed his lips against her neck, taking what she offered as he sank his teeth into her.

Her body froze, paralyzed, as pleasure consumed her. She couldn't move and couldn't breathe as he pumped his venom into her bloodstream. All she could do was lay there and feel the rapture coursing through every cell of her body.

When her ability to move returned a few seconds later, her orgasm slammed into her, and she cried out, her entire body convulsing beneath him.

He drank deep, and she let him, feeling her blood leave her body, as she surrendered to the sensation. Sophie had described the experience to her many times, but nothing could have prepared her for the overwhelming rush of arousal and pleasure that washed over her.

Tears prickled her eyes as she was overcome with love for this man, this vampire she had loved for as long as she could remember. When she started to feel lightheaded, she pushed against his shoulders. "Aden, that's enough."

He pulled his fangs from her neck and licked the deep punctures he'd left in his wake. Her eyes fluttered closed, her head spinning.

"Aly." He choked her name, his voice a mixture of desperation and fear.

Her lashes swept open to meet his eyes again, and she gasped, her breath catching in her throat. His eyes had darkened. They were no longer blue, no longer gentle. The crimson that had overtaken them was fierce, full of bloodlust and something else she couldn't place.

His penetrating stare never faltered as his eyes bore into hers.

"I need more," he said through clenched teeth.

Locked in his gaze, a prick of icy fear spread through her entire body.

He tore his eyes away from hers and buried his face in her neck. Before she could stop him, he sank his fangs into her again. There was no gentleness this time, just a brutal hunger she felt in every tense muscle pressed against hers, in the searing pain as his fangs sank deeper.

A gasp escaped her lips as the grip of his venom on her body loosened. "No. Aden. Don't do this-"

She pushed against his shoulders, desperate to stop the assault. Pain surged through her body, searing and intense, overwhelming her senses and obliterating any trace of the ecstasy she'd experienced minutes earlier. "Please, come back to me-" She choked through the blood filling her throat, gagging her, suffocating her and silencing her plea.

"No." She pleaded again, tears streaming from the corners of her eyes.

His teeth tore at her neck and he growled against her skin as he pumped into her, breaking her body with each ruthless, powerful thrust.

With her vision fading and darkness closing in, she summoned the last remnants of her strength to whisper his name, "Aden," her voice heavy with surrender, as everything in her world faded to black.

Aden

475 V.E.

"Kane, get out of my way. I'm in no mood tonight."

His sister's shrill voice was the first sound that penetrated Aden's consciousness, bringing him back from the edge. Not even the gasping breaths and soft pleading cries of the human girl beneath him gave him pause. When he fed, Aden felt and tasted nothing except the warmth wrapped around him and the sweet blood that flowed down his throat. The low growl in his chest was a purr of satisfaction as he drank long and deep. The only sounds in Aden's world were the slap of flesh against flesh, mingled with the gurgling of warm blood bubbling against fang—until Keeley's voice echoed through what should have been soundproof walls.

Fucking hell!

Once again, Aden found himself disappointed with the girl brought to him for his nightly meal. Of course, she was beautiful, soft, and innocent. The staff wouldn't dare send one who wasn't. But like all the others, she couldn't live up to *her* memory. And the girl beneath him paid for it, enduring his rage and frustration as he battered her body in a desperate attempt to forget.

He pressed his hands into the mattress beside her head as he braced above her. The only parts of his body that touched hers were his fangs, buried deep in her jugular, and the point where their bodies joined. The girl gripped the sheet below her as she jerked beneath him. She knew better than to touch him. They all did.

Aden abhorred physical contact. Even as a child, he'd despised it. He could endure a casual touch, but even that made his skin crawl. He could shake a vampire's hand in greeting and crush an enemy's windpipe with his fingers. And he could endure the occasional hug from Keeley and his mother because he knew it hurt them when he pulled away.

But in his almost three hundred years, there was only one person whose touch Aden could bear. She was the only one whose touch didn't make him want to crawl out of his skin, the only one whose touch he not only enjoyed but came to desire and crave. And she was the only one whose touch he'd never feel again.

Aden growled and tore his fangs from the girl's neck, licking his lips. Blood bubbled on the surface of her skin. The temptation was too much and he sank back in. She jerked and stiffened as Aden's venom seeped into her bloodstream, paralyzing her once again. He was almost there and he'd be damned if he let his sister ruin his meal.

Despite his determination, the argument outside his suite echoed in his ears as he strove for completion inside the poor girl who had the misfortune of not being *her*.

"I don't give a rat's ass what he wants right now. Step aside, Kane, or I'm gonna have to hurt you."

The thrall whimpered, and her body convulsed around him as she climaxed. A few more thrusts and Aden shuddered, his orgasm ripping through him. He removed his fangs and licked the puncture wounds for one last taste. He was going to kill Keeley for interrupting his dinner. Why the fuck was she in his wing of the compound, anyway?

He pushed off the bed and grabbed his jeans, sliding the worn fabric up his legs.

"Aden." Keeley's piercing voice echoed through the door. "If you don't get out here in ten seconds, I'm gonna tear his fucking head off."

He snorted under his breath as he walked toward the door. She was such a drama queen.

As he approached, it slid open on its own, and Aden leaned against the door jamb, his arms crossed. He hadn't bothered with a shirt, and his jeans, unbuttoned at the top, rested low on his hips. He smirked down at his older but much shorter sister.

"What the fuck do you want, Keeley?"

She gave him a once over, her lips pursed. "You couldn't even bother to get dressed? Jesus, Aden. I have no desire to see you half naked."

Her petite body vibrated with rage. She was a vision, with her long black hair loose and wavy and her blue-green eyes flashing with indignation. Even in her irritation, her beauty remained as captivating and ageless as ever. Like all vampires born from the vampire procreation program, they both stopped aging at twenty-five, forever frozen in eternal youth.

He narrowed his eyes at her, but she didn't flinch.

"Don't give me that look. It may terrify everyone else, but it doesn't scare me." She jabbed a finger at him. "You and I need to talk."

The sides of his mouth quirked upward. "I'm kinda busy."

With his hunger satisfied, he was feeling feisty and there was no one he enjoyed sparring with more than his sister. Keeley reacted as he expected and punched him in the gut, pushing him out of the way so she could walk into his suite.

"Oof." He coughed, doubling forward. Damn, she was strong for such a little thing.

Aden side-eyed the man beside him. Kane, his personal guard since birth, stood seven and a half feet tall. He was a product of the breeding program developed before the Great Vampire Wars.

Kane's scruffy beard concealed his olive skin, his tousled black hair only adding to his disheveled look. Despite his casual appearance, Kane was fierce and dedicated to his job, protecting the son of the second most powerful vampire in the world.

"Some guard you are."

"She's scarier than you."

"Coward."

Kane's deep-chested laugh echoed after Aden as he turned to follow Keeley into his suite.

Aden walked around the corner into the living area and found his sister standing over the unconscious, naked girl. The white sheet beneath her was stained red with the blood still dribbling from the puncture marks on her neck.

"You've taken too much of her blood."

He grabbed his shirt and shrugged it on. "She'll be alright."

"Why do you always do this, Aden?" Keeley tossed the sheet over the girl's body. "Do you have to batter them so badly?"

"It's not my fault human flesh is pliable and bones are brittle. Bruises and breaks are inevitable, Keel. At least I leave them with as few scars as possible." Aden motioned to the bite marks on her neck and breast. "Oh, for fuck's sake," he snapped as her lips spread into a grim line. "I haven't accidentally killed a thrall in over a hundred years."

"Do you even know her name?" The anger in Keeley's eyes had morphed into disappointment and it set Aden's teeth on edge.

"No."

He could count on one hand the number of thralls whose names he knew, and it was only because their blood had a unique flavor he craved. All the others remained nameless.

"She doesn't look old enough to be a feeder."

The girl looked twenty. He liked them *her* age. Not that anyone would dare verbalize it. No one who was around then dared to speak her name. Not unless they wanted him to go on a rampage of destruction.

"Why do you have to compel all your thralls?"

Compulsion was one of the drags of being a vampire. Drinking from a human or half-breed during sex created a permanent obsession that neither could resist. If they didn't fulfill the compulsion, both would go mad.

"I feed my way. You feed yours."

Keeley placed her hands on her hips. "Doesn't it bother you at all, leaving them like this?"

He walked to the bar in the corner and poured a glass of whiskey. "I don't need a lecture, okay? Just because I don't give them a second thought after I finish with them doesn't make me a monster." He strolled back to the bed and grabbed the girl's wrist, sinking his fangs in and then holding it over his glass. "And I don't deliberately hurt them. It just happens sometimes."

"That's why civilized vampires keep sex and blood separate, except with their mates. Vampires and half-breeds can take it, but human bodies are too fragile."

That was one thing they agreed on. Humans were weak. Too weak.

Aden licked the puncture wounds on the thrall's wrist before dropping it back to the bed. "Either those civilized vampires have never savored the flavor of dopamine-infused blood or they lack taste buds. A little recovery time is to be expected, Keel." He scoffed at her appalled look. "I have to take our parents' righteous indignation, because they used to be human, but I don't need it from you. We treat our thralls better than most. They're not starved or abused like most other regions."

"Yeah, you only injure your pets."

"I don't have pets. I have feeders I fuck."

They weren't going to agree. But at least he'd stopped the carnage that dominated his early years, accepting that nothing, including punishing his weak thralls, would purge him of his pain.

"Infirmary."

A woman's face appeared in a floating hologram. "How can I serve you, Mistress Keeley?"

"My brother's thrall is about to bleed out on his bed."

"Yes, ma'am. We have a medical team standing by."

The door buzzed and opened. Two nurses came around the corner with a medical pod hovering between them. Aden looked on, indifferent, as they lifted the almost lifeless girl from the mattress before guiding the pod out of the room.

"You could at least act concerned whether that girl lives or dies."

"They'll give her BloodStone and she'll be fine."

He gulped the last of his drink as Keeley's anger flared to life again. She grabbed the empty glass from his hand. "Dad didn't create BloodStone to keep your thralls from dying after you feed from them."

"It's just a benefit."

Keeley set the glass on his bedside table and scrunched up her nose. "Your room always reeks of blood and sex."

"You don't have to come in here." Aden walked over to the sofa and sat down, lifting his bare feet onto the table. "What do you want? You know I hate having my dinner interrupted."

With narrowed eyes, she followed him across the room and plopped down beside him before punching him in the arm. "Why is Zoe in the hospital wing with puncture marks on her neck?" She hit him again, a little harder. "What the hell, Aden? Leave my thralls alone. I'm tired of you biting every freaking girl you see."

"I don't bite every girl I see. Besides, it's not my fault she was still in my room when I got back."

Keeley moved to punch him a third time but he jerked his body out of reach, laughing.

"I'm serious, Aden. That's the fourth one this year. Feeding on underage thralls is illegal. Who you are doesn't give you the right to break the law."

Aden's cocky smirk faded into a frown. "Does Sophie know?"

"She's the one who found Zoe, jackass." One corner of Keeley's mouth pulled up in a smug smirk of her own. "I figured she would beat me here but she knows your typical feeding time. She's gonna tear you a new asshole again."

"Fuck." Aden raked his fingers through his hair as Keeley leaned against the back of the sofa.

"You deserve it this time. Zoe is just a kid."

He jerked his chin in defiance. "This shit wouldn't happen if the housekeeping staff stopped sending underage thralls to tend to my rooms."

"This shit wouldn't happen if you'd learn to control your blood lust." She mimicked his petulant tone. His lips curled into a snarl but he didn't reply because they'd had this argument for centuries.

Keeley let her head drop onto his shoulder and his spine went rigid. Keeley and his mother were the only ones who regularly ignored his aversion to touch.

He willed his body to relax.

"Keeley, you can't just invade my personal space, especially when you know how much I hate it."

"We're best friends, so I can do anything I want."

"That's only because we have no other siblings."

His tone sounded cold and detached even to his own ears. They were the only children of Aurick Westcott, the Gerent of Réimse Shíochánta, and his half-breed wife Sophie. Born from the vampire procreation program launched in the second century, they had been raised in seclusion and privilege. Only two years apart, they were each other's primary playmates as children and confidants as adults.

She raised her head and glared at him. "Are you saying I'm only your best friend because we had no one else?"

"You said it. Not me." His lips curved into a smirk. "If I were anyone else, you'd loathe me, and you know it."

"Probably," she said with a shrug and dropped her head back onto his shoulder. "You are kind of a dick most of the time."

He didn't disagree because she was right, but he stiffened again. A few seconds passed before the tension in his muscles eased, and he sank back into the cushion behind him.

"Are you coming to Arcipelago with us?" He asked.

"No."

"Why not?"

Keeley pressed closer to his side and Aden grunted his displeasure. "I can't get away right now. I'm still preparing for the BloodStone board meeting on the tenth."

"So? The Council gathering is only a week."

"We've got the new drug to unveil and I have to get ready."

"What new drug?"

She lifted her head, her eyes narrowing as she glared at him again. "Maybe if you came to the office once in a while, you'd know."

He shifted far enough away that she wouldn't be able to lay her head on his shoulder again. "I've got a fucking job too, Keel. BloodStone is your territory."

Keeley sighed as she leaned closer, clearly needing something from him. He studied her face. "Why is your eye twitching?"

"My eye isn't twitching," she said as her hand shot to her face.

He barked out a laugh and swatted it away. "Yes, it is. What's the matter?"

She tucked her bottom lip between her teeth. "Ryan and I have our insemination in three weeks and I guess I'm anxious."

"Why? I thought you wanted a baby."

"I do. But it won't be like you and me. Mom and Dad didn't need a surrogate to carry us." Keeley ran her fingers through her hair in a gesture reminiscent of their mother. "Our child won't really be ours. It will be his and someone else's."

The vampire procreation program launched in the second century developed LIBER, a drug that made vampire sperm viable. Human females could conceive, but their bodies couldn't sustain the pregnancy. Only bitten half-breed females could carry vampire children to term.

Aden couldn't help but notice the way Keeley wrapped her arms around what would be her eternally empty womb.

"Keel, we can't change any of that."

"Easy for you to say. You don't have a wife. You'll feel differently when you do."

"I'll never have one, so it doesn't matter." He reached out and patted her knee before pulling his hand away. "It'll be fine. When the baby is born, get rid of the incubator. Problem solved."

The smile that curved her lips at his touch faded away. "Why are you always so heartless?"

"It's a gift." He grasped her wrist and pulled her off the sofa. "Now come see my new portrait. I just finished it today."

He dragged her across the room and through the archway that led to his private studio. He knew how to ease her annoyance, especially when it came to his lack of empathy. But that's who he was. He'd loved once and it nearly destroyed him. He'd never do it again.

Resting on an easel in the center of his studio, the watercolor painting was five feet tall. The woman was breathtaking. With her back arched, she stood bare to her waist. Her head was tilted back and to the side, her long auburn hair flowing between her fingers. With her face hidden in shadow, her captivating emerald green eyes were the centerpiece of the painting. The haunting memory of *her* eyes was always the focal point in every portrait that Aden painted.

"So?" When she didn't answer right away, he growled. "Well?"

Keeley's opinion mattered most to him. She angled her head and walked around the canvas, her eyes sweeping from top to bottom. She loved keeping him in suspense because he was insecure about his art more than anything else in his life. He folded his arms over his chest and growled out her name.

"The lighting is good, but aren't you tired of painting naked women?"

Aden's lips curved up into his signature smirk. "I like naked women. And the correct term is nude. Naked is just crass."

A gentle laugh escaped Keeley's lips, and he waited for her to say more. She always did.

"I thought you stopped painting redheads."

"Keeley," he ground out through clenched teeth as his impatience got the better of him.

"The eyes are perfect."

The swift, excruciating pain that always accompanied Keeley's soft comment engulfed him. He welcomed it. His voice was a whisper as his throat tightened and constricted.

"Yes. They were."

Keeley wrapped her arms around his waist, but he wrenched out of her grasp.

He didn't want the comfort she offered. He didn't deserve it.

Ellie

Ellie's brisk footsteps carried her down the dark street. The two other kitchen thralls, Adam and Brant, clambered after her, shadowed by the three half-breed guards, always close, always watching, ready to step in if one of them tried to flee.

"Slow down, Ellie!" Adam panted, trying to keep up with her.

"No. We have less than two hours." She barreled ahead without so much as a backward glance.

"We wouldn't be late if you hadn't overslept." Brant's heavy breathing drowned out his accusation as he also struggled to keep up with her. "For someone who never sleeps, it was a pain to get you out of bed today."

The frightening world her dreams conjured plagued Ellie. Her mother's murder, at the hands of the most vicious vampire in existence, was always at the forefront. Even after eighteen years, every time she closed her eyes, she relived it. Between that and the mysterious blue eyes that haunted her since childhood, it's no wonder she never slept. But she could only go so long before her body crashed, as it did yesterday.

"Shut up, Brant. You know she was stuck in her nightmares again."

Ellie's night terrors, as her best friend Carrie called them, were well known around the thrall's quarters. Sometimes she got trapped and when she couldn't wake up, her screams woke everyone else.

Ellie stumbled and her throat rippled as she swallowed back the bile that rose in her throat. Dreams of her mother always made her feel this way. Her inability to forget anything plagued her in both her waking and sleeping moments. Every sight, action, and sound etched permanently into her memory.

"Why don't we take a warp port?" Brant asked. "Master Matthais lets us use them for emergencies."

"Do you really think he'll consider our running late to be an emergency?" Ellie asked.

She glanced across the street where a handful of vampires and their human pets still wandered. The pets stumbled behind their owners, dragged on invisible leashes connected to the collars around their necks, weak from a night of use, abuse, and blood loss.

A wave of revulsion shuddered through her body. "Come on, keep up."

Ellie navigated through the vast underground maze of dirty and dimly lit streets, bathed in the muted glow of flickering neon signs outside hundreds of vampire clubs. Ellie suspected the horrors that took place within, having seen enough battered thralls stumbling out of them. Her stomach churned as a mix of conflicting emotions washed over her: fear, sadness, and a flicker of morbid curiosity.

Their route, on the lowest street level Master Matthais required his thralls to use when heading to the weekly market, was the most dangerous. But Ellie plunged ahead, ignoring the prick of fear and the bead of sweat on the back of her neck.

She turned the corner and her stride faltered again as she was swallowed by the ominous darkness of an alleyway, the quickest route to the escalator that would take them to the surface level. If the guards hadn't been following, she never would have dared to go this way. It wasn't safe for thralls to wander the city's lower levels alone.

The alley smelled of old, stale blood and sex. The scent saturated much of the underground levels of the city, but it was the only path to the market escalator. Ellie slowed her pace on the slick and sticky concrete. It took what seemed like weeks to get the putrid scent of blood and venom out of her uniform and off her skin the last time she'd slipped and fallen.

One more turn around a sharp corner, and she halted in front of a tall, moving stairway between two buildings. She exhaled a breath, relieved to make it unscathed.

"Damn, girl." Brant panted, his breaths heavy as he and Adam caught up and nearly bumped into her. "You move fast on those short legs."

Ellie bristled as he reminded her of her short stature. It's not that she was exceptionally short. Most vampires were over six feet, and all male half-breeds were over seven feet. But at just under five feet, six inches, Ellie was often looked down on by most people in her life.

She stepped onto the escalator and tapped her foot, feeling the slight vibration beneath her. As it rose and passed by the next street level, the rancid stench grew less foul, but still turned her stomach. At last, the surface level came into view. The tension in her body melted away as she stepped into the muted light.

The dome that covered the city, opened each night for fresh air, was already closed. Ellie inhaled a deep breath, sucking in the untainted air thanks to the city's advanced filtration systems that kept the topmost level cleaner and more livable.

"I'll get the vegetables and fruit," she said as she stepped onto the street, Brant and Adam falling into step beside her. "Brant, you get the meat from the butcher. Make sure you tell him it's for Master Matthais' thralls, so he gives you the best cuts." He nodded but Ellie continued before he could respond. "And smell it all so he doesn't pass off anything spoiled. Maybe I should get it."

Ellie led them across the street, past a group of farmers unloading crates filled with bread, fruits, vegetables, and herbs. Opposite them was a line of large refrigerated trucks containing an assortment of fresh fish, meats, and dairy items.

"I can handle it," Brant said. "He knows who I am now."

"He still gave you tainted meat last month. Half the thralls got sick."

"I got it."

Ellie skidded to a stop at the market entrance and jabbed a finger into his shoulder. "I'm the one who got punished when a thrall threw up on Master Matthais' floor, not you, so please check it first." The memory of her broken arm lingered under her skin, causing a pulsing ache.

"I said I got it." Brant's tone softened and his eyes echoed with the faint hint of remorse.

Ellie turned toward Adam. "Go to the bakery. I told the baker what we needed so he should have it ready. Take as much as you can carry and tell him to have the rest of it delivered to the compound no later than two. We'll meet back here in one hour."

"We do this every week. You don't need to keep telling us how," Adam said before taking off in one direction as Brant headed in the opposite, each followed by one guard.

Ellie eyed the one still with her before she turned and dashed off toward her destination.

The market's fruit and vegetable section was located right next to the city gate, a massive structure made of steel and tempered glass with two large panels that slid open to admit the thralls from the surrounding villages. Armed half-breed guards admitted only those with approval to deliver and sell their goods on market day.

The gate was still open. Daylight streamed through unfiltered, unlike through the tinted dome, which enclosed the city and protected vampires from sunlight, the only thing that could harm them.

Ellie tightened her sweater around her thin frame, squinting against the biting winter wind. While most city thralls were born and raised inside the dome, Ellie had been born in a village, but the warmth of the sun on her skin was a distant memory. It was only in these moments, when it reflected off the snowy landscape outside, did the sun's brightness stand out in the eternal dimness within the city.

A fleeting longing to flee washed over her, filling her with an intense yearning to break free from her domed prison. But the thought of leaving Carrie and her dad behind was a crushing weight, pressing on her chest. And the tracking chip in her neck served as an ever-present powerful warning against any thoughts of escape.

The market hummed with its usual activity, the booths overflowing with fresh produce in a rainbow of colors. The scent of freshly picked herbs permeated the air as thralls rushed along the busy walkways, filling their reusable baskets and bags.

"Hi, Ellie."

She turned at the sound of her name and her face lit up at the sight of a man with a warm, toothless grin. "Hi, Rodney."

His dark, weather-beaten skin was a stark contrast to her pale, unblemished flesh. His dirty, tattered clothes barely covered his skeletal, malnourished body.

She glanced down at her clean, freshly pressed gray uniform, and Ellie's grin faltered. City thralls were well fed because they needed to provide healthy and abundant blood for the vampires. Most country thralls weren't so lucky, denied most of the food they grew.

"What have you got for me today?" she asked as she stepped closer.

Rodney's weakened hands shook as he held out a tray of strawberries. "I saved you all the best ones."

Ellie reached out to steady his fingers. "Strawberries in the winter are always a treat." She took the tray from him, setting it on the table before picking through apples in one of the baskets, selecting several to fill the bag that hung over her arm.

"I'm going to need ten bushels of these apples. Do you have that many?"

"Of course." He nodded. "I'll deliver them to the compound myself."

"Do you have any kale?"

"I've got it back here." Rodney turned toward the back of the booth. "I have cauliflower and parsnips, too."

Ellie watched him sway on his feet and she stepped into his booth, grasping his elbow as his legs threatened to give way.

"Rodney!" She tried and failed to stop him from falling, her bag forgotten as the apples spilled onto the ground.

"I'm okay, Ellie." His words trailed off into a groan as his knees hit the concrete.

She kneeled beside him, trying to lighten the moment with a smile. "You sure know how to scare a girl."

"You okay, Rod?" The man in the next booth called. He was years younger than Rodney and looked stronger but was still skin and bones. "Oh hey, Ellie."

Ellie waved as she helped Rodney to his feet. "Hi, Jimmy. He's okay."

"Hunter?" Ellie turned to her guard. He threw an annoyed look her way as she motioned to a rickety wooden chair a few feet to his right. "Please bring me that chair?"

Embarrassment bloomed on Rodney's face. "I don't need a chair, Ellie."

"Humor me, please," she said to him before glancing back toward Hunter, who had yet to move. "Hunter? Hello? Did you hear me?"

"I'm not the thrall here, Ellie."

She bit her tongue to stifle her rude reply and turned back to Rodney. "Can you stand by yourself for a minute?"

"I'm okay, hun." Rodney patted her hand.

She released his arm, and once he was steady, she walked over to get the chair.

"We'll be late if you don't hurry." Hunter's hard tone made Ellie's fingers itch with the desire to slap him. Not that she'd ever dare unless she wanted to be whipped again.

"You can be a real jerk sometimes."

She carried the chair into Rodney's booth. He leaned against the table, attempting to gather up her fallen apples.

"Here, sit, Rodney. I'll get those." Rodney dropped into the chair as she crouched down to gather up the fruit, pressing one into his hand. "Take this."

"No, Ellie, I can't—" Rodney shook his head and darted worried glances around.

Ellie followed his eyes before she slipped the apple into the pocket of his sweater. "Please, Rodney. You're not gonna get through the day if you don't eat."

"I'll be alright." He squeezed her hand. "You're a good girl."

Ellie gathered the rest of her apples before standing and brushing the dirt off her dress, now stained at the knees, but there was nothing she could do. She moved over to Jimmy's booth.

"Don't worry, Ellie. I'll take his stuff with mine later."

"Thanks, Jimmy."

"How much do you want of everything this week?"

"One hundred pounds, please."

"You got it, kiddo."

Ellie whipped around when she heard a scuffle behind her. Two large guards yanked Rodney out of his chair. He stumbled and a wince of pain flashed across his face as they dragged him toward the booth's exit. His eyes met Ellie's, and the fear in them was unmistakable.

"Hey, what are you doing?" She hurried over and stepped into their path.

"Stay out of this, you stupid thrall," one guard warned and shoved her aside. She lost her balance, falling backward over the chair and smacking her head on the concrete.

Ellie blinked, blinded by the spots that danced in front of her eyes. She reached behind her head, blood clinging to her fingertips when she pulled them away. Fear for Rodney overrode the sharp, throbbing pain in the back of her skull, and she gave her head a quick shake before scrambling to her feet. Her body swayed, and she gripped the chair leg to steady herself.

Hunter yanked the guard's arm, halting his retreat. "She belongs to Master Matthais. She's not to be touched."

"You can't take him." Ellie rushed forward again but Jimmy grabbed her from behind.

"Don't, Ellie. You can't do anything and you'll only make it worse."

Tears stung Ellie's eyes, her heart breaking, as the guards shoved Rodney towards the gate. He stumbled and fell several times before they dragged him through. Ellie spun in Jimmy's arms and clutched his shirt in her fingers. "What are they going to do to him?"

"If he can't man his booth, Ellie, he can't have it. They'll give it to another farmer who can."

"No. They can't." A sob clogged her throat.

"Take your hands off her!"

Jimmy released Ellie, holding his hands up as he backed away at Hunter's sharp command.

"Come, Ellie. It's time to go," Hunter said.

"Here, take this for your head." Jimmy handed her a handkerchief before stepping back into his booth.

Ellie blinked back tears and whispered her thanks as she used the cloth to mop up the blood trickling down her scalp. She took a minute to compose herself before grabbing her bag and forcing herself to walk out of the booth.

Two hours later Ellie burst into the kitchen, followed by a frazzled Brant and Adam.

"Put those on the counter and go." Ellie panted, out of breath. "I'm right behind you."

The two guys bolted from the room without looking back. Damn! They were late. Dread tightened her muscles, anticipating Master Matthais' wrath. She tossed her sweater onto the counter before racing out of the kitchen. Maybe he'd be too wrapped up in his lecture to notice her. Oh, who was she kidding?

Ellie turned the corner and crashed to a halt, colliding with her worst nightmare. Strong fingers bit into her arms as the scent of freesia filled her nose. Ellie blew out a long breath, her body sagging in defeat.

Mistress Kira.

She was one of Master Matthais' underlings. The rumor was he sired her over a thousand years ago but regretted it as soon as he realized what an insufferable bitch she was. Ellie knew very little about how vampires were sired. All vampires were born now, and thralls were forbidden to discuss anything about them. But

Ellie often wondered why Master Matthais kept her around because it seemed like he couldn't stand her most of the time.

"And where the hell do you think you're going?"

Ellie's body tensed, the shrill voice sending a chill down her spine. Could her day get any worse?

"Mistress Kira, ma'am, I'm on my way to the meeting."

Ellie averted her eyes. Making direct eye contact with a vampire was forbidden, but Mistress Kira had made it her mission to get Ellie to slip up. She had no idea why the vampire hated her so much. Before she'd turned eighteen, Mistress Kira had barely even acknowledged her existence.

"Too bad for you. You're already late. Pity."

Cool breath blew past her cheek as Mistress Kira leaned closer, a sneer on her face. Ellie's heart pounded against her ribcage as a flash of red hair and flawless, pale skin filled her vision. Learning to focus peripheral vision was essential for any thrall and Ellie mastered it at a young age. Now, she could see almost everything around her even when her eyes were lowered. Every thrall had to learn it unless they wanted to trip every time they were in the presence of a vampire.

"I hate January," Mistress Kira sneered. "For weeks on end all Matthais can do is obsess over his pointless little gathering. And all you stupid thralls run around like the filthy rats you are. The games are the only good thing about it. They get rid of the most repulsive of you."

Ellie clamped her teeth shut, biting her tongue until she tasted the faint metallic taste of blood. She was in enough trouble already and didn't need to make it worse.

"Don't ignore me, you little bitch!" Mistress Kira screeched. "I'll scratch those filthy eyes right out."

She grabbed Ellie's hair by the roots and yanked her head back before leaning in to inhale the dried blood that clung to the long strands. Ellie bit back a cry and squeezed her eyes shut as fingernails dug into her left cheek, breaking the skin under her eye. Her traitorous body trembled, fear coursing through her veins, and she braced herself for the pain she knew was coming.

"Kira, Ellie is required at Master Matthais' meeting."

Relief flooded Ellie at the sound of Ivan, Master Matthais' executive assistant. She'd never been more grateful for his presence.

"Since it's already begun, I suggest you let her go so she can make her way there." Ivan's tone was firm, leaving no room for argument.

Ellie winced, feeling a sharp pain shoot through her scalp as Mistress Kira gave her hair one final vicious tug. She leaned in and hissed into Ellie's ear.

"This isn't over, bitch."

Mistress Kira shoved her hard and Ellie stumbled, her shoulder colliding with the wall. But she caught herself before she face-planted. She opened her eyes to see Mistress Kira licking the blood from her fingernails as she stormed away.

Ivan shot her a stern glance. "You best be on your way, Ellie."

"Yes, Sir. Thank you," she whispered before turning to dash down the hallway.

With a soft swish, the door slid open, and Ellie slipped into the meeting room. Hundreds of thralls stood side by side in silence in the chilly and sterile room, their heads lowered. Adam and Brant were tucked against the back wall, avoiding going deeper into the room and risking being noticed.

Ellie heard the low hum of whispers before a hand reached for hers. Her only friend, Carrie, tugged her into the crowd and out of the spotlight.

As the daughter of one of Master Matthais' Elite Guards, Ellie was disliked by most of the other thralls because they believed she received special treatment. Maybe she did, but only to a small extent. Ellie's father's rank ensured that she rarely faced the harshest punishments. Except for once.

As long as she followed orders and completed her chores, she was fine. Of course, she still rebelled in small ways sometimes, when she believed Master Matthais wouldn't find out. The illusion of control, however slight, gave her a sense of satisfaction that felt almost real. Until she was caught, or reported, by the other thralls, which happened more and more often.

At the front of the room, Master Matthais sat on a large throne on a raised dais, the only furniture in the expansive space. Despite the interruption, his voice didn't falter. "Gerent Westcott and his family will be the first ones to arrive. Master Aden will bring his own pets, as usual. Veronika," Master Matthais singled out the thralls' head nurse. "Make sure there are at least a dozen beds available in the infirmary for his thralls. He will bring his medical team but have one standing by in case they need assistance."

"Yes, Sir."

"The other Gerents will arrive tomorrow before midnight. I expect everything to be ready. I haven't been working you around the clock for weeks to have less than perfect hospitality."

Ellie shivered as she felt Master Matthais' eyes on her. She was always skating along the edge, relying on her father's position to protect her. One night, it was going to catch up with her. Ellie just hoped it wasn't tonight.

"Camilla," Master Matthais addressed the head thrall. "I expect the great hall to be ready by sunset tomorrow. I want the east wall prepped and ready for the wine bar. Have a minimum of one hundred thralls available to provide blood as needed."

"Yes, Master Matthais."

He slapped his hand down on the arm of his chair. "Now get to work, or you'll wish you were never born."

"Where were you?" Carrie leaned over and whispered as the thralls filed out of the room. Ellie shook her head and pulled on Carrie's hand, desperate for a swift escape.

"Elliana." Master Matthais' voice echoed through the room and Ellie cringed. He was the only one who used her full name. "You will remain here."

Carrie held her hand until the exiting crowd pushed her along, forcing her to let go. Ellie remained in her spot, arm extended toward the door until the last of the thralls exited.

"Come to me," Master Matthais said, quieter now. Too quiet.

Ellie moved at once, keeping her head and eyes lowered. No thrall in their right mind would dare look into Master Matthais' eyes. Or keep him waiting. He rose from his chair and stepped down from the dais. "Do you have something to say to me?"

"I'm sorry, Master. I was late returning from the market. It won't happen again, Sir."

He glided closer, and a wave of fear and dread washed over Ellie, making it difficult for her to take a breath. She fought hard to suppress the shudder that threatened to escape as he invaded her personal space.

"Why is your uniform dirty?" His calm demeanor contradicted the rage emanating from his eyes.

"I dropped some apples at the market."

"You are aware that it's unacceptable to be dirty in my house. Why did you not change your clothes before attending this meeting?"

"I didn't want to be any later, Sir."

"Late is late, child." The sound of his silky voice was bone-chilling and a trail of cold sweat trickled down Ellie's back. "Now you have two transgressions for which to be punished."

"I am truly sorry, Master." Ellie's voice quivered with the dread coursing through her.

Master Matthais grabbed her chin, his fingers digging into her flesh. He jerked Ellie's face higher, but she kept her eyes down. "Very good, girl. Perhaps you're learning." He leaned closer, his breath brushing against the delicate skin of her jaw as he inhaled deeply. Ellie gulped as his eyes turned red and his fangs lengthened, a feral smile spreading across his face. "I am so looking forward to the day you reach your peak."

He pushed her to the floor. Ellie stifled a groan as her knees hit the marble with a crack. Searing pain shot up her thighs and slammed into her abdomen.

"In the meantime, if you are ever late to one of my meetings again, I will whip you to within an inch of your life."

Ellie forced herself to swallow and nod, her throat constricting with the effort as she recalled the agonizing pain from her last whipping, the memory still so vivid it made her knees weak.

"Yes, Sir."

"As punishment, you will have no food for three days."

She knew she should have eaten before she left for the market. "Yes, Sir."

"If I find your father or little friend sneaking you any food at all, my wrath will be swift."

"Yes, Sir." It was the only answer he expected and to disappoint him meant more punishment.

Master Matthais kicked her in the side, and Ellie grunted under her breath. The sound of her ribs cracking echoed in the otherwise silent room, and she couldn't contain the gasp, despite her efforts.

While she usually avoided the most extreme consequences, Master Matthais' punishments were becoming more severe. The only thing she could do was try to numb herself to it.

"Now get out of my sight."

Ellie scrambled to her feet, ignoring the pain radiating through her body as she fled the room.

Aden

"Good evening, Horatio."

Aden greeted his father's head guard as he approached his parents' suite. Horatio stood at attention outside the door, a commanding figure in his suit, as the ceiling light reflected on the smooth mahogany skin of his bald head. He stood over seven feet tall and was part of the first generation of half-breed guards created from the breeding program. Horatio had been with his father since before the Great Vampire Wars, and like Kane, he had later been turned into a sired half-breed. As long as he received a daily dose of his father's blood, he would never age or die.

"Good evening, Sir."

The door slid open. The sound of several young hearts beating filled the air as Aden made his way down the hall to his parent's sitting room. He rounded the corner and found his father sitting on a long, cream-colored sofa, enjoying his nightly meal. A line of three female and two male thralls kneeled on the floor in front of him.

His father's hand clasped the wrist of the first thrall in the line, his fangs piercing the delicate flesh beneath her palm. The girl's head lolled to one side, her mouth slack as his venom coursed through her veins. The tips of his jet-black hair fell over his closed eyes. Thanks to his Celtic roots, his father's Irish skin had always been fair. But his lack of exposure to the sun since becoming a vampire, over seventeen hundred years ago, made him appear even paler.

Like the other Ancient Ones, his father was a turned vampire, born-again in Áth Cliath, shortly before the Viking invasion of Ireland, thirteen hundred years before the Great Vampire Wars. A monk, crusader, and eventual religious scholar, he was one of the oldest vampires in existence. Only Matthais, Chancellor of the Vampire World Council, Rashidi, the Gerent of Afara, and Katsumi, the Gerent of Asu, were older.

His father's eyes opened as Aden approached, his irises red from his feeding. He retracted his fangs and brushed the tip of his tongue over the puncture wounds until the bleeding stopped and the small wounds sealed. He raised his head and his irises faded back to blue.

With a nod, he turned to the next thrall. She crawled forward and settled on her knees before lifting her wrist. He brought it to his lips as his fangs lengthened and pierced the skin. The girl's body jerked and then stilled, as the venom from his fangs raced through her bloodstream, paralyzing her. Ten seconds later her body jerked again as movement returned to her static body. She sighed and her head lolled to the side, her mouth slack as his father drank long and deep.

Aden crossed the room and sat on the chair beside the sofa. As he waited, his eyes wandered around the room. His mother had redecorated again, something she did every few decades. She went with a cream and blue color scheme this time.

As always, their rooms were cozy and inviting, with a mix of modern and antique elements. She'd replaced everything in the room, except her husband's Celtic crosses and several of his ancient swords. The overall effect created a sense of balance, seamlessly blending the old and the new. Aden couldn't give a fuck about design, but he had to admit she had taste.

His father removed his fangs from the last thrall's wrist and wiped his mouth. Aden didn't know how he tolerated it. The only time he could stand to drink from a thrall's wrist was when it was required in polite company.

The line of thralls stood and exited the room without a word, assisting the last thrall, who was still unsteady on his feet.

"Keeley and your mom are on the warpath."

"Yeah, I already saw Keeley."

Aden bristled at the disappointment in his father's voice. But he said nothing else about Aden's slip with Zoe. His mother would give him enough hell for both of them.

"How was your trip to the western villages?"

"I found several caves filled with rogues. We exterminated them, but I suspect there are more we didn't find. When we get back from Arcipelago, I'll go back and handle it."

A grim expression crossed his father's face as his lips pressed together. "How many humans did they kill?"

"Roughly a thousand."

His father made his way over to the bar. "Drink?"

Aden nodded.

"I think you should handle it before we go to the capital. We don't want things to get out of hand here the way it did in Abya Yala."

"Abya Yala got out of hand because Cecilia refuses to get off her commanding officer's cock long enough to let him do his job."

"Yes, it would appear so," he said as he handed Aden a glass of Irish whiskey before returning to the sofa. "Either way, we don't leave for the capital until the day after tomorrow. You should take care of the problem before we leave."

It was not a suggestion. Aden gulped down his drink, the fiery liquid scorching his throat. He hated when his father told him how to do his job. He was the head of his father's military for a reason. He was damn good at it. After two hundred years, you'd think his father would trust his judgment on when an insurgency needed immediate attention and when it didn't.

"I've got it handled, Aurick. Don't worry."

His father's mouth opened, but then it snapped shut again at the sound of heels clicking on the marble floor. His mother's purposeful and clipped footsteps echoed down the hall, and Aden braced himself for the onslaught of her wrath.

She rounded the corner, and Aden looked up, feeling the heat of her glare. His mother was one of the most beautiful women Aden knew. Long, golden blonde hair framed her oval face. Her honey-colored skin was radiant, and she had the second-most beautiful eyes he'd ever seen, her heterochromia making them all that more captivating. Her smile could light up a room, and her laugh was so contagious that it was impossible not to join her once she got started.

But she wasn't laughing now. Fury burned in her eyes, and they blazed with the same disappointment that was in his father's.

"Aden!" His name sounded like a curse on her lips.

"Evening, Sophie."

In his twenties, as he spiraled deeper into darkness, Aden started calling his parents by their first names. It took them decades to accept that he wouldn't stop, no matter how much they demanded otherwise. It wasn't meant as a deliberate act of disrespect, but rather one of defiance that eventually became the norm.

His mother walked over and slapped him upside the back of the head. He reached up to rub the spot, though it didn't hurt. "Ow."

She sat next to his father, her back straight. Aden gave her his signature cocky smirk, and he saw her fingers twitch, no doubt itching to hit him again.

"Aden, I am so angry with you right now."

"I've already heard it from Keeley. Let it go."

"This has to stop." Her voice was tight and controlled. "There is no more room in any of our compounds to keep your girls."

Aden waved his hand. "I only bit her. She's not compelled. I won't need to drink from her again."

"That's not the point." She leaned back and crossed her legs. "She's underage, Aden. Why do you have to be such a—" She paused. "Dickhead."

Aden barked out an abrupt laugh. A dickhead? Really?

"We can't keep looking the other way as you defy the law, Aden."

"I am the law."

"No!" His father, who up to that point had ramained silent, interrupted. "The VWC is the law. I uphold it. You enforce it. And you're going to obey it."

"Then keep underage thralls out of my bedroom," Aden snarled.

"Watch it, Aden." His father's eyes flashed crimson before returning to their natural blue.

Disappointment and sadness flickered in his mother's eyes. "Aden, please. I know this isn't you. It's been almost three hundred years. Al—"

Aden surged to his feet. "Don't say her name!" He bellowed, unable to keep the anguish from his voice. He released quick, jagged breaths, clenching both hands tight. Neither of his parents reacted to his outburst. His father would often bellow right back about respecting his mother, but they both knew the depth of the grief and pain that was still a living thing inside him, despite how much time had passed. "I need to feed again before I head back out to take care of the rogues."

Despite his insistence that the rogue problem didn't need immediate attention, Aden would heed his father's recommendation and take care of it now.

"Do you want me to go with you?" His father asked.

"No." His tone was sharp. He didn't need a babysitter. "I'll see you both on the plane tomorrow."

He spun around and strode toward the door

"Come on, mo ghrá. It's time for your blood."

Aden turned the corner leading to the hallway but stopped dead in his tracks as he heard his father's gentle words. Gaelic was his native tongue, and Aden had heard his father speak it his entire life. But those words left a gaping wound in his body so deep, he doubted it would ever heal.

Aden glanced over his shoulder, watching as his mother nestled into his father's arms. He leaned back and dragged the nail of his index finger across the vein in his neck, tearing the skin. She smiled and pressed her face against his throat. She ran the tip of her tongue along his skin, catching the drip of blood, before closing her mouth over the wound. His father growled and clutched her closer as he tilted his head back and let the pleasure overtake him.

A pang of regret filled Aden's chest, and he spun around, exiting their suite. He'd once wanted what his parents had. Watching them together when he was growing up, he vowed to one day find a woman like his mother and worship her for eternity. But one cruel, violent moment ripped eternity away. Now he was destined to walk the world alone because he'd never love again.

Instead, he used his thralls to dull the pain. And right now he needed to dull it something fierce. He barked Georgina's name and a hologram of her image appeared.

"I want Chelsea brought to my room in thirty minutes. Make sure her blood alcohol level is point two five percent. I want to taste whiskey in her blood."

Aden stomped down the hallway of his parent's wing.

"Kane!" He barked, and a hologram of his guard, bare from the waist up, appeared.

"Yes?"

"Fuck, Kane! Why are you answering a hologram naked?"

"I'm not naked." Kane grunted a laugh before he slid a needle into his abdomen. "I'm taking my injection. And I can't exactly ignore your calls."

"Put your fucking shirt on and meet me at the hangar in an hour. We're going back to make sure we got all the rogues."

"Okay." Kane shrugged back into his shirt. "By the way, this is my last vial."

"What? Why the fuck didn't you tell me sooner?"

"I did. Two weeks ago."

Aden exited his parent's wing and the cool breeze from the open roof above ruffled his hair as he strode across the courtyard to his wing. "I'll get with Mina, but I don't have time to give her blood before we leave."

"That's okay. I can go a day or two without a hit."

"No, you can't. You age when you don't have my blood every day, and those spotty gray hairs in your shaggy beard are already making you look too fucking old. I hate when I have to feed you my blood myself."

Kane snorted as he grabbed his go-bag and exited his room. "I don't know what to tell ya, boss. I gave you fair warning."

Aden's steps came to a halt as he reached the hallway that led to his wing. He lifted his hand and straightened the crooked painting on the wall.

The painting was one of his favorites by Steve Hanks, a renowned watercolor artist who lived long before his grandmother, a once-famous artist in her own right, was born. It captured the beauty of a woman in a contemplative pose on a disheveled bed. Her sheer sheath left little to the imagination. Her round, full breast, and hard-tipped nipple clearly visible through the flimsy material. It was an erotic and breathtaking piece, one of the first artworks that had ignited Aden's passion for painting as a teenager. His admiration and affection for the nude female form was born from the sensual figures Hanks brought to life.

"You still there, boss?" Kane asked.

Aden stepped back, satisfied the painting was now set to right, before continuing down the hall. "Call Roderick and have him and three fresh teams meet us."

"Got it."

Aden swiped the hologram away before barking, "Mina!"

An older woman with short brown hair and glasses appeared in a new hologram. "Yes, Aden?"

"Why didn't you tell me Kane was running low?"

"I did, but, as usual, you didn't listen."

"When?"

"Last week, when we took Tiffany away in a medical pod."

The memory tightened Aden's gut. Yeah, that hadn't been his finest night.

The door to his room slid open as he approached. "Well, he just took his last injection."

"Can I come see you now?"

"No. I have to leave the city and take care of something but I'll call you when I get back."

"Okay."

"Mina?" Aden tried to soften his tone. "Has Tiffany recovered?"

The weight of Mina's disappointment was so heavy he almost regretted asking.

"She'll be fine, but even with BloodStone, she'll need an extended break to recover fully."

Aden gave her a sharp nod and swiped the hologram closed.

The temporary command center set up at the base of the mountain range gave Aden the ability to be close but not directly involved in the action. Not that he didn't enjoy a good fight, but the sun had just risen, so he had to leave the combat to the half-breed army.

He watched his troops on a hologram as they moved into position. The confirmation that his instincts were right only irritated him more. In the less than twenty-four hours since he'd left, rogues had wreaked more havoc and decimated one more village to the northwest before settling back in a series of caves halfway up the mountain.

"What's the fucking hold up?" Aden asked.

Roderick, Aden's Major General since he'd taken the reins of his father's military, appeared in the hologram. "Clearly, they know we're coming. They've moved higher."

"So, send a contingent up on a plane and drop onto them from above. It shouldn't be taking so fucking long."

Aden leveled a hard glare at Kane, who stood by the door in his usual stoic manner. "Why the fuck do you half-breeds have to make everything so complicated?"

"I don't understand why you just don't launch UV missiles into the caves and be done with it. Seems to me you're the one making it complicated."

Kane was the only half-breed Aden would let speak to him that way. Anyone else would have had their head removed.

"Because the missiles will obliterate them, and I want to talk to at least one of them. UV bullets will incapacitate them, allowing me to gather intel. There have been zero rogues in this region for fourteen decades. Why the fuck are they popping up now? And where are they coming from?"

Aden studied the hologram as Roderick's team climbed higher, scaling over the dense, snow-covered terrain. Armed with Helios guns, which were designed to utilize UV light-infused bullets, the soldiers also had swords strapped to their backs. Since traditional weapons didn't kill vampires, the half-breed soldiers used the Helios to immobilize the rogues. Then hand-to-hand combat, often with swords got the job done. Half-breeds weren't as strong as vampires, though their ability to overpower weak, hungry rogues made them a formidable force. Once overpowered, a rogue could be killed by decapitation.

Fifteen minutes later, as he'd instructed, a plane appeared above the mountain peak, and four dozen additional soldiers dropped into the trees. Roderick and his team met up with the extra troops, and Aden signaled for them to proceed. He and Kane watched as Roderick took the lead, with Drake and the other soldiers forming half circles around the entrances of half a dozen caves. Aden's views of the events were from a camera built into Drake's helmet, along with multiple holograms that followed the soldiers.

In a blur of movement, a group of rogues poured out of several caves, leaping with their fangs bared and red eyes glowing. The soldiers sprang into action, opening fire on the rogues. The UV bullets streaked through the air, leaving ethereal blue trails in their wake. Despite their weakness, the rogues moved with extraordinary speed as they evaded most of the soldiers' shots.

Several vampires stumbled as the rounds struck them, their skin sizzling and smoking where the bullets made contact. But the effect was temporary, and within moments, the vampires' bodies expelled the foreign matter, healing rapidly.

"Fuck!" Aden growled. "They're not as weak as we thought."

Drake dove behind a tree trunk, reloaded, and stepped back into the fray. A rogue leaped at him, his claws raking across Drake's body armor, fangs snapping at his exposed flesh. Drake quickly tossed the rogue aside, then holstered his gun and reached for his sword from his back. With a single strike, Drake carved a deep gash into a vampire's chest. It let out a deafening roar, the wound oozing with dark, thick blood before Drake decapitated it.

The other soldiers, including Roderick, had similar encounters, as it became obvious the rogues knew how to dodge the bullets.

Roderick and his team switched to swords, steel glinting in the sunlight as they clashed with the vampires. Again, despite their weakness, the rogues swiftly dodged many of the soldiers' blows.

Were they soldiers too?

"Push them back into the caves and corner them." Aden snarled before shooting a glare at Kane. "I should have sent you up there."

"Yup." Kane agreed with a fierce look as he watched the chaos on the holograms. "It would be over by now."

Aden smirked despite his aggravation. "You're nearly as arrogant as I am."

Kane let out a snort, the sound rumbling deep from within his chest.

"Form a line," Roderick commanded. "I want half with the Helios and half with swords. Don't stop shooting or swinging for any reason."

Half the soldiers formed a line, advancing and firing their Helios. The others used their swords to cut down rogues in their path. The battle flowed into the caves. Holograms followed the troops, their boots crunching on the frozen ground as they entered in synchronized formation.

The confined space echoed with snarls, screams, and the rapid rhythm of gunfire. UV bullets ricocheted off the stone walls, creating a disorienting light show. The soldiers emptied one magazine after another into the vampires. Some, riddled with hundreds of UV rounds, collapsed, their bodies overwhelmed by the effort to expel the deadly particles.

Finally, Roderick commanded the soldiers to stop shooting. With their sharp, almost vampire-like eyesight, aided by the glow of the holograms, the half-breeds advanced further into the dark caverns, led by Roderick and Drake. Swords decapitated any injured rogues in their path.

Faint hisses were the only warning before more rogues lunged out of the darkness. In a frenzy of steel and teeth, the soldiers defended and attacked.

A rogue took one soldier by surprise and sank its teeth into his neck. A gurgling scream burst from his lips before Roderick grabbed the rogue by its collar and tossed it into the cave wall. He swung his sword, decapitating it before it could stand.

As Aden had trained them, the soldiers fought with exceptional precision, driving the rogues further into the caves, eliminating them one by one.

It took less than two hours, but Aden's army triumphed. Followed by Kane, he stomped to the warp port in the corner. "I hope you left one of them alive."

"Yes, Sir," Roderick said as Drake and another soldier held a struggling, snarling, hissing vampire in the background. Ultraviolet-infused handcuffs were clamped around his wrists to restrain his hands and weaken him.

"I'll be right there."

Aden entered the warp port and swiped his fingers over the screen, entering the coordinates and arriving inside the cave a few seconds later.

"Where did you come from?" Aden hoisted the vampire by his neck, suspending him in midair, but the vampire didn't answer. Aden tightened his grip, crushing his throat, relishing the powerful sensation that surged through him as he felt the rogue's windpipe collapse under his fingers.

"I asked you where you came from." Aden's dangerous growl and the deliberate flashing of his eyes from their normal blue to red would have left even the fiercest vampire trembling. The rogue just spat in Aden's face.

So that's how he wanted to play it.

Aden hurled the rogue against the wall of the cave, knocking him out.

"Take him back to the city and lock him up. Then use your powers of persuasion to find out who he is and what the fuck he's doing here."

"Yes, Sir," Roderick replied with a wicked gleam in his eye.

"Burn the rest of them." Aden snarled before striding into the warp port.

Ellie

Ellie dabbed at her knees as she sat across from Carrie on her bed. "Jeez, that hurts."

"Here." Carrie handed her a bandage.

"Thanks."

The shallow scrapes stung and throbbed, but the intense pulsing pain in her side was worse, making it hard to move or breathe.

The thralls' quarters were empty except for the two of them. Rows of single bunk beds, stacked three high, filled the massive room. Devoid of personal touches, color, or comfort, it reflected the thralls' dismal lives. The narrow beds lacked any cushioning, so the metal springs poked through the thin mattresses. However, as Master Matthais often reminded them, thralls were fortunate to have any beds at all.

A loud rumble echoed from her stomach, reflecting her overall achy and foul mood.

"I wish you'd let me get you something from the kitchen. I can sneak it out with no one knowing."

"No. I don't want you to get caught. It's not worth it. I've gone three days before. No big deal."

Ellie suffered the pangs of hunger more than a few times because of what her father called her rebellious nature.

"It's not fair. It wasn't your fault you were late."

"Yeah, it was, but that never matters, Carrie." Ellie stretched her legs out and poked at the bruise on her knee. "Ow."

"I'll sneak something at breakfast then," Carrie said to herself. "As soon as the Gerents get here, it'll be a madhouse, and if you're hungry and weak, it'll be hard to keep up."

"Carrie, I mean it. Don't take any chances. You need it more than I do. The last thing you need is to pass out from hunger and blood loss."

Thralls could legally become feeders at eighteen. Only pretty girls became feeders, and as one of the prettiest, Carrie had been chosen.

Unlike her own wavy, long brown hair, Carrie's blonde hair fell in short layered, wispy waves around her face. She was taller and curvier than Ellie and had legs that seemed to go on forever. At least she hadn't become a private pet yet, but she was used to provide cocktails for the vampire guests. Before the welcome party, she'd be plied with alcohol and then seated at the refreshment table, where glasses of the finest crystal were filled with blood, upon request.

Ellie shifted and flinched as pain shot through her side. "I think he cracked a rib."

"I wish you'd let me look at them. Or Veronika. Why are you so stubborn, Ellie?"

"It's one of my more charming qualities. Besides, I don't need any more attention on me, okay? Everywhere I turn lately, Master Matthais is there watching and waiting for me to screw up."

"He's watching you, alright. But I doubt it's because he's waiting for you to screw up. He can't wait to get his hands on you."

Ellie's face twisted in disgust. "Ew, Carrie. That's just... gross."

"I'm telling you, Ells. There's a reason he didn't offer you up to be a pet four years ago. And not just because your dad asked him to wait. He wants something in return and he's waiting to collect."

"Okay, double ew. Are you trying to give me more nightmares?"

The mere thought of Master Matthais touching her and drinking from her was almost too much to bear, sending shudders of revulsion down her spine. Death would absolutely be better than that.

"I dreamed about my mom last night. I haven't done that in weeks. But it kept switching back and forth with the eyes."

Carrie reached for Ellie's hand and laced their fingers together. "You want me to sleep with you today?"

"Yeah." Ellie nodded and sank back against the cool, rough wall in relief. She always slept better with Carrie next to her.

The thick mist swirled around Ellie as she walked forward, each step cautious as she struggled to find solid ground through the white haze that enveloped her. But somehow, she knew where she was going. It wasn't a destination, but an inexplicable pull that guided her through the heavy fog, and even though she couldn't quite define the emotion, she knew it wasn't fear.

At the sound of shuffling a few feet behind her, she spun around.

"Hello? Is there anybody there?"

There was no response but the hairs on the back of Ellie's neck stood up. She squinted her eyes to see the pair of piercing blue eyes emerge through the mist, their intensity unwavering as they focused on her. Startled, Ellie's heart raced with a mixture of fear and excitement, but as she stared back, curiosity replaced her initial panic. Unable to resist the hypnotic pull of the eyes, she found herself drawn closer.

Somehow, from somewhere, she recognized this was a dream. It wasn't real. Still, her heart fluttered in her chest.

"Who are you?" Her breath stirred the mist.

She took a hesitant step, and then another, her feet carrying her closer to the mysterious presence. But just as she was within reach, the eyes faded away, retreating into the fog until they disappeared.

"Wait." Ellie cried as she reached out. "Come back."

Tears gathered on her lashes as the words clogged her throat. She ran into the mist.

"Please, don't go."

Her broken pleas echoed in the haze surrounding her, suffocating her. She gasped for breath, and the mist swirled, enveloping her, but Ellie didn't care. She succumbed to the engulfing emptiness, allowing herself to be consumed by the void.

Ellie bolted upright with a gasp and let out a low groan, her body throbbing with pain. Her eyes whipped around the room, blinking as they adjusted to the dark.

There was no mist anywhere.

Pressed against the wall, she could feel Carrie hogging most of the narrow mattress. The loss and emptiness that engulfed her as the eyes faded away persisted, even in wakefulness. Ellie rubbed a hand over the center of her chest, her heart constricting and sinking in disappointment.

She pushed against Carrie, who grunted and shifted to the left. Ellie lay back down, the hard springs beneath the mattress digging into her, resigned to the fact that she wouldn't be able to go back to sleep.

The raging headache pounding behind Ellie's eyes was a combination of hunger and a lack of sleep. The lingering aches in her knees and side every time she moved didn't help. Neither did the bustling activity around her.

Just the thought of the council gathering and the impending vampire invasion filled Ellie with anxiety, but her feelings meant nothing in a world ruled by vampires.

"Ellie, quit standing around."

She jumped at Veronika's harsh voice behind her, almost dropping the vase she carried.

"The Gerents are arriving any minute. Camilla said to put those flowers on the banquet table and find Carrie. She should be in here by now. Master Matthais will drain us all if everything isn't perfect."

"I'm going. I'm going," Ellie said under her breath and limped into the great hall, wincing as her aching knees and ribs protested with every step.

The large room, like the rest of Master Matthais' compound, was luxurious and filled with lavish furnishings. Oversized black sofas and chairs were arranged in clusters around the room, complemented by blood-red accents.

Long banquet tables with centerpieces of red, white, and black orchids, covered in red tablecloths, lined one wall. Rows of long-stemmed glasses stood ready for the evening's guests, and in front of the tables, chairs waited for the thralls who would be tapped for their blood during cocktail hour.

The room hummed with energy as thralls scurried about, putting the finishing touches on the preparations. Ellie set her vase on the table, brushing a few pieces of lint off the tablecloth, before turning around when she heard her name.

"Ellie, your dad is looking for you."

Carrie walked toward her, looking like a dream. Her hair was curved around her face, her makeup accentuating the blue of her eyes and the soft features of her face. She wore her formal thrall uniform, a long black dress with a blood-red sash over the shoulder, and black heels that clicked on the patterned stone floor. Quite the contrast to Ellie's everyday thrall uniform of white pants with a gray button-down shirt and matching shoes.

Ellie smiled as Carrie reached her. "You look really pretty."

"Thanks." Carrie ran her hands down her body. "It looks okay?"

"Yeah, but you've got a smudge. Look up." Ellie reached up and rubbed her fingertip under one of Carrie's eyes. "You don't want to look like Heather, all raccoon-eyed," she said as Carrie snickered. "Hold still."

Carrie had been a party feeder for a few years, so she didn't get nervous anymore, but Ellie worried enough for both of them. Every time she did it, Carrie risked the chance of a vampire taking a liking to her and asking Master Matthais to take her as a pet.

"Carrie, get over here." Veronika called from the doorway. "You need your BloodStone shot."

All thralls received a daily dose of BloodStone. The pill kept humans healthy and sped up their blood regeneration, allowing them to be fed from more often. Feeders took concentrated shots before parties to increase their blood flow and provide the maximum amount of blood.

"I'll see you later." Carrie pulled Ellie into a brief hug before releasing her.

"Be careful." Her words were barely audible, and as her eyes followed her friend, Ellie's fingers itched to reach out and pull her back.

The door to the command center slid open with a whooshing sound as Ellie approached. Her father, Myles, had programmed it to recognize her years ago. Discreet strips of ambient lighting integrated into the ceiling and walls, illuminating the room. Her dad sat at a massive console table in the center, its surface embedded with rows of small, touch-sensitive screens that controlled everything in and out of the room. Above the table, a wall of holograms hovered, their shimmering images casting a muted glow throughout the space. With each touch or voice command, the holograms displayed a dynamic feed of live images, smoothly transitioning between scenes from inside and outside the compound.

Everything in Master Matthais' city ran like clockwork, and her father handled all the technical aspects of it, monitoring the various systems and displays from this one room.

"Hi, Dad."

He swiveled his chair and stood. He wore his standard Elite Guard uniform—a charcoal gray suit, white shirt, and blood-red tie. Elite guards ranked higher than other half-breeds, and her father was second in authority, only to Lorcan, the most vicious of Master Matthais' guards. But Lorcan wasn't a half-breed. He was one of only a handful of vampire guards under Master Matthais, and just the thought of him caused Ellie's skin to break out in a cold sweat.

"Hi, Ellie Bellie."

"Dad." Ellie let out a sigh at her father's childish nickname for her. "I'm almost twenty-three. I thought we agreed you were going to stop calling me that."

"Sorry. Sorry."

He flashed her a sheepish grin as he pulled her into a hug. As always, she was dwarfed in his embrace. Her father's over seven-foot-tall frame made him unique for a human. Well, a half-breed who was turned rather than born through the breeding program.

Ellie gritted her teeth and tried not to flinch as her sore body protested. He didn't need to know what Master Matthais had done to her. She only saw her dad a few times a week, and she didn't want to worry him.

Or get a lecture.

Her father was rare. Vampires stopped making half-breed guards out of humans once the breeding program was introduced. But her dad was born to human parents. When Master Matthais saw him while touring their village almost two decades earlier, he murdered her mother, turned her father, and took both of them back to the capital. That moment had changed their lives forever.

Ellie pulled out of his embrace and sat in his chair.

"Carrie said you wanted to see me."

"Yeah, before it got too busy." He tilted her head to the side as the smile slipped off his lips. "What happened to your face?"

She pulled away. He didn't need to know what had happened with Kira.

"Wrong place, wrong time with one of the house cats."

"Those don't look like cat scratches."

In need of a distraction, she shifted her gaze towards the console table. "Did you get that error with the program fixed?"

He nodded and folded his enormous frame into the chair next to her. "Yeah," he said, lowering his voice. You never knew when someone is listening. "Thanks to you remembering which operating manual it was in."

Reading was illegal for humans. Most didn't even know what books were, never mind how to read them. But her dad learned when he joined Master Matthais' Elite Guard. And he taught her.

"Your flawless memory has been a lifesaver, Ells. It got me out of more than a few tight spots, that's for sure."

"Who knew secretly teaching your kid to read would be so useful?"

"Your brain is too incredible to waste."

That's what he said to her that night, a year after they came to the capital. He took her on his lap, gently tapped her forehead, and whispered, "You're special, you know. You have the gift of remembering everything you see and hear."

Then he taught her to read, too. And she didn't waste her brain. She read anything she could get her hands on, mostly those instruction manuals. Although she didn't always understand everything she was reading, she heeded her father's words.

She felt his intense gaze on her and recognized the familiar expression on his face—a mix of longing and affection. His sad smile betrayed the sadness he tried to hide.

He reached out and tucked a stray hair behind her ear. "You remind me so much of your mom."

Every time he said those words, it felt like a vise tightened around her heart, a suffocating grip, making it almost impossible to breathe. He said it more and more lately. At twenty-two, Ellie was only two years younger than her mom when Master Matthais murdered her. And the closer Ellie got each year, the more apparent her father's sorrow became.

She was saved from replying when the mic in his ear came to life. He glanced at the hologram of the airplane runway outside the city. A private jet was approaching the hangar as the first of their vampire guests arrived.

"Tell them to use hangar one." He looked back at her, his eyes echoing regret. "You should get out of here. That's Gerent Westcott's plane. The others will be here soon."

Ellie nodded and stood up. He kissed the top of her head. "Get Veronika to check those scratches. Maybe I can try to squeeze out a few minutes tomorrow morning and we can have breakfast together, huh?"

"Uh, sure. I'll see you later, Dad."

Ellie hurried out of the room. She had one more day before she could eat again, but he didn't need to know that either.

Aden

Aden relaxed on one of the large sofas in the middle of the hall, tuning out the mind-numbing activity around him. Andrei, Matthais' Commander General since the Great Vampire Wars, sat across from him, sipping blood from a wine glass.

"I'll never know how you can bear to drink it that way. It gets too cold outside the vein."

Andrei took another sip with a casual shrug. "You get used to it. Warm blood is nice, but room temperature is an acquired taste."

Chelsea kneeled at Aden's feet on the cold floor with her head down, waiting to feed him. He beckoned her closer, and she crawled forward before lifting her arm. He sank his fangs into the spot beneath her wrist, barely touching her with the tips of his fingers. Her body jerked and then stilled, paralyzed, as he drank deep. After a few gulps, he retracted his fangs and sat back. Chelsea listed sideways, and, in seconds, another thrall was there to help her stand.

"Make sure she gets BloodStone and is in my suite by eleven."

"Yes, Sir."

"Also, give her at least four glasses of Jameson."

"Yes, Sir."

Aden grabbed a napkin from the table, erasing the evidence of blood that lingered at the corners of his lips.

"Why don't you keep your pets on a leash?" Andrei asked.

Chelsea wasn't his pet. Aden didn't keep pets. He fed from and fucked all his thralls.

"I don't need to. Mine don't run."

Andrei gave him a doubtful glance but changed the subject. "Get ready for some insane action at this year's games. Matthais brought in a few Arctic bears."

"What fun is that? Humans are no match for them."

"But it's much bloodier."

Aden saw Matthais making his way around the great hall. In contrast to the Westcott's, Matthais' cities and compounds blended classical Roman architecture, infused with subtle elements of state-of-the-art, modern design.

The walls of the great hall were beige marble and granite blocks, stretching up to vaulted ceilings, displaying intricate frescoes, and supported by tall columns with fluted shafts and capitals. Draped over the stone, embroidered tapestries in red and gold added color to the otherwise monochrome walls. Ornamental sconces and a mantelpiece made from the same marble as the surrounding walls flanked a towering fireplace.

Ornate furniture, covered in black silk, blended ancient design with optimum comfort. The polished floors were a colorful mosaic of individual tiles, featuring geometric shapes ranging from sharp lines to elegant spirals. The designs were masterfully crafted artwork that showcased the technical skill and artistic vision of ancient Rome.

It wasn't his style, but as an artist, Aden could appreciate the aesthetic.

Ever the attentive host, Matthais glided around the room. He greeted his Gerents personally, taking the time to catch up on each of their lives. Despite technology that enabled instant contact at all times, Matthais allowed his Gerents to rule each of their regions with little interference, provided they enforced all laws.

Hence the reason for the annual council gathering. It allowed the Gerents to give him a status report and address any business. The week-long gathering was Matthais' way of maintaining control and ensuring world peace.

Of course, the week was not all work. It was also a time to socialize and play in the world's capital. Besides the meetings, there were parties, HEW games, and slave auctions to keep the vampires entertained.

"Are we going to need to intervene in Abya Yala?"

Andrei's annoyed expression required no further interpretation. "Fucking moron. Paolo's troops should be able to handle this, but that coven of rogues has grown too large. Cecilia's going to catch hell for that at the meeting tomorrow."

"I just took out a coven in the northwest a couple of days ago."

"How large was it?"

"About ninety."

Andrei set his empty glass on the table. "Do you know their origins?"

"No. I kept one alive and Roderick is interrogating him while I'm here. But why the fuck have rogues started popping up?"

"Bring it up tomorrow. It would be interesting to know if anyone else has had any encounters."

Aden shifted so he could watch a tall, leggy redhead as she passed behind Andrei. She wore no collar, so she wasn't a pet. Was she for sale?

"I can take my troops down to help, but will piss me off if I have to clean up Paolo's shit."

"That's probably what will end up happening. I can send a team to assist."

Aden turned his attention back to Andrei, his lips twisting into a conceited smirk. "I've got it covered."

"Don't smirk. Wait until you hear about it tomorrow. You might change your mind."

Aden's gaze moved to his father who was standing near the fireplace speaking to Rashidi. Aurick Westcott was an impressive figure in his dress kilt in shades of red, forest green, and blue. He wore his family's colors and crests at formal events. Aden sometimes did as well, but tonight he'd chosen his more casual standard black pants and button-down shirt, with the sleeves half rolled up his arms.

While their posture appeared relaxed, his father's serious expression suggested the conversation was far from casual. As Matthais approached, their conversation ceased.

From the corner of his eye, Aden caught sight of his mother speaking to Indira, the Gerent of Vindhya. As one of only three female Gerents, Indira was a respected member of the Council, and she and his mother had been friends for centuries. Sophie wasn't a vampire. She was a sired half-breed, but as Aurick's wife, she commanded the same level of respect as her husband. She could have become a vampire centuries ago but chose to remain a half-breed, something Aden never understood. Who wouldn't want to be a full vampire?

The sound of his name drew Aden's attention back to Andrei. "What was that?"

"I said I'm surprised she's not here."

"Who?"

"Kira. She's been talking about seeing you for weeks."

Aden jerked when a hand touched his shoulder. He looked up to find his mother standing behind him.

"It's almost sunrise. I'm heading to bed."

She smiled as she looked down at him. They made up on the plane because she could never stay mad at him.

"Are you going alone?" he asked. "Do you want me to walk you to your rooms? Or better yet, take a warp port."

The Westcott's guest quarters were in the farthest north wing of Matthais' compound, which spanned almost a mile along the capital's coast.

"I'm more than capable of walking myself. Your father and Cecilia are in a heated discussion, so I'm not waiting. It could go on for hours."

Aden looked over and saw Cecilia waving her arms, while Rashidi and Katsumi watched the theatrics with hesitant looks.

"Will I see you tomorrow evening?" she asked.

"We've got the opening night games," Andrei said, and Aden shot him a what-the-fuck look. Anyone in their right mind knew not to mention the HEW Games to Sophie Westcott. The Human Extinction Warfare games were held twice a year to commemorate vampires' victory in the Great Vampire Wars.

"Hmmm." His mother pursed her lips before turning and walking away without another word.

Aden caught Kane's eye, where he stood by the door and motioned for him to follow Sophie before turning his gaze back to Andrei. "Real nice, jackass."

"She needs to get over that, man. The games are a way of life here. We have them every month now."

"What?"

"Yeah. They alternate between here and Völkberg."

"Hmmm." It wasn't lost on Aden that his response was an echo of his mother's. The games were enjoyable, but was it necessary to have them more than twice a year?

"They want to start a regional rotation. Each month a different region will host and every eight months it starts over again. It's one of the things on the agenda tomorrow."

Aurick wouldn't take that well. At all.

"Well, I'm gonna head back, too." Aden stood and stretched. "Chelsea should be ready for me. I'll see you at the meeting."

"Hello, handsome."

Kira's sultry voice wrapped around Aden from behind as he walked down the hallway leading to his family's guest quarters.

It was only a matter of time before he ran into her. With a slow spin, he turned and gave her his signature cocky smirk. Kira was one of the most gorgeous vampires he'd ever seen. Unfortunately, she was batshit crazy.

They had a very brief, violent fling a century ago, but it didn't last long. She'd refused to adhere to his no-touching rule. They hadn't parted on the best terms, but over the last century things thawed between them.

"Kira," Aden drawled as she approached him. Her smile was even more alluring than her voice.

"You're not leaving the party already, are you?" Her tongue darted out to lick her full lips. "I've been looking forward to seeing you."

"Then you should have come to the party earlier."

"A woman is always fashionably late."

And just like that, desire for her surged through his body like wildfire. His eyes raked over her. "You look exquisite."

Her fiery red hair had grown longer and was curled around her face in sultry waves that matched the curves of her voluptuous body.

"Of course I do." Modesty was not in Kira's vocabulary. "Andrei said you were going back to your room."

"Yes. Do you want to join me?"

Her lips curved into a seductive smile. Aden stepped to the side and motioned for her to walk ahead of him.

"Did you bring your favorite pet?" she asked.

"Of course."

"Mmmm... you know how I enjoy playing with her. Maybe she can join us?"

He grinned as they turned down the hallway to his suite, where Chelsea would be waiting. "She'll be full of Jameson when we get there."

"Perfect."

Opening night of the HEW Games filled Aden with excitement. The capital's outdoor arena was a massive circular structure, dominating the landscape with walls of weathered limestone and polished granite. Modeled after the Colosseum of Rome, the city of Matthais' birth two thousand years ago, the massive amphitheater was a magnificent spectacle built to host the savage celebratory games to commemorate the end of the Great Vampire Wars.

The stands surrounding the arena overflowed. The tiered seating provided unobstructed views for the thousands of spectators waiting for the games to begin. Humans watched through bars at ground level, while half-breeds occupied the levels above and vampires the levels above those.

The Gerents and their families enjoyed private skyboxes on the highest level with a hologram of the arena below, at eye level, for their viewing pleasure. The Westcott's skybox was next to Matthais', indicating the family's importance in society, but Aurick hadn't stepped foot in it for almost five centuries.

"This is probably a stupid question, but is there any chance Aurick will attend this year?" Andrei asked from his seat beside Aden.

He was Matthais' gamer and always joined Aden in the skybox. They had an ongoing rivalry for almost two and a half centuries.

Aden's lips curved into an amused smirk. "Yeah, that's not gonna happen."

"He doesn't have to play, but as a Gerent, he should support them by showing up. Or at least give you players."

Although at first, Aden only attended the games in Aurick's absence, his decision to take part had caused a chasm between him and his parents. The Westcotts didn't offer their humans for the games, but Matthais provided the required number for Aden to control when he was in the mood to play.

"You keep living in your fantasy world," Aden said.

Aden enjoyed the games, especially when he was younger, during what everyone referred to as his "dark years." Watching humans fight to the death was a welcome distraction from the unending torment that plagued him.

The energy in the air was electric. Vampires came from around the world to attend the games. Held twice a year, summer and winter, the January games drew the most crowds. Vampires enjoyed watching humans suffer, and it was more difficult to fight in the bitter cold.

The dusty, packed dirt of the center fighting pit was empty except for four massive bears, three grizzly, and one polar. They lounged in individual cages, each with its half-breed attendant.

"They breed them larger every year, don't they?" Aden said.

Andrei pointed to the white one. "That's Zurina. Matthais bred the largest male and female polar bears in existence, and she was the result."

The animal was sleek and twice as large as the grizzlies. Her fur was pristine and impeccably groomed.

"She's magnificent. Why is he using her in the games?"

"Showing off."

The open-air arena was located a few miles outside Arcipelago. With an average of twenty hours of night in January, the games took place outside the dome city, unlike the summer games, which were held in a smaller underground arena inside it.

The night was icy cold. Snowflakes from the pitch-black sky above left a dusting on the ground below. Unlike humans, who could freeze to death at these extreme temperatures, vampires were unaffected, their bodies adapting to match the frigid surroundings.

Aden looked at his thrall kneeling on the wood floor. Her head was down, awaiting his needs. Andrei's thrall, also on her knees, shivered, but tried to hide her discomfort. Sophie insisted that their thralls dressed appropriately for the weather, but Andrei's thrall wore only a light coat, insufficient for the current conditions.

"Wrist," Aden said, and his thrall lifted her arm. He sank his fangs in and drank.

The noise in the arena grew louder, and Matthais walked out to a glass platform in front of his skybox.

"Welcome my friends to the opening night of the winter Human Extinction Warfare Games."

Matthais' voice boomed through the arena. Zurina roared when she heard it and the other bears joined in, their roars blending with the crowd's thunderous cheers, creating an almost deafening cacophony of sound.

"Yes, yes, my sweet," Matthais cooed at the bear. "You will get to play soon."

Aden sat back, relaxed and warmed by the blood now coursing through his body.

"Thank you all for coming tonight to celebrate the four hundred seventy-fifth HEW Games, commemorating our victory in the Great Vampire Wars. Humans once thought us inferior, even after we saved them from extinction twice. First, we gave them BloodStone, eradicating the second pandemic in a decade and curing them of all human illnesses. Then we rebuilt civilization following a catastrophic shifting of the world's continents. Yet, they still refused to show us the respect and gratitude we deserved. However, with courage and determination, we liberated ourselves from their tyranny and claimed our rightful place in this world. Tonight, as we do every year, we celebrate our freedom by reminding humans of their place in the evolutionary food chain, affirming nature's law of survival of the fittest."

Aden chuckled. Matthais recycled the same speech every year.

"In honor of this milestone, I'm introducing my cherished Zurina." She roared again at the sound of her name. Her guard led Zurina out, parading her along the length of the field. "My beloved girl is eager to give her master and his esteemed guests a show to remember." The other bears roared again, eager to be released. "So, without further delay, let us begin our annual week-long celebration."

Matthais retreated from the platform as more cheers filled the arena. He had a tendency to ramble, so Aden was surprised but grateful that his introduction was over.

Aden looked at the hologram. Ninety humans, ten for each region, both male and female, of various sizes, ages, and races, were led onto the field. They were chained, barefoot, and barely clothed. Each wore a metal collar embedded into their neck, giving the vampire complete control over the humans' actions through a wireless console in the Gerents' skyboxes.

Their region's crests were branded on the humans' skin, with men bearing the mark on their chests and women on their backs. Guards led them to nine cages, also bearing each region's crest, and forced them onto their knees.

Each cage had twelve-inch rods that emitted a weak electrical charge when pressed against the humans' skin or the bears' fur. Animal abuse and cruelty were punishable by death, so the players were only given non-lethal weapons to defend themselves. Their weapons couldn't hurt the bears, only make them pause and give the humans a chance to escape, prolonging the action.

Each region was permitted one hundred humans, ten per game, to participate in each night. Their vampire masters pitted them against each other, controlling their actions in a brutal display of hand-to-hand combat.

Aden swiped his finger over his hologram and brought up images of each of his players. There were eight men and two women. Humans had to be at least twenty to play, and the ones Matthais gave to him varied in age.

Unless otherwise euthanized, because of BloodStone, humans remained healthy and strong and lived to the average age of one hundred fifty years. Two of the males Matthais gave him looked to be close to that. Because of Aden's skill, Matthais never gave him the advantage of younger and stronger humans to control.

Aden picked up his console and selected his first player, one of the older males. He might as well get rid of the weakest first.

The cheers rose in volume as one human from each cage stepped out, their movements manipulated like puppets on strings. Aden directed his player to grab his stunner and exit the cage. The humans circled one another, their eyes wide with fear, knowing what was about to happen yet powerless to do anything to stop it, as each of the controlling vampires assessed their opponents.

"Get ready to have your winning streak shattered," Andrei taunted him, a mischievous glint in his eyes. "You're about to be dethroned."

"Don't hold your breath." Aden's voice oozed with confidence. He'd been winning for almost one hundred years, and his exceptional skills as a player ensured that the Westcotts' region often had their annual financial tribute waived. But Aurick never once thanked him for it.

The fighting began, and two men charged toward each other, their movements stiff and unnatural. As the vampires fine-tuned their control, the players' actions became more fluid. Barefoot, they circled each other, their feet sinking into the dirt and light snow.

In a sudden move, one player lunged, thrusting his stunner against the other's chest. The man's body jerked like he was being electrocuted. It was short-lived, and he retaliated before dropping his stunner and charging at his opponent again. He threw a punch, and the opposing player ducked under the swing, retaliating with an uppercut, sending blood spattering through the air.

Nearby, two women fought. One executed an awkward roundhouse kick, her leg swinging through the air. Instead of her foot connecting with her opponent's face, it landed against her neck. The force of the impact knocked the other woman down, gasping for air and clutching her throat.

Aden kept his player on the sidelines, moving him around the perimeter as the fighting concentrated in the center. Patience was the key to survival.

Once two of the humans were dead, Aden unleashed his player, sending him into the fray between a man and a woman. With a forceful jab, he thrust the tip of his stunner against the woman's neck, sending her to her knees. He turned on the man who was watching and he attacked. Despite the man's age and somewhat frail physique, Aden got him to outlast three other players before Zurina and the other bears were released from their cages.

The scent of blood and human fear rose from the ground as the three brown bears charged into the arena, attacking their prey. The increased screams of the players were almost inaudible over the roar of the crowd.

Hot breath steamed in the cold air as Zurina strutted around the perimeter, almost as if she were surveying her options. Aden kept his player to the side until one of the brown bears turned toward him in what felt like slow motion. It charged toward his player, but Aden directed him to stand his ground. At the last moment, Aden had him sidestep and grab the bear's fur, using its momentum to swing onto its back. He wrapped his arms around the bear's neck, squeezing as the bear thrashed wildly.

A female player wasn't so lucky. As her vampire had her attacking another player, Zurina caught her unaware. Massive claws raked across her back, and she fell face-first into the bloodstained snow.

"That pristine white fur of hers is going to get awful bloody before it's over," Andrei said with a laugh.

Aden murmured his agreement as he sat back, indifferent to the suffering in front of him. His player could only hold on to the bear's neck for so long until the bear bucked him off. The bear turned on him and tore the old man to shreds.

Frustrated, Aden let out a string of fucks. They echoed through the skybox as Andrei's deep chuckle filled the air.

The battles between humans and humans, and humans against beasts, raged on through the night. Bones cracked, blood flowed, and bodies fell. With each victory, the sole surviving human was directed to the arena's edge, while the dead were dragged away, leaving dark trails in the now snow-covered ground.

The winner of each round advanced to the next one, giving that region an additional player. The one left at the end of the night advanced to the next night. And so on until the end of the games.

As dawn approached, only two players remained—Aden's and Andrei's. Andrei's was a burly man with a broken nose, and Aden's was a slender woman who was stronger than she looked, although she favored her left leg. Their final showdown was swift and brutal. The man charged, but the woman used his momentum against him, flipping him over her head. As he lay stunned, she struck his throat with a powerful blow and crushed his larynx, breaking his neck.

She swayed on her feet, what was left of her clothing, torn and bloody. The crowd erupted in cheers as Aden sat back. In a fit of anger, Andrei chucked his gaming console across the skybox. Aden shot him a smug, gloating smirk, confident that he'd be crowned the champion again this year.

Ellie

The mist was back, and it engulfed her.

Ellie fought the urge to panic. She'd been here before, but this time felt different.

She was being watched. And the sensation of eyes on her was unsettling, like an invisible hand pressing against the back of her neck.

She turned, and the mist parted, revealing an endless void of darkness that seemed to stretch on forever. A shiver ran down Ellie's spine as she sensed someone moving closer.

A sudden, sharp pain shot through her neck as she felt something pierce her skin, and she reached up to swat it away. When she pulled her fingers back, they were slick and sticky, coated in a thick layer of blood.

Fear coursed through her veins and her breath quickened, coming out in short, shallow gasps. Then, out of the dark abyss in front of her, the eyes appeared.

She met the gaze of those piercing blue eyes, so familiar and comforting, and her anxiety melted away as relief flooded her body.

But then they hardened and darkened, like storm clouds rolling in, and Ellie's heart sank into her stomach.

The eyes turned a chilling shade of red like they always did, and Ellie's breath caught in her throat. The now red eyes and their haunting stare faded into the blackness.

"Wait! Come back," she murmured, her voice barely a whisper, her heartache echoing in every word.

Ellie's eyes snapped open. She stared at the metal bed frame above her, a queasy sensation churning in her stomach. At least it was the eyes in her dream again and not her mother.

The lights inside the thralls' quarters were already on, but the room was silent. That meant she was late.

Why hadn't Carrie woken her up?

Ellie jumped out of bed, casting a worried glance at the one Carrie always slept in when she didn't sleep in hers. It didn't look like it had been slept in at all.

Worry twisted Ellie's stomach into knots. That meant Carrie probably spent the night in the infirmary, getting a blood transfusion.

She tugged on her clothes and dashed down the never-ending row of beds, leaving behind the lingering uneasiness from her dream, her sole focus on making sure Carrie was okay.

Aden

The temptation to bang his head on the bronze and marble table was staggering but Aden had no desire to call attention to himself or risk breaking the table. The meeting dragged on, and they were no further along than when they started. Except the current argument between Matthais and his father grew more heated.

"Aurick, be reasonable. All the regions should take part in the rotating games."

"No, Matthais. I've never agreed with the games and that's no secret. I don't want that kind of violence within my borders. It's barbaric."

"You don't have to attend. It won't be any different from now. But you should host them, like the rest of us, Aurick," Dietrich, the Gerent of Erebu, said as Aden and Andrei exchanged a stare across the table. They attended these meetings in their capacity as the top two commanders of the world's military. But Andrei looked like he also would prefer to be anywhere else.

Banjora, the Gerent of Terra Australis, spoke from the other end of the table. "Each region should participate. It's a sign of solidarity if nothing else."

"Yes, Aurick," Yuri, the Gerent of Sever Sib-Ir, said. "Banjora is right. It reflects poorly on all of us when a single region chooses not to take part."

"I don't want to host the games in my region either," Rashidi said, his thick accent and deep voice leaving little room for debate.

"That's enough!" Matthais heaved himself out of his chair in a rare display of uncontrolled anger. "I'm tired of talking about this. We're getting nowhere. Clearly, we will not agree on this, so let's table it for now. Those who want to host the games will and those who don't can abstain. We'll revisit this at next year's meeting. We have more important things to discuss today." Matthais took his seat. "Now, Cecilia, this rogue problem is out of hand. You and Paolo should have handled this."

"It wasn't a problem until recently. This coven has grown to an unmanageable size," Cecilia said.

"It never should have been able to grow that large," Indira said, unable to hide her distaste for the other woman. The contentious relationship between them was infamous, dating back half a millennium.

"I agree," Katsumi said. "How did you not know this was happening?"

Cecilia's eyes flashed with anger but, with his usual diplomacy, his father intervened. "The how or why doesn't matter. We have to deal with it now. Your failure to control your vampires compromises the security of my borders. I want those rogues taken care of immediately."

"If Paolo can't handle this, you will find another Commander General who can. Or I will," Matthais said, effectively closing the subject.

Seated in a chair against the wall, Paolo bristled but remained silent. Cecilia, however, did not. She pushed away from the table and stood. "I won't tolerate being reprimanded like a child. I will rule my region as I see fit and hire who I want to command my military."

"Cecilia." Matthais' voice was dangerously low. "Calm down. And sit down."

She crossed her arms and remained standing.

"You have neglected your responsibilities. Feigning ignorance doesn't suit you. If you cannot govern your region effectively, you will lose it."

"How dare you speak to me this way?" Cecilia marched toward the door. "Paolo, vámonos!"

Paolo followed her, but two guards on either side of the door blocked their exit. When Matthais said her name again, she turned to glare at him.

"You have one week to get this situation resolved, or Andrei and Aden will do it for you. Your region will not only be required to cover the cost but will also face fines. Do I make myself clear?"

Cecilia cursed in Spanish, then pushed past the guards and exited the room with a flourish.

"Well, that went well," Aden muttered, receiving a sharp glare from his father in response.

"Aurick, if you're so concerned about your borders, you should have a contingent standing by to take point." Matthais turned to Aden. "You can handle this I assume? Or do I need to send Andrei?"

"Consider it handled," Aden replied.

He couldn't wait to see how Cecilia reacted when she heard about that.

"Good. Now, let's move on to the next order of business."

The slave auction was in full swing, but Aden was bored. The meetings earlier had left him with a raging headache, a sensation he was unaccustomed to as a vampire.

Of course, Aurick reacted to the games' suggestion as Aden had expected. His father was nothing, if not predictable. Then, after Cecilia's meltdown, the last order of business for the day had been a discussion of a group of rebelling humans banding together in Eastern Erebu. Dietrich's troops had quelled an earlier uprising but there were rumors of a larger insurgency building.

Andrei dropped into the seat beside Aden after slipping into the skybox. "Aurick left the meeting pretty heated today."

"When does he not?" Aden looked at the hologram. A male slave was on display, being led around the arena on a leash, wearing nothing but a collar. He was shivering in the cold night air as, again, light snow fell from the sky, dusting the dirt floor.

The arena's transformation erased any traces of the bloodshed from the previous night and gave no hint of the blood that would stain its grounds later in the evening. Beside the stage stood several rows of men and women, all dressed in black robes, as they waited their turn on the auctioneer's block.

"Humans are no match for the half-breed army," Aden said. "I understand the need to eliminate any potential threat before it gets out of control, but bombing three thousand miles of Erebuian countryside seems like overkill."

It was only when Andrei chuckled Aden realized the irony of what he said.

"Aurick made his opposition very clear."

"He doesn't subscribe to Matthais' ideology of exterminating rebelling humans. As a military commander, I can see the efficiency of it, but I have to agree it's a disproportionate response."

Andrei lowered his voice so only Aden could hear him, even though there was no one else in the skybox except Kane, standing near the door, and Maggie, sitting at his feet.

"Dietrich told Matthais privately that this was the third uprising in the last year."

Aden glanced away from the hologram to meet Andrei's eyes. "Why didn't he tell everyone on the Council?"

"I don't ask. I just listen."

Aden understood that perspective. Although they often sought the opinions of their military commanders, the Gerents disliked being openly questioned.

"Concealing that information seems foolish," Aden said as he grabbed the tablet and brought up a smaller hologram to scroll through the catalog of slaves for sale.

"I don't ask. I just listen," Andrei said again, drawing out each syllable.

"Have any other regions had uprisings?"

"Not that I know of, but it's probably best to wipe them all out and the word will get around. If any other humans are thinking of doing the same thing, that should quell it."

Aden nodded. The odd look that overcame his father's face during that discussion seemed more puzzling, and Aden suspected there was more to it than simply being disgusted with Matthais' lack of regard for human life. He'd have to ask his father about it when he had time, but right now he needed to find a couple of thralls to buy so he could go back to his room and feed.

"Are you staying for the games later?" Andrei asked.

"Depends on the outcome here."

Aden's eyes returned to the hologram. He swept his finger over it to once again peruse the catalog. The skybox door slid open and Kira glided in before slipping into the seat beside him.

"Hello, Aden. Andrei."

Andrei nodded in greeting as Aden shot her an irritated glare.

"What are you doing here?"

They had fun the day before, feeding from Chelsea, and then fucking her before each other. But he'd gotten his fill of Kira. She'd gotten pretty rough with Chelsea, who had to be rushed to the infirmary, and it reminded him just how unhinged she was.

Kira's eyes flashed. "Fuck you, Aden."

"What?" he barked as he looked back at the hologram and swiped past more thralls for sale. "We had our fun last night, Kira, but I've got a busy week. I'll see you next year."

"The hell you will, asshole." Kira stood and stormed out.

Aden's eyes didn't stray from the hologram.

"Wow, that was harsh, man," Andrei said with a dark chuckle.

"Why do I always forget how fucking crazy she is?"

"When you're that hot looking, you can make men forget their own names."

Aden didn't disagree, but beauty only went so far. There was nothing wrong with being a little rough. Pleasure could be more intense with a touch of pain, but Kira always took it over the line.

Maggie shivered at his feet. She'd been plied with wine before accompanying him to the auction but the false sense of warmth from the alcohol in her blood was fading.

"Kane, take Maggie back to the city."

As Kane and Maggie exited the skybox, Matthais walked in, his entrance so sudden and quiet that Aden almost didn't notice him. "Ah, Aden, shall I have a replacement feeder brought to you?"

"No thanks. I'm good for the moment."

Matthais sat in the chair Kira had vacated. An exotic redheaded slave caught Aden's eye and he watched as she was led onto the stage. He placed a bid for her. A bidding war ensued between him and Yuri until the other vampire conceded.

Aden stood and he saw annoyance flash across Matthais' face as he rose out of his seat.

"Don't you want to stay for the games?"

"I have other games taking priority tonight. I'll play tomorrow."

Matthais rose. "I'll have your new pet delivered to your suite at once."

"Thanks." Aden gave Andrei a nod of farewell and left the skybox. He had no intention of thinking about business again until tomorrow.

Aden barely registered Kane's presence outside the door as he approached his guest suite. He'd left Kane behind tonight, not wanting to be shadowed.

The second day of meetings was less dramatic than the first. Cecilia was calmer and assured Matthais that Paolo would handle the rogue problem as soon as they returned home. After each region's commander provided a brief update, the meeting focused on determining the number of half-breed soldiers needed in each region to replenish those who aged out.

Half-breeds lived for two hundred fifty years, give or take. As they aged, the military retired the soldiers and replaced them with younger versions. Retirement meant euthanasia, except in Réimse Shíochánta. Aurick didn't believe in disposing of otherwise healthy half-breeds, so he sent them to the outlying villages to oversee the human thralls.

The door to his suite opened, and the scent hit Aden like a freight train. There was a human female in his room and her scent was mouthwatering.

He walked around the corner to find her leaning over the raised antique platform bed, smoothing the sheet. The previous day's bloody sheets lay in a pile on the floor at her feet. Waves of dark chestnut hair piled on top of her head in a messy bun, revealing the graceful curve of her neck. Aden's throat tightened as he swallowed, his fangs lengthening at the sight of her flawless, unblemished skin. He took a deep breath, inhaling her intoxicating, overwhelming scent. Its mixture of honeysuckle and jasmine hijacked the entire room.

She was pure, untainted, a virgin in every sense, and venom pooled in his mouth. She turned to grab the pillow and jumped when she saw him.

"Oh!" The girl lifted her hand to her throat even as she dropped her head. "I'm sorry, Sir," she said before regaining her composure. "I'll be out of your way in a minute."

She whirled back to the bed to resume her task. Unable to tear his eyes away from her, Aden walked toward her, his eyes devouring every inch of her.

She was petite, at least a foot shorter than his six-foot-five frame. Her heart-shaped face narrowed at the bottom, giving her a mature appearance, yet her full mouth and the cleft above her upper lip gave her a youthful air. He couldn't see her eyes but a set of full, bushy eyebrows hovered over them, the left arching slightly higher than the right. Her cheek bore several deep scratches, leaving him curious about their cause.

She couldn't be much older than twenty and although overall she was rather plain, there was a captivating allure about her that took his breath away. It irritated him.

Aden enjoyed the sight of beautiful women, and while all of his thralls were attractive, they were nothing compared to female vampires. But this small slip of a girl—a human girl at that—was stunning in her simplicity.

Aden continued to circle her and a wary expression crossed her face as she registered his movement. But she didn't cringe away the way most thralls did in his presence. Her actions, or lack thereof, intrigued him. In less than a minute, she stunned, irritated, and intrigued him. Not an easy feat.

Aden took a deep breath, his nostrils flaring as her intoxicating scent filled his lungs. "A vampire has never drunk from you?" The question slipped out before he could catch himself.

Her body froze. "No, Sir," she said with a slow shake of her head.

"Why not?"

"Master Matthais forbids it."

Interesting. Matthais wanted her for himself, which meant she was off limits. Even though she wasn't his usual type, he couldn't help the subtle pang of disappointment coursing through him. But Matthais' claim on her didn't mean Aden couldn't have a bit of fun.

"Turn around."

Her eyes closed and her heart thumped wildly in her chest. Fear emanated from her pores, but she turned toward him, bending to pick up the bloody sheets, keeping her head bowed as she stood.

"How old are you?"

"Twenty-two, Sir."

She was four years beyond the acceptable age for a human girl to become a pet and it baffled him that Matthais hadn't taken her yet.

"What's your name?"

"Ellie, Sir."

"Light." Her brow furrowed, and his lips curved into a bemused smile. "Your name means light." He cocked his head to the side. "Ironic, considering you're destined to live in a dome city shrouded in perpetual darkness."

But she wouldn't know that. Humans weren't educated; ignorance kept them docile.

"Your bed is ready, Sir. May I go?"

A subtle shift in Ellie's scent, now a blend of trepidation and embarrassment, made him want to consume her whole. He moved closer and leaned his head down toward the crook of her neck. He breathed deep, filling his lungs with her scent again and she gasped, stepping back, clutching the sheets to her chest. Her head whipped up and she looked at him, wide-eyed.

Aden's cocky smirk faded when he saw her eyes. Eyes that had haunted him for almost three centuries. Pain ripped through his chest, stealing his breath and making his knees want to buckle.

"Who are you?"

She stood motionless, shoulders tight, her face turning ashen. Her eyes scanned his face before meeting his once more. She inhaled a startled breath before dropping her eyes to the floor again.

"Who are you?" He grabbed her arms and yanked her body toward him, shaking her slight frame.

"Ellie, Sir," she squeaked as she stared at his chest. Aden's fangs lengthened and his eyes turned red as he tugged her closer. Ellie's eyes snapped back up to his face, wide and brimming with fear.

"Please."

Her soft plea and the fear in her eyes, fear he'd seen in eyes identical to those once before, jolted Aden back to reality. He shoved her away, and she stumbled over the sheets, smacking her face against the marble floor.

"Get out!" Aden thundered as he reeled away, his fingers curling in on themselves as his nails dug into his palms. He heard her feet scurrying and the door to his room slide closed before he spun back to where she'd been standing. A small smear of blood marred the otherwise pristine floor.

Anger and agony tore through him and he roared, reaching down and flinging the bed, with its extravagant frame and headboard, through the wall.

Ellie

Ellie burst through the laundry doors and flung the bloody sheets across the room. Her legs buckled, and she sank to her knees, ignoring the sharp jolt of pain that shot through them when they hit the marble. She leaned forward and pressed her forehead against the cool tile, fighting over her ragged breath, her chest heaving with each inhale as she tried to calm herself.

Those eyes! The eyes she'd been dreaming about her whole life were Aden Westcott's eyes.

How was that possible?

She knew of him. Everyone knew of him. His reputation preceded him, but she'd only ever seen him from afar, and she never would have dared look him in the face. So how could she have been dreaming of someone she'd never met?

Ellie's heart pounded, and she took slow, deliberate breaths through her nose, trying to calm her racing thoughts. The cool tile against her face was a balm for the swelling she could feel on her forehead. She swiped her fingers under her nose and was startled to see blood coating the tips. The minutes crept by until her heart slowed, and she could think straight again.

She'd done nothing wrong.

Except look in a damn vampire's eyes without permission.

Damn. Damn. Damn. Master Matthais was going to whip her for sure.

Ellie pushed to her feet. She peeked in the mirror above the wash sink and the reflection looking back startled her. A wide gash on her forehead was the source of the blood, an angry purple bruise forming on the surrounding skin.

She snagged a cloth from the fresh pile in the corner and washed the blood away before pressing a clean one against the open gash. Tremors rippled through her body as her shaky legs carried her down the hallway toward the command center, where she knew her father would be. She had to tell him before Master Aden told Master Matthais. Maybe he could plead her case.

Ellie stepped inside when the door opened.

"Dad." Her voice was barely a whisper.

Her father swiveled in his chair. "What are you doing here, Ells?" He stood, his eyes widening in horror. "What happened to your face?"

"I screwed up, Daddy."

He strode over and pulled her hand away from her face. She winced as her forehead throbbed. She blinked and reached up to swipe away the blood dripping into her eyes.

"Who did this to you?"

Ellie took a step back, startled by the unexpected harshness in his tone and the fierce anger in his eyes.

"I didn't mean to do it. It was an accident."

His face softened, and he took her arm, his touch gentle as he led her to his seat. Ellie sank into the chair and took a deep breath, trying to steady her racing heart.

Her father dropped to his knee in front of her, pulled a handkerchief from his pocket, and pressed it against her head. "Tell me what happened, Ells."

"I looked him in the eyes."

"Who?"

"Master Aden Westcott. I looked him in the eyes."

Ellie's breaths quickened, becoming shallower as her heart pounded in her ears.

"What? I don't understand." His brow furrowed. "What were you doing near him?"

"Heather gave too much blood last night and was too weak to work, so Camilla sent me to her room cleaning assignments. I was still there when he came back."

"Why would you look up at him?"

It wasn't an accusation, but Ellie still bristled at his words.

She took the handkerchief from him, keeping it pressed against her forehead. "I didn't mean to. He sniffed me, and I was so startled, I just looked up."

She didn't tell her dad she couldn't tear her eyes away from him or that she recognized his eyes from her dreams. He'd think she was crazy.

"How did you get that cut? Did he do that to you?"

"No. He didn't hurt me. He grabbed me and yelled at me to get out. I stumbled and hit my face on the floor."

Why hadn't she told him that Master Westcott shoved her? Why would she keep that a secret?

"He's going to tell Master Matthais. I know he is. What am I going to do, Dad? He'll whip me for this."

The look in her father's eyes mirrored the terror pulsing through her own body. It was a tingling sensation building up beneath her skin, threatening to erupt.

Ellie gripped her father's wrist, fighting to suppress the tears welling up in her eyes. "I don't know if I can take it, Dad. Do you think he'll go easier on me if I tell him before Master Aden does?"

He pushed to his feet. "Let me go speak to him. I'll explain it was an accident."

She shook her head, her eyes widening in panic. "No. I should confess. He'll consider it as disrespectful if I'm not there with you. If I don't confess to him face-to-face, the punishment will be much worse."

His knuckles turned white as he clenched his fists, unable to disagree. "Damn it!"

She looked up at him and saw the familiar towering giant who seemed invincible, but the dread on his face told a different story. Their combined fear hung in the air, thick and tangible, knowing Master Matthais' punishment was inevitable, no matter what her father said.

Ellie's body trembled as she wiped the tears and blood from her cheeks, her last whipping replaying in her mind. Then she leaned forward and clutched her belly, her body swaying to the rhythm of that haunting memory.

CRACK!

Ellie's body jerked as the whip snapped against her back. She clamped her tongue between her teeth, refusing to cry out, unwilling to give Master Matthais the satisfaction. But she couldn't prevent the tears from pouring down her face as excruciating pain tore through her entire body with each lash.

Helpless, she strained against the chains that bound her wrists above her head, her feet spread eagle, and shackled to the snow-covered travertine tile, stripped down to her bra and panties. Modesty was irrelevant as she hung there. The whip had torn through the back strap of her bra with the first lash and it was now barely clinging to her breasts.

CRACK!

Warm blood coursed down her back and her teeth bore into her bottom lip as her body jolted again. In her peripheral vision, she saw her father standing across the courtyard, his face a mask of anguish, his eyes blazing with anger as he was forced to watch, powerless to intervene. That rage wasn't directed at her. Still, the sight of it made her flinch.

CRACK!

The whip connected with Ellie's back again, slicing through the already torn flesh and muscle, splattering more blood onto the stone beneath her. Even though no one was allowed in the courtyard during a thrall's punishment, Master Matthais had invited his guests to watch from the ramparts above. He punished all his thralls personally and publicly, his intention to always put on a show. Ellie was unsure how many were watching because she didn't dare look up. But Master Matthais forced all the other thralls, who were not entertaining his guests, to watch, to witness the consequences of disobeying him.

CRACK!

The final lash tore through her skin and a broken sob escaped her lips, a whimper of relief it was over. Her knees gave out and her mutilated body slumped, her weight pulling on the chains holding her. Her body convulsed as her shoulder popped out of its socket.

Tears and snot clung to Ellie's face. Footsteps glided closer, and a hand pushed on her chin, lifting her face as Master Matthais' fingers wrapped around her jaw. But she knew better than to look him in the eye.

"Oh, so now you obey my rules." He tightened his fingers, bruising the soft flesh. Ellie trembled but remained silent. He squeezed her chin harder and Ellie bit back another cry.

"This is your last warning, girl. Next time I will not be so merciful." He leaned closer to her face. "I will break you, Elliana. And when I do, you will finally be ready for me."

Revulsion, fear, and pain flooded Ellie's body as he shoved her away, causing her body to sway in the chains that held her captive.

"Take her down and clean her up. I have neglected my guests long enough for this."

He turned and walked out of the courtyard.

Hands released the shackles on her wrists. The ground drew closer, but before she hit it, a soft blanket surrounded her, and powerful arms encircled her. A ragged cry she was powerless to stop tore from her lips as the pressure on her shredded back and dislocated shoulder wracked her body with so much pain that spots flashed in front of her eyes. Familiar fingers released the bonds at her ankles, and then she was lifted and pulled against a hard chest. She buried her face in the familiar muscular neck and let the soul-wrenching sobs take over.

The last sound Ellie heard was her father's voice as everything faded to black.

"I've got you, baby. Daddy's here."

His face was clear now. How hadn't Ellie seen it before?

The mist was gone, and he stood in front of her. Just out of reach.

Laughter rumbled from the depths of his chest as he looked at her, his blue irises shimmering in the light.

She adored his eyes like this and would do anything to keep them on her. To keep him looking at her. Just like that.

She took one step forward, her hand outstretched, beckoning him to her, but in an instant, his eyes changed.

They darkened and hardened until the once brilliant blue faded away and was replaced with an angry, fiery red.

Stunned and heartbroken, Ellie's hand trembled as she pulled it back, shattered by the loss of the warmth in his eyes.

Ellie's lungs screamed in protest as she dragged in a heaving breath of air. A low, pained groan slipped past her lips as her eyes shot open and reality came crashing back. She was on her stomach, sweating, panting, and gasping for air. She pushed up onto her hands and whimpered as fresh pain radiated through her entire body.

Her arms gave out and she sank back to the mattress, sobbing, unsure if the tears were a response to the searing pain or the overwhelming relief that she was still alive. Her back was on fire, but it was the remembered heartbreak in her dream that had her choking and soaking the pillow with tears.

"Stay still, Ellie." Carrie's pleading voice came from beside her. The sound of her only friend's voice made Ellie cry harder.

"Shit, I think we should get her dad."

Ellie's body shook as she sobbed until her throat was raw. It had been years since she cried that hard. She remembered crying only twice in her life—the night her mother died and the last time Master Matthais had whipped her.

Another voice filled the room that Ellie recognized as Veronika's. "He's not here. He went to the games with Master Matthais. Let her be. She needs to let it out and she'll be fine."

Nothing would ever be fine again. Ellie's body jolted as a wet cloth brushed down her back.

"No." The word came out as a strangled cry.

"Let me clean them, girl." Veronika's less-than-gentle touch sent fresh waves of pain through her torn flesh.

"Please." Ellie shuddered. "It hurts."

"It's gonna hurt worse if they get infected."

Ellie buried her face in the pillow and bit her tongue. Sometimes she really despised Veronika.

After what felt like forever, Veronika's painful cleaning stopped, and Ellie sighed with relief. She turned her face away from the pillow and opened her eyes, her eyelashes wet and sticky. Carrie was sitting on the floor beside her bed, watching her, her blue eyes filled with worry.

"Are you gonna be okay?"

Ellie nodded her head, sniffling and hiccuping, because that was all the movement she could muster.

"He whipped you so hard."

"That's enough, Carrie. She doesn't need to hear that." Veronika gathered up the blood-soaked towels. "I swear I don't know what's wrong with you girls. Looking a vampire in the eye. When will you ever learn?"

"I didn't mean to," Ellie snapped at the older woman, but even that effort sent fresh waves of pain through her. "He grabbed me and I couldn't help it."

"It doesn't matter what he did. You never look them in the eyes."

Veronika left the room as Carrie reached up and took Ellie's hand in her own, linking their fingers, offering the only comfort she was able.

"Is it as bad as it feels?" Ellie asked.

Carrie nodded.

"I hate him so much," Ellie whispered, emotion clogging her throat. Carrie was the one person Ellie trusted besides her father, so she didn't hesitate to say what was on terminal repeat in her head. "It hurts to even breathe."

Fatigue overwhelmed her but she didn't want to go back to sleep. The last thing she wanted was to see the eyes of the man who had caused her so much pain. Ellie shot a quick glance at the door and tugged on Carrie's hand, urging her to move closer, grateful they were alone. Carrie rested her chin on the bed beside Ellie's face.

"They're his eyes." She had confided in Carrie about her dreams years ago. "Aden Westcott. They're his eyes."

Carrie gave her a puzzled look. "How? Have you ever met him before?"

"No. But when I looked into his eyes, it was just like my dreams."

"Maybe they look alike because they both have blue eyes."

Ellie felt her throat tighten, but she took a deep breath, swallowed, and shook her head. "I've seen those eyes my whole life, Carrie. I'd know them anywhere."

"How?" Carrie asked.

"I don't know."

Carrie sat back as Veronika entered the room. She handed Ellie a small cup of water and two pills. "Take these. It's all Master Matthais will let me give you."

Ellie recognized BloodStone. "What's the other one?"

"A sleeping pill. It won't stop the pain, but it will help you rest. He expects you to do your chores tomorrow so you best get some sleep."

"He can't make her work tomorrow. She can't even stand."

"He can make her do anything he wants," Veronika said with a snarl as she stormed away.

Ellie dreaded going back to sleep but she swallowed both pills. Arguing was futile. She had no idea how she was going to do her chores, but if she didn't, she'd be in worse shape than she already was.

Aden

Aden paced like a caged animal, unable to get the girl out of his mind or his nostrils. It had been less than twenty-four hours since he found her in his room. Less than a day since he was tempted by her intoxicating scent and saw her eyes. Eyes that had haunted him for centuries.

Nothing could distract him—not the tedious meetings he had to attend or the trip to the outlying areas with Andrei to watch his troops practice their drills. Even his thralls, accustomed to enduring his anger and frustration, couldn't get his mind off the girl.

He looked for her today, his eyes scanning every dark-haired thrall who came within two hundred feet of him. He thought he'd found her once, following the unique scent down a long corridor, but all he'd found was the laundry room, where several large industrial washing machines churned linens in a sea of pink water.

What the fuck was he doing?

Losing his damn mind. That's what he was doing.

He needed to see her eyes again to make sure he hadn't imagined it. How could an inconsequential human girl in Matthais' household have *her* eyes? The need to see this girl was so intense, he was ready to crawl out of his skin.

A hologram popped up beside him with Andrei's face. "The games are about to start. Are you coming?"

"Not tonight. I have other plans."

"Your loss. I'm edging closer to dethroning you, my friend," Andrei said, a mischievous grin spreading across his face, before closing the hologram.

Aden didn't give a fuck about the games anymore. He had to forget about the girl and her eyes. There was only one place he could do that. He headed toward the door. Kane was standing at attention outside.

Aden didn't look at him, walking past him. "You can stay here tonight."

The strobe lights from above were the first thing Aden registered as he entered the dark space. Almost two centuries had passed since he stepped foot in the club, but the familiarity of it enveloped him.

He forgot how seedy the lower levels of the capital were. Civilized vampires didn't come here. The kinds of establishments the underground levels harbored were for a particular breed of vampires who wanted to shake off the constraints and expectations Matthais and his brand of cultured society put on them. Sex and blood play clubs were the most popular, and Aden had spent over a century dwelling in their depths.

The air was heavy with the scent of blood and sex, and the sound of pleasure and pain, mixed with the throbbing beat of the music, echoed in Aden's ears. Around the room, thralls writhed, displayed for all to see, both on top of and beneath their masters. A raised stage on one side featured vampires and their pets performing sexual acts for the viewing pleasure of others. Aden never understood the thrill of being watched but to each his own.

A row of cells was built deep into the opposite wall, with both male and female thralls cowering, huddled together, waiting to be chosen by a vampire. Doors along the back wall led to Aden's preferred private rooms.

The atmosphere was one of hedonistic indulgence, an unmistakable combination of the illicit and forbidden, everything civilized society deemed unacceptable.

Aden never brought his thralls here and never once took a private pet. This place gave him the space he needed to unleash his dark side. He couldn't use his thralls here, because if he brought them home broken or, worse, failed to bring them home, his family would have known the truth of the monster that lived inside him.

His family saw him through his dark years and didn't turn their back on him despite the destruction he caused. But they were oblivious to what he was truly capable of. Aden had made sure to bury that monster a long time ago. He vowed to never return to any of these clubs, but tonight, he could feel it rising once more. And the clawing in his gut had drawn him here—like a moth to a flame.

Despite the repulsive memories of this place, Aden's lips curved as he sensed a familiar female presence before he saw her.

"Soraya."

Her name was a sexy drawl as she stepped into his view.

"Well, fuck me. If it isn't Aden Westcott. What's it been, almost two hundred years?"

Her sultry smile sparkled under the lights and Aden's eyes drank her in. Her painted blood-red lips, stark against her pearlescent skin, matched the skintight dress she wore.

"Something like that."

"I never thought I'd see you again," she said as her eyes raked over him.

"Neither did I. You look enchanting, as always."

"Don't try to flatter me. Your sexy smile can't make up for draining three of my girls in one night and destroying my finest room."

Her rebuke spread like ice through his veins, leaving a knot in the pit of his stomach. "I paid for it."

"Yes, quite generously, if I remember." Her lips curved. "But that doesn't mean I forgive you yet."

That made two of them.

"I heard you mellowed over the years, so what brings you back?"

Because the recesses of his heart were in shreds once again.

"Just wanted to let loose."

Her eyes swept over him again as she assessed him. "Do you want your old room?"

"Let's try a different one."

"Your usual, I assume?"

"Do you still have one?"

"I have all types, Aden. And I've always kept one on reserve in case you came back."

"Is she fresh?"

"As if I'd dare give you used goods." She motioned him to follow her. "One red-headed, green-eyed girl coming up."

Aden raised his voice above the noise in the room as she led him through the crowd. "Actually, do you have one with dark hair and green eyes?"

She gazed at him with curiosity. "Of course."

"Let's try that instead."

Aden looked up from his spot on the leather sofa as the girl shuffled into the room, keeping her head and eyes lowered as she walked toward him. Her dark hair was a momentary distraction as an image of Ellie flashed in his mind, but he pushed it aside.

"Drop your robe and kneel," he commanded, and the girl obeyed.

He hadn't seen her eyes yet, but he could already feel the weight of both anticipation and foreboding settling in his gut.

What the fuck was he doing in this place again?

Ever since his encounter with Ellie, he couldn't shake the persistent sensation of fire creeping under his skin.

He shouldn't be here. He knew it. And he couldn't help the pang of guilt, knowing that the girl before him would soon be subjected to his merciless cruelty. She didn't deserve it. But he didn't deserve to have his heart wrenched out of his chest by some insignificant slip of a girl with *her* exact eyes.

Almost three hundred years. Hadn't he suffered enough?

Aden gazed at the naked girl at his feet. Her head was bowed, her dark hair cascading around her face and draping over her shoulders in long waves. The absence of red hair was an odd and unsettling sight.

She remained silent, awaiting his instructions, her training evident, yet her body quivered, betraying her underlying fear.

"Come closer."

She shuffled forward until her knees were inches from his bare feet.

"You're not to touch me. Do you understand?"

"Yes, Master."

"Tilt your head and bare your neck."

She swept those long, silky locks over her shoulder. With a quick lunge forward, Aden sunk his teeth into her neck. She cried out, but her voice caught in her throat as her body froze.

For several minutes, Aden drank deep, focusing on the soothing sensation of the liquid sliding down his throat, a brief respite from the suffocating ache in his chest.

Then he leaned back against the cushion, his eyes fading from red to blue as he licked his lips, savoring the blood that pooled in the corners. The metallic flavor lingered on his tongue as his body absorbed it like a drug.

The girl kneeling on the floor in front of him swayed, her head dipping forward as blood flowed from the puncture wounds on her neck. Her eyes fluttered and her dark curls again surrounded her face as her head lolled on her neck. Her naked body shifted forward and a weak moan escaped her lips as her forehead dropped onto the cushion between his legs.

Aden's bare chest barely moved, his breathing shallow, as he looked at her through hooded lids. He took more of her blood than he'd intended, but he hadn't quite finished with her yet. He wouldn't release both of them from their torment until he was.

Aden reached over and grabbed the syringe of red liquid from the table, plunging it into the girl's vein. Her body jerked, a groan escaping her lips. She lifted her face and her eyes fluttered open, clearing as the BloodStone coursed through her.

The green eyes, so different from *hers*, caught him off guard, and for a moment, he imagined Ellie was kneeling before him instead. As always, the green depths sent a fresh wave of pain through him, tearing through his gut and ravaging him from the inside out.

The girl pressed her hands on the sofa and sat up, steadying herself, the BloodStone in her system revived her.

Aden stood. "Get up."

She struggled to stand, swaying, but stayed on her feet.

"It's almost over." His words weren't meant as a comfort, but a warning of what was coming.

"Master." The girl croaked, her voice weak.

"Get on the bed." He led her across the room. "Lay back."

His voice was harsh and she scurried onto the bed. Aden shoved his pants down his thighs but didn't bother removing them. This wouldn't take long.

Aden crawled over the girl, her body trembling in fear. He braced his hands on either side of her, not letting his body touch her as she turned her face and tilted her chin to present her neck to him again. He slid a finger along the trail of congealed blood that painted her skin before licking it clean.

"Don't touch me!" he snarled as he thrust into her, tearing through her virginity and sinking his fangs into her neck all in one motion. Her body froze and a cry caught in her throat, his venom paralyzing her.

Aden drank deep, savoring the blood as it flowed down his throat. When she could move again, her fingers gripped the sheets. He blocked out her sobs as he surrendered to the darkness inside him. The pain started in his gut again and crawled up his body, gripping his heart. He welcomed it. Reveled in it. Let it consume him until all he felt was the agony.

Her cries lessened, softened, and her heart slowed, as did the flow of her blood down his throat. Aden tore his mouth away, even though he hadn't come yet, and saw the light in her wide green eyes fading. He hurled his body away from her, skittering across the floor until his back hit the wall.

Aden's head fell back and he looked up at the mirror on the ceiling. The sight that met his gaze was reminiscent of the one from two hundred years earlier when he drained three green-eyed, red-headed girls.

He'd buried that monster, but now, his encounter with Ellie and her familiar eyes had driven him to the depths of his depravity again.

Remorse clawed out of his chest and he yanked his pants up before calling for a medical team through a hologram.

Less than a minute later, Soraya walked in, followed by two nurses and a medical pod.

"Again, Aden?"

Aden

Aden stalked down the hallway, his skin feeling more on fire than it had before he'd gone to the club. The girl Soraya sent him had needed an emergency blood transfusion, but she survived. He'd only just kept the worst of the monster at bay. And going back to that club and using that brown-haired, green-eyed girl to sate his demons had done nothing to erase Ellie's memory from his mind.

The sound of a scuffle and then a girl's pained cry filled his ears seconds before the scent of blood hit his nostrils. He turned the corner as Kira pushed a thrall to the floor, a pile of fresh linens scattering around her. It took only a second for Aden to realize who she was. His gut tightened, and he bolted forward, just as Kira's foot connected with Ellie's back.

"Kira, what the fuck are you doing?" His voice echoed through the hall as he grabbed her arm.

Kira's face registered her surprise at his touch before she pulled her arm away and her lips curled into a snarl.

"Stay out of this, Aden. This doesn't concern you. I have a score to settle with this bitch."

Kira kicked Ellie again, and she grunted in pain. The scent of her blood slammed into him, almost as if she had open wounds. Aden looked down and saw blood seeping through her shirt.

"She's bleeding, for fuck's sake." Aden yanked Kira away before she could kick Ellie again.

"What the fuck do you care? She's a stupid thrall."

Kira jerked away from his grip and moved to kick Ellie again, but Aden shoved her, sending her stumbling into one of the hallway's columns.

"Touch her again and you'll answer to me."

Despite Kira's place in Matthais' household, she still ranked lower than Aden. He was the son of Aurick Westcott and the second in command of the world's military, below Andrei. Kira was a vampire, but she held no power or authority of any significance in their world and was required to follow Aden's orders.

Not that she cared.

"How dare you?" she screeched as she lunged for him, scratching her nails down his face. She left shallow scrapes in his cheek but they were already closing by the time she reached his chin. Kira was never one to back down from a good fight.

Aden grabbed her hands and pushed her away. Their shared history made her feel she could defy him and normally Aden wouldn't give a fuck. But he would not let her hurt the girl crumpled on the floor. The girl with *her* eyes.

"Get a grip."

Kira stumbled and then launched herself at him again. Aden grabbed both arms and pinned them behind her back as he leaned over her. Despite her six-inch heels, she was still shorter than him.

"I mean it, Kira." His dangerous growl reverberated from deep within his chest. "Get a fucking grip. I'm not in the mood to fight with you right now."

"How dare you defend her? She's a filthy thrall."

Kira's screech pierced his ears as she squirmed in his grasp, but she was no match for his strength.

"She's hurt. I doubt Matthais will want you damaging his thrall any more than she already is."

Kira stopped squirming. "You clearly don't know him. Let me go, Aden."

"Are you going to calm down?"

She glared at him, refusing to answer. Aden loosened his grip and she pulled away. He raised an eyebrow daring her to defy him again.

"You and your fucking family." Kira did nothing to hide the disgust in her voice. "Always so concerned about stupid humans. It's going to catch up with you one of these days. Mark my words."

Her threats meant nothing to him. Aden looked down at Ellie. She was rocking back and forth, and the muscles in his jaw twitched.

"What did you do to her?"

"Nothing the little bitch didn't deserve."

"Kira, enough. Walk away."

Kira's eyes filled with fire and she screeched once again in frustration. "You'll pay for this, you little bitch. I promise you." She turned back to Aden. "And so will you, asshole."

Aden watched Kira stomp down the hallway, knowing he'd hear about this soon enough. His gaze shifted back to Ellie. Her face contorted with effort as she struggled to find purchase on the smooth stone wall. Halfway up, her hands lost their grip, her legs gave out, and she slid down, grunting as she landed on her knees.

He dropped to one knee and reached out, his hand hovering in the air, inches away from her. "Are you alright?"

She flinched away from him. "I'm fine, Sir."

He wanted her to look at him again, so he knew he wasn't losing his mind. He needed to know he hadn't let the beast out for no reason.

"You don't look fine." A large gash and fresh bruises on her forehead and chin were visible under the muted hall light.

"Please don't bother with me, Sir."

"Someone should see to your injuries."

"They're being looked after."

She struggled to stand, her hands slipping against the smooth wall as she sought leverage. Her legs trembled, unable to support her weight. Aden's instincts took over, and he scooped her up in his arms before she hit the floor, lifting her off her feet. His body went rigid with surprise, and he braced himself for the usual wave of revulsion that accompanied any physical contact. But it wasn't there. A surge of comforting warmth spread through him at the feel of her in his arms, and his eyes locked onto her face.

A sharp cry of agony escaped her lips as she jerked her head up and she inhaled a sharp breath, her wide eyes locking on to his.

And his entire world shifted.

There was no mistaking her eyes now. He knew them better than his own. Those eyes filled with horror and Aden's heart froze mid-beat before she looked away.

"I'm sorry, Sir. I didn't mean to look at you again. Please don't tell my Master." Her broken plea tore through his chest. She struggled in his grip, weak and whimpering, terrified. "Please, Sir, forgive me. It won't happen again."

Aden turned and strode down the hallway. The way she felt in his arms was foreign and unfamiliar but didn't make his skin crawl as he'd expected. It was almost a balm for the agony he'd endured for centuries.

"Where are you taking me, Sir?"

"The infirmary."

"No! Put me down! Please!" Aden stopped as Ellie's terrified voice echoed off the walls. Her eyes flashed with stark terror, and even though she was clearly in pain, her body writhed against his grasp, desperate to break free. "He'll whip me again. Please!"

Whip her again?

"Stop moving!"

She froze at his harsh command.

"Why don't you want to go to the infirmary?"

She sagged in his arms as the fight left her. "Master has forbidden any more medical treatment. Please just let me go and I'll be fine."

"Fucking hell!"

Aden turned back the way he came. Ellie's head lolled to the side and her forehead pressed against his neck.

"I'll be fine," she murmured before her eyes fluttered closed.

Aden registered the shock on Kane's face as he approached his room with the broken girl in his arms.

"Don't even fucking say anything right now. Go get Sophie and don't use a hologram. Tell her to bring Mina and a medical bag."

Aden strode through the door, carrying Ellie to the bed. He set her down, keeping one hand on her shoulder to keep her from falling over.

Her eyes fluttered and she shook her head, but the slightest movement looked like it was agony. When he was sure she wouldn't topple over, he removed his hand and shook it to relieve the tingling sensation creeping up his arm.

"My mother will be here in a few minutes with a nurse. She'll help you."

"I don't need it." Ellie pushed on her hands, trying to stand. She swayed and grasped the edge of the bed for balance.

"Sit down before you fucking fall."

Ellie obeyed, but Aden suspected it was only because she was about to crash to the floor.

"I'm just—I just—I have to finish my chores, Sir."

"Forget your fucking chores!"

Ellie scowled at the floor. She said nothing, but he could tell by the way her lips pursed that it was not from a lack of something to say. And her words would be most certainly far from polite. He couldn't contain the smirk tugging on his lips for a second before it disappeared.

"What happened to you?"

"Like you don't know." She slapped her hand over her mouth. "I'm so sorry, Sir, for my disrespect. It won't happen again."

"You say that a lot. Now answer my question. What happened to you?"

She cringed, but she had to answer because refusing to answer a direct question from a vampire was forbidden.

"Master whipped me because I looked into your eyes."

The cords of his neck tightened. "What did you say to me?"

"Punishment for looking a vampire in the eyes is twenty lashes."

Revulsion shot through him. "How did he find out?"

Ellie's body went rigid. "Didn't you tell him?"

"Of course I fucking didn't."

"Oh, no." Ellie dropped her face in her hands with a moan. "I was sure you were going to—"

"You stupid little girl," he roared, fury exploding out of him. "Why would you tell him?"

Ellie scowled and yelled back at him. "Because it would have been thirty lashes if I hadn't." Her green eyes again doubled in size and it would have been comical under any other circumstances. But there was no humor in the way she slumped on his bed, her body broken and bleeding, trembling from blood loss. Her shoulders sagged, and her voice was a whisper. "You were so angry that I looked at you."

Aden couldn't tear his eyes away from her as the hammering of her heart echoed in his ears. What thrall would confess to breaking the law, knowing she would be whipped? She was a fearless little thing; he'd give her that. A foolhardy, fearless little thing who got whipped because she was too damn honest.

"Let me see your back."

"No," Ellie said, then winced. "I didn't mean that, Sir. I apologize again for being disrespectful."

"Stop fucking apologizing already. You don't have to remove your shirt. Just lower it in the back. I want to see what he did to you."

"Please, Sir, it's nothing."

"Your shirt is soaked with blood. It's not nothing. Now I won't tell you again." He threw up his hands in exasperation. "Are you always this defiant?"

"Sometimes, Sir."

Aden couldn't stop the sardonic laugh that burst out of him. Her honesty was as refreshing as it was unexpected. It was going to get her fucking drained one day.

He took a deep breath and groaned as the scent of her blood assaulted his senses, making his eyes cross. He attempted to soften his voice. "Let me see your back, Ellie."

She closed her eyes, accepting her fate, and turned away from him. Her hands trembled as she unfastened the buttons on the front of her shirt. His mother would kick him out as soon as she arrived. If he didn't see now, he would never know what this girl had suffered because of him.

The congealed blood prevented her shirt from sliding down her back. She wiggled, whimpering. "I can't get it to go down, Sir."

Aden sat on the bed beside her, making sure not to get too close. Ellie flinched but otherwise remained still.

"Why are there holes in your shirt?"

Ellie's lack of response spoke volumes as she shrugged, her face showing the pain she was trying to hide.

"What caused these holes?"

"Mistress Kira's fingernails, Sir."

"Mother fucking hell!" Aden snarled and hooked his finger into her collar, careful not to touch her, as he pulled the shirt down, revealing her back to his gaze.

A wave of unrivaled fury surged through him. He wanted to scream and rage. He wanted to kill, maim, and bring the roof down. Ellie's back was a mess of shredded flesh. The skin gaped, muscle and sinew exposed, the long angry gashes weeping with fresh blood.

The sight before him was sickening. He'd inflicted a lot of damage on thralls over the years, but it was always in the heat of the moment during feeding. He was never deliberate or vicious in his destruction.

Her name slipped past Aden's lips before he could catch himself, and she stiffened.

The blood oozing from her open wounds was overwhelming and intoxicating, tempting him. It filled every one of his senses. Aden's fangs lengthened and venom filled his mouth. He wanted to lick every inch of her back from top to bottom and let his venom relieve her pain as he feasted on her blood.

He should move away from her, but he was rooted in place, unable to tear himself away. The snap was coming. He could feel it come alive inside him, pulsing and rushing through every cell in his body.

He was drawn to her neck. She was intoxicating, and he wanted to drown in her scent. His proximity caused Ellie to shift uncomfortably.

"Don't move!"

She froze in place at his command.

Before he could stop himself, Aden lowered his head and brushed his nose against the tender skin of her neck, opening his mouth and sinking his fangs into the side of her throat. His eyes rolled back in his head as her blood hit his tongue.

Ellie's body jerked, then froze.

Aden moaned as her warm blood flowed down his throat, each tug matching the rhythm of her heartbeat. The taste of her blood hit him like a lightning bolt. His body responded, fire rushing through his veins.

As soon as the paralytic effect of his venom was gone, Ellie cried out. "No!"

Aden retracted his fangs, removing them from her neck and she pulled away, shoving at him as she lost her balance and fell off the bed. She sank to her knees, leaning forward and pressing her face against the tile.

The enormity of what he'd done hit Aden like a tidal wave, as he watched her body tremble violently.

Ellie

Ellie's body jerked and shook, convulsions coursing through her like jolts of electricity.

It was too much. All of it was just too much, and for the first time in her life, Ellie wanted to die. She just wanted an end to all this pain.

Her battered and torn body rocked back and forth as she knelt in the fetal position on the cold tile floor. She tugged the front of her shirt closed, crying out as her shirt came in contact with her back.

Strong arms surrounded her and lifted her off the floor. She didn't fight him, just sagged in his grasp. He would do with her what he wanted, so fighting was futile.

He laid her on her side on the bed, more gently than Ellie would have thought him capable, and she buried her face in the pillow.

Blood trickled from the holes in her neck. As the warm liquid glided across her skin, another shudder wracked her body. The sensation was strangely familiar as if she'd felt it before, but she'd never been bitten.

"I have to lick the punctures or they'll keep bleeding." His voice was too close to her ear.

Before she could respond, his tongue swirled over the bite, sending shockwaves of both pleasure and pain through her body. Her muscles tensed and throbbed as he moaned against her skin and the vibration rippled down her body, all the way to her toes.

Was it possible to feel more pain?

He moved away, and the tension in her muscles eased.

"Please, just kill me." Her broken plea filled the otherwise silent room.

"No." His voice came from somewhere near the foot of the bed.

"I won't survive it the next time he whips me. He'll kill me for sure, so please, I'm begging you, just do it yourself."

"No. I own you now so I won't allow him to punish you for this."

A wave of nausea rolled over Ellie and bile leaped into her throat as she realized the truth of Master Aden's words. When a vampire bit a thrall, ownership instantly transferred.

She was his now!

"My god, Aden, what have you done?"

Startled by the loud screech, Ellie sat up and groaned in discomfort as her body protested.

"Why is everything always my fault?" His snarl sounded almost inhuman. "Never mind. Don't answer that. Help her. She needs urgent medical attention."

"Why didn't you call the infirmary?"

"She's terrified to go."

The bed beside Ellie shifted as a woman sat down beside her.

"She needs serious medical attention."

"I already fucking said that."

Ellie swore she heard his teeth clench when he spoke.

"The mere mention of it sends her into a panic. Why do you think I called you here?"

"How could you do this to her?"

"I didn't do this to her," he roared. Ellie flinched, but the woman didn't seem fazed.

"Aden, there's a bite mark on her neck and your scent is all over her."

"I fucking lost control, alright? Can you hold off accusing me of anything else until you've taken care of her?"

"There's so much blood. What happened? If it wasn't you, who did this to her?"

"Matthais." The disgust in his voice was surprising. No one said his name like that.

The woman released a resigned sigh. "Mina, come help me."

Gentle hands covered hers.

"It's alright, child. I just want to check your injuries."

The woman's voice was kind, a tone Ellie was not used to. It wrapped around her and tears stung her eyes. It was pointless to resist.

"Aden, you need to go so we can look her over."

"No."

"Aden, we can't help her if we can't examine her injuries."

"I'm not leaving."

"Aden, give us some privacy."

The woman's firm tone left no room for argument. But Ellie feared an argument would erupt and she would be caught in the crossfire.

"It's alright ma'am," Ellie said, despite not being directly addressed, even knowing that speaking in the presence of vampires wasn't allowed. Was there any rule she wouldn't break?

"What's your name?"

"Ellie, ma'am."

"My name is Sophie and I won't hurt you, okay."

"Yes, ma'am."

What a minute. Sophie? As in Mistress Sophie Westcott, the wife of Gerent Aurick Westcott? Why would she bother with a thrall?

"Mina, hand me that pillow." She knelt on the floor in front of Ellie. "Place this in front of you. Mina is going to cut your shirt down the back so we can remove it and see how badly you're hurt."

Ellie's breath snagged in her throat as Mina pulled her shirt away and scissors sliced the back open. One at a time, Mistress Sophie helped her pull her arms out of the shirt until her upper body was fully exposed. Ellie pulled the pillow back to her chest, watching Master Aden pacing out of the corner of her eye.

"Good lord."

"My God." Mistress Sophie gasped as she leaned over Ellie's body. "You poor child. What has he done to you?"

Ellie closed her eyes and held as still as she could, not used to such compassion. She jolted at the sound of several loud crashes and glass breaking. She turned her face away, reluctant to look.

"Aden, get yourself under control. Destroying the room won't help."

"There isn't much I can do," Mina said. "She needs to be in the infirmary."

"I'll be fine," Ellie said, looking down.

"Stop fucking saying that already," Master Aden roared, but Ellie didn't have it in her to be afraid anymore. As soon as Master Matthais found out about this, she was dead anyway.

"Aden, stop it." Mistress Sophie admonished. "You need to get your father."

"Kane!"

The door to the suite opened, and the giant man Ellie saw standing in the hallway the other day came around the corner.

"Go get Aurick. Tell him it's important. But if he's with anyone, especially Matthais, only tell him I need to speak with him when he's free."

Ellie's body lurched forward as something cold and wet pressed against her back. Only Mistress Sophie's hands on her arms kept her from falling off the bed.

"Try to hold still. I know this hurts but I have to get a better look," Mina said from behind her.

"Are they infected?"

"They're on their way. These need to be stitched and she needs BloodStone. A lot of it."

"Did you receive any BloodStone today?" Mistress Sophie asked.

"Yes, Mistress."

Mistress Sophie sat beside Ellie as she helped steady her. "That's alright. You can take it again. You need to replenish your blood to help you regain your strength."

"She'll need an antibiotic too, so infection doesn't set in."

Ellie heard Mina rummaging around in her bag.

"Give her something for the pain, too."

"Master won't allow it," Ellie said, her voice a soft whisper.

"I don't care what he allows."

Ellie bit her lip at Mistress Sophie's blunt words. "Yes, ma'am."

She dared a glance toward Master Aden. He was pacing and growling as shattered glass crunched under his feet.

"Can you look at me, Ellie?"

"No, ma'am. I'm not allowed."

"I'm not a vampire, so it's okay."

Ellie hoped she could hide her surprise. Master Westcott's wife was a half-breed? But she commanded the same respect he did.

Unable to refuse, Ellie slowly raised her eyes. The woman in front of her was blonde and beautiful and her multicolored eyes shone with sympathy. Then her smile faded and her eyes filled with shock.

"Who are you?" Mistress Sophie gasped in a disbelieving tone. She had the same stunned expression that Master Aden had the first time she looked at him. Ellie lowered her eyes, embarrassment and confusion flooding her body.

"Aden, what is this? Who is she?"

"I don't know, Sophie," Master Aden seethed through clenched teeth. "Do you understand now why I lost it?"

Mistress Sophie studied her through the rapid blinking of her eyes for a few moments. Ellie remained still, unwilling to even breathe. She winced as a needle punctured her hip, then another.

"You have permission to look at me, Ellie. You don't have to be afraid. No one in this room will tell Master Matthais."

Ellie's lips curled up on one side. "I'm used to looking at the world this way, ma'am. But there isn't much I don't see."

What the heck was she thinking? Why would she ever admit that?

"She needs something to eat. These pain meds will make her nauseous," Mina said.

Master Aden barked Kane's name again and Ellie wondered if that was the only way he knew how to communicate. Kane entered the room.

"Go to the kitchen and get some food."

"Something light, crackers, maybe," Mina said. "Nothing too heavy. Have you eaten anything today?"

"No, ma'am."

"Bring soup as well," Mistress Sophie said. "When did you last eat?"

Ellie hesitated. "Three days ago, ma'am."

The door opened again. Ellie sucked in a breath as she watched Master Westcott's commanding figure enter the room. As the Gerent of Réimse Shíochánta, one of the most powerful of the regions, every vampire, half-breed, and human knew Master Westcott's name. He was almost as powerful as Master Matthais.

He had a reputation as a stern but kind master, unlike Master Matthais, who used fear, pain, and punishment to rule. His thralls always spoke with respect for both Master Aurick and Mistress Sophie. It was Master Aden who had a reputation for cruelty.

"What's going on here?"

His eyes fell on her, and Ellie kept her head down and closed her eyes.

When nobody answered him, Master Aurick roared in a language Ellie didn't recognize.

So that's where Master Aden got his temper.

Ellie heard struggling, and several loud crashes, and then it felt like the whole room shook. She whipped her head up and saw Master Aurick holding Master Aden against the wall by his throat. Both men glared at each other but Master Aden didn't struggle against his father's hold. She quickly looked down before anyone could notice.

"Aurick, let him speak and he'll tell you."

Mistress Sophie didn't sound as frantic as Ellie thought she should considering her husband had her son by the throat.

"Matthais whipped her because she looked in my eyes."

"What?" Mistress Sophie screeched and turned horrified eyes toward Ellie. "That's why?"

Ellie nodded.

"Why would you ever report that to him?" Master Aurick asked.

Master Aden pushed his father's hands away from his throat. "I didn't."

"It was my fault, Sir," Ellie said, not knowing why she felt compelled to defend Master Aden. "I thought Master Aden would tell my Master so I confessed first. My punishment would have been worse if I hadn't."

"Oh, Ellie," Mistress Sophie's murmur sounded broken.

"Why does she have a bite on her neck?"

"Yeah, well, there was too much blood exposed and, for fuck's sake, Aurick, don't give me that look. I haven't slipped in ages."

Ellie tried not to squirm as Mina rubbed something cold around her wounds.

"You're going to fix this." Master Aurick's voice was low and serious. "You will go see Matthais and apologize for marking his thrall without permission. Damn it, Aden. I'm tired of cleaning up after you."

"Then don't. I'll handle Matthais myself."

"I won't allow you to condemn this child to Matthais' whims. You will make this right, Aden. But first—" Master Aurick walked over to the bed. "Mina, take her to the infirmary and get her proper medical attention."

"No!"

Ellie couldn't stop the small snicker that escaped her lips as Master Aden roared again. She smacked her hand over her mouth.

"Aurick," Mistress Sophie said. "She's terrified of going to the infirmary."

"I can't treat this," Mina said. "She needs a surgeon to close these wounds. And she's going to need more than BloodStone."

"Sophie, she's not our thrall to treat," Master Aurick said. "Matthais should determine her care."

"No. I bit her. She's mine now and I will decide."

Ellie resisted the urge to jump up and run as far and fast as she could at the reminder. But she was woozy and couldn't do anything more than sway.

She watched Master Aurick glance back and forth between Mistress Sophie and Master Aden, then over to her. He sighed, calmer than his son. Why was Master Aden so angry all the time?

"Okay. Infirmary."

A hologram appeared. "Yes, Master Westcott, how may I assist you?"

"Have a portable surgical bay brought to my son's room at once. I have a human who needs urgent medical attention."

"Yes, Sir. I'll send a surgical team right away."

Master Aurick turned to Master Aden. "If you're going to insist she's treated here, she's going to get the proper treatment. Sophie, you'll have to take her as one of your thralls. I'll speak to Matthais to make the arrangements after Aden apologizes."

"No, she's mine!"

Ellie turned her head toward Mina. "Does he always yell so much? It must be exhausting."

Mistress Sophie chuckled beside her.

"Oh no, they heard me, didn't they?" Ellie dropped her head.

"The meds have kicked in. Where is that food?" Mina asked just as Kane walked back into the room carrying a tray. He handed it to Mistress Sophie, who set it on the bed beside her.

"Wow, he's as big as my dad. And he's very handsome, isn't he? Oh, did I say that out loud?"

"Kane, get out!"

Mistress Sophie pressed a cracker into Ellie's hand. "Take a bite of this."

Ellie shook her head even as her stomach growled. "I can't ma'am."

"Why not?"

"Master forbade me to eat until tomorrow."

"Ellie, you will eat this cracker right now."

Ellie complied, lifting it to her lips. "Did you give me that stuff that makes you tell the truth?" Ellie asked, appalled that she couldn't stop saying things she would never dare say. "Master gave it to me once. I put glue in his shoes." Ellie snickered again as she nibbled on the cracker. "He was always losing them and I was supposed to keep track of them. So I filled them with glue. I thought it would help him keep them on his feet. But he got so mad. That was the first time he whipped me." She released a quiet sigh. "I was ten."

The room grew eerily quiet. She lifted her eyes. Master Aden's expression of horror made it impossible for her to look away. A mixture of anger and revulsion and something else she couldn't identify blazed in his blue eyes, causing her breath to catch in her throat.

"Her eyes."

At his gasp, Ellie's eyes shifted to Master Aurick, where she once again saw horror, shock, and confusion. What the heck was wrong with her eyes? She swallowed the last of her cracker. "I feel sick."

"She's going to be out any second. Sophie, help me lay her on her side in case she vomits."

"No." Ellie's words slurred. "I can't rest. I have chores."

"But she didn't really eat anything," Mistress Sophie said at the same time.

Gentle hands guided Ellie down onto the mattress. The last words she heard as she closed her eyes reminded her of her mother.

"Just sleep, child."

Aden

For only the second time in his life, Aden couldn't breathe. Vampires didn't need to breathe, not deeply at least. A handful of oxygen is all they needed to survive, but he always enjoyed the sensation of air filling and leaving his lungs. But Ellie's words were a crushing weight on his chest that held his lungs hostage.

Could a vampire go into shock?

Sophie tucked a pillow underneath Ellie's head. Motionless, she appeared small and broken, like a shattered doll. That was the problem with humans, they were fragile.

Aurick was the first one to break the silence. "Well, this is unexpected."

The suite door buzzed, then opened. A surgical team of one doctor and two nurses dressed in scrubs entered the room. Behind them, a portable surgical bay floated, complete with an operating table and all necessary diagnostic and surgical equipment.

"How can we assist you, Master Westcott?"

"She was whipped," Aden said. "You need to tend to her wounds."

The doctor approached Aden's bed to examine Ellie and the color drained from his face. "I'm afraid I can't do that, Sir."

"Excuse me?"

The doctor retreated a step at Aden's menacing tone. "Master Matthais gave me strict instructions that she was not to receive medical treatment. Her wounds are to heal on their own."

He was teetering on the edge of a meltdown. It had been coming since he first saw this girl in his room yesterday. He wasn't sure how he'd been able to hold it back as long as he had. Aden grabbed the surgeon by the throat.

"You will do whatever is necessary to fix her. Are my instructions in any way unclear?"

"No, Sir," the surgeon choked.

"Good." Aden released him with a hard shove that sent the man stumbling.

The surgeon instructed the two nurses to lift Ellie onto a stretcher, which floated into the surgical bay. They sealed it and Aden watched as the surgeon prepped Ellie for surgery.

"I'll come back later and check on her," Mina said.

As she passed him, Aden reached out, his fingers flexing before dropping to his side. "Thank you, Mina."

She nodded her reply. His words were unnecessary. Mina had been his caretaker as a child, a second mother of sorts to him, always there when he needed her and when he didn't. His parents looked at Aden when the door closed behind her. He stared back, an uncomfortable silence filling the room.

"Okay, let's put aside the question of her eyes for now. We'll get back to that. Start at the beginning, Aden. What happened here?" Aurick asked.

Couldn't they just give him time to think? He needed time to process what happened with this girl he only met twenty-four hours ago. Why did he care if she lived or died? What was this pull he felt to her? It was more than her eyes. He'd sensed it the second he found her in his room yesterday. Before he ever saw her eyes.

Aden cracked his neck and dropped into the chair. He hadn't been this out of sorts for over a century. Being out of sorts wasn't good for him. It led to blood and carnage everywhere.

"She was changing the bed when I got back from the meetings yesterday. She was uncomfortable with me so I harassed her a little. I wasn't going to do anything, but you know I can't help being a dick sometimes."

"Yes," Sophie agreed as she sat on the sofa.

Aden ignored her dig. "I startled her and she looked up at me. I saw her eyes and I freaked. So I yelled at her and she ran out."

"This is why you were so agitated at the meeting earlier?"

"Obviously. Did you see her fucking eyes?"

Aurick joined Sophie on the sofa. "Focus, Aden, we'll get back to that later. How did she get here tonight?"

"When I got back from—" He hesitated, revealing where he'd been wouldn't go over well. "I found Kira assaulting her in the hallway."

Sophie made a sound of disgust. There was no love lost between her and Kira.

"Anyway, Kira and I got into it when I told her to leave the girl alone. It was clear she was hurt and Kira was making it worse. After Kira stormed off, I was going to take her to the infirmary but she freaked out. So I brought her here and got her to tell me why Matthais had whipped her. The stupid girl thought I was going to tell him, so she told him first. What kind of stupid—" Aden tried to reign in his anger. "He whipped her for no fucking reason."

"Aden, you really can't blame her. Anyone but us would have gone straight to Matthais," his father said. "That doesn't explain the bite."

Aden heard the judgment in Aurick's voice and he counted to ten inside his head. "It just happened, okay. I was trying to do a good fucking deed and it ends up biting me in the ass."

Aden glanced over to see the surgeon stitching Ellie's back, a holographic display hovering above her showing the surgeon's every movement. It was clear from her pinched expression that she was in pain, even though she was unconscious.

"I didn't intend to bite her. I can't explain it. I don't know if it was the blood or—" Aden paced the length of the room, glass crunching under his feet. "I shouldn't have gotten that close to her."

"Something is pulling you towards her." Sophie's tone was quiet and their eyes met.

"Don't start with me, Sophie. It drives me insane when you do this. Trying to make something out of nothing. The scent of her blood hit me, and I gave into temptation and bit her. End of story."

Aurick growled, his typical reaction when Aden disrespected his mother.

Sophie shushed him with a hand on his arm. "Aden, have I ever shared with you what my mother once told me about eyes?"

"I can't stop you, can I?"

Sophie ignored his question. "I was six years old and the kids at school were teasing me about my heterochromia. She said that you can see a person's soul through their eyes."

"Don't tell me shit like that about my grandmother. I lose respect for her every time you do."

"Enough with the impertinence, Aden." His father's voice turned sharp, as it always did whenever Gabby Newman came up.

"There's something about Ellie," Sophie said. "I saw it in her eyes when she looked at me."

Aden's jaw hardened as he sat on the edge of the bed. "You've got to be fucking kidding me? I know you both have this fascination with heaven and hell and souls, and all that shit, but I never believed it."

"That doesn't make it any less true."

"You can't tell me you think—" He couldn't bring himself to say her name, hadn't been able to since that night, when he screamed it in agony.

"Aden, souls can be reborn. I believe that. I also believe every person has their other half. Their soul's mate. And those souls are forever destined to reunite."

Aden remained silent.

"Don't you think there's a reason, even after all this time, the pain is still so raw for you? You can't tell me you didn't lose part of yourself that day."

That day he lost the best part of himself, but his heart couldn't entertain this idea. "She's not her."

"No, she isn't Alysia—"

Sophie got her name out before Aden could bellow at her to stop. The torment of hearing the four syllables hit him full force and burned through his veins. A hiss tore through his teeth and he surged forward, buckling in on himself where he sat.

The darkness surrounded him as his vision blurred. A whooshing reverberated in his ears, blocking out his mother's frantic voice now closer, beside him.

"Aden, can you hear me?"

Her voice sounded muffled and disjointed as his body rocked back and forth of its own volition. He recognized her hands on him, trying to soothe him, but he was too lost in his mind to move away from her.

"Aurick, do something."

"Give him a minute, Soph. He'll be alright."

Aurick's words registered in the back of Aden's mind but his father was wrong. The blackness closed in. It surrounded him, blocking out the pain, and he welcomed it as his mind shut down.

Reality came back to Aden in increments. Everything ached. His body. His mind. His soul. That word set his teeth on edge. He was too brutal and heartless to have a soul.

His mother's hands still touched him, but he didn't have the strength to pull away. She held his head against her chest, murmuring soothing words against his hair. Under the pressure of her tight grasp, he struggled to breathe. His half-breed mother didn't realize her own strength sometimes.

"Let go, Sophie."

"Oh, Aden." She exhaled a shaky breath as he pulled her arms away and sat up, moving away from her. "Thank God. I'm so sorry. I didn't know that still happened."

"Yeah, well, there's a reason I always scream at everyone not to say her name. But it hasn't happened in a long time."

"Oh, Aden, don't you see?"

"Fuck! Sophie, please. Do you really want me to lose my shit again?"

"Okay, okay. I'll stop. There's enough to figure out right now without this. But you know in here—" Sophie rested one of her hands over his heart. "That I'm right."

He removed her hand before moving away from her. "No, I don't."

"I've waited so long for this day." Sophie looked over at Aurick, her eyes blinking with unshed tears.

Aden stood and tugged on the short strands of his hair. "I can't deal with this shit right now."

"Well, we have to deal with Matthais. I'm surprised he hasn't sent someone here by now," Aurick said.

"Kira probably went straight to him," Sophie said with a sour look.

"The law says she's mine now." The moment the words left his mouth, Aden recognized their undeniable truth. "I won't let anyone take her from me."

"Is that why you bit her?" Aurick asked.

Aden looked over at his father. He'd barely said a word, letting Sophie lead the conversation. But he had to agree. Otherwise, he'd contradict her. To Aden's surprise, Aurick's eyes now held curiosity instead of judgment.

Aden shook his head, at a loss for an answer.

"Aden, you've condemned her. She'll carry your scent forever. No other respectable vampire or human will have her. If you decide later she isn't who or what you want, you can't take this back. If you try to give her back, Matthais will euthanize her."

Aden stared at Ellie's unconscious form across the room. He focused on her slow heartbeat and her shallow breaths. The sound filled his ears until it was all he could hear.

"No one will touch or hurt her again or they'll answer to me." The conviction in his voice surprised even him.

"You better go speak to Matthais. He'll be looking for her I'm sure."

Aden moved closer to the surgical bay. The doctor was bandaging Ellie's back while the nurses cleaned up after the surgery. Aurick stepped up beside him.

"I knew Matthais was cruel to his humans, but how could anyone do this to a child? Just for looking a vampire in the eyes?"

"She's not a child. She's old enough to be held responsible for her actions, but there's no reason for this kind of inhumane punishment."

Sophie joined them. Their reflections looked eerie in the glass. "It's an asinine law."

"It's not. It's just common practice. Why do you think we don't enforce it at home?"

Aden glanced over at his father. "I figured your soft spot for humans got the better of you."

"Compassion and respect for all of God's creatures are not flaws, Aden."

Aden smirked but didn't respond because they'd spent centuries disagreeing on that.

"Aden, you have to be strategic when dealing with Matthais. Are you certain you don't want me to do it?

"No. I did this. I'll deal with it."

With one last look at Ellie, Aden walked out of the room.

Aden nodded at Lorcan, Matthais' personal guard, as he entered his office. Just as lavish and ostentatious as the rest of his compound, the room was built over the ocean, offering unobstructed and breathtaking views of the crashing waves below. The rising sun bathed the space in a warm glow through the floor to ceiling windows. All the windows in Matthais' compound were made from the same ultraviolet light-filtering polymer as the dome.

Matthais waved him in as he sat behind his cedar wood desk talking on the phone, speaking Italian, his native language. Few vampires spoke Italian. The world's universal language was English, and all vampires and humans were required to speak it. But as Ancient Ones, the Gerents retained the language of their ancestors and spoke it with their closest advisers to maintain secrecy.

No doubt Matthais did that now. He didn't know that Aurick and Sophie spoke all the Gerents' languages and insisted their children did as well.

Aden sat on the sofa in the middle of the room, below a diamond crystal chandelier that projected prisms onto the walls. Zurina, napping beside the window, lifted her head and looked at him before lowering it again and closing her eyes. She was an exquisite animal.

Aden half listened to Matthais speaking about details for the HEW games' closing night ceremonies. He had to remain calm. If he didn't handle this carefully, it could blow up in his face. Matthais had to think Ellie was just another thrall Aden had indiscriminately bitten. It wouldn't be the first time.

He needed to keep his anger in check. But every minute that passed was another Aden could see Ellie's battered and bloody body at his feet, broken by Matthais' hand. He still couldn't fathom how she had endured it. Then she confessed to being whipped when she was only ten. What kind of monster whips a ten-year-old child?

Matthais' cruelty was renowned in the vampire world. Despite their differences, Aden always respected Matthais, even if he thought he went too far. He was the Chancellor of the Vampire World Council, and it was under his leadership that vampires had claimed their power. Maintaining order was crucial, but what Matthais had done took human punishment to the extreme.

"You've caused quite a stir in my household." Matthais sat on the sofa across from Aden as Zurina loped over and laid down at his feet.

"I hope I haven't caused you any problems."

Matthais waved his hand. "Of course not. Thralls don't cause problems in my household. Kira on the other hand…"

"She and I have a very volatile history."

Matthais reached down and stroked Zurina's fur. "Your interruption of Elliana's discipline left her feeling quite irked."

"It looked like more than discipline to me. Since when do you allow others to punish your thralls?"

"I don't, but Kira, well, you know Kira. Sometimes it's easier to let her have her way."

Why would he give Kira so much leeway? Any other vampire would have faced extermination.

"Why did you stop her?" Matthais asked.

"I could smell the girl's blood. She had a lot of open wounds and I've always had a weakness for AB Positive."

"I thrashed her well, didn't I?" Matthais' grin was feral. "Although I must say, I would have expected to hear of Elliana's indiscretion from you directly," he commented, his tone tinged with suspicion. "Why didn't you report her?"

Aden shifted, crossing his legs in an attempt to keep his temper in check. "No need. She did nothing wrong."

"She made direct eye contact with you."

"I startled her, so she likely perceived it as worse than it actually was. But there was no eye contact between us," Aden lied through his teeth.

A quiet "hmm" passed Matthais' lips. "Elliana isn't typically prone to hysterics. It seems I punished her for nothing."

Matthais' casual disregard for the extreme damage he'd inflicted on Ellie's fragile body was beyond disturbing.

"She never ended up in the infirmary. Where is she?" Matthais was trying to appear casual but Aden saw right through him.

"That's why I'm here. I'm afraid I succumbed to the temptation and bit her before I could stop myself."

Matthais' eyes glowed a vibrant red, and his hands tightened before relaxing as if nothing had happened. "I thought you were over such youthful rebellions, Aden," Matthais said with a scornful twist of his lips.

How did Aden never notice what a condescending fuck he could be?

"Yes, but that amount of blood out in the open just hit me. I know I've slighted you. I want to make it right." Aden considered his next words. "Tell me though, I'm curious. Why hadn't you or anyone else taken her yet? Her scent is intoxicating, her blood exquisite tasting, and she's well over the legal age. Yet she was pure."

"There are those of us who prefer our fruit to be more ripe before indulging."

"How can I make it right with you?"

"Don't worry. I'll take care of her."

That didn't sound good.

"You see, the thing is. Now that I've had a taste, I want to invoke the sovereignty law. Remuneration isn't an issue."

Compensation for a damaged thrall was the norm. It was a reasonable proposal. So why was Matthais looking at him with amusement?

"She's one thrall. There are millions of them. The loss of one is nothing."

In principle, Aden shared Matthais' view. He said something similar to his father last week about the humans the rogues had slaughtered. But rage and possessiveness prickled at the base of his spine at the thought of Ellie suffering the same fate. How had his world turned upside down so quickly?

"I've marked her. Aurick's feelings about such things are clear. If I don't make this right, I'll never hear the end of it. Eternity is too long to listen to that."

"Indeed, Aurick has always had a strange fondness for humans. I fear it's his one true character flaw."

Aden nodded his head, but the muscle in his jaw clenched. He and Aurick may not always agree, but Aden respected his father and didn't appreciate anyone speaking ill of him.

"Of course I'll owe you a girl. I have several I bought I have yet to drink from. Perhaps you may find one to your liking."

Aden instantly regretted the words as soon as they left his mouth. His mother was going to murder him for offering one of his thralls for Ellie.

"She's the daughter of one of my elite guards, Aden. I can't simply barter her off so easily. And how would Aurick feel about that, condemning one girl to save another? That's something *I* would never hear the end of."

"Honestly, it's not Aurick's wrath I dread."

"Yes, I imagine not."

Matthais was quiet for several moments, tapping his lips with his finger, his eyes unreadable. Aden refused to squirm under his gaze. Finally, Matthais' face relaxed. "No need to anger your mother. Neither one of us, I dare say, wants to deal with that. Take the girl. She's yours. No need to trade another. I have plenty."

Aden looked at him. Matthais always expected something in return. "Surely you want compensation for her?"

"No. Consider her a boon," Matthais said, his gaze growing darker. "But there may be a day I require a favor from you and I would hope you remember my generosity."

That didn't sound good either.

"That seems more than fair," Aden said.

Matthais stood, signaling that the conversation had come to an end, prompting Aden to do the same. "A word of advice, however. She's a defiant little thing. You'll want to nip that in the bud."

Aden

Aden was the last to board the plane. After his meeting with Matthais, he'd met with Andrei to discuss the number of troops to be sent to assist Paolo, if it became necessary.

Humans were easy to control. Rogue vampires were not. They were stronger than the half-breed army but typically stayed in smaller groups, so they could easily be subdued. The ones in Abya Yala hadn't. These differed from the rogues Aden dealt with before visiting the capital. This group amassed quite a coven and was slaughtering the human population across the countryside.

Cecilia had let the skirmishes go on too long and now he would have to clean up her mess. Like he needed one more thing to deal with right now.

Aden sat on the sofa without acknowledging his parents and the cabin door closed as the crew readied for departure. The plane's front section, true to his mother's style, exuded an air of sophistication. Aurick let her decorate as she pleased, and the current décor matched the blue and cream color scheme she seemed to favor, punctuated with his ancient Celtic artifacts and style.

Sophie sat at a table writing in one of her journals while Aurick relaxed in a chair across from her, reading one of his leather-bound books. Physical books were rare since almost everything these days was digitized. But his parents preferred the weight and texture of them, enjoying the experience of turning the pages and feeling the paper beneath their fingers. His family was the only one he knew to still possess actual books because they were technically forbidden.

Aden's legs shook, agitated. He wasn't a fidgeter. Was that even a word? Regardless, Aden slammed his fist onto his thigh to stop his leg from shaking.

He needed to see Ellie and it pissed him the fuck off. Aden hadn't seen her since she was taken from his room that morning and he felt her absence acutely. He needed to get a grip on himself. She was a thrall. Nothing more. He wouldn't let Sophie's ramblings convince him otherwise.

In a moment of weakness, she made him wonder, but he was long past that now. So what if Ellie had her eyes? It meant nothing. Neither did the prickling in his fingertips whenever he touched her. Neither did the way his entire body hummed when she was near him. Nor did the way all the missing pieces in his life had seemed to fall into place when he'd tasted her blood.

But what if his mother was right?

Fuck! No! He slammed his fist on his leg again. She was just a thrall. He bit her so now she was his, but what the fuck was he going to do with her? He hadn't compelled her, so he never needed to drink from her again. So, why did the thought of never tasting her again make his stomach clench in revolt?

He should give her to Sophie with explicit instructions that he never wanted to see her again. That's what a sane vampire would do. But no one would ever accuse him of being sane.

With his mind made up, Aden thought he'd feel better, but his anxiety ratcheted up a notch. He had no idea how to deal with this, but one thing was certain—there was no way in hell he would last the entire flight without checking on her.

Fuck! It had been barely a minute since his decision and he was already backtracking on it. How loathsome could one vampire be?

"How did your meeting go?"

The cushion next to him sank as Sophie took a seat. Grateful for the distraction, Aden focused on her.

"I suspect I'm going to have to go to Abya Yala myself."

Aurick set his book down, looking over and sipping his blood-spiked whiskey. "Matthais shouldn't have given Cecelia a week to quell this. It will only give the coven time to kill more humans."

"And increase in size," Aden said, only making it more obvious to all of them the differences between his and Aurick's priorities.

As the plane ascended into the sky, Aden brought up a hologram of the recruit training he'd instructed Roderick to oversee in his absence. Sophie remained on the sofa beside him, her eyes fixed on him.

"Is there something you want?" he asked without looking at her.

"She's sleeping." Sophie chose to answer the question he hadn't asked instead. "She's still in tremendous pain so Mina gave her another shot. She'll sleep the entire trip."

Aden's lips formed a tight, stern line as the hologram vanished. Despite his aloof demeanor, the thought of Ellie still being in pain bothered him. Sophie reached out to touch him but he shifted away.

"Don't. I know you think I need comfort, but you're wrong. I don't buy into your insanity either. I have too many things to deal with, and I can't contemplate your craziness, so please, just don't."

"Okay. I said I'd let it go." She settled back on the sofa. "But you won't be able to ignore it for long."

"Wanna bet? You know I can avoid things for centuries. She'll be long dead before I think of it again, and then there will be no reason to."

"Aden, don't be callous. That isn't you, despite how much you pretend."

He didn't need to look at her to know she was frowning. They sat in silence for a few minutes. Her presence always comforted him, even when he didn't want it.

"You did the right thing."

"Biting her was the right thing?"

"Well, not that." She pursed her lips. "But getting her out of there was. At least now, away from Matthais, and with your scent on her, she'll be safe from other vampires."

"And I should care about this why?"

"She's very pretty," Sophie said as if he hadn't spoken. It drove him crazy when she did that. "I can't imagine why Matthais didn't allow her to be marked."

"He wanted her for himself, but was waiting for her to get a little older."

"In her condition, it's unlikely she would have." Aden shifted his gaze to meet hers. "If you hadn't stopped Kira, and we hadn't treated her, I suspect she might have died from the blood loss."

"I'll be right back," Aden said before he stood and walked toward the back cabin. He was going to go crazy if he didn't see her.

And that right there was proof he already was.

Aden stalked through the half-breeds' cabin. Kane, Horatio, and a group of guards were huddled around a table, their faces tense as they played poker. He halted when he reached the last row before the door to the thrall's cabin.

"When did you last check on her?" Mina glanced up at him. She could always see right through him, just like his mother, and it annoyed the fuck out of him. "I don't want any wise-ass comments out of you, woman. I simply asked when you last checked on her."

She looked back down at her tablet. "Right before we took off. She's fine for now."

"Did you pull out a bed for her?"

Damn it! Why did he care?

"Yes. She's in the last bed at the back. I have Chelsea sitting nearby with instructions to come get me if she wakes."

He flexed his fingers above her shoulder but refrained from touching her. He knew she recognized the gesture as an apology for snapping at her.

"By the way." Mina narrowed her eyes. "Chelsea is going to need a break for a few weeks. She needs recovery time."

Mina was the only one who knew of Kira's mistreatment of Chelsea the other day, but she still held him responsible.

He waved his hand. "Okay, whatever."

When he'd left home five days ago everything in his life was in order. Now chaos reigned. Everything he knew and believed about the world he lived in no longer made sense. Nothing felt right anymore. Who was this thrall to have such a profound impact on him?

He should turn around and walk back to the main cabin, take Mina's word that she was fine, but his nerves were too frayed. The last seventy-two hours had taken their toll and Aden never took the easy road in anything. He had to see her for just a minute. Then he'd be calm again.

He entered the thrall's cabin. His thralls sat in a grouping near the back. Several of them sat up and pushed their shoulders back, waiting for his command.

He didn't acknowledge them, walking down the narrow aisle. Chelsea was sitting in the seat closest to the small bed. She saw him approach and mimicked the other thralls' posture. But his eyes never left the girl lying on the bed.

Regret washed over him as he watched her. Her face was pinched, not smooth and relaxed as it should be in sleep, suggesting the medicine Mina gave her wasn't working.

He thought seeing her would make him feel better, but with each passing second, he could feel his next snap getting closer, coming alive inside his body, prickling under his skin, waiting to explode. Her injuries were covered, but he doubted he could forget them. The scent of her blood was still potent and filled his nostrils as he clenched his hands at his sides. If he listened close enough he could hear the blood flowing in her veins.

A haze clouded Aden's vision and his fangs lengthened. He swallowed the venom flowing into his mouth. Chelsea flinched beside him. He chose her more often, and so she knew his moods better than any of his other thralls.

"Stand up Chelsea," he said and she obeyed his harsh command in an instant.

With one last glance at the sleeping girl, Aden turned away. He gripped Chelsea's arm and yanked her closer, despite what Mina had said. The last sound he heard was her cry as he sank his teeth into her neck.

Aden spent the rest of the flight in the thrall's cabin, sitting in the small seat Chelsea had occupied. It was much too small for his frame and he was uncomfortable. He'd told himself more than once to get up and get the hell out of there, but his body refused to cooperate. The warm, delicate hand that held his captive didn't help his resolve.

Chelsea was now in a bed of her own, recovering from his attack. He'd almost drained her before he realized what he was doing and pulled back. He immediately sent a thrall to get Mina. And, as usual, she dealt with his destruction without involving his parents. She never hid her disapproval of his violent tendencies, but the extent to which she enabled him was yet one more thing to ponder by a mind ready to break.

The plane began its descent as Mina walked into the cabin again. Chelsea sat up, getting her bearings. She had recovered, for the most part. The BloodStone drip and transfusion Mina gave her replenished her blood so she no longer looked pasty and gray. He'd licked the additional tear marks on her neck, but it would still take a while to heal. Mina had covered them with a large bandage, the unsightly thing reminding him of how badly he'd lost it. He'd been seconds from killing her and only when he'd opened his eyes and saw Ellie sleeping on the bed had the madness receded.

Ellie slept peacefully now, but she hadn't been calm for most of the flight. That's one reason he'd stayed back here. Once Mina had Chelsea settled with her transfusion, Aden had turned to leave. But small whimpers had stopped him in his tracks.

"No," she'd murmured in her sleep. "Don't do this."

Aden spun and looked at her, his eyes wide. She'd started to thrash on the mattress and then groaned in pain, rolling onto her back. Without a second thought, he'd reached out and rolled her back onto her side. Had she been dreaming about her whipping?

"Please," she begged, almost choking.

His eyes had locked on her and Aden watched, spellbound, as her breathing sped up. Her heart thrummed wildly and the scent of fear wafted from her pores. Whatever she was dreaming about terrified her.

She'd thrashed harder, her hands reaching up to her neck to grab it as if trying to pull something away, but the pain medication dragged her so far under she couldn't surface from her nightmare.

"Don't do this. Please," she'd pleaded again.

Aden had choked as her words pierced his ears. Words that were stuck on repeat in his memory for centuries.

He'd worried she'd hyperventilate and gouge her neck with her fingernails, so he'd reached out and touched her hand. She stilled, his touch calming her, but she'd continued to whimper, gripping his fingers. Until finally, she sighed.

"Aden."

Impossible!

She was dreaming of him.

Aden staggered into the small seat beside her and that's where he remained. Her fingers clung to his. He was unable and unwilling to pull away. Her touch didn't make him uncomfortable. Quite the opposite. Despite his aversion, it calmed him and he had no desire to pull away.

Mina walked Chelsea to a seat near the front of the cabin, and then she walked back to the bed, never once acknowledging his fingers entwined with Ellie's.

"I need to wake her, give her oxygen, and check her vitals."

"Let her be, Mina. She's fine."

"Aden, I need to check her and at least make sure she's strapped in for landing."

"I said leave her alone," he said louder than he intended.

Ellie stirred at his voice. She let go of his fingers and Aden felt the loss. He jerked his hand back. There was no need for her to know she'd been holding it.

Ellie

“**W**here am I?”

Ellie’s eyes fluttered open. She tried to stretch, but her body protested and she groaned as the pain echoed through her. “Oh, that hurts.”

She blinked and gasped, surprised to see Master Aden beside her. The intensity in his eyes was unsettling. They were so familiar, like distant memories tugging at her mind.

“How are you feeling?” Mina’s voice drew her attention from him.

“Like someone’s been using my body as a whipping post,” she said in a bland tone, surprised she could speak so lightly about what happened to her. She stiffened at the deep sound of Master Aden’s growl beside her.

“Do you think you can sit up?” Mina asked.

“Do I have to?”

“Otherwise, I’ll have to strap you down during landing.”

“No, I’ll sit.” Ellie pushed on her hands. Her back muscles seized up and it took several tries to get upright. She swung her legs off the bed, trying to shake off the grogginess.

She stole another glance at Master Aden. He watched her closely as if expecting her to pitch forward and face plant on the floor.

She licked her dry lips. “Can I have a glass of water?”

“Here.” Mina handed her the oxygen mask. “Put this over your mouth and take a few deep breaths. I’ll get you some water.”

Mina walked into the small kitchen area to the right. Ellie did as she was told and the oxygen helped clear her head. She looked anywhere but at Master Aden, who remained silent and still beside her, rubbing the fingertips of one of his hands together.

Mina handed her a small cup and Ellie removed the mask. "Just take sips."

The cool water soothed her parched throat.

"You should go back to the front for landing," Mina said to Master Aden. He shot her a nasty glare but she didn't even blink. Their eyes locked in a tense standoff until he stood and stomped out of the cabin.

"Whoa," Ellie said under her breath as she looked at Mina with awe.

"Let's get you in a seat for landing."

"I don't think I can lean back."

"Then you can sit forward but you need to be seated and belted in."

Ellie stood up and her legs threatened to give way. Mina grasped her arm to steady her.

"How long will it take for my back to heal?"

"Longer than you'd like. At least without vampire blood."

"Won't that turn me into a half-breed or vampire?" Ellie asked.

"No, you haven't lost enough blood for that, but it will heal you."

Ellie started down the aisle, bracing herself with a hand on the top of the seats. Her legs wobbled and she was dizzy. She could feel the other thralls' eyes on her, assessing and judging her.

A feeling of overwhelming sadness and loss came over her. She was barely conscious when she'd been sent to the Westcott's guest thrall quarters. She hadn't even been allowed to say goodbye to her dad or Carrie before being brought to the plane. And now she would probably never see either of them again.

Her breath hitched, and she blinked to keep the tears at bay as Mina helped ease her into a seat before sitting next to her. She braced a hand on Ellie's shoulder so her back didn't press against the seat. But it didn't stop the pain from rippling through her body as the plane landed.

She gritted her teeth and waited for the plane to come to a stop. She'd only been on a plane once in her life, and the shaky movement made her queasy. Mina waited for the other thralls to leave before helping Ellie up.

"Can you walk on your own?"

"Yes, ma'am. I think so."

"The first thing you should know is we're not so formal here unless there are guests in the compound. My name is Mariana but everyone calls me Mina because Aden couldn't pronounce my full name as a child. It just stuck."

"Does he always yell so much?"

Mina laughed. "Yes. He always was a hothead, even as a kid. But you'll soon figure out when he's furious or just blowing hot air. When he's truly angry, it's best to stay out of his way."

Ellie ambled down the aisle toward the exit. The door to the next cabin slid open and Master Aden entered, followed by his guard, Mistress Sophie, and Master Aurick. They all looked flustered and Ellie wondered what was going on. Mina looked as confused as she was.

"Kane is going to take Ellie to my rooms," Master Aden said to Mina. "She will stay in my concubine suite."

Ellie swayed on her feet. He was taking her as a pet.

"Aden, be reasonable. Mina can monitor her recovery better in the thrall's quarters," Mistress Sophie said.

"No. Mina can tend to her in the concubine suite."

"Can the three of you argue somewhere else?" Mina said. "I don't care where you put her, Aden, but she needs to rest. I'll speak to Zach and he'll examine her tonight."

"Aden, you should think about this," Master Aurick said. "Let her heal, then you can decide what to do."

"No!" His roar echoed through the plane.

Ellie took a seat. This was going to take a while.

"What are you doing?" Master Aden asked her.

"Sitting, Master, while the three of you work this out." She kept her eyes down.

"Stop doing that already," he snapped. "You will look at me when I speak to you."

"Yes, Master." Ellie looked up, startled. Every time she saw his eyes, it shocked her all over again.

Her eyes skimmed over his face, taking him in for the first time, noting the sharp contours and the intensity of his gaze. She couldn't deny he was attractive despite his intimidating and angry demeanor. His face was well-defined, with a sharp jawline and chin, covered with the lightest touch of stubble that accentuated his rugged features. His lips were full and firm, and she couldn't help but imagine the heart-stopping smile they could form if he ever let himself.

His nose was narrow and slightly crooked in the middle like he might have broken it once. Vampire children were born as mortal as humans and, as they aged, grew stronger like half-breeds before becoming fully vampire around the age of twenty-five. Any injuries or scars they received as children stayed with them, serving as a permanent mark on their bodies.

His hair was short and light brown, and it looked soft to the touch, effortlessly tousled. The urge to run her fingers through it surprised her.

"Don't call me master!" Master Aden bellowed. Ellie cringed, torn away from her perusal of him, as his angry personality once again overshadowed his good looks.

"I'm sorry, Sir." Ellie was unsure of how to act around this volatile vampire. Clearly, nothing she did was right.

"Aden, stop yelling at her," Mistress Sophie said. "Give her a chance to learn things here."

"Then perhaps Mina should educate her while she accompanies her to my room."

His petulant tone might have been amusing under different circumstances, but the fact she would stay in his pet room made her want to throw up.

"You'll want to think this through, Aden. There is no going back if you cross that line."

"Sophie, I will not yield on this."

Mistress Sophie released a heavy sigh and nodded her head. Damn. Ellie was hoping his mother would win.

Aden stormed off the plane before anyone could say anything else.

Ellie's eyes darted around the small room. It was modest with a bed, a dresser with 4 drawers, a small round table, and a chair in the corner. It was stark and white and the walls were blank, reminding her of Master Matthais' thralls quarters. But the mattress beneath her was comfortable, much softer and thicker than the one she was used to.

A door across from the bed led to a small bathroom with a shower, and one on the left, Mina told her, led to Master Aden's room. The door she used to enter from the hallway would remain locked. She would have to go through Master Aden's room to reach her own unless he specified otherwise. It didn't thrill her and only confused her. Why would he want her to invade his personal space?

"What am I supposed to call him if not master?" Ellie had asked Mina before she'd left her alone.

"Aurick and Sophie dislike that term so they insist thralls use their name after it, making it a little more informal. Aden and Keeley are the same."

"Who's Keeley?"

"Aden's sister. Here, sit." Mina helped her into a chair in the corner. "You look like you're going to fall."

"They let you call them by only their names?" Things were very different here.

"I raised both those children from the day they were born so, yes, I call them only by their names. I've never called them anything else, even when I was human." Mina looked inside the dresser. "Oh, good. They put clothes in here for you."

"So what should I call him?" Ellie asked again.

Mina removed a set of pajamas and put them on the bed.

"The term master irritated him, so adding his name after it will still anger him. Why don't you start with sir and see what happens from there?"

"Why do my eyes upset all of them so much?"

Mina shook her head but Ellie suspected she knew the answer.

"Why does he want me here? Why not keep me with the other thralls?"

"I don't know. But try to remember, he may be volatile, but he's not so bad when he can get past his own ego. You'll see that soon enough."

Ellie had her doubts but she nodded. Even if it meant facing Master Matthais' wrath, she just wanted to go home. She missed her dad and Carrie. These kinds of rooms were for private pets, to keep them close and accessible for sex. The mere thought of it made her feel sick.

Ellie pushed to her feet, the effort making her legs wobble. Had it really been only three days since her whipping? No wonder she still felt like an exposed nerve that kept getting irritated. So much had happened, and it was hard to wrap her mind around it. This punishment had been ten times worse and had twice as many lashes as her last. She never got a good look at it herself, but from everyone's reaction, including Carrie and Mistress Sophie, her back must be completely ruined.

Ellie was at a loss for what to do. Was she supposed to wait here for Master Aden to come get her? Mina said to rest but she wasn't used to being so inactive. Even when injured, thralls worked in Master Matthais' household. The only excuse for not reporting for your chores was death.

She pressed a hand to her stomach when it growled. Apart from a handful of crackers from Mina, she had gone without food for days. The medicine was bothering her stomach and her hunger pangs were getting stronger. It had been five days, and the most she had ever gone without food was seven.

Why didn't she ask Mina if she could have something small to eat? Maybe she should look for the kitchen. Mina had only told her to rest, not that she was required to remain in her room.

Ellie walked to the door, bracing herself on the wall. It slid open. Master Aden was in the room, pacing back and forth. His head snapped up, and his intense gaze locked onto her.

Ellie stepped back, her response purely instinctual, as she took a deep breath to slow her racing heart. Don't be a coward, she thought, as she urged herself to walk through the door. Sure, she was scared, but she had to face him sometime.

What's the worst that could happen? He already bit her. And if he was going to make her his pet, then the least he could do was feed her first.

Aden

Aden paced, listening to her breath coming from the next room. He'd passed Mina on her way out and she shot him a knowing look. He hated the way her knowing looks still made him feel like an errant child, even after nearly three hundred years.

"I haven't given her any rules. That's all on you." She'd tossed over her shoulder as she walked away. Sometimes he really wanted to wring her little neck.

No one agreed with his choice to keep Ellie in his concubine suite. He wasn't sure why he'd done it. It had been a split-second decision once the plane landed.

Having her this close was likely a huge mistake. He may not be thinking clearly right now, but he knew that much. He should have let her stay with the other thralls. But the idea of her in the communal thralls' quarters bothered him. Perhaps it was just the effect of her eyes on his psyche, but he needed some fucking time. This kind of crazy was too much for even a vampire to process so quickly.

He was so wrapped up in his thoughts he didn't hear the door open. It was her stomach growling that caught his attention. When he whipped his gaze over to her, she immediately stepped out of sight. He kept his eyes trained on the door as he waited to see what she'd do.

Her heart slowed, and then she appeared again, her footsteps cautious and hesitant. She was still unsteady on her feet and she leaned against the doorframe as she stepped into the room. As he instructed her, she kept her head up, but her eyes remained lowered. She looked around the room, taking in her surroundings as if they were the most interesting thing she'd ever seen.

So that's how she was going to follow his orders. After a minute of silence, it was obvious she wouldn't speak first. She was forbidden to do so in Matthais' house and carried that expectation here. She would soon discover the rules here were different, but like him, she needed time to adjust.

"Hello, Ellie."

"Hello, Sir," she said, slowly lifting her eyes.

It was like a kick to his gut again. She sucked in a breath. But he didn't know if it was in response to his reaction or her own. He couldn't stop looking at her, so after a long moment she looked away first. At least it wasn't down. That was progress, right?

"I'm sorry to interrupt you, Sir. I was going to look for the kitchen to get something to eat."

"When was the last time you had a full meal?"

She pushed away from the door frame and looked like she might fall on her face. She regained her balance just in time, saving him from having to step in to catch her again.

"Almost six days ago."

"Kitchen!"

A hologram of a thrall appeared. "Yes, Master Aden?"

"What do you eat?" Aden asked her, unsure of what to order for a human after all this time.

"Anything, Sir. But I can go to the kitchen and get something myself."

"No. You can barely stand. You'll stay here. What do you want to eat?"

"I think something mild would be good until I know what my stomach can handle."

"Such as?" he asked, his voice dripping with impatience.

"Maybe soup and crackers."

"That's not enough food."

"Master Aden?" the kitchen thrall said. "Why don't I bring a few options for Miss Ellie and see what she likes?"

"Fine. And hurry up."

"Yes, Sir." The hologram vanished.

Ellie looked surprised that the kitchen thrall had called her Miss Ellie. His mother must have already informed the staff of Ellie's name and status as a second-level thrall.

First-level thralls were the lowest of humans. They were the servants and workers, performing menial labor and serving as feeders. Second-level thralls worked as personal assistants to vampires in authority. They received a modest education, with a focus on basic reading and writing skills. Most second-level thralls were those who had tested high as children, and vampires often turned many second-level female thralls into either pets or half-breeds for breeding purposes.

"You should sit down," he said, trying to keep his commands to a minimum. Although he enjoyed making thralls nervous, she was much too skittish, and it was going to drive him crazy if she didn't stop jumping every time he spoke.

"I can wait in my room, Sir."

"Sit down, Ellie."

He'd never invited a thrall to sit on his furniture. What the fuck was going on with him?

She walked around the couch and sat down slowly. The oversized sofa seemed to swallow her slight frame as she sunk into it. Aden sat in the chair to her right. Damn Mina for not doing this for him. She may not have known what rules he planned to set, but she could have covered the basics. Ellie continued to stare anywhere but at him.

"Ellie, look at me," he said with all the patience he could muster. She looked at him with wide and uncertain eyes. The sight stole his breath once again. How the hell was he going to deal with seeing her eyes all the time? "I am only going to tell you this once. You are to never call me master. Not even Master Aden. When you address me, you will call me sir."

"Yes, Sir."

"I realize I've taken you from the only home you've known and brought you to a foreign place. You don't understand the rules. And I know the last few days probably don't make you feel safe with me but you have nothing to fear. I won't hurt you."

"Yes, Sir."

"I can see you want to ask me something. It was different in Matthais' house, but thralls are allowed to ask questions here."

She nibbled on her lip and scrunched up her forehead.

"There's no need to be afraid to speak up when you have one, Ellie."

"What will you do with me?"

A frown etched into the side of his mouth. "Don't let your mind run wild with all sorts of horrifying scenarios because I'm keeping you in my concubine suite. I haven't decided what I'll do with you but, I'll say it again, I have no intention of hurting you."

In that instant, Aden was struck by undeniable truth of his words. Ellie looked at him, her eyes reflective, assessing the honesty in his words. The edges of her eyes relaxed as she accepted them. Her eyes were so easy to read, revealing her every emotion. Just like...

"Thank you, Sir," she said, before shifting in what was obvious discomfort.

"Are you still in pain?"

"It's getting better."

He didn't need to be a mind reader to know she was lying. "I'll have Mina bring you more pain medication."

"No thank you."

"Why not?" he snapped. Why the fuck would she refuse pain medication when Matthais had obviously denied it to her?

"I don't like how it makes me feel. It makes me dizzy and sick."

"It's foolish to remain in pain," he scoffed. Then his voice softened, almost amused. "You're quite the martyr, aren't you?" A laugh escaped her lips and he narrowed his eyes as his tone dropped to an insulted growl. "And that's funny why?"

A flush of pink spread across her cheeks. "I'm sorry, Sir. I didn't mean to laugh. It's just you're not the first person to call me that."

"I bet." He grunted. "Another thing, stop apologizing all the time. I won't snap at every little thing you say." She arched one of those full eyebrows in disbelief and this time he snorted out an unexpected laugh. "Well, I probably will until I get used to you at least. Even then—" He scowled. "Stop apologizing. It irritates me."

"Yes, Sir."

The trace of a smile touched her lips and it tugged at something in the center of his chest.

"I'm sure I don't need to go over the basic rules with you. Most rules for thralls are universal, but I need to make one thing clear. Other than my rule about not calling me Master, there is only one other rule you must follow."

Ellie looked at him.

"You are never to touch me. Do you understand?"

"Of course, Sir. Touching vampires is forbidden."

"No, Ellie." He snarled before nodding. "Yes, touching vampires is forbidden. But what I am telling you is that under no circumstances are you ever to touch me without permission. Is that clear?"

"Yes, Sir."

"Ellie," he barked. "I need you to understand this rule implicitly."

"I can understand simple instructions, Sir."

If her expression wasn't so earnest, he might have snarled at her for her impertinence. Instead, he sighed. "Ellie, I don't wish for you to fear me but this rule is for your own safety."

She nodded but didn't answer him.

"I can tell you have something else to ask so you might as well spit it out."

When she didn't speak up, he snapped at her. "Fucking ask it already. I'm not getting any younger here."

"Mina said something I didn't quite understand."

Aden's lips twisted into a frown. "She often speaks out of turn. What did she say?"

"She said vampire blood could heal my back almost instantly."

"That busybody will never learn to keep her damn mouth shut," he muttered to himself.

"If it's true, why didn't she give it to me? Surely I'm being a bother."

"You're not being a bother." A mix of annoyance and frustration swept over him, prompting him to take a calming breath. "The medicines you've been given already contain vampire blood and are speeding up your body's natural healing."

"But Mina said—" she started and Aden shot to his feet.

"Vampire blood is not an option. Do you know the consequences of drinking it? No, you don't. So, don't ask again."

"Yes, Sir, I'm sor—" she stopped mid-sentence when he narrowed his eyes at her.

"I have business to attend to. I'll send Mina to give you something for your pain." His voice softened. "Something that won't make you so dizzy."

"Thank you." Ellie tried to stand.

"You can stay here on the sofa until she gets here."

She settled back on the cushion.

"This evening, after Zach examines you, I will have one of my other thralls show you where you can and cannot go."

"Okay," she said.

There was a buzz at the door.

"Enter."

A male thrall guided a cart with several covered plates into the room.

"Leave it," Aden said. "Return in an hour to retrieve the dirty dishes. I don't want the odor of food in my rooms all night."

"Yes, Sir." He hurried out.

"Come over here and eat something."

Ellie rose, taking a moment to steady herself. She walked over and pondered her choices before picking up a muffin.

Aden's eyes dropped to the vein in her neck, pulsing beneath her skin and he couldn't contain the groan that rumbled up his chest. Her body tensed up and he caught a whiff of the unmistakable scent of fear. He had to get out of there before he sank his fangs into her tantalizing flesh again.

He spun and strode out of the room to avoid giving in to the temptation.

Aden slammed his drawer so hard that the wood along the top of his desk splintered and cracked, leaving a visible fracture in its rich, dark grain. Much like his suite, Aden's office was a blend of modern and masculine elements, the furniture oversized and sturdy. His large desk, typically formidable against his aggression, seemed to quiver under the weight of his heightened intensity tonight.

He glanced at the clock with a low growl. He was leaving for the training field in five minutes, but he couldn't focus. Every interaction with Ellie, and each time she looked at him with those eyes, knocked him off balance. No matter how much he tried to deny it, maybe his mother was right.

Aden didn't believe in an afterlife. Dead was dead and there was no bringing a vampire or human back. But his father and mother were certain there was something after death, and their deeply held beliefs governed everything they did in their lives.

If souls existed, perhaps his mother was right. There was no other reason Ellie had *her* exact eyes. No other explanation for why she dreamed about him—dreams that caused her to talk in her sleep, saying words he hadn't heard in centuries. And being near her both calmed him and lit him on fire, a sensation he had only experienced with one other person.

He dropped into his high-backed leather chair and glanced at the frameless sliding glass doors to his left, looking through to his private gym. Maybe he should work out. He'd have to leave the training in Roderick's hands for one more night, but it might be better to get this agitation out of his system. He had the tendency to unleash his temper on the recruits, and the last few days had taken a toll on him. His frustration was ready to erupt, but his office door opened and Keeley walked in before he could decide.

"Hey, welcome back." She smiled and then pointed to his desk. "What happened here?"

He grunted. "None of your fucking business."

Unfazed, she sat across from him. "So Mom tells me all hell broke loose in Arcipelago."

Leave it to his sister to go straight for the jugular. "Keeley, I'm in no mood."

"Why does the good stuff always happen when I'm not there?"

"There is nothing good about what happened to that girl," he roared as he stood and pushed the entire top of his desk to the floor.

She held up her hands. "Whoa, calm down. Sorry. I didn't mean it like that. I just—"

"I know what you meant."

His mother obviously told her about Ellie's eyes and her theory. Aden turned and looked out the window. He could see the training field and Roderick already working with the new trainees in the distance.

She regarded him cautiously. "Does she really have Aly's eyes?"

"Keeley," he bellowed, spinning and slamming his fists on the desk again, splitting it in half. The sound of her nickname, the one only he and Keeley used, plunged like a knife into his chest.

She jumped out of her chair and out of the way of the flying debris. "Jesus, Aden!"

Clenching his hands at his sides, he waited for the darkness to descend. But it didn't. He hissed out a sharp breath. "Don't fucking say her name!"

"I'm sorry. I'm sorry." She moved closer. "I just thought—"

Aden held up a hand and headed to the bar in the corner. "Don't fucking think then."

He filled a glass with whiskey and gulped it down, welcoming the burn in his throat. His words were harsh, but she knew better.

Unwilling to let the subject go, Keeley's voice lowered, but he expected nothing less from her. "Mom said her eyes are identical."

He poured another glass and guzzled it down. Then another. "They are."

"But?"

"But nothing." He downed a fourth glass, poured a fifth, and then took a seat in the chair beside the sofa. Keeley crossed her arms, giving him a pointed look that spoke volumes. "Keeley, let it go."

"It's kind of strange how similar their names are, though, huh?"

"Don't create significance where there is none. You're so much like Sophie sometimes, it makes me want to pull my hair out."

"I need to meet this girl."

"No! You fucking don't. Stay away from her, Keeley, I mean it."

"You can't stop me from meeting your new thrall."

He clenched his teeth at her words. "She's not a fucking thrall."

"What is she then?" She sat on the sofa, tucked her feet underneath her, regarding him with a curious gaze. "Aden, all humans are thralls. She'll always be one as long as she's human."

"Then I'll make her a half-breed or a vampire."

Wait! What?

Keeley leaned forward. "Okay, back the hell up a minute. First, creating a vampire is illegal. So is creating a half-breed, unless it's for breeding purposes. And both require dispensation from Matthais. And maybe she doesn't want either. What if she wants to stay human?"

"Don't be ridiculous," Aden scoffed. "Why would anyone want to remain human?"

"How would I know but she could?"

"She'll die one day."

"All humans do."

"That's not an option."

"Are you even listening to yourself? You went to Arcipelago relatively normal, well, for you anyway, and you come back acting like a crazy person."

He gulped the last of his drink before tossing his glass onto the table. "Keeley. I feel like I'm going out of my mind."

"I think you are." Keeley's eyes reflected the sympathy in her voice.

"Don't fucking pity me!"

"I don't," she snapped right back before her voice softened. "I can sympathize with what you're going through without pitying you. Hey—" Her voice grew fiercer. "I'm on your side. Always. Even when you're a dick."

"I know." Brushing off her snide remark, he released a deep sigh. "I'm in a foul mood and I need to be alone so I can think. Don't you have an empire to run?"

"Nope. But speaking of, the BloodStone Board of Directors meeting is on Friday. You should be there."

Glad of the change of subject, he asked, "Why? I never attend."

"Dad said to make sure you're there."

"Is this about that new drug you mentioned? Keeley, I have too much shit to deal with right now." He stood. "In fact, I have to go. I have training, then I need to go kick rogue vampire ass in Abya Yala in three days. My calendar is full. I'll see you later."

She rose and put her hand on his arm. "You know I'm just giving you a hard time."

He shrugged her off, flinching away from the discomfort her touch caused.

"I shouldn't have joked about the trip. I didn't mean it like that. Mom told me how badly she was whipped."

"You never need to apologize to me, Keel."

"Can I ask you something before you kick me out?"

"I thought I already did." He fixed her with an annoyed stare. "Clearly, my 'I'll see you later' didn't register in that big beautiful brain of yours."

"Oh, it did." She quirked her lips. "I just ignored you."

"As usual. Ask, but make it fast. I have to go."

"Why did you bite her? Really? This is me, so no bullshit."

Aden furrowed his brow, his eye twitching as he racked his brain for the answer. He'd thought that his lack of self-control had driven him to bite Ellie. He was no stranger to moments like that. But a nagging sensation in the pit of his stomach suggested otherwise. There was something unique about her. And that made him feel like an asshole because the perpetrator always blamed the victim.

"I couldn't stop myself," he said, settling on the truth. "She smelled so fucking good. It put me off-balance. It was like I was outside my body watching. But I needed to taste her."

"And?"

"It wasn't the same."

"Is that good or bad?"

"Both."

She wrapped her arms around him and Aden stiffened. Fucking hell! Why did she always have to hug him? He wrenched out of her grasp and she took a step back.

"Well, if it means anything, I like her already. Mom told me she's feisty, and once this girl gets over being afraid of you, there's no way she's going to take any of your bullshit."

"Get the fuck out of my office, Keeley."

"You have to let me meet her before you go, or I'll do it while you're gone, and you probably don't want that," she sang as she headed to the door. She was attempting to lighten his mood, and a rush of love for her filled him, though her words sent a surge of panic through him.

"Don't you fucking dare!"

"Glad you're back, baby brother! See you at the meeting on Friday!" Keeley chuckled as she turned and waved as the door closed.

She was absolutely going to seek Ellie out. And there was not a damn thing he could do about it. Aden glanced at his splintered desk. And his mother was definitely going to hear about that.

He was two for two.

He walked toward the door on his right. It slid open as he approached, revealing a room that was an exact replica of his office, only smaller. This was his private space, a place he could go when he didn't want to be disturbed. There was a sitting area with a sofa and a sleek fire-glass fireplace. Above it, a six-foot-by-eight-foot portrait of *her* took up almost the entire wall. She was reclining on the beach, smiling up at him from under the enormous hat she had loved to wear.

Aden reached out and ran his fingers over her face, just beneath her green eyes, feeling the texture of the watercolor canvas against his fingertips. He could almost feel the soft warmth of her skin against his.

She'd been eighteen years old then. It was one of the last times he'd been able to go into the sun without feeling its effects. His vampire physiology overtook his human physiology that year, forcing him to spend less and less time outside the city during daylight hours. And that was the last time they'd visited the beach together.

After she was gone, he'd taken his photos of her and painted for months, until there were thousands of canvases with her image. But he had them all put in storage, her image simply too painful to look at.

Except for this one.

It was his favorite and deserved a place of honor—a spot only he would see it, though it felt like his heart was being torn from his chest every time he did. It was a perfect likeness of her. She was happy and smiling, with her flowing auburn hair and brilliant green eyes shining.

The way he loved to remember her.

Now he saw those identical eyes on another woman's face. But it wasn't the same. And for a brief moment, it sent him into a downward spiral, transporting him back to that torturous time filled with haunting memories.

Aden never thought he'd see her image and not feel agony. But for the first time, as he gazed upon the woman he loved more than life, with the dark-haired girl in his room not far away, the pain it evoked in him had lessened a fraction.

Aden stood on the sidelines, watching as the newest half-breed cadets practiced their drills. Kane hovered a hundred feet from him, as always. The moonlight cast an eerie glow over the open field as Roderick ran the trainees through their paces before sparring practice. But Aden couldn't focus. His mind was not on the military exercises or the mission to Abya Yala. It was on the girl back in his room.

In the distance, the lights of the dome city flickered. The training ground was only five miles south, but it might as well have been on the opposite side of the world.

Aden glanced up at the sky. It looked like it might snow. Like every night, the retracted dome flooded the city with the frosty night air. Normally it was closed when it snowed or rained, but tonight, after their plane landed, Aurick instructed it to remain open. His father always felt trapped and on edge after a trip to the capital.

The lights from a line of military vehicles reflected off the snow-covered ground as they approached in the distance, and Aden recognized his father's truck. They hovered above the ground as they glided closer. He snapped his teeth in aggravation. Couldn't his family just fucking leave him alone for once? There was no reason for Aurick to come to training tonight. There was nothing he needed to see.

Everyone, and by everyone, he meant his parents, Keeley, and most likely Mina, and Kane too, that traitor, all thought he was on the verge of losing it. Not that he blamed them. But it still pissed him the fuck off.

The trucks stopped, and the wheels dropped to the ground several feet away. Horatio exited one and glided to stand next to Kane as Aurick exited the other and approached Aden.

"How are things going tonight?"

"Fine." Aden hoped he sounded as annoyed as he felt.

"They look good."

"Roderick and Drake have been running them all week. They won't be ready for combat for a while but they can provide city security, especially when I'm in Abya Yala. By the way, Andrei called and moved up the timeline."

"So, when do you leave?"

Aden motioned with his hands for Roderick to start the drills again. "Friday."

"We have the BloodStone board meeting Friday."

"Keeley told me. I never go. What's the big deal this time?"

"You're on the board of directors, Aden. You have a fiduciary responsibility to show up occasionally."

"What does it matter if it's this one? I have to go get this handled. I'm tired of cleaning up other people's shit."

"Now you know how I feel."

Aden narrowed his eyes and scowled at the obvious dig.

"You need to attend this one," his father said.

"What's with all the mystery around this new drug?"

"Be there, Aden."

"Fine," he said with an indignant fold of his arms. "I'll leave after the board meeting."

"Is Andrei planning to meet you down there?"

"No. I don't need him. But he's sending a thousand soldiers."

The sound of the trainees sparring filled the air as they watched the drills.

"Did Roderick get anything out of that rogue? Do we know where he's from?"

Aden's scowl deepened. "No. But Roderick's interrogation techniques require patience. They can't be rushed."

"Do I want to know?"

"Nope."

"So, your mom said Mina got Ellie all settled in." Aurick changed the subject. "That's her name, right?"

"Yes, and she's wreaking havoc as usual."

"Who? Mina?"

Aden clenched his teeth at his father's low chuckle.

"She told Ellie vampire blood would heal her."

Aurick's smile slipped away. "It's true. You should let Mina give it to her. You've seen what Matthais did to her. BloodStone and the pain meds can't be enough. She has to be in agony."

Aden frowned. Ellie had admitted she was still hurting, but she hadn't let on that it was that bad.

"Aden, vampires are only forbidden from giving blood to humans who aren't their mates."

"She's not my mate."

"Whatever you say. But having her underfoot is probably going to cramp your style, don't you think?"

"What do you mean?"

"I heard you're requiring her to use your entrance. What are your plans for feeding?"

"Fuck." Aden rubbed the back of his neck.

"Didn't think that one through, did you? You could always unseal the other entrance."

"No. I'll just have to lock her in her room when I'm feeding."

"That's cruel, Aden. You should send her to the thralls' quarters."

"I said no, Aurick!"

"What will you do then?" He pressed the issue and Aden's temper erupted.

"What would you have me fucking do? Let her walk in on that? She'll be fine locked inside. Once she's healed, she can move."

"Uh-huh."

"What the fuck was that 'uh-huh' for?"

"No reason. You'll figure it out I'm sure," Aurick said before turning his attention back to cadets.

Ellie

Ellie took the last bite of the best omelet she had ever had. Maybe it was because she was so hungry, but she couldn't remember anything tasting so good. She leaned back and a sharp gasp escaped as her damaged back met the sofa cushion. But after a few seconds, she sank into its comforting embrace.

Once she had selected what to eat from her choices, Master Aden stormed out without saying another word. She'd tried a little of everything on the cart, surprised that her stomach didn't protest, not only because of how empty and tender it was, but because she wasn't used to eating so much food in one sitting. Now, for the first time in days, she felt full and somewhat comfortable.

Ellie glanced around the room. There was no doubt this was a man's room—a vampire's room. The chunky wood furniture made it feel masculine, but the comfy materials and natural accents softened it. The colors were brown, beige, and a shade of green that matched the color of her eyes.

The room felt familiar as if she had stepped into a forgotten memory, even though everything looked completely different. But like the sensation when he bit her, that was impossible.

To the left of the sitting area was the biggest bed she'd ever seen, larger than the ones in Master Matthais' guest rooms. On the far wall were two open doors—one led to a bathroom and the other to a closet, where rows of black clothes hung neatly. On the opposite wall, behind the sofa, was a bar and a corner desk. Paintings of women, naked and in various states of undress, covered the walls. But they weren't indecent. They all had a sensuality to them that was captivating and beautiful.

Ellie's legs trembled as she stood up, and a rush of dizziness swept over her. The momentary wooziness passed, and she placed her dirty dishes back on the cart.

A book was sitting on the desk. Although she was alone, she glanced around before shuffling over, bracing herself on furniture as she made the trek across the spacious room. Ellie picked it up and flipped through a few of the pages. Several images matched the artwork on the walls, but she was still too uncomfortable to focus on anything, so she put it back.

To the left of the desk was an archway. Still knowing she shouldn't, but unable to tamp down her innate curiosity, she made her way over and peeked around the wall.

Her eyes widened at the sight of multiple paintings on easels and resting on the floor, propped against the wall. She stepped into the room to get a better look.

Master Aden was clearly obsessed with naked women, red-headed naked women since they were the only subject in this room. Ellie looked closer at one painting on a stand in the middle, but Mina's voice echoing down the hallway drew her attention away.

"Aden told me to bring her different meds."

Ellie turned, then stopped dead in her tracks as she took one last glance at the painting. All the air rushed out of her lungs as she stared at the women's eyes. She stepped closer to the canvas, her heart racing.

Her hand moved on its own, lifting towards the woman's face. The face and hair looked nothing like hers, but the eyes were a perfect match. It was like looking in a mirror.

Ellie's eyes darted across the other paintings, and she was stunned to see that they all had the same eyes.

Her eyes.

The sound of footsteps echoing down the hallway jolted Ellie back to reality. She hurried back to the sitting area as fast as her battered body would allow and settled on the sofa just as Mina came around the corner. Ellie focused on her breathing, the sound of each inhale and exhale helping to drown out the pounding of her heart, as she hoped to mask her shock and confusion from Mina.

"Oh, good, you're still awake."

Ellie's groan morphed into a whimper as her battered flesh came into contact with the mattress. She twisted back to her side, blinking away the tears stinging her eyes. After Mina had cleaned her stitches and changed her bandages, she'd given Ellie another shot of BloodStone and some additional pain medication. The new drugs didn't make her feel tired, but her body gave out on her anyway. She didn't recall falling asleep, but for the first time in a long time, her dreams hadn't plagued her. She sank into the mattress beneath her. The softness and comfort were unfamiliar. Until now, the beds she always slept in were saggy, with mattresses so thin that the metal springs poked through them.

Ellie closed her eyes and thought of her dad and Carrie again. She missed them so much that it left a desolate hole in her chest. She was completely alone in a strange place with people she hoped wouldn't hurt her. Mistress Sophie told her she was safe, and Mina said the Westcotts weren't like other vampires. And Master Aden said he had no intention of hurting her, but after a life of pain and misery, she didn't have an abundance of trust to give.

What was she supposed to do? Who could she turn to now that she'd been ripped away from her father and her only friend?

Out of nowhere, groans reverberated from beyond the door, mixed with soft crying. The sound of banging mingled with other noises.

Ellie listened closer, her brain grasping what she was hearing, and she covered her mouth with her hand. Master Aden was feeding.

The bloody sheets she changed in his room that day were proof, but the sounds of pain and pleasure she heard through the wall confirmed his reputation.

The thuds grew louder, the groaning intensified, and the cries sounded muffled. She tried to block it out, lifting the pillow over her head, but it didn't work. How long would she have to endure the wretched sounds? But they continued, stopping only briefly before starting over.

After what seemed like an eternity, the groans and growls stopped, and Ellie drifted off into a fitful sleep again.

Ellie was trapped in her pajamas.

Mina helped her into them the day before, but the pain meds had worn off and she couldn't lift her arms over her head.

She gave up after a few tries and nibbled her lower lip, debating what to do. Mina said she would take her to the infirmary, but she didn't say what time she'd come by. Since the room had no clock, Ellie had no way of knowing the time.

Ellie shuffled toward the door, intending to find the infirmary. Or at least someone to help her get changed, but the door remained closed when she reached it. She hesitated. What if Master Aden was in there? What would he be doing? Before her imagination could run wild, the door slid open, and she took a step back in surprise. Mina stood facing her, and beyond her, Ellie saw two nurses placing an unconscious girl on a stretcher into a medical pod.

"How did you sleep?" Mina entered the room.

"Fine," Ellie said as the door slid shut again, trying not to dwell on what she had seen.

"Are you still in pain?"

She loathed admitting it, but Ellie answered. "A little. I'm a little weak, too, and I need help changing. I can't lift my arms above my head."

"You still look very pale."

Mina tilted Ellie's head to the side. Ellie was glad she didn't grab the still-tender bruises on either side of her chin.

"That gash is probably going to leave a scar. Why didn't anyone stitch you up?" Before she could answer, Mina continued. "Zach will check it. Let's get you dressed."

Mina walked over to the dresser. "Which color should you wear?" she murmured, rummaging through the drawers.

"Shouldn't I wear teal? Pets are supposed to wear teal, aren't they?"

"No one has been told you're a pet."

Relief flooded Ellie's body at Mina's words. Private pets wore the distinct color to identify them in their dual role as both food and sex slaves. It was too bad because Ellie liked the color, but if it meant avoiding that fate, she would forgo wearing it forever.

"They've left both blue and green here. I think green. It will complement your eyes."

The uniform Mina gave her was a lovely jade green top over white pants. Ellie looked in the mirror. The uniform was cheerier than Master Matthais'. But Mina was right. Her skin looked washed out.

They entered Master Aden's living area. She glanced toward his bed. It was a mess of bloody sheets and a broken headboard. Yet one more confirmation of his reputation.

It was barely twenty-four hours since she left the capital, but so much had happened Ellie thought she might crumble under the weight of it.

Although as big and luxurious as Master Matthais', the Westcott's compound was warmer, both in temperature and atmosphere. One of Master Aden's other thralls was supposed to show her around after her visit with the doctor. Ellie was still unsure what would happen to her here, but she hoped it wouldn't be something bad.

Ellie let out a sigh, her eyes wandering around the stark, white room from where she sat on the examination table waiting for Mina and Dr. Zach, as he told her to call him. He spent over an hour examining her, running full body scans, blood tests, breathing tests, and eye tests. Their thralls' health was apparently very important to the Westcotts.

After determining that the cut on her forehead didn't need stitches, Dr. Zach examined her back and cleaned the wounds again. He was less gentle than Mina and it had been excruciating. Ellie thought, at one point, she might pass out from the pain until he gave her another shot of meds. He said her healing would take time. He then told her to wait while they went over her test results. Once again, the room had no clock, so Ellie was unsure how much time had passed.

What did this family have against clocks?

She was used to being busy, so having nothing to do was odd. But then the door opened and they walked in together. Mina carried two syringes and Dr. Zach held a tablet.

"We've reviewed your tests, Ellie," Dr. Zach said. "And we need to treat a few of your conditions."

"Roll up your sleeve," Mina said.

"What are those?"

"This one contains concentrated BloodStone."

"Are humans supposed to have so much BloodStone?" Ellie asked.

"Don't worry," Mina said. "You lost a lot of blood and your body needs help to replenish it."

She flinched as Mina slid the needle into her vein. "What's in the other one?"

"Nothing you need to know," Dr. Zach answered.

"It's vampire blood," Mina said at the same time. He glared but didn't contradict her. "You're bleeding internally and this is the most efficient and least invasive way to stop it."

Mina removed the first needle, and Ellie tried to pull her arm away. "But Master Aden doesn't want me to have it."

"He will when he knows your condition."

Ellie placed her hand on her arm as Mina tried to insert the second one. "He won't like you giving me blood from another vampire."

"Be careful," Mina said. "I can't give you blood that isn't his. It would taint you."

Wasn't she already tainted?

"I don't understand."

"When a vampire bites a human, the wound absorbs the vampire's venom and scent, which they carry forever in the scar."

Ellie knew this. It was why no one drank directly from the humans at Master Matthais' parties. So they can be used again and again.

"Human senses are too dull to smell it," Mina said. "But vampires do, leaving no doubt who marked them. The scent fades over time, but other vampires won't drink from them."

"Mina, enough."

"Zach, shut your ears if you don't want to hear. There's no reason she can't know this."

He scoffed his disapproval as he walked up behind Ellie and pressed his thumbs against the base of her skull. "Hold your hair up please."

"I can't lift my arms that high," Ellie said, keeping her hand over her arm so Mina couldn't stick her.

"Lift it as high as you can."

Knowing she couldn't refuse, she reached up and grasped her hair from him, holding it to the side as best she could with one hand.

"Are you still dizzy?"

"A little."

Ellie fixed a distrustful gaze on Mina, who continued talking instead of finding a vein for the needle in her hand.

"When a vampire feeds a human his blood, the blood and all the tissue in the body absorb the vampire's scent. It's permanent. It's how vampires claim a human in the most primitive way, confirming ownership."

Mina grasped Ellie's arm again.

"Wait a minute. Are you sure about this? He was pretty insistent about me not getting his blood."

"Trust me, he would want this."

Mina prepared to insert the other needle, but it wasn't right. Not without Master Aden's consent. Ellie dropped her hair and pushed Mina's hand away.

"I think he should know before you do this."

The door opened and the vampire in question entered the room, eyes blazing and lips curled in a vicious snarl.

"What the fuck is going on in here?"

Aden

Aden surveyed the room, his eyes blazing. They swept over Ellie where she sat on the examination table. Her heart galloped in her chest as she stared at him wide-eyed. His eyes snapped to Mina, and he leveled an accusing glare at her. "What the fuck are you giving her?"

"Master Aden," Zach said. "I haven't finished her examination, but I intended to contact you once we were done here."

Aden ignored him and addressed Mina. "Don't make me ask you again, woman?"

"Perhaps we should talk in my office." Zach tried again and Aden grabbed him by his neck. "Someone better answer my question or I'll rip your throat out."

"Aden, we're trying to help her," Mina said with an exasperated sigh.

He felt Ellie's eyes on him, watching him. Her scent changed, but it wasn't fear he detected. He caught her gaze and saw a flicker of curiosity mixed with hesitation in her eyes.

"Kylie." One of his mother's thralls hurried into the room when he barked her name.

"Yes, Sir?" she squeaked.

"Take Ellie back to my room."

"She needs treatment," Mina said.

"From now on, all her treatment will take place in my room, with me present. You will accompany me there after we're done speaking."

Ellie stepped down from the table and rolled her sleeve down her arm before making her way toward the door without a word, using the wall for support.

"Kylie, help her," Aden snarled, and the girl scurried over. Her hand gripped Ellie's elbow as she ushered her out of the room. Aden's eyes followed them until the outside office door closed. He tossed Zach to the floor and his fierce gaze found Mina.

"If you were about to give her vampire blood—"

"Aden, she needs it."

"You told me her back should heal on its own."

Mina set the needle down on the table and turned to him. "She still needed a thorough exam, and we've uncovered a multitude of underlying issues."

"What else is wrong with her?" The hiss that escaped his lips would have frightened almost anyone else. But not Mina.

Zach stood, clearing his throat. "Her back sustained extensive damage," he said. "It goes beyond her external wounds, Master Aden. Someone should have brought her to me as soon as she arrived. Apart from stitching her up, the doctor in the capital provided no internal treatment. Her tendons, muscles, and nerves are mutilated."

Aden's face twisted into a sneer as he bared his teeth. "So why does she need vampire blood? BloodStone should be sufficient."

"In the absence of vampire blood, she needs surgery to repair her injuries. Without intervention, she'll have permanent damage."

"What kind of damage?" His patience was wearing thin, and Zach's neck looked ripe for snapping.

"Permanent paralysis of many of her back muscles is possible. Given her current condition, it's astonishing she's able to remain upright and walk."

"Aden," Mina said. "She will be horribly disfigured. But even more importantly, she has internal bleeding that requires urgent attention."

Mina's words slithered like a snake through his belly.

"Is it life-threatening? I didn't hear any hemorrhaging."

"It's so slight we almost didn't see it on the scans. But it will worsen if we don't act."

"So you were just going to give her blood without my permission?"

"Mina and I decided it would be best to treat her first since you were not in the compound," Zach said.

"I decide how she's treated! And have you heard of a fucking hologram, Zach? Whose blood is it?"

Mina's eyes flashed with annoyance and resentment. "I'd never give her blood that wasn't yours."

"I still should have been told before you gave her anything. I will be informed before she receives any treatment in the future. Is that understood?"

"Fine. Let's go to your room."

Mina started for the door but Aden blocked her path, his arms crossed across his chest. "You won't be giving her that shot."

"Aden, be reasonable."

"I'll give her my blood as soon as we're done here. Now, how is she other than that?"

Mina's face betrayed her shock as Zach listed off all of their findings. "She's anemic and a little underweight but other than what we discussed she is healthy overall. The cut under her left eye and the scratches down her cheek shouldn't scar. The gash on her forehead doesn't need stitches. Of course, your blood will lessen any scar she may have from it. And the bruises will fade. There is, however, one other issue."

"What?" Aden was losing what little patience he still possessed.

"Her microchip is implanted at the base of her brain stem."

"Okay. So what's the problem?"

Zach swiped his finger over the screen of his tablet, searching for something.

"Do you know if she belonged to another vampire before Master Matthais?"

"No, why?"

"She has a scar on the back of her neck. It's clear she had a previous tracking chip, but it was removed and replaced with the one in her head."

Aden leaned against the examination table and buried his hands in his pockets, to keep from grabbing Zach by the throat again.

"Is it still activated?"

"Yes."

"Well remove it."

Zach and Mina exchanged an uneasy glance.

"Normally we would replace it with one of our own, but it's not that simple."

"Why not? Are you telling me with all the technology we have, you're unable to remove a quarter-inch microchip from her head?"

Zach turned the tablet to show Aden an X-ray. "Its location makes it extremely challenging to extract."

"Find someone capable of doing it."

"The person who put it there positioned it near her brain stem to prevent its removal."

Aden pushed away from the table, propelling it across the floor, and the sound of it colliding with the wall echoed through the room. "Mother fucker! What can be done? Can you deactivate it?"

"We can probably reprogram it, but—"

"I don't want it reprogrammed. I want it fried."

"There are risks."

"I want to be clear here, Zach." Aden clenched his teeth so hard he was surprised they didn't crack. "I want it fried, and I don't want one hair on her head damaged."

"We can use an electromagnetic pulse, but she may experience some physical effects for a few days."

"EMPs don't affect the brain."

"It's not the EMP. Short-circuiting the chip next to her brain stem could cause her to have a seizure and—" Zach paused. "Certain other after-effects."

Aden felt Mina's eyes on him. It was unusual for her to be so quiet. "What after-effects?"

"Her speech and her equilibrium could be affected," Zach said. "Perhaps sight and hearing, too. But it should only be temporary."

"Should only be temporary?" Aden's growl was a warning and Zach retreated a step. "Do I need to find a more capable doctor?"

"No, Sir. I am a trained neurosurgeon and I will handle it."

Aden stepped forward, his voice low and measured with restrained fury. "I don't care what you have to do, but if she is injured in any way, there will be no escape, no matter how far you run."

"Yes, Sir." Zach swallowed.

"I want it done by the time I return from Abya Yala."

Zach nodded and left the room. Aden turned his hard gaze to Mina. She jerked her chin in defiance.

"Just say what you want to say."

The weight of his disappointment in her settled in his bones, making him feel heavy and drained. "Why would you do something like this? You are one of the five people I trust, and you were going to betray me."

Mina's stance softened. "I wasn't betraying you, Aden. I was trying to protect her for you." She laid her hand on his arm. He shook her off. "We're fortunate we found this now. But she'll be fine once she gets your blood."

Ellie's scent hung in the air and his need for answers compelled him to stay, rather than storm off like he wanted to. Instead, he paced.

"How bad will her scars be?"

"Although we can't see them, the scars from her previous whipping are still there. But any new ones should be minimal after your blood heals her."

"What about the chip? What are the risks of deactivating it?"

"It's more dangerous to keep it active. We can reprogram it, but it has an internal override, so he can always find her. Now, come on. Let's go to your room so I can give her this shot."

Aden stopped pacing. "I said no! She will take my blood only from me."

Mina eyed him warily. "Are you sure about that? You've never shared your blood with anyone before."

"So?"

"It's an incredibly intimate act."

"There will be nothing intimate about it. She's not in any condition for—"

"That's not what I meant. This isn't about sex. Blood sharing creates a bond. You know this."

"I don't form bonds with my thralls, Mina, so you don't need to worry about her."

"She's not the only one I'm worried about, Aden."

He walked to the door, uncomfortable with the direction of the conversation. "We're done talking about this. I'm giving her my blood, and you can check on her in a few hours."

Ellie startled in her chair as her door slid open, and Aden walked into her room. She sat at the table in the corner finishing a salad.

"Good, you're eating again," he said when she met his gaze. "The doctor says you're underweight. You will eat more often and I'll have a nutritionist assigned to you."

"I don't need a nutritionist. I know how to eat properly. My appetite is just coming back."

A half-smile curved his lips as she gazed at him with defiance.

"If you haven't put on weight by the time I return, you'll have one."

"You're going away?"

"Yes. I leave tomorrow after sunset. You'll be well taken care of in my absence."

Ellie looked unsure, biting her lip. "Oh."

"What? You look like you want to ask me something again."

It was incredibly easy to read her face.

She hesitated only for a moment. "Why was Mina going to give me your blood? I thought you said no."

"I did." His reply was curt as he shoved his hands into his pockets. "But they discovered internal bleeding during your exam, and Zach believes that you'll have permanent damage to your back without it."

"Is that why I keep getting dizzy?"

"Yes. You're also anemic but that's likely a direct result of the blood loss and your malnutrition. My blood will heal you. In a couple of hours, all your injuries will be healed."

Ellie looked down, her fingers playing with the fabric at the bottom of her sleeve. "But why were they giving it to me without your permission?"

"I told Mina your health is the top priority. She believed she was following my instructions."

"Is she going to bring it here or do I have to go back to the infirmary?"

She shifted in the chair as if she was going to stand.

"I'm going to give it to you."

She looked at him warily. "You're going to give me the shot?"

"No, you're going to drink from my vein."

"Oh." Ellie couldn't hide the shock on her face. "But you said I was never to touch you."

"I said you were never to touch me without permission. I'm giving you permission." He eyed her with a curious dip of his head. "Does drinking my blood scare you?"

"No." Her hesitation was momentary.

"Then what's that look on your face? Most thralls would be excited to have a vampire feed them."

"I'm not like most thralls."

"Clearly," he muttered.

"Why doesn't Mina just give me a shot?"

"Because if you're to have my blood, you will take it from my vein," he snapped, then softened his tone. "It's most effective that way. I have things to do, so let's get this done. Come over here and sit on the edge of your bed."

Ellie stood and moved closer. Her discomfort was obvious. An unexpected and unfamiliar pang of emotion tightened his gut, a strange mix of sympathy and regret for not realizing the extent of her suffering.

"All your pain will be gone soon. You'll be glad I did this." Aden rolled up his sleeve. "You will tell no one about this. Do you understand?"

"Yes, Sir." She sat, trying and failing to hide her wince.

He stepped closer. "I'm going to bite my wrist and then you need to latch your mouth onto it. You need to do it quickly because it will start to close immediately. Your saliva will keep the bite open. Close your lips around it and suck. My blood will flow freely, so drink slowly."

She looked nervous.

"It won't take much, and I'll tell you when to stop. You're only to touch my wrist. Is that clear?"

She swallowed. "Yes." Her eyes drifted closed, and she took a slow breath before opening them again.

Aden looked at her. His palms were sweating. He'd never shared his blood before. Although pure vampire blood could be used to heal a half-breed or human in emergencies, it was treason for vampires to share blood from their veins with anyone but their mates. It should have been given as a shot, as Mina had been about to do. Aden would ponder his willingness to commit treason for Ellie later.

"Are you ready?"

Ellie nodded again and he bit his wrist. Blood bubbled on his skin and he moved his hand closer to her.

"Take my wrist now."

She grasped it with shaking hands, pulling it to her mouth, closing her lips around the wound, and her eyes as she drank.

A shudder ran through Aden's body, and, despite his best intentions, a muffled groan escaped his lips. He couldn't tear his eyes away from her. Was that a tremble from her, too?

Ellie opened her eyes and her eyelashes swept upward. Their eyes locked. Her gaze was dark and intense. She gripped his wrist tighter, pressing her mouth firmer against his flesh as her tongue flicked against his skin.

A low growl erupted in his chest. Her eyes fluttered closed and her soft moan vibrated up his arm and lodged under his ribs.

"That's enough." Aden could barely form the words. She didn't stop.

"Ellie, you've had enough."

He jerked his arm out of her grasp. She dropped her hands to her lap, her breaths coming in shallow pants as she licked her lips. Her heart hammered in her chest, and he heard the blood rushing through her veins. His blood.

Aden took a step back, rolling his shirt down his arm. The bite sealed before his cuff reached his wrist. Ellie opened her eyes, and he was stunned to see the swirling intensity in them.

"I likely won't see you again. I leave tomorrow night."

Was that a tremor in his voice?

She nodded, the disappointment in her eyes unmistakable.

"Mina will look after you."

"What should I do while you're gone?" Her voice was hoarse.

"Nothing. Rest until you are told otherwise. Iris will come show you around soon."

He had to leave before he did something he would regret, so he turned without another word.

"Thank you, Sir."

Her soft whisper followed him through the door as it closed behind him.

Ellie

Ellie sat there in a daze, unable to move as she relived the last several minutes. It was done.

She was his now.

Although she'd been hesitant, drinking his blood was like nothing she had ever experienced. It had a tangy metallic taste, similar to her own, but there was a sweetness and a sharpness to it that was contradictory and hard to define. The flavors exploded on her tongue, making her whole body come alive, and a rush of energy flowed through her muscles and brought her senses to life.

A staggering, tingling sensation rushed through her, from the top of her head to the tips of her toes, before her veins felt like they caught fire. Ellie had savored the warm liquid as it slid down her throat, her body absorbing it and the relief it brought to her aching body.

A flurry of images flickered in rapid succession behind her closed eyelids. Images of his face—smiling, happy, laughing. More images of unknown places and people flickered through her mind. Then his face appeared again. His eyes. The allure of the eyes she saw in her dreams was captivating. But this time, there was a depth of emotion in them she hadn't seen before.

His gruff voice had barely registered when he told her to stop, but then he yanked his wrist away, and she released him. She took a moment to steady herself, blinked, opened her eyes, and met his gaze. He'd looked as shaken as she'd felt. Could he have experienced the same intense sensations she did?

Now that he was gone, Ellie was unsure and confused. How could she feel like this? How could a vampire make her feel like this?

She pressed her fingers to her still-tingling lips, and all she could do was stare at the door he'd exited and wait for her heart to slow.

The female thralls' living space differed from Master Matthais' quarters. Although it was still one large room filled with rows of bunk beds, partitions separated each one. The partitions didn't provide total privacy, but it was better than nothing. The walls were painted a subtle peach, and the floors were covered with a plush, cream-colored carpet. Like the rest of the compound, the temperature was warmer and the beds looked more comfortable. The mattresses were thick, and the linens looked soft. Not as comfortable and thick as the bed Ellie woke in this evening, but definitely nicer than she was used to.

"The female thralls sleep here, and the males are on the floor below," Iris said.

She was a tall girl with ginger hair and bright blue eyes. She was nice enough but seemed almost as lost for words as Ellie felt.

"Most of Master Aden's thralls sleep in that room." Iris gestured to a door beside them as it opened. The room was twice as large, with three times as many beds. "His cleaning thralls, the ones he doesn't drink from, are on this side. His feeders sleep over here." She waved her hand to the right. "He also has others on several of the lower levels."

How many thralls did he have?

A curtain hung at the end of every bed. "Why are they closed up like that?" Ellie asked.

"It takes a while to recover from one of his feedings, so it gives them more privacy."

"What does that mean?"

Iris looked at her with a puzzled expression. "You should know. He drank from you."

Ellie's hand touched the puncture marks on the side of her neck. They healed after she'd had Master Aden's blood but she could feel the bumps, a lingering reminder of what he had done.

"Are you one of his feeders?" Ellie asked.

"No, I'm a cleaner. Me and six other thralls clean his rooms and offices. I've never heard of him thrashing a pet as much. The thralls on the plane said you were in terrible shape."

Ellie gasped. "He didn't do that to me."

"But you have a bite mark on your neck and you can barely walk?"

"He bit me, but my former master whipped me."

"Oh, I just thought—" Iris shook her head. "Never mind."

"No. What? What did you think? Is he always that violent?"

Iris shrugged. "The way Chelsea came back I figured he'd lost it again."

"What did he do to Chelsea? Which one is she?"

Iris pointed to one bed halfway down the room. The curtains were closed around the bed, so Ellie didn't see anyone. "She's his favorite. He uses her a lot and she comes back weak most of the time. But something happened over there. She was pretty beat up and then he tore her neck apart again on the plane home. Didn't you see it? All the thralls did."

"They put me to sleep." Ellie's brows furrowed. "Why would he do that to her?"

"He loses control sometimes." Iris gave her a bland smile like it wasn't a big deal. "So he's keeping you in his pet room, huh? I've never seen him do that with anyone."

"He said it's just until I'm healed."

"So what makes you so special? Chelsea is probably hurt more than you."

Ellie shook her head. "I don't know."

Ellie approached the door to Master Aden's room after her tour with Iris. Her body felt stronger and more energized with each step she took. He was being honest when he'd said she would be healed in a couple of hours. For the second time in less than a day, a vampire had told her the truth. She wasn't used to that.

Kane's dark eyes met hers. "You can't go in there."

"I thought the door was programmed for me."

"It is, unless he overrides it. You're going to need to—"

Before he could finish, two nurses rushed up with a medical pod. A buzzing sound came from the panel beside the door and it slid open.

Ellie's stomach plummeted when she realized why they were there. The urge to run was almost overwhelming, but her innate curiosity compelled her to follow the nurses into the room.

"Don't go in there."

She ignored Kane's warning, walked down the hallway, and stopped, gaping at the sight in front of her. Aden was standing in a loose-fitting pair of jeans, his chest bare, and under any other circumstances, Ellie might have spent more than a second admiring him. His body was chiseled and hard, like a work of art brought to life, but the sight of the two nurses removing another unconscious, naked girl from his bed pushed aside the stray thoughts about his unnerving attractiveness.

And her stomach sank like a stone, leaving her feeling nauseous.

"What are you doing here?" Aden snarled and Ellie's eyes snapped to his face. His fierce red eyes locked onto hers, and she took a small step backward, her chest tightening with fear.

All the air in her lungs evaporated, but she stammered out, "Um—I'm, uh—sorry, Sir. I—I was, uh, going to my room."

But her feet remained stuck to the floor, pinned in place as her eyes whipped back to the gruesome sight on his bed.

Ellie stumbled as four thralls hurried past her. They replaced the stained sheets with crisp, clean ones as if they had done it a hundred times before.

They rushed back past her with the soiled sheets as a red-headed woman wrapped in a short robe came around the corner.

"You need to go into your room now." Aden's harsh voice startled Ellie out of her trance and her eyes whipped back to his face. Though the fire in his eyes had faded and they no longer burned with anger, the white-knuckled tension in his clenched fists and the stiff line of his jaw hinted at the storm that still raged within him.

"Yes, Sir."

She darted across the room, moving faster than she had in days, and threw herself through the door, seeking solace from the horrifying scene she'd witnessed. Ellie wrapped her arms around her heaving stomach when she heard Aden tell the girl to strip and get on the bed as the door closed behind her.

Aden

Aden arrived on the top floor of BloodStone's worldwide headquarters via warp port. The modern steel and glass building dominated the center of the dome city. A military helicopter waited on the roof, ready to take him to his jet, which would then fly him to Abya Yala. A fleet of ten transport planes carrying his troops would follow, accompanied by five cargo planes carrying equipment.

He couldn't shake off the way his body had reacted when Ellie drank his blood. Even fucking and feeding from a dozen of his thralls couldn't drive the memory from him. It was the most arousing thing he ever experienced. Mina had been right. There was a profound intimacy to it that had nothing to do with sex. He witnessed his parents sharing blood over the years, and although part of him yearned for it, the intimacy unsettled him. He never gave Aly his blood before she died, so he never realized how personal and pleasurable it could be.

Aden froze and waited for the familiar agony that always accompanied the thought or sound of her name. There was a sharp ache in his chest, but he didn't feel like he might black out. That was a first.

Technically, what he'd done was illegal. Vampires could only feed their mates from the vein. No one but him, Ellie, and Mina knew. But somehow he suspected his mother would know sooner than later. Mina would cave and blurt it out long before he told either of his parents.

Sophie would argue he hadn't broken the law, and Aurick would support her as he always did. Aden was finding it difficult to deny that there was something different about Ellie. He still didn't believe his mother's insanity, but he also couldn't explain the pull Ellie had on him. It was getting exhausting. But he needed time to think through the consequences of what he'd done. Yes, her internal bleeding had been serious but was not life-threatening. And now, their connection was irrevocable. They drank each other's blood. Anyone who was near her would smell his blood flowing through her veins, just as everyone could smell her scent on him.

It's not like he had a choice. She needed his blood, but he didn't have to let her feed from him. He could've had Mina give her a vial. But he wanted her to drink from his vein. When she'd latched onto his wrist, he'd sworn his knees would buckle. Her touch made him tremble, and only one other person had ever elicited the same reaction.

Aden had to fucking shake this off. He had to sit through this meeting, then head to Abya Yala to help Paolo deal with his rogues. Then he could come back and figure out what to do about the young woman who turned his world on its head.

He entered the boardroom and saw Keeley and his parents standing off to the side, talking. A long rectangular table, made from a single, seamless sheet of tempered glass, dominated the space, with oversized executive chairs surrounding it. Holograms of the other Gerents, who were all board members attending remotely, hovered above several of the seats.

Three sets of eyes met Aden's as he approached. "So, can we get this meeting going? I have shit to do."

"It will start when I'm damn well ready." Keeley shot back before walking away.

"What's got her panties in a twist?"

"Last-minute preparations. You know she gets tense before speaking to the board," Sophie said. "Are you leaving straight from here?"

"Yes."

"How long do you think you'll be gone?"

"Only a couple of days if all goes as planned."

"Mina tells me there's an issue with Ellie's tracking chip?"

"Yes." He started but Keeley called the meeting to order before he could say anything else.

Aden took his seat. Hannah, BloodStone's chief scientist and his mother's best friend, was already in her chair.

Aden gave her his most charming smile as he greeted her

She grinned, leaning closer. "I hear you've been wreaking all sorts of havoc lately."

His smile disappeared, replaced by an intense glare. Clearly, he would need to have a conversation with his mother about keeping her mouth shut.

Hannah laughed. "Aww, come on, your face is too pretty to scowl."

"I despise you."

Hannah's grin widened, and she turned her chair toward Keeley.

"Thank you for coming tonight," Keeley began. "Although our quarterly board meeting is still two months away, we wanted to provide you with this update in advance because we will make this announcement public in two weeks."

Aden tried to pay attention. He really did. But his mind was consumed by the memory of Ellie's tongue swirling against his wrist as she finished drinking from him.

Aurick kicked him under the table.

"As you all know, we have been working for centuries to synthesize an individual vampire's blood into a viable independent form for sired half-breed maintenance. Currently, half-breeds require a daily dose of blood from their sires to suspend the aging process. Even if it's administered by injection, it still must be pure blood."

She swiped her finger across a tablet in her hand, and a hologram appeared above the table.

"I am thrilled to tell you all that we've finally developed a drug that replaces this. Through the use of a sire's blood as the primary component, we have successfully developed AEON. This drug, in injectable form, will give the vampire relief from having to provide a constant supply of blood to a half-breed. With only a single pint of the vampire's blood, we can synthesize enough of the drug to sustain a half-breed for five hundred years. It will have the same effect as drinking their sire's blood directly."

At first, Aden was only half listening to Keeley's speech, but his interest grew from indifference at the beginning to genuine fascination. His father had long desired to create something like this. He wanted Sophie to have the choice of whether or not to drink from him. But the last Aden had heard, the trials they'd been conducting were still unsuccessful.

He leaned toward Hannah, whispering, "Why didn't I know this?"

She glanced at him over her shoulder. "You're too wrapped up in yourself most of the time."

"Have I mentioned I despise you?" He scowled at the sound of her quiet chuckling and sat back.

Aden remained behind after the meeting. Once the last board member left, he turned to Keeley.

"Fuck, Keel. This is going to be huge."

"That was a great presentation, hun." Aurick's pride was clear as he put his arm around Keeley.

"I think everyone walked away with a good impression," Keeley said with a smile.

"Why didn't you tell me you solved the dissolution issue?" Aden asked.

"I've tried multiple times, but you never want to hear what's going on here."

She was right. He nudged her with his elbow. It was the most contact he could initiate on his own unless they were alone. "You're going to make us so freaking rich. Well, richer than we already are."

"Aden, this isn't about money." Aurick shot him a disapproving look.

"Everything is about money."

"This is about half-breeds no longer needing to depend on their sires for long-term survival," Sophie said as she smiled.

"This is the first step to full blood independence, Aden," Keeley said. "We're so close to—"

"Hun." Aurick tugged Keeley to his side. "Let's not get ahead of ourselves."

"Full-blood independence is a fantasy, Keel." Aden scoffed. "It'll never happen."

"People said AEON would never happen," Keeley fired back.

Aurick released Keeley, but he was still beaming with pride. "AEON is a success. Let's focus on that."

"On that note, I'll be on my way to make the world a safer place. You did great, sis. I'm proud of you." He started to walk away but stopped and turned back. "Damn, you know what this means, right? I won't have to give Kane blood every fucking month anymore. That alone makes it priceless."

"I heard that," Kane said from the doorway.

"Good. Tell the pilot to start the chopper. I'll be right there."

"Why are you so mean to everyone?" Keeley asked, hitting him.

"Because I can. I'll be back in a few days."

Sophie reached out and wrapped her arms around Aden's torso. He stiffened before awkwardly reaching up and patting her back. "Be careful," she whispered before adding. "I'll watch over her."

He pulled away from her with a scowl to see her eyes crinkling with her smile as his father and sister exchanged amused looks.

"Stop fucking smiling. You look like fools—all of you," he snarled, stomping away.

Acanas was twenty-nine hundred miles north of San Allena, the capital of Abya Yala, Cecilia's region south of the Westcott's. As the most northern of only four dome cities on the continent, it served as the military hub for the north. Although a much smaller city than San Allena, Acanas provided state-of-the-art military facilities and was only fifty miles west of the coastal mountains, where the rogue problem was concentrated. Before he left, Aden had instructed Paolo to meet him with two thousand of his soldiers. Andrei's contingent of a thousand had arrived and were standing by along with Aden's fifteen hundred men. But he'd been here for over twelve hours, already, and Paolo and the troops had yet to arrive.

He was such a fucking hack.

Drake, Roderick's Major General, and three hundred of the soldiers had scouted the area, both on foot and with thirty drones. And they believed they'd found the rogues' den.

"They've concentrated in this series of caverns." Roderick pointed to a mountain range as he and Aden stood next to an electronic table in the command center, maps of the mountains displayed on several holograms above it.

"How far up and how many caves are we talking about?"

"Three to five clicks and at least fifty, but there could be more."

"And the number of vampires in each cave?"

"Based on the drone pictures, we're thinking maybe sixty to seventy." Roderick swiped his finger over the screen and a hologram of the inside of the mountain caves appeared.

"If you're right, we're talking about three thousand rogues?" That was more than Aden had expected. He should have brought more half-breeds. "You're sure about this?"

"Yes."

"Fuck! No wonder they've decimated six hundred square miles. How the hell did this coven get so big?"

Drake entered the room. "The men are standing by and ready when you are, Sir. Still no sign of Paolo's troops."

"Get me Paolo," Aden barked at the soldier seated at the table controlling the holograms.

"Yes, Sir."

Roderick and Drake huddled together, their voices barely audible as Aden's thoughts wandered for what seemed like the tenth time in the last two hours.

Ellie had been constantly on his mind. He spoke to his mother, who said that Zach planned to deactivate her chip this evening. He was confident in Zach's medical ability, but he still worried. It had been centuries since he worried about a human, and it was unnerving.

"I'm not getting any answer on the hologram, Sir."

"What exactly is he pulling?" Roderick asked with an irritated growl.

"He and Cecilia are pissed I'm down here. Get me Cecilia," Aden said to the soldier. "Drake, get five thousand more men on a plane. I want them airborne within the hour."

Drake nodded and exited the room.

"Our troops should be able to take them. They're likely weak," Roderick said. "We'll move into position at first light, wait until mid-day, and lure them out, cave by cave. As they scramble out, we can pick them off one by one."

"How do you suggest we do that? Even starving rogues won't come out during the day. They'll wait until after sunset," Aden said.

"Not if they scent humans nearby. If they're hungry enough and humans are close by, they'll risk it."

Roderick's suggestion intrigued Aden. "You want to use humans as bait?"

"I don't think we have a choice. They'll be fixated on their prey and the sun will weaken them enough for us to exterminate them easily."

Drake re-entered the room. "They'll be wheels up in sixty."

"Have you reached Cecilia yet?" Aden asked as he swiped his fingers over the hologram to see the inside of the caves again.

"No, Sir. No answer on any of her numbers."

Now Aden was livid. "Pull up the GPS on their phones. He turned to Drake. "Roderick suggested we use humans to lure the rogues out."

"It would work," Drake said. "But with the additional five thousand men I don't think it will be necessary."

The soldier swiped his finger over his table and two red dots appeared on the hologram. Both were in the same location in San Allena.

"Fucking hell! Call Cecilia!" Aden commanded and his personal com appeared beside him. Cecilia's image materialized in the hologram above. When the voice-mail connected, her smiling face told him to leave a message.

"Cecilia." He hissed her name through clenched teeth. "What kind of fucking game are you and Paolo playing? The only reason I'm here is because the council doesn't trust either of you to deal with your rogue problem. And you're proving them right. You refused to take responsibility and threw a tantrum when you were called on it. Grow the fuck up."

Roderick and Drake looked at him with shocked expressions. Cecilia was an Ancient One and the Gerent of Abya Yala. No one but an Ancient One spoke to another Ancient One that way, but at that moment, Aden didn't give a fuck.

"I made it perfectly clear I needed Paolo and two thousand of your soldiers to accomplish this mission. I will now handle this on my own and you can deal with the Council when I tell them of the lack of cooperation I received trying to solve your problem. Get the fuck off Paolo's cock and act like the fucking leader of a major world region for once!"

Aden grabbed his com from midair and threw it across the room. All these delays kept him from getting back home. He spun around to face Drake.

"I want ten humans outside each cave and ninety of your men in formation behind them."

"That's five hundred humans. We only need one or two for the rogues to get a scent."

"That's not enough. I want this finished."

Aden sensed Kane's eyes on him from where he stood at the door.

"That's a lot of humans to sacrifice," Roderick said.

"We'll likely lose half of them," Aden admitted. "But more will die if we don't destroy this coven. And don't fucking look at me like that, Kane!"

"Where are we supposed to get them?" Roderick asked. "Without Cecilia or Paolo here, we can't just take them."

"I'll deal with Cecilia. Drake, pull them from the villages outside the city. Roderick, have the men parachute in tandem with the humans above the caves. I want everything ready to go by noon. I'll meet you both there."

Drake nodded and walked out, exchanging a look with Roderick and Kane that didn't go unnoticed. Roderick remained behind.

"Are you sure you want to do this? You know Aurick's thoughts about—"

"I command this military," Aden roared, his eyes blazing. "It's up to me to decide how we'll accomplish this mission."

"Yes, Sir." He turned to go, but Aden's voice stopped him.

"Don't underestimate the rogues. Even with the number of villages they've decimated, they're likely still starving, but they'll be stronger than you think."

Aden walked into his private room in the military quarters, needing to feed before he went into battle. This would not be the quick and simple cleanup he expected. He should call Andrei for reinforcements. He loathed to do it, but he couldn't rely on Cecilia and Paolo to provide help.

Agitated and hungry, he realized that the one person he wanted to see was thousands of miles away.

"Kane!" His guard's face appeared in a hologram. "Send me Kristina."

Kane nodded and his face vanished. Less than two minutes later, a red-headed girl entered wearing nothing but a robe. Kristina was one of his preferred feeders, second only to Chelsea.

He commanded her to approach in a gruff tone, and she obeyed without hesitation.

"Get on the bed."

She dropped her robe and climbed onto the bed, settling on her back in the center. Aden fed from her and fucked her quickly. A nurse took Kristina away, and a new thrall replaced her. Then another. Then another. But nothing satisfied him.

Centuries of fucking and drinking from thousands of girls was getting old. He was tired of the effort it took to keep them from touching him. They were all taught what to do and how not to move before being brought to him. The ones who failed to follow instructions never made it out of his bed alive. But the ones who adhered to the rules suffered a worse fate.

The fourth girl entered his chamber and took her place beneath him, and Aden braced his body over her. Like the others, she closed her eyes and turned her face to give him access to her neck. He was about to sink into her when he suddenly lost his appetite.

He could still fuck her, but what was the point? He only fucked them to make feeding more pleasurable. And tonight he hadn't found pleasure in any of them.

"Get out!" He pushed up and off the bed, heading into the bathroom.

He showered quickly. Despite not really enjoying his meals, the blood his body absorbed energized and strengthened him, making him feel like he could tackle the rogues single-handedly.

Kane met him outside his door and fell into step with him.

"Are the humans in place?"

Kane nodded. "The additional troops arrived. They're just waiting for you."

He walked down the hall toward the hangar. "Good. Any word from Cecilia?"

"No. But after that message you left, we'll hear something from someone soon."

"Fucking hell. This is deliberate."

"Are you sure about this?"

Kane's voice held no judgment but it was solemn.

"Sometimes hard sacrifices have to be made."

Kane nodded as they reached the transport vehicle. He settled into the backseat as Kane guided it out of the hangar and into the daylight. The sun was strongest in the middle of the day, and even inside the vehicle, Aden could feel the heat. Roderick had a temporary structure erected at the base of the mountain so Aden could be close by, but he hated being out during the day. Yet another fucking reason to be pissed at Cecilia.

"Find Ellie," he said and a hologram opened to show Ellie sleeping in her bed. She thrashed around in the throes of a nightmare before she jolted upright, screaming. Her eyes flew open, wide with terror, and she clamped her hands over her mouth. She rocked back and forth, her breaths coming in ragged gasps as she fought to regain control.

Aden held his breath, waiting for her to burst into tears, but she only collapsed onto the mattress and flung her arm over her eyes.

He swiped the hologram closed, unable to stand the sight.

Ellie

Ellie's body hummed with annoyance as if there were bees buzzing around inside her.

She was better, no longer dizzy or in pain. So why was she in Dr. Zach's exam room? In the time she lived in Master Matthais' house, she'd only seen a doctor once, when she'd first arrived.

Aden left the previous night and she tried to ignore the slight pang of loss that echoed inside her chest. Physically, she never felt better. His blood erased any trace of her brutal whipping. Yet, she was back in the infirmary, instead of out exploring her new world.

The door opened and Dr. Zach entered. "How are you feeling, Ellie?"

"Great. All of my pain is gone."

"Good."

"So why am I back here? Making sure I'm okay to work?"

"Something like that. Put your hands on the arms of the chair."

Ellie obeyed, and he secured straps around her wrists. "Uh, Dr. Zach, what are you doing?"

"I'm securing you for your own safety."

She pulled against the restraints as fear slithered up her spine. "What are you going to do?"

He fastened straps around her ankles, pulling them tight.

"You don't have any reason to worry. I'm taking extra precautions because Master Aden insisted your well-being was paramount."

Ellie's heart pounded in her chest. "I don't feel safe right now."

"This will only take a few minutes. The side effects should be minimal and last for a day or two at most."

Ellie pulled harder at her restraints, trying to break free. "What side effects?"

"Relax, or I'll have to sedate you."

"Don't you dare," she warned through clenched teeth, shocking them both. "I knew he was lying. He plans to do something weird and perverted to me."

"Ellie, calm down." Dr. Zach grabbed her arms. She tried to jerk out of his grasp, but he was too strong. The door opened and Mina entered.

"Zach, what are you doing?"

"Mina." Ellie's shoulders sagged with relief. "Help me."

"Take those things off her." Mina frowned as she walked over. "Relax, Ellie. He's just going to deactivate your tracking chip."

"What?"

Mina released the restraints from Ellie's wrists. "Aden wants your tracking chip deactivated."

She crouched, freeing Ellie's ankles from the straps, and Ellie sprung out of the chair. She scrambled to the other side of the room, pressing her back against the opposite wall. "I don't understand. Why aren't you just replacing it? That's what Master Matthais did."

"We can't replace it, so Zach's going to deactivate it."

Her brow furrowed. "Why?"

"It should be in the back of your neck but yours is in your head," Mina said.

Ellie's eyes swept toward the door. Could she make it before Mina or Dr. Zach tackled her? "And that's not good?"

"No," Mina replied. "And it means Zach can't remove it. But he'll disable it, implant a new one in your neck, and everything will be fine. Ellie, come back over here and sit."

She couldn't refuse, despite how much she wanted to, so Ellie took a few faltering steps forward. "So what's with the straps, then?"

"To keep you from getting hurt if you convulse and fall to the floor," Dr. Zach said.

"What?"

"Sit." Mina pointed at the chair.

Ellie took a seat and eyed Dr. Zach warily as he grabbed a hairdryer-like object.

"I'll hold on to you to make sure you don't fall. Don't worry. You won't feel anything and when you wake up it will be over."

She swiveled her head to look at the older woman for assurance. "Wake up?"

"Yes. There's a good chance you'll seize and lose consciousness." As brutal as her answer was, Ellie appreciated her honesty. "Just sit back and breathe."

Ellie inhaled a deep breath before letting out a long drawn-out exhale. Her eyes followed Dr. Zach as he moved around to stand behind her.

"Tilt your head forward." He pinned her hair on top of her head.

For a second, she thought about refusing, but it wouldn't stop him. She was only a thrall and he could do whatever he wanted to her, including forcing her to lean forward. But she was determined to keep at least some control of her fate.

Mina held her wrists down on the arms of the chair.

"It's really not going to hurt?" Ellie had a pretty high tolerance for pain, but this was getting ridiculous.

"It won't hurt. You may feel a little heat on your head right here." He pressed his fingers to the left side of the base of her skull. "Ready?"

She nodded and locked eyes with Mina. A warm tingling sensation crawled up her scalp and her body jerked violently towards Mina.

Then everything went black.

Ellie woke with a start, but she couldn't speak. It was almost like she'd forgotten how. She tried to grab at her throat, but she couldn't lift her right arm. She couldn't move the entire right side of her body. Everything was blurry and dark, except for a faint glow of a distant light somewhere in the room. Her left hand fumbled with the blanket, struggling to push it off, but an overwhelming sensation of heaviness weighed her down.

Then the memory slammed into her. It was hazy, but she remembered Dr. Zach strapping her to a chair, then Mina showing up and explaining they needed to deactivate her tracking chip. She groaned, then jerked when a hand touched her arm.

"It's alright, Ellie. It's just me, Sophie."

Ellie turned her head toward the voice but it wobbled and only a dark fuzzy shape was visible.

"Do you know who I am?"

She tried to nod her head but she was unsure if she'd succeeded.

"Are you having trouble speaking?"

She nodded again, blinking rapidly.

"You're having trouble seeing, too." This time it wasn't a question and Mistress Sophie's voice ended on a sigh. "Don't be scared. Zach said to expect something like this, but it shouldn't last long."

Ellie tried to pat her right arm with her left hand, but it flopped back against the mattress.

"The paralysis will go away too. I know this is frightening, but you're going to be alright. Mina, is there nothing we can do for her?"

"No."

Ellie turned her head toward Mina's voice.

"We just have to wait for it to pass."

Ellie's eyes slipped closed and she gave up trying to see.

"I'm sorry Aden didn't tell you what Zach was going to do," Mistress Sophie said, her voice laced with frustration. "Sometimes I want to wring my son's neck."

Wringing that vampire's neck sounded pretty good to her, too.

"Mina will stay with you until you can see and speak. Go back to sleep. You'll heal faster if you do."

Ellie felt a prick on her left arm and drowsiness settled over her, lulling her back to sleep.

Ellie could see the world around her again. Mistress Sophie had kept her word, and either she or Mina were always there. They helped her to eat and even carried her to the bathroom. Mistress Sophie could have easily left her in Mina's care or one of the other thralls, but she didn't. In many ways, she reminded Ellie of her mother, and several times over that first day, she ached with longing for the mother she'd lost.

Ellie's ability to move the right side of her body returned in increments, and when she could sit up on her own without listing sideways, Mistress Sophie carried her out to the courtyard Iris showed her. She could feel her fingers again, even though lifting her hand was still difficult.

The courtyard was a beautiful oasis in the heart of the Westcott's compound. Carved in the center of the marble floor was an elegant family crest, featuring delicate leaves intertwined with intricate knotwork, with a rabbit head on one side and a dragon on the other. Comfortable-looking padded sofas and loungers, along with small round tables and chairs, were arranged along the edges. In between the furniture, oversized pots filled with vibrant green trees and cascading flowers added a burst of color to the otherwise minimalist space.

A greenhouse was connected to the courtyard, its glass walls revealing an even greater abundance of flowers and trees. Ellie had yet to see inside, but she hoped Mistress Sophie would allow her to explore it one day. The courtyard was shielded from the falling snow by the closed dome. Ellie enjoyed the change of scenery as she settled back in a lounger, watching the large flakes accumulate into a pile on top of the dome, Mistress Sophie beside her.

"Hopefully your ability to speak will return today," she said, her tone soothing and pleasant.

Ellie nodded.

"I heard from Aden, and he's going to be a few more days." She continued her one-sided conversation. "He ran into problems, but he'll get them sorted. He always does."

Ellie's lips slipped into a scowl at the mention of Master Aden's name, but his mother didn't seem to notice, her attention on a sleek black cat that strolled up, rubbing against her leg.

"Hi, Vlad," she purred at him when he stretched his front paws up her calf. She picked him up. "Do you like cats, Ellie?"

Mistress Sophie set him on her lap and scratched under his chin. The cat purred in return.

Ellie nodded. There were a few cats in the thralls' wing of Master Matthais' compound and she and Carrie fed them table scraps.

"This is Vlad. He's spoiled rotten." Mistress Sophie held him out and set him beside Ellie. "Would you like him to keep you company?"

A small smile crept over Ellie's lips and she nodded as he settled against her thigh and curled into a ball.

"He thinks he's king of this castle, and I guess he probably is." Ellie flexed the fingers of her right hand, wishing she could pet him. "Here." Mistress Sophie took her hand and placed it on the cat's back. Ellie's fingers stroked over his fur, and the left side of her mouth curled higher.

"Oh, hi, Keeley," Mistress Sophie greeted a woman with long black hair and dazzling blue eyes.

"Hey, Mom."

"Ellie, this is my daughter, Keeley,"

Ellie lifted her gaze, careful to avoid making direct eye contact.

"Hi, Ellie." She grinned, revealing a row of perfect white teeth. "I'm glad to meet you." Despite the casual curve of her mouth, her face mirrored the same mixture of shock and uncertainty all the others had when they'd first seen Ellie's eyes.

"Can you stay with Ellie for a few minutes?" Mistress Sophie asked as Mistress Keeley sat in the chair on the opposite side of her.

"No problem. It's about time we got acquainted."

"I won't be long. Vlad and Keeley will take good care of you."

As she walked away, Mistress Keeley reached out to Vlad and stroked her fingers down his back and tail. He stretched before curling back against Ellie's thigh.

"Hi, Vlady." Her eyes dropped to the cat, and then she raised them to look at Ellie again. "My mom must really like you because she doesn't let anybody near her baby."

Ellie rubbed Vlad's silky fur as Mistress Keeley settled back in her chair and tucked her feet beneath her, diving right into a one-sided conversation.

"I've been wanting to meet you. My mom kept me away because she didn't want me to overwhelm you. She said my brother didn't tell you what they were going to do. What a dickhead." She scoffed.

Ellie's eyes widened.

"Knowing him, he probably didn't think it was important or that it would affect you so badly. I don't think Zach thought it would either. After everything you went through, they should have given you a couple of days. Your entire system was on overload. It's no wonder your brain shut down."

Ellie shifted a little to get a better look at the vampire beside her. She looked like Mistress Sophie but with black hair like Master Aurick. It was long and pulled off her face, twisting down her back in an intricate braid. Her eyes were as blue as Master Aden's, but now that she had a better view, Ellie noticed they also had a slight hint of green. Her features were softer, and less severe than her brothers.

Mistress Keeley continued to chatter beside her and Ellie realized she had stopped listening.

"I'm probably overwhelming you." Her lips curved in a wry smile.

Ellie shook her head, not wanting to offend her. She petted Vlad, and his strong purr vibrated beneath her fingers.

"It's okay. There's plenty of time to get to know each other."

Her words surprised Ellie. Why would Mistress Keeley want to get to know her?

A thrall walked up carrying a glass of juice and a sandwich. "Mistress Sophie asked me to bring this to Ellie."

She was tall, with light auburn hair, but seemed kind of fragile. She must be one of Master Aden's feeders, given the bandage on her neck.

"Give it to me."

When the girl left, Mistress Keeley leaned closer and whispered, "I don't know why my brother keeps her around. She's a little snot." Ellie's eyes popped open as she failed to hide her surprise that a vampire was confiding such a thing to her. Mistress Keeley burst into laughter. "You'll feel the same way about her soon enough. Can you eat on your own?"

Again, using her only form of communication, Ellie nodded and held out her left hand.

"I'll put the juice on the table and you can signal when you want it. You eat and I'll just keep talking."

Lifting half of the sandwich to her lips, she listened to Mistress Keeley tell her about the baby she and her husband, Ryan, would have in the fall through a half-breed surrogate.

The right side of Ellie's mouth still wasn't working. She had to chew slowly so her food didn't tumble out. A piece of turkey did drop, but Vlad was only too happy to clean it up for her.

Ellie

The next night Mistress Keeley visited her again. By then, Ellie had regained control of her right side. She still slurred some words, but if she spoke slowly, she was understandable.

And boy did she want to rant something fierce. But she held her tongue, cursing Aden Westcott in her head every second she was awake. Lucky for him he was still away because if he'd been there, she might have just told him what she thought of him and his empty promise never to hurt her.

She could walk, thanks to the cane Mina had given her, but her steps were unsteady.

"It's not that cold tonight. Let's get real fresh air," Mistress Keeley said as she led Ellie through Master Aden's room to his balcony, guiding her towards the railing. "You're doing well."

"Yes, ma'am. As long as I go slow, I'm okay."

Ellie's gaze dropped to the busy street below. It looked different from Master Matthais' city. The buildings, a combination of glass, steel, and smooth stone, created a multi-level skyline against the backdrop of the dark night. The streets were clean, well-lit, and filled with vampires, many with pets on leashes, walking along and going about their lives. Cars hovered over the pavement, moving silently through the bustling city streets.

"We're not up that high," Mistress Keeley said. "What I like is that you can still see what's going on down below, but we're high enough that we can't hear the street noise. And we can feel the breeze."

"It's nice." Ellie looked up through the open dome, captivated by the myriad of stars and just the sliver of a moon, all winking in the otherwise dark abyss above them. She shivered in the cool air and pulled her sweater tighter around her body.

Unlike the previous night, Mistress Keeley wasn't chattering nonstop. She hardly said a word. Finally, the weight of her stare became unbearable.

"Is there something wrong with my face, ma'am?"

"No. I'm sorry, I don't mean to stare but your eyes are just so—" She stopped when Ellie cringed. "No one has told you why we can't stop looking at you, have they?"

"No, ma'am."

"Aden will probably kill me for this." Mistress Keeley looked around like she was afraid someone would hear, but no one else was around. "Here, let's walk. Mina said you need the exercise."

The balcony, like the courtyard, had a polished stone floor and an identical crest. Couches and lounge chairs scattered across the space, offering a peaceful escape from the fast-paced city life below.

Mistress Keeley held her elbow as they walked, their pace slow but steady. The feel of her cool fingers was odd because Ellie was not used to a vampire's touch.

"A long time ago Aden was in love with a girl who had your eyes."

Ellie blinked in disbelief, her mind racing to process Mistress Keeley's unexpected words.

"I don't mean eyes like yours. I mean your exact eyes. That's why we can't help staring."

"Oh." Why was she telling Ellie this? "Where is she?"

"She died."

"She wasn't a vampire?"

Mistress Keeley shook her head. "No. She was human."

Ellie's eyes widened in surprise, but she tried to mask her shock. "How did she die?"

"That part of the story isn't mine to tell, but her death destroyed him."

"Why did he take me if my eyes remind him of hers?"

"My brother is a masochist." Mistress Keeley paused, and Ellie could see the internal struggle in her eyes. "This is going to sound crazy but he thinks you might be her... well, her soul."

Out of nowhere, Ellie was overcome by a familiar sensation, as if a dormant memory had been awakened. That happened a lot lately.

"I know that sounds bonkers, believe me. I'm not sure if I buy into the whole thing, either, but my mother is convinced. And Aden, as much as he denies it, is on the fence about it. My mom has him all in a tizzy." Mistress Keeley urged her to walk again. "Have you ever heard of soulmates, Ellie?"

"No."

"How about reincarnation?"

Ellie shook her head, her long hair swaying with the movement.

"Never mind." Mistress Keeley waved her hand before reaching for Ellie's when she stumbled. She led Ellie to the sofa. "Here, let's sit for a minute."

Ellie let out a sigh of relief as she sat. Right away, Mistress Keeley picked up where she left off.

"Soulmates are two people who are destined to be together, their souls forever intertwined as they're born time and time again, always finding their way back to each other."

"But vampires don't die. How can they keep being born?"

"That's just it, isn't it?" Mistress Keeley asked. "Aden is stuck here waiting for his soul mate to be reborn, hoping he finds her. Vampires suffer even more than humans or half-breeds because they don't die, so there is no escape from the loneliness and longing for the person who makes you whole."

Ellie looked down, trying to digest Mistress Keeley's words. "Was she his soulmate?"

"If soulmates are real then, yes, I believe she was. She was a burst of color in a world of black and white, and she didn't take shit from him." Mistress Keeley's smile was tinged with a hint of sadness. "She had a crush on him from the time she was a kid and when he realized he felt the same, she told him it was about damn time he pulled his head out of his ass. He vowed from that moment to worship her for eternity."

Surprise washed over Ellie at Mistress Keeley's words. She couldn't believe that the man she had heard so many awful things about was capable of such deep emotion.

"So he bit me and brought me back here because he thinks I'm her?"

Mistress Keeley leaned back and crossed her legs. "Not exactly. You aren't Aly. But if you believe in the concept, then you're the same soul. It's your soul he's drawn to. It sounds weird but do you understand what I'm saying?"

"I guess." Ellie's brow furrowed, and she paused. "Why are you telling me this?"

"Because I imagine you're baffled by his behavior."

Ellie shrugged, not wanting to admit how confused she was.

"He probably acted like a crazy person, right? Nice one minute, yelling at you the next."

"He does yell a lot."

Mistress Keeley laughed. "Yeah. Don't let it get to you. He likes to yell and intimidate people. But don't be afraid of him. He won't hurt you."

"He already has."

Where did she get the courage to speak so boldly to a vampire?

"From what I heard, he saved you from a much worse fate by whisking you away from Matthais," Mistress Keeley said, her gaze fixed on Ellie.

"You mean taking me from my father, my family, everything I've ever known?" Ellie slapped her hand over her mouth and mumbled into her palm. "I'm sorry, Mistress Keeley."

Mistress Keeley leaned forward and grinned. "Don't be. I like you. I like that you're not afraid of me. Or my brother, from what I hear."

"I'm terrified of him." Ellie hesitated, unsure if there was more to her emotions than just fear. After drinking his blood, it changed into something else, but she couldn't quite grasp what it was.

"There's no need," Mistress Keeley said. "But a word of advice. If you want the upper hand with him, don't let him know that."

Ellie was restless and over being confined to her bed. Her mobility was back and she longed for the freedom to move about. She was used to doing everything for herself. So, having others wait on her didn't feel right. With her stomach grumbling, she set off to find the kitchen and make herself something to eat.

It took her several tries to find the thralls' warp port to take her to the lower level. The courtyard had six connecting hallways, and she'd gone down two without success, only finding locked door after locked door. Too embarrassed to ask, she wandered until she found the right one.

Ellie entered the kitchen and saw four thralls sitting around a circular table at one end. She recognized Iris, but not the other three. Each of them had a unique shade of red hair, ranging from bold red to soft auburn.

"Hi, Iris."

Iris didn't return her greeting. She kept talking to the thrall next to her, but her lips twisted into a halfhearted smile. Ellie felt all eyes following her as she walked to the wall of stainless steel refrigerators to gather the fixings for a salad. They were all whispering, their voices carrying just enough for Ellie to hear them.

"She doesn't look like there's anything wrong with her."

"I told you she doesn't look any worse than me," a raspy voice said.

"She has brown hair?"

"I said she did."

"What's she doing down here?"

"I can't believe she has brown hair."

"You said that already, Janessa."

"But Master Aden never takes brown-haired thralls."

"If she's his pet, why didn't Master Aden take her with him? And why isn't she wearing pet colors?"

Ellie released a slow exhale, closing her eyes. Finding friends here was going to be as hard as it was in Master Matthais' house. Her heart ached for Carrie, yet again.

Her salad in hand, Ellie took a deep breath and approached the table. "Hi." She smiled, sitting down, trying to be friendly. "I'm Ellie."

"We know who you are." The thrall sitting to her left shot her a less-than-welcoming glare.

"And you are?" She was used to other thralls disliking her, but she refused to be pushed around by anyone who wasn't a vampire.

"None of your business."

"Janessa, don't be a jerk. You heard Mistress Sophie," Iris warned.

She glared at Iris before turning to Ellie. "What are you doing down here?"

"I was hungry."

"Second-level thralls don't use this kitchen. Besides, don't you eat in your private room?"

It was clear Janessa resented her, but why? She didn't even know her.

Ellie brushed off the rude question and shot Iris a curious glance, but Iris wouldn't meet her eyes. "What are your names?" she asked as she took a bite of her salad.

The girl who sat across the table introduced herself. "I'm Mandi. Don't mind Janessa. She can be a bit of a bitch."

"Shut up, Mandi," Janessa said.

Ellie looked to the thrall on her right.

"That's Chelsea," Mandi offered when Chelsea didn't acknowledge her. "She's not supposed to talk a lot because her voice is still healing,"

Ellie recognized her as the girl who brought her food to the courtyard the other day. The bandage was gone from her neck, which looked mostly healed, yet still had a red, raw scar from Master Aden's attack. But it was the multiple old jagged scars on Chelsea's neck that Ellie couldn't look away from.

"What are you staring at?" Chelsea asked, her voice hoarse. "You'll look like this someday, too."

Bewildered by her outward hostility, Ellie tried to change the subject. "What do each of you do?"

"We're cleaners," Mandi jumped in when no one else spoke up. "I clean Master Aden's rooms and Janessa cleans his office. Chelsea serves Master Aden. She's one of his feeders."

"That's all you do?"

"All," Chelsea scoffed but didn't elaborate.

"Master Aden likes his feeders available whenever he wants them, so he forbids them from doing anything else," Mandi added. "Unless he's away. Then Mistress Sophie will have them do other things."

So that's why she'd brought Ellie her breakfast the other day.

"We all did more than one job in Master Matthais' house."

"How old are you, anyway?" Mandi leaned forward.

"Twenty-two."

"And you weren't a pet already?" Janessa's suspicion of Ellie's answer was apparent in her tone.

"No."

"Why not?"

Ellie didn't want to admit that her father was the reason for her being spared. It would make it worse if everyone thought she got special treatment where she came from.

"I guess I don't smell good."

"All humans smell good to vampires," Mandi replied. She was the only one who was talking to Ellie. The others just stared.

"You obviously smelled good to Master Aden," Chelsea said in a sour tone.

A male thrall wandered into the kitchen, saving her from having to respond. He was tall with a head of messy blond hair and a crooked smile. He looked older than the girls but not by much.

"Hey, Finn," Iris said and Ellie caught the breathy tone of her voice.

"Ladies," he said as he waved before stooping and hefting three large pans onto the stove.

"Are you cooking today?" Mandi asked.

"Please say yes," Janessa said. "Emma cooked yesterday, and it was terrible."

"Making my specialty," he said as he opened the fridge, pulling out ingredients.

Mandi leaned across the table and whispered. "Finn is one of the best cooks we have. He works upstairs in the half-breed kitchen too."

"I wasn't shown any other kitchen," Ellie looked at Iris.

"Yeah, sorry about that." Iris didn't seem sorry at all. "I know you're in his pet room but Master Aden didn't say you were a second-level thrall so I thought you were one of us. The second-level thralls use the same kitchens as the half-breeds, two levels up."

"We didn't have levels in Master Matthais' house," Ellie said as she picked at her salad.

"Second-level thralls get treated more like half-breeds. They get better jobs. And no drinking from them," Mandi said.

"Oh." Ellie glanced over her shoulder at Finn, who chopped what looked like root vegetables on the gleaming marble countertop.

"But since you're his pet, he'll probably start feeding on you when he gets back." Janessa gave her the once over and Ellie swallowed thickly as her words sunk in.

"Hey Finn," Mandi called. "Have you met the new girl, Ellie, yet?"

His face split into a wide grin. "Nice to meet you, Ellie, the new girl."

"Hi," she replied, taken aback by how good-looking he was.

She caught sight of Iris's scowl. Fed up with these girls, Ellie stood and took her plate to the sink.

"Don't worry about that," Finn said as she rinsed her dish. "I'll do that when I do the rest."

"That's okay. I can do it. I used to work in the kitchens." Ellie placed it in the dishwasher. She stopped as she turned to leave, unable to resist peeking into the pot. "That looks like you're making soup."

"Good guess. Garden vegetable," he said, a smile playing at the corners of his lips.

"Sounds good."

"You should come back later and try it."

"Maybe I will." He seemed nice, and she appreciated the kindness. "Thanks."

"See you around, Ellie, the new girl." Finn grinned again before turning back to his chopping.

She headed toward the door, waving to the girls on her way. "Bye." The only one who replied was Mandi.

As she exited the kitchen, she couldn't help but overhear, "You're right, Chelsea, she's not special at all."

By the time Master Aden returned a few hours later, Ellie's anger and resentment had reached dizzying heights. Her emotions were a chaotic tangle of confusion. What Mistress Keeley told her about the human girl he loved was a shock, not only because he once loved a thrall, though that was shocking enough. But if he thought Ellie was her, what would he want from her?

And what had happened to her?

Ellie was in the greenhouse when Mistress Sophie came in to tell her his plane was landing. She'd invited Ellie to help tend to her plants. Ellie had eagerly accepted, unable to resist the chance to explore the hidden world within. It was everything she imagined it would be, and more.

The living, breathing paradise had surrounded her the moment she stepped through the arched entryway. Thousands of vibrant flowers and towering trees filled the vast space, creating a lush canopy of green with bursts of color blooming overhead. Smooth stone pathways wound throughout the space, curving around the plants. To the right of the entrance, a warp port provided transport to a network of suspended walkways above, permitting access to the higher levels of the thriving enclosure.

Nestled in the farthest corner, a waterfall flowed into a pool full of colorful fish. The greenhouse's open roof allowed the plants and trees to absorb the fresh air.

"It's nice to have you here with me."

Ellie looked up, surprised at Mistress Sophie's words.

"As much as I love tending the plants, it gets lonely because neither Aurick nor my children join me."

Ellie wanted to ask why but hesitated to speak without being asked a direct question.

"Vlad is the only one who comes in, but that's only because of the koi fish."

Ellie's lips quirked. There was no question in her mind about the cat's motives.

"I can switch off the daylight bulbs and use normal lighting but they still avoid it," Sophie said as they worked, stripping thorns from a pile of roses. "There isn't a great deal vampires fear, but a light that replicates sunlight is one of them."

There were lights that could harm vampires like the sun? She never learned that while living in Master Matthais' household.

"These lights aren't exactly legal," Mistress Sophie said in a hushed tone.

Unable to contain the weight of her curiosity, Ellie asked. "How can you have them?"

Mistress Sophie's lips twitched as if she knew she'd broken down Ellie's walls. "This section of the compound is part of our private quarters. We don't invite other vampires into this wing. All visitors stay in the west annex."

"Sophie?" Master Aden's voice carried over from the doorway to her right.

Ellie turned to see him standing outside the door. She was off to the side so she didn't think he could see her. She remained where she was as Mistress Sophie walked over to him.

"Aden, welcome home. Let me switch over the lighting so you can come inside. Ellie is in here with me."

"Yes, I know."

Of course, he knew. Stupid vampire senses. A deep sigh escaped Ellie's chest, carrying with it the weight of her emotions. She had hoped to have a little longer before she had to see him again.

But no such luck.

Aden

The lingering anxiety that had consumed him for days left Aden's body the closer he got to her. His eyes drank in the sight of her. Despite checking on her through a hologram and his mother's assurance that she was better, he only believed it after seeing her with his own eyes.

Ellie's body stiffened, and she refused to acknowledge him. Focused on her task, she pruned the roses, removing thorns and laying the stems in a basket. But as he drew nearer, her heart thudded louder.

"Hello, Ellie."

Her fingers slipped on the stem she held and she pricked her thumb. "Ouch." She slid the digit between her lips.

The sweet scent of her blood hit Aden like a ton of bricks. It took all his strength not to grip the edges of the table and groan. Aden's head swiveled around, looking for his mother, but she slipped out. He swallowed back the venom pooling in his mouth.

"You look better."

"Yes, Sir."

Her short, curt reply was not altogether unexpected. His mother warned him she was angry about not being told what Zach would do. He hadn't meant to keep it from her. He just hadn't thought to mention it. She obviously harbored her anger, but he was out of patience. He couldn't bear another minute of her not looking at him.

"Ellie, look at me when I'm speaking to you."

The gruff command came out more harshly than he intended. She tore her thumb from between her lips and her eyes snapped up to meet his. The anger blazing in her eyes stunned him. Not only had he never been looked at that way by a thrall, but the familiarity of those fiery green depths rendered him speechless.

As soon as their eyes met, her breath hitched. For a split second her eyes softened before they burned hot again. Although shocking, it pleased him to see her gaze didn't waver. Maybe making her angry was the key to getting her over her hesitation to look at him. He fought the clawing urge to yank her against him and sink his teeth into her.

"Spit out what you want to say to me already."

"I have nothing to say, Sir."

"I own you," he snarled. "I don't owe you an explanation."

Hurt flashed in Ellie's eyes and her lower lip trembled before she bit down on it. She looked like he slapped her and the sight sent a sharp pang of regret through him. He sucked in a deep breath.

"But I'm giving you permission to speak as you wish right now. I wouldn't waste the opportunity."

Her eyes hardened again and she tossed the rose onto the table. Anger flickered across her face as she cocked her head, planting her hands on her hips. She was beautiful in all her fury and the inexplicable urge to kiss her consumed him as he braced for the onslaught of her ire.

"You could have warned me they were going to zap me like a lab rat."

"What do you know about lab rats?" A wry smile pulled at his lips.

"All you vampires put so little thought into the thralls around you, expecting them to be like dumb animals. You talk about things like we're not there or can't hear you or are just too dumb to understand. I've always seen and heard more than anyone realizes, and I'm not as stupid as you think I am."

Aden's eyes trailed up and down her rigid body. "I don't think you're stupid. Foolish, yes. But not ignorant."

She hiked a stubborn chin at him. "You called me stupid."

"When did I do that?" He picked up a rose, twirling it just to give his fingers something to do. Otherwise, he feared he was going to give in to the temptation to shake her.

"The night I told you I confessed to Master Matthais."

The memory rushed back. He forgot he said that to her. "I said what you did was stupid."

"No, you didn't. You called me a stupid little girl."

"And how do you remember that? You were virtually unconscious from blood loss." She was right, but he wouldn't admit that to her.

Those flaming green eyes narrowed. "Because I remember everything."

His amusement at her bold behavior vanished in a flash and his gaze hardened as he dropped the rose on the table.

"Apparently, not everything."

He turned and stomped out of the greenhouse, unsure and uncomfortable with what he'd meant by those words.

Aden retracted his fangs, licking the punctures on the girl's neck to stop the bleeding. He leaned back on his office sofa, bracing one hand on her shoulder. Her eyes fluttered open, and she assessed her surroundings before her head slumped forward onto the cushion beside him.

He might have taken a little too much of her blood, but he was so hungry. His hunger seemed to consume him constantly now. He'd only been home for a few hours, but it had been two days since he decided he'd take a break from fucking his thralls during feeding. He wouldn't have to lock Ellie in her room any longer, but feeding this way always left him wanting, edgy, and unsatisfied.

His encounter with her after he arrived home had made him feel restless. Of course, she was observant and remembered him calling her a stupid little girl. Perhaps he'd underestimated her.

Aden looked up as his father stormed into the room, his eyes red and bulging with anger.

"Hi. I was planning to come see you," he said.

"Cén cineál ollphéist atá agat?" Aurick roared in Gaelic as he reached down and flipped the chair near the door, sending it flying across the room and through the glass wall that separated Aden's office from his workout room.

"What the fuck?" Aden pushed to his feet. Everyone always wondered where he got his legendary temper because Aurick was always so calm and level-headed. But few had seen his father when he was in the throes of a tantrum. It was a spectacular, rare occurrence indeed.

"What kind of monster have you truly become?" Aurick bared his teeth as he asked again, in English this time.

"What are—" Aden started.

"How dare you use humans as bait?"

"Is that why you're flipping out?"

Aurick's eyes shifted back to their normal blue color as his temper receded. "That is not how we live our lives, Aden."

Aden walked around the thrall still leaning against the sofa. "I had to do something drastic. Paolo and his troops flaked, and I was tired of waiting for them."

"That's no excuse," Aurick said, his voice measured.

"Cecilia misled everyone about the size of the rogue infestation. It was far larger than we thought. The only solution was a massive, simultaneous strike on all the caves. I needed something to lure them all out at the same time."

Aurick walked to the window, the tight set of his shoulders loosening. "Humans are not expendable, Aden."

"You're not listening to me. Drastic measures were necessary."

"Sacrificing human lives in such a blatant and indiscriminate manner is unacceptable. There had to be another option."

"There wasn't." Aden made his way to the bar and poured himself a drink before gulping it.

Aurick let out a sigh as he gazed over the expanse of land that disappeared into the horizon. "Aden, I gave you the position as head of my military because you're smart and I believe you have the potential to be a brilliant leader someday. Don't make me regret my decision."

"Then don't always question mine," Aden snarled and crossed his arms over his chest. "I know we have different... views on certain things, but you have to trust me to do my job. Otherwise, I shouldn't be here."

Aurick didn't look at him. "It's more than just our philosophies, Aden. How many did you sacrifice?"

"That coven had already slaughtered ten times the number of humans."

"How many?"

"Only five hundred."

"Only?" Aden saw Aurick's eyes flash red again in the window's reflection. "Damn it, Aden."

"Collateral damage." Aden took a seat behind his desk. "If you want to blame someone for this, you should focus on Cecilia. She's the one who let the problem get out of control."

"She is responsible for her part in letting the situation get as unmanageable as it did, but only you are accountable for your actions in handling it. And speaking of Cecilia, threatening an Ancient One is forbidden. You know this."

Aurick turned to face him and Aden saw the disappointment swirling in his eyes.

"I didn't threaten her." Aden pinched the bridge of his nose. "I warned her there would be consequences for her failure to act."

"That's semantics. You should have called me when Paolo didn't show up. I would have dealt with them."

"I'm a grown man. I don't need you fighting my battles," he scoffed.

Aurick walked over to stand in front of Aden's desk. "Well, I've spent the last three hours smoothing this over with both Matthais and Cecilia. You not only threatened her, you took her humans without her consent."

"I used the resources I had at my disposal to clean up her mess."

"By slaughtering more innocents? Are you even listening to yourself?"

"I did what I had to do under the circumstances. Cecilia wasn't there. That's her fault, not mine. I stand by my decision."

"You're going to need to apologize to her."

"The fuck I will." The thought of apologizing to Cecelia was repulsive.

"Aden, this isn't a request."

"Are you fucking kidding me? I didn't threaten her."

"Well, she says you did. There are very few laws imposed on vampires. You've broken two. Matthais has agreed to overlook the humans, but threatening an Ancient One is treason."

Aden pushed to his feet. "This is bullshit. I'm not the one in the wrong here."

"I've assured Matthais you'll apologize to her tonight. Don't test him on this, Aden. I think he's still vexed about Ellie, so you need to set your ego aside and do this."

Aden squeezed his hands into fists, growling under his breath. "Fine."

Aurick turned to leave, but he stopped in the doorway. "I've never needed to question your methods or your motives with military strategy, but you've disappointed me with your decisions on this mission. The man I raised would never be so callously cruel."

Aurick glanced at the girl struggling to stand near the sofa, then walked out without giving Aden an opportunity to respond.

"Get out," he roared at the frightened thrall, and she scurried out the door.

Aden stood in the same spot for a long time, seething, before he trashed his office, breaking every piece of furniture in his path before throwing it through the glass wall.

Aden drove his fist into the heavy bag that hung from the ceiling in the center of his workout room, releasing his anger and frustration with every strike. Glass still covered the floor and crunched under his feet, but he returned his chair and the other broken furniture to his office.

He'd foregone gloves and wrist wraps because he needed to feel a bit of pain. He thought about sparring with Kane or Roderick, but given his intense rage, hitting an inanimate object seemed like the safer option.

Groveling to Cecilia pissed him off, particularly when all he wanted was to tell her to go fuck herself again. She'd enjoyed it far too much. It left a bitter taste in his mouth, one he doubted even Ellie's blood could remove. Politics and kissing ass to keep peace with the other Ancient Ones were definitely not his thing. He didn't envy Aurick's position and could never do what he did.

With each strike, Aden's fists hit the coarse canvas before he added in several kicks. Each forceful blow caused the bag to sway, the D-rings that secured it to the ceiling squeaking in protest.

His encounter with Aurick also pissed him the fuck off. His father was so damn judgmental sometimes. Despite what everyone thought of him, protecting his family and his region was Aden's top priority. Okay, he occasionally bent the law a little, but he refused to apologize for it or for who he was.

His core muscles contracted with each strike, releasing more of his pent-up fury. But with everything happening tonight, he feared the bag wouldn't endure his wrath much longer. It wouldn't be the first time it tore from the ceiling in tatters.

He fed again after his confrontation with Aurick, but he was still hungry and irritated, reeling from the encounter with Ellie. He'd thought about her too much while he was gone. It distracted him more than it should have. Even Roderick noticed, but it hadn't kept Aden from doing his job. Despite the initial challenges, the troops easily found and dispatched the rogues. With the humans as bait, it went far more smoothly than he thought it would, but it had just taken more time than he wanted.

Paolo's inability to handle it on his own made Aden doubt his suitability as Cecilia's commander. After they both calmed down, he would speak to his father and suggest he look into the matter. As the Vice Chancellor of the Vampire

World Council, Aurick carried out the necessary investigations before presenting problems and solutions to Matthais. Paolo clearly wasn't fit to run a marathon, never mind a military.

He expected Ellie's anger after his conversations with Zach and his mother, but it was the hurt in her eyes and her accusations that had thrown him off balance. Aden was usually unshakable, but in the short time he'd known her, she had unsettled him. He didn't know why she affected him like this.

He'd let his mother's insanity get into his head. That's why.

Aden focused on increasing his striking power, driving punches straight off his chin. He moved into a cross, front and back hooks and uppercuts, and the bones in his fingers cracked. He welcomed the pain, but he should have worn gloves. His hands were going to fucking ache when he was through.

The squeaking of the D-ring above echoed in the room before it snapped. And with one last powerful thrust of his fist, the bag exploded and flew across the room, bouncing off the wall as Kane entered.

"What happened in there?" He jabbed a thumb toward Aden's destroyed office. "Are you still testy? Why didn't you call me to spar?"

Aden shook his arms so they didn't cramp. "I didn't want to smash your face in tonight. What do you want, Kane?"

He could feel Kane's eyes on his bloody, broken fingers as he went over to the sink in the corner.

"I wanted to let you know Ellie never returned. Did you find her?"

"Yes, I fucking found her." Aden turned the water on and ran his hands under it, feeling the bones knitting back together under his skin. "But she should have returned to her room by now."

"You want me to track her?" Kane asked.

"No! Fucking find Ellie!" A hologram of her appeared. She was still in the greenhouse, alone. "You can go now."

Kane nodded and left.

Aden watched her for a few minutes before swiping the floating orb closed. The workout helped, but the prickling in the back of his neck persisted. He needed to shake off the remnants of his irritation, or he couldn't guarantee he wouldn't drag her to his bed and lose himself in her until the world around him blurred.

It was time to do what always cleared his head better than kickboxing.

Ellie

Stunned, Ellie stood frozen, her eyes fixed on the door long after Master Aden had stormed out, his words echoing in her mind.

What in the heck did that mean?

And where had she gotten the courage to talk to him like that? She always had a little bit of a smart mouth. It got her into trouble with Veronika more often than not. But she'd never dared to speak to a vampire like that.

She was starting to feel safe here, and she believed him when he said he wouldn't hurt her, but it was foolish to provoke him. His yelling she could handle. Mistress Keeley said that was just how he communicated, but pushing him was like poking one of Master Matthais' bears. The bear would wake and take a bite out of you. Master Aden had already bitten her, but he could have hurt her worse. He could have torn into her neck like he'd done to Chelsea.

Ellie finished stripping the last of the roses, the thorns pricking her fingers as she replayed her conversation with Master Aden in her mind, his parting words still confusing even after what Mistress Keeley told her. That was something she couldn't wrap her mind around.

Ellie placed the basket in the walk-in cooler Mistress Sophie showed her and walked out of the greenhouse. She didn't want to go back to her room yet, so she made her way to the kitchen to make a sandwich. She opted to eat alone, even though several tables were occupied by other thralls, her last encounter making her wary of them.

She was still learning her way around, not yet familiar with where each hallway led. They all looked the same—white marble floors, white ceilings, and white walls covered in various artworks. She only realized she had gone the wrong way when the hallway came to an abrupt end at a set of double sliding doors. They slid open with a whoosh just as she was about to turn around.

"Hello?" she called but was met with silence.

When the doors remained open, she approached, peeking into the room, her eyes darting from side to side. The room was dark except for the subtle glow of a gigantic stone fireplace in the far right corner. She squinted, trying to make out the room's features, curiosity getting the better of her. Several soft overhead lights embedded into the ceiling flickered to life as she stepped inside, illuminating the room. Her breath left her lungs in a rush as she took in the sight in front of her. To say the room was huge would be a major understatement.

It was enormous.

Elle turned in a slow circle, her eyes scanning the space. Every wall was lined with mahogany shelves filled with books from floor to ceiling except one that had large windows draped with a deep green fabric. The curtains were pulled, framing the windows on either side.

Even though the room was massive, the dark wood paneling gave it a cave-like feel, complemented by the rich tones of burgundy, olive, and brown in both the furniture and flooring. Plush area rugs covered the hardwood floors, adding warmth and comfort to the space. All around the room were sofas and chairs covered in dark leather. They looked luxurious and comfortable, and incredibly tempting, inviting her to sink into them and get lost in a book. Several coffee tables overflowed with books, and a sense of wonder washed over Ellie as she took in the breathtaking sight.

She shouldn't be in here. She'd overstepped all boundaries, invading the Westcott's privacy and breaking what she was sure were at least half a dozen laws. But she couldn't get her feet to move. Overwhelmed by the urge to touch and smell every one of those books, Ellie longed to curl up on one of the comfortable-looking chairs and find out if she could remember how to read.

Unable to help herself, she moved deeper into the room but her steps faltered as a strange sensation washed over her. Her brows furrowed as an inexplicable feeling of familiarity enveloped her, stronger than the one she'd felt in Master Aden's room.

Ellie reached out, and her fingers brushed against the velvety fabric of a nearby chair. She steadied herself as the room seemed to shimmer as if obscured by a sheer curtain. She gasped as the study transformed around her. The room looked the same, but the furniture was rearranged and the color scheme was different. Ellie saw herself, but not herself, sitting on the sofa closest to the fireplace.

Only she wasn't alone. A man sat beside her, his features indistinct yet somehow achingly familiar. They were huddled close, a heavy book open across their laps. Ellie could almost feel the warmth of his body pressed against her side. He read aloud, and she hung on his every word, captivated by the story unfolding before her.

The vision faded as suddenly as it had started, and Ellie found herself still standing in the dimly lit library. Her heart raced, and she was overcome by a profound sense of loss mixed with lingering sensations of love and contentment, leaving her both exhilarated and confused.

As if drawn by an irresistible pull, she moved towards the sofa and cautiously sat down in the same spot the Ellie in her vision had been.

Was she losing her mind?

Was what Mistress Keeley had told her and Master Aden's cryptic words causing her mind to play tricks on her?

Ellie took long, deliberate breaths, as she stared into the flickering fire, willing her heart and mind to settle.

Maybe her brain was still recovering.

She stood, intending to leave but as she turned, her eyes swept past the windows. Thousands of snowflakes fluttered down from the sky, glinting in the moonlight like sparkling diamonds. Without a second thought, Ellie walked over and pressed her nose to the glass.

She'd loved snow as a child. Those were the most cherished memories she had with her parents before Master Matthais had taken them. A sad sigh, filled with longing and regret, escaped her lips. What she wouldn't give to be back there in their little village with them again.

Ellie wasn't sure how long she gazed out the window before she stepped back, moving over to the overstuffed chair beside it, and sat down, watching the snow gathering on the windowpanes. A book on the table beside her caught her attention. She reached over and picked it up, feeling its solid weight in her hand before flipping it open. She scanned the first several pages and frowned. It had been a long time since she'd read anything and there were a lot of long words, ones she wasn't sure she understood. She would love to have the time to read this book. What kinds of stories did it have in it?

She closed it and placed it back on the table before leaning over and resting her head on the chair's arm, suddenly very tired. The snow was coming down harder now, creating what looked like a solid white wall outside the window. Ellie watched it sleepily, her eyes growing heavier as she tried and failed to remember the feeling of snowflakes landing on her eyelashes.

Aden

Aden stepped back from the canvas and set down his brush, wiping the paint from his fingers with a rag. After a quick shower, which helped wash away most of his residual irritability, he'd headed into his studio. Painting was his refuge, and it calmed and settled him. Aden looked back at the portrait, shocked at what he saw.

He'd painted Ellie.

She crouched on her knees, like that night in his room at Matthais' compound. It was the view he had of her as she gasped for breath on the floor before she collapsed in the fetal position. With her head lowered and tilted to the left, she gazed up at him through the corners of her eyes. Her eyes in the painting differed from the reality of that moment. He'd painted them sultry and full of secrets, not fear.

Her hands were flat on the ground in front of her knees, her thighs bare and spread, but her shirt covered what lay between. It draped off her shoulder, open in the front and torn in the back. Unlike reality, her back was unblemished and her breasts hung exposed over her thighs, firm and lush. Her skin was flushed, and the portrait was so lifelike, it was as if she were sitting there before him, tempting him.

Too stunned to move, Aden stared at the painting for what seemed like hours. He lost track of the time, and when he tore his eyes away to glance at the clock, it was almost morning. And Ellie still hadn't returned to her room.

He shouldn't be, but he was worried. She was safe inside the compound. But he refused to go to bed without her in her room, if only because she would disturb his sleep when she returned.

Rather than using electronic means to locate her, he opted to stretch his legs and hunt her down.

Where the fuck was she?

There were only so many places she should be, but he had yet to find her.

He was no longer angry with her. In truth, he'd never been. His fury, as always, burned inside him until he could no longer contain it, and it exploded, leaving him with no one to blame but himself for the carnage he caused.

He was less concerned about his fight with his father. This wasn't the first time Aden suffered his disappointment. He'd been doing that for hundreds of years. But damn, he hadn't seen his father that furious since the bender he'd gone on during the first fifty years after—

Aden shuddered, unable to finish the thought.

Vampires were known for their perfect memories, but those years were a blur for him. He'd been so consumed with grief and rage, his actions filled with violence and blood, that he'd blocked them out for self-preservation. And, if he was being honest, so he could look himself in the mirror again.

His workout accomplished most of what he needed it to, but his fingers still ached. He'd done quite a number on them this time. Ellie was probably still angry, and though he was still a bit on edge, all he wanted was to see her.

He tracked her scent from the greenhouse to the kitchens. At least she'd eaten. Then he followed it in what seemed like a random pattern through the courtyard and down several hallways she never should have entered, ending up outside the library. He heard her steady heartbeat beyond the door.

What the fuck?

He'd granted her extreme leeway since she arrived, more than he gave any other thrall. The weight of his guilt over her whipping and the conflicting emotions her eyes caused had him all tied up in knots. But she overstepped her bounds by invading his family's personal space. His mother didn't allow thralls access to the library unattended. Those who cleaned it still needed her or one of her assistants to be present.

He needed to put a stop to this before it got out of hand. She was his thrall and both of them would have to get used to that.

The doors slid open, and he prepared to confront her when he stopped in his tracks. Ellie slept, nestled in a chair beside the window, bathed in the muted glow of the moonlight seeping through the tinted glass and heavy snowfall outside. Flames flickered in the stone fireplace, casting dancing shadows over the walls and her peaceful face. His mother insisted on keeping the fire in this room burning, ready for any of them to escape into the hundreds of thousands of books the family possessed.

Floor-to-ceiling shelves lined the walls, packed with only a fraction of his parents' extensive collection of books, but most of them were hidden in the depths of the lowest levels of the compound. Driven by their deep-rooted reverence for the written word and his father's intuition, his parents hoarded and hid one original copy of every book they could find. His father's instincts about Matthais proved true when the Great Vampire Wars ended. To erase the history he wanted kept secret, Matthais burned most of the world's physical books.

Aden entered the room, the scent of aged paper and leather greeting him. But Ellie's gentle scent, a delicate blend of honeysuckle and jasmine, enveloped him, overshadowing everything else, and drawing him closer. Her heartbeat thumped, matching the rhythm of her slow breaths. His eyes drank her in. She was so beautiful that looking at her left him with an ache in the center of his chest.

As he watched her eyelashes flutter against her cheeks, he understood why. He didn't have to see her eyes. He knew who she was deep down in his gut. He hadn't known this kind of certainty since the day he'd admitted he was in love all those years ago.

Aden's heart stumbled out of his chest and fell at his feet—at her feet. The weight of the realization hit him, and he sank into the chair across from her.

He was fucked.

Ellie stirred as the sun rose over the horizon, the muted light crossing over her face. Her eyes fluttered, her heartbeat speeding up as she came awake.

Aden had remained in his spot for the last few hours, watching her sleep and trying to figure out what the fuck he was going to do. He was in love with a human again. How could one vampire be so fucking unlucky?

She opened her eyes and stretched, her scent wafting toward him. He inhaled, stifling a groan, overcome with the longing to bury his nose in her neck and breathe her in. Her blinking eyes wandered from the window to him, and she gasped as they widened in surprise. A strange expression crossed her face, a mix of recognition and confusion, but she schooled her features so quickly Aden was unsure if he'd imagined it.

"Oh, Sir, did you need me for something?"

Aden didn't care who she was. Or wasn't. It didn't matter to him what her eyes looked like. All he knew was that he wanted to spend the rest of eternity getting lost in their depths.

Years ago, Matthais granted an exception for him to marry and turn Aly. Given the circumstances of how he acquired Ellie, Aden doubted he would do the same again. He believed he'd done Aden one favor, and he made it clear Aden owed him for it. If Matthais granted him a second exception, not only would he owe the man another favor, but he would have to sign away the soul that already belonged to the girl in front of him.

Aden cursed his fucking parents and their belief in souls.

"No," he said as her questioning eyes skimmed over his face.

"Then what are you doing here?"

He arched a brow at her. "I could ask you the same thing."

She cringed, realizing her situation, and a smirk tugged at his lips.

"I guess I must have fallen asleep watching the snow."

"Apparently. But that's not what I meant."

Contrition flashed in her eyes. "I know I shouldn't be in here. I was looking for my way back to your room and got lost in the hallways."

"Most of the halls look alike. Only the artwork on the walls distinguishes them."

"I saw the art but didn't realize it was different in every hallway. The doors slid open when I approached, so I was curious. That's gotten me into a lot of trouble over the years."

"I have no doubt."

Why were the library doors programmed to grant her entrance? He'd have to talk to his mother and see who screwed up.

"I've overstepped my bounds." She dropped her feet to the floor. "I'll apologize to Mistress Sophie and take whatever punishment you give me."

"I don't plan to punish you, Ellie."

Surprised eyes met his. "You don't?"

"No. I won't punish you for getting lost and being curious."

"You might be sorry for that," she muttered to herself, but he heard her and hid a smile.

He suspected she was right.

"It won't happen again, Sir."

"Ellie, when you and I are alone, or we are with my family, you have permission to call me Aden."

Shock washed over him at his own words. Only a handful of non-vampires had permission to call him by only his name, and all of them were half-breeds. Only one human had used his given name. But that was far too long ago.

What the fuck was he thinking? But he knew it was the right choice. His instincts rarely failed him so he decided to just go with it.

"But, Sir." Ellie's eyes flooded with shock and confusion.

"No buts. I don't care what you did in Matthais' house. You're not in his house any longer. These are my rules and you'll follow them."

"Yes, Sir."

He narrowed his eyes at her. "It's really going to be a challenge for you to call me by my name, isn't it?"

"It might take me some time, but I'll try, Aden." She said his name slowly as if testing it out. "I'll get out of your way." She stood to leave, and he held up his hand.

"Sit. I want to speak with you about our conversation earlier."

She nodded and lowered herself back into the chair. "I'm sorry," she said through pursed lips, and she looked like she would rather chew off her tongue than say those words to him. "I was disrespectful. It's not my place to question you."

"I should have told you what Zach had to do. I was more concerned with stopping your internal bleeding but it was still my responsibility to tell you. You shouldn't have had to fear he was going to do something weird and perverted to you."

He smirked when a blush crept up her cheeks. She looked toward the window. "Nothing is a secret here, is it?"

"Not from me. Although it's usually my mother who no one can hide anything from. You'll want to remember that if you plan to sneak into the library again."

Her eyes tightened at the corners as they whipped back to glare at him. "I said I wouldn't do it again."

"Yes, you did, but I don't believe you."

She looked insulted, and he laughed as he settled back in the chair. "Tell me, can you read?"

Panic flooded her eyes though she tried to conceal it. "Thralls aren't taught to read."

He admired the careful way she phrased her answer and his suspicions were all but confirmed. "Did you practice that line?"

She kept her face impassive. "I'm not sure what you mean."

"I think you do. And I suspect you know how to do many things that are off-limits."

Her face remained emotionless but this time her eyes gave her away. They always gave her away.

"Few thralls would dare enter this room." He watched her facade slip as she swallowed. "Yet I found you here, curled up with a book on your lap."

Her jaw dropped in panic. "But I put it back on the table before I laid my head down."

There was no book on her lap, but he noticed the book on the table beside her. His smile widened and her shock turned into a scowl when she saw his smirk.

"That was unfair," she said under her breath, resignation in her voice.

"You're not in trouble, Ellie, but I would like the truth. Do you know how to read?"

Her hesitation was brief. "Yes."

"Who taught you?"

Another pause. "My father."

"He sounds as rebellious as you are. He's one of Matthais' Elite Guards, right?"

"Yes. But please don't report him, Sir. Er, I mean, Aden. I'm begging you. My dad knew he wasn't supposed to teach me, but he said—"

She stopped mid-sentence, panic glistening in her eyes. It was obvious she thought she was saying too much so he let it go.

"How well do you read?"

"Not very."

"Would you like to improve your reading skills? I'm sure my mother would help you."

"Oh, that's alright. Why would I need to read?"

"Do you enjoy it?"

"Yes."

"Then that's a reason." He glanced at the shelves behind her before meeting her eyes again. "We have a lot of books here that you'd probably find interesting.

Although many would be off limits to you." A short laugh escaped him at her look. "Have I shocked you into silence?"

"I think so."

Her troubled expression made him want to reach out and smooth the lines between those bushy eyebrows.

"So, what do you have trouble with?"

She hesitated before answering slowly. "I don't know most of the words or what they mean."

"What book were you reading?"

Ellie's shoulders sagged, and she reluctantly picked up the book from the table, handing it to him. Aden yanked his hand back as her fingers brushed his, the contact leaving a lingering tingle on his skin.

A deep laugh escaped his lips. "Well, you don't start small do you?"

She bit her lip as her eyes shone with embarrassment.

"That's an excellent book but you might want to choose one that's written in English. Dante's Inferno is in Italian."

"I knew the words looked strange. But some of them seemed so familiar. And I understood a little of what I was reading, I think."

He'd been teaching Aly Italian when she—his stomach clenched. NO! He couldn't allow his mind to go there!

"I think maybe I heard Master Matthais speaking it."

Yeah, that had to be it.

"Well, you let me know if you want my mother to help you," Aden said. "She can recommend the best ones for you to start with. But I'll leave the decision up to you."

"Why?" Ellie blurted out.

"Why what?"

"Why would you do that? Thralls aren't allowed to decide." A puzzled frown formed on Ellie's face as her brows knitted together. "But since coming here I don't really understand what being a thrall means anymore."

He arched an eyebrow. "Go on."

She nibbled her bottom lip anxiously. "Thralls are treated so differently here. And I still don't know what you want from me. You're keeping me in your pet room but before you left you didn't drink from me or use me. Mistress Sophie had me help her in the greenhouse but other than that I had no chores."

He bristled at her words. "And this bothers you? Kindness bothers you? You've barely recovered from your injuries. Would you rather we treat you like Matthais? As nothing more than my servant?"

"But isn't that what I am? I don't know what you plan to do with me. My imagination is running wild and the waiting is nerve-wracking."

What the fuck did she want from him? Aden pushed to his feet.

"When I make my decision, I will tell you what I expect from you. But you will sleep where I tell you to and for now, you'll remain in my concubine suite."

How dare she complain he wasn't mistreating her? And why the fuck couldn't he keep his emotions in check when dealing with her?

"Clearly you're recovered so you can rest one more day but then you will report to Sophie tomorrow night. Until I decide your future, you'll assist her in whatever way she needs."

He took a few steps toward the door, but something compelled him to turn back to her.

"I'll tell her I've given you permission to come in here when you have free time, but you'll only read the books she permits you to read. Is that understood?"

"Yes, Sir."

"Ellie, what is my name?"

She looked up, confusion swirling in her emerald eyes.

"What is my name?" He asked again, his impatience clear in his tone.

"Aden," she said.

"I won't tell you again to call me Aden when we're alone."

He spun on his heel, needing to get away from her.

"I won't forget, Aden."

Ellie's voice halted him in his tracks, tempting him to turn back. He didn't want to leave her. But the overwhelming scent of her was making it hard for him to resist the yearning to kiss her. He fled without another word.

Ellie

For the first time in her life, Ellie woke up excited. She was going to the library to find a book in English. Aden's unexpected permission to let her read still seemed unreal to her, but she'd decided not to question it.

The more she thought about it, the more she wondered why she'd been so furious with him. He didn't owe her an explanation. He owned her. She had to remember her place.

Aden assured her he wouldn't hurt her, but he never said he wouldn't take her as a pet. She hoped he wouldn't, but considering his reputation, it was only a matter of time. She needed to prepare herself for when it happened, but she would be grateful for how things were right now.

And maybe, just maybe, life might be different here.

She showered and dressed before heading to the kitchen for breakfast. To her surprise, several of the tables were full of thralls, including Mandi, Janessa, and Iris. What were they doing in this kitchen?

She stepped over to Finn, who was washing dishes. She grabbed an apple from the bowl on the counter.

"Hey, Finn."

"Hi, new girl." His smile was always genuine when he saw her.

"What's going on?"

"A pipe on the lower level burst, so everyone is using this kitchen tonight."

"Oh." She peeked into the pot on the stove. "Something smells good."

"Chili."

"Yum." Ellie bit into her apple as Mandi, Janessa, and Iris approached.

"Hi, Ellie," Mandi greeted.

Ellie gave her a hesitant smile in return.

"Did you hear what happened?"

Ellie swallowed. "What do you mean?"

Iris leaned forward. "Master Aurick and Master Aden got into a huge fight last night."

"They did?"

"Yeah," Janessa jumped in. "Tina was feeding him in his office when Master Aurick came in and started throwing furniture around. It had something to do with Master Aden using humans as bait."

"Bait for what?" Ellie's stomach sank with dread.

"Well, Chelsea overheard Master Aden talking before he left about some rogue vampires," Janessa said. "And Tina said it was something like five hundred humans."

Ellie's chest tightened, and her breath caught in her throat. She dropped the apple on the counter.

"Are you okay?" Finn reached out to her, but she pulled her arm away, shaking her head.

"And I heard Mistress Sophie knows," Janessa said, ignoring Ellie's reaction. "She yelled at him in her office a little while ago. She called him a monster."

"We get it, Janessa." Finn scowled at her. "You should stop gossiping about it before someone overhears you."

"What's the big deal? Everybody's talking about it." Mandi said. "You won't say anything, right?"

"Huh," Ellie said, rubbing her arms.

"You're not going to tell anyone we're talking about this, right?" Iris asked. "Thralls aren't allowed to gossip."

"No, I won't say anything."

"You better not," Janessa spat. "No one around here likes you. If you snitch, everyone will hate you more."

Ellie blinked, startled by her outburst.

"Don't be such a bitch," Finn said as Mandi smacked her arm.

"Yeah, shut up, Janessa."

"I have to go." Ellie backed away from the counter and rushed out of the kitchen.

Ellie stared out the window, stroking Vlad's fur. As if he could sense her despair, he hovered, tucking his small body into her lap and resting his paw against her thigh. She'd been in the library almost all night but couldn't think about anything except what Mandi and Janessa had said.

"Finn told me you didn't eat breakfast."

Ellie startled at Sophie's soft voice from the doorway. "Oh, Mistress Sophie, I'm sorry. I didn't see you there."

She set her book down and prepared to stand, but Aden's mother held up a hand.

"Don't get up. I wouldn't want you to disturb the king." Her eyes twinkled as she looked down at Vlad, who reached out and swiped Ellie's hand when she stopped petting him. "I thought you might be hungry since it's almost sunrise."

Mistress Sophie handed her a bowl and then sat in the chair opposite her before reaching out to stroke the cat.

"Thank you." Ellie set it on her lap. Vlad poked his head over the edge and sniffed, then settled back on his paws. "I hope it's okay that I let him come in here with me."

"Of course. He goes anywhere he wants. Although I'd keep him out of Aden's room, they don't exactly get along."

That was no surprise.

"I'm sorry you went to any trouble, ma'am." Ellie wasn't hungry, but not wanting to insult Mistress Sophie, she took a small bite.

"It was no trouble. I was heading this way. And you know what? I've always despised that title. When we're alone, why don't you call me Sophie?"

Ellie looked at her, unsure. Why did this family insist she call them by their first names? Was it a trick?

"Is there something I can do for you?" She asked as she put the chili aside.

"Not today, but I was happy when Aden told me you'll continue helping me now that he's back. I enjoyed our time in the greenhouse."

Although his name sent a rush of anger and sadness through her again, Ellie was grateful he was going to let her work with his mother. "Me too."

"I'd like to have you help in my office, too. Does that interest you?"

"Yes, of course," Ellie replied. "Whatever you want me to do."

Sophie crossed her legs, settling back in her chair. "Having trouble?" Her voice was kind as she motioned to the book Ellie had set aside.

Ellie nibbled on her bottom lip, nodding.

"I was surprised when Aden told me you'd been able to get in the library."

Ellie squirmed under Sophie's intense gaze as an uneasy sensation crept up her spine. "I don't know why the door opened for me."

"I have my suspicions, but it was probably just a glitch. I was also surprised when he said you can read."

That uneasy sensation increased. "Like I told him, I'm not very good."

"He said you tried to read Dante's Inferno."

"Yes. I understood some of it, I think, but that doesn't make sense."

"What book are you reading tonight?" Sophie gestured toward the book with a nod.

"I hope this one is okay." Ellie handed it to Sophie, and she chuckled.

"Aden's right. You don't start small. The Marriage of Heaven and Hell is one of Aurick's favorites."

Ellie shifted her eyes, stealing a glance at the snowfall outside, her cheeks flushing with embarrassment.

"Most of the books you'll find in here are illegal." Sophie stood and approached the bookshelf, running her fingers along the spines before selecting one. "Here, why don't you start with this one?"

"Five Great Dialogues by Plato."

"Yes," Sophie said as she sat again. "I know Keeley told you who I think you are."

Uncertainty flickered in Ellie's eyes as she nodded. She still couldn't fathom the idea that Master Aden had ever loved a human. Not after witnessing the way he treats his thralls. Or any human.

The idea that she could be the soul of his past love if such a thing were possible, and that she had loved him, a vampire, seemed even more unimaginable.

"It's okay, Ellie. Both of my children think I'm a little crazy, too. But I believe souls and soulmates exist. Plato wrote on the subject. He lived a very long time ago. In Symposium, which is one of the five dialogues, a character named Aristophanes gives a speech about soulmates and how each of us is a matching half of a human whole and is always seeking the other half."

Again, Ellie found the courage she never had in Master Matthais' house. "Why would vampires want to read about humans? They don't care about humans."

"Some do." Sophie gave her a reassuring smile. "Anyway, I thought you might like to read what he wrote. He was very intelligent, and his writing covers many subjects, not just soulmates."

"Thank you," Ellie said, her throat tight with emotion.

"Aden said you can read most words but don't always know what they mean. Is that right?"

"Yes."

"Have you ever used a tablet?"

Ellie stilled, debating whether to be truthful. "Yes, a little, ma'am. I mean, Mistress Sophie." She cringed. "I mean, Sophie."

"It will get easier." Sophie patted Ellie's knee. "So you've used one?"

She nodded. "My dad would let me use his when he taught me to read."

Sophie moved back to the bookcase. She brushed her hand over a glass surface in front of a shelf. As the books slid to the side, a sleek tablet emerged from a hidden compartment. She carried it over to Ellie.

"Here, use this then. It will be simpler than dealing with the heavy books we have around here." She swiped her finger across the screen, and a hologram popped up. "Here's the Five Dialogues. You can read it on the hologram or the screen. The books on this tablet are all ones you can read. They're listed alphabetically by the author's last name." She swiped over a few more screens, and another book appeared. "This is a dictionary. You can look up any word you don't know, and it will tell you what it means."

"Really?" Ellie's eyes lit up.

"Here," Sophie handed the tablet to Ellie. The hologram flickered as it reset to recognize her touch.

"Now, if you don't know a word in the definition, then you can look that one up too by swiping your finger over it."

Sophie sat down as Ellie brought up several words in quick succession. She looked over at Aden's mother, her chest tight with emotion. "Thank you."

"You're welcome." Sophie gestured around the room. "I like books I can hold in my hands, but printed books are a thing of the past. Everything is digital now, so tablets do the trick."

"I never saw an actual book up close before yesterday, but I like the tablet." Ellie smiled. "It's light."

"And more compact for you to carry. Also, you won't have to confine yourself to this room to read. I'm giving it to you. It's yours, but please keep it private. Working with me, you'll need to use one, but the other thralls don't need to know you're using it for more than just work."

"Oh, of course. I won't tell anyone. I'm at a loss for words." Overwhelmed, Ellie's chest tightened. She had never received a gift from a vampire before.

"You don't have to say anything."

"Are you sure there is nothing I can do for you?" Ellie felt compelled to ask.

"No. I just wanted to make sure you weren't forgetting to eat. It's easy to get lost in books, and suddenly the entire night is gone. It happens to me often."

"I didn't realize so much time had passed," Ellie admitted.

Sophie stood and reached over to pat Vlad again. He head-butted her hand as he purred. "I'll see you tomorrow night. I'll meet you in the courtyard at six."

"Okay. Miss— Um, Sophie. Thank you," Ellie said, over the lump in her throat.

"You're very welcome, child."

It felt as if time sped up, and before she knew it, two weeks had gone by. Ellie expected to be sent to the thralls' quarters and hoped she would since she could hardly bear to look at Aden after what he'd done. Just when she thought maybe he wasn't as cruel as all the other vampires she'd known, she was shocked back into reality. Her disgust had morphed into disillusionment and a dull ache in her chest when she thought about those poor humans.

It was almost dawn when she returned to Aden's room, followed by a trotting Vlad.

"Hi, Kane," she greeted as she approached the door.

"Hey, Ellie."

Unlike most of the half-breeds she knew in Master Matthais' house, Kane was always nice to her. Although handsome, he was fierce-looking, with scruffy facial hair, sharp features, and a jagged scar intersecting one eyebrow. But there was a gentle kindness behind his eyes that made her feel at ease around him.

He motioned to her tablet. "What are you reading today?"

"Cloud Atlas."

"Do you like it?"

"Yes. Mistress Sophie recommended it."

"I bet she did."

His smirk reminded her of Aden's, and just like that, her good mood was gone. She reached down and swept Vlad into her arms. "Well, goodnight, Kane."

"Night, Ellie."

She found Aden sitting on his sofa, reading. Her stomach twisted and her chest tightened at the sight of him, leaving her feeling uneasy. She felt his eyes following her as she passed, and a shiver ran through her body.

"Hello, Ellie," he said when she was almost to her door.

She stopped and looked at him. "I'm sorry to interrupt you. I didn't think you'd be back this early."

His eyes met hers, and he looked like he had something to say, but his face contorted with a hint of hesitation as he furrowed his brows. She turned away.

"I'll get out of your way, Sir."

"Okay, that's it," he snapped, his voice filled with frustration, as he abruptly stood. "I told you to call me Aden when it is just us." His irritation was palpable as he circled the couch. "Did I say or do something to upset you?"

"No, Sir," she said as she clutched Vlad and the tablet against her chest. "I mean, Aden."

"Then why do you look at me like I kicked that mangy ball of fur in your arms?"

She didn't answer, but her grip on the cat tightened, causing him to hiss in protest.

"Ellie." Aden's tone was low, like a warning.

She set Vlad down on the floor, and he scurried toward her room, sitting by the door, licking his paw.

"Are you sure you don't want me to move in with the thralls? That way, I won't be in your way anymore."

She had asked him several times in the last two weeks, and, as he'd done each time, he exploded in a rage. "If I wanted you gone, you would be. I forbid you from ever asking me that question again."

His bellow made her flinch. It was an automatic response that she couldn't help, although it didn't happen as much as before. The familiar apology caught in her throat, knowing that it often made him as angry. Aden's chest heaved as he locked eyes with her, challenging her to defy him.

"Fine, I'll never ask again. May I go to my room now?"

"Not until you tell me what your problem is." When she said nothing, he exhaled in frustration. "When I give you permission to speak freely, I would suggest you take advantage of the opportunity."

Unable to stop herself, Ellie's anger burst out of her. "I think you're a monster for what you did to those humans."

Aden did a double take. "What? What humans?"

"The ones you used as bait."

His face grew even paler than normal. "How do you know about that?"

"I just do."

"Who told you?" He stepped closer to her and snarled, his eyes blazing. She shook her head, standing her ground as a bead of sweat trickled a slow path down her back. The anger on Aden's face morphed into shock. "You're refusing to tell me?"

"Yes."

"Who are you protecting?"

"No one."

"So you refuse, even at the expense of my wrath?"

"I'll accept whatever punishment you want to give me," she said, hoping he wouldn't whip her.

He looked away from her as the muscles in his jaw twitched. Irritation and annoyance flashed over his face. Ellie thought she might have seen hurt too. She couldn't be sure, but the sight of it made her heart ache a little, despite how disappointed and angry she was with him.

"You have absolutely no clue about what you think you heard. Go to your room, Ellie."

She hesitated for a second before turning around and walking through her door. As the door closed behind her, she heard the sound of his snarl and what she suspected was the table being kicked over.

Aden

"Did you tell Ellie about Abya Yala?"

Aden walked into his parent's suite without warning. They sat on the sofa, Sophie nestled against Aurick's side as she drank from him. Aden was so furious that he didn't feel any remorse for interrupting them.

Sophie pulled her lips away from Aurick's neck, her gaze shifting to Aden, her eyes fluttering as they cleared.

"Aden, what are you talking about? And why didn't you announce yourself?"

"I asked you a question. Which one of you said something to her?"

Aurick growled, shaking his head as he recovered from Sophie's feeding. "Watch it, Aden."

She turned to face him. "Your father doesn't talk to Ellie. Also, why would I ever tell her what you did? I'd like her to fall in love with you someday, and her knowledge of what you're capable of could very well derail any chance of that."

Aden blinked at her harsh tone, filing away her words about Ellie falling in love with him for future deliberation. "Are you still mad at me about that?"

"Yes, but I wouldn't tell Ellie about it. Why do you think she knows?"

"Because she told me she did. She called me a monster."

"She didn't?" Sophie asked with more amusement than Aden believed was appropriate.

"You don't have to find that so humorous."

"Did you ask her where she heard it?" Aurick asked, joining the conversation.

"Yes, and she refused to tell me." Aden let out a bitter laugh as he paced in front of the sofa. "Where the fuck did she get the courage?"

"I believe Ellie is more courageous than any of us are aware," Aurick said.

"You didn't threaten to punish her, did you?" Sophie asked.

Aden came to a halt and shifted his gaze to his parents. "No, but what does that have to do with anything?"

"I'm just curious."

"I can't figure out how she found out."

His father stood and walked to the bar. "There was a thrall in your office when we argued. It likely got around that way."

"Why would she protect another thrall?" Aden asked.

"She was probably afraid of how you would punish them," Sophie said, offering her wrist to Aurick when he returned to the sofa. He bit her, and she held it over his glass, letting several drops of her blood fall into the amber liquid.

"So she would rather be punished herself?"

"I thought you said you didn't threaten to punish her?"

"I didn't, but she offered to take whatever punishment I deemed appropriate. Why are you smiling?"

"No reason," Sophie said with a twitch of her lips.

Aden stopped pacing and sat. He and his parents had settled into an uncomfortable truce after the events in Abya Yala. That was the modus operandi for them whenever Aden went off the rails.

"Every decision I make these days seems to come back and bite me in the ass."

"Aden, how can you not see how wrong it was?" Sophie's eyes implored him.

"Are we going to have this argument again?"

"Arguing with you is futile if you don't see the cruelty of your actions."

Deep down, he knew she was right. He'd known it when he used the humans as bait, but it had taken too long to lure the rogues out of the caves, and his only focus was getting back home. He didn't care what it took. But he would never share that knowledge with anyone. Even he recognized that his actions that day probably made him more of a monster than they already thought he was.

"We're at an impasse, Sophie," Aden said. "How about, instead, you give me some advice on how I can persuade her to get over it?"

"It won't be that easy," Sophie said with a frown.

"So, what do I do?"

"What every man in history who pisses off his mate does?" Aurick said as he gave Aden a long, knowing look. "Grovel."

Aden exited his closet, shrugging into his shirt, to find the room set to rights. Aside from the lingering scent of blood and sex that filled the air, there was no evidence that he had just finished breakfast. Following his fight with Ellie, he returned to fucking and feeding from his thralls but only did it when she was with his mother.

Aden had rejected Aurick's suggestion that he grovel for Ellie's forgiveness. That was exactly what he did not need to do. Groveling wasn't in his nature.

Why should he grovel? She had no right to judge him, not when she didn't know the circumstances of what happened. He didn't need to justify himself to her.

And if he kept telling himself that, maybe he'd believe it.

Over the next several weeks, Aden spent more time away from the city than in it. He left several times, traveling to Terra Australis to conduct drills with Banjora's soldiers and meeting up with Andrei in Afara to oversee the training of a new contingent of generals in Rashidi's military.

He had just arrived home after being away for five days and was having dinner when he heard Ellie's voice through the haze of his feeding.

"Hi Kane," she greeted.

"Ellie." Aden didn't need to see Kane to know he was giving Ellie his most charming smile.

"Is he here?"

He couldn't miss her hesitant tone.

"Yes."

"Is it okay to go in?"

"Yeah, it should be."

"Well, goodnight, Kane."

"Night, Ellie."

Her footsteps echoed down the hallway. Aden hadn't seen her since their fight. Not in person. He'd checked on her via hologram, but it wasn't the same. And her absence left him feeling bereft.

After almost three weeks of fucking and feeding from his thralls again, Aden changed his mind. It had lost its luster for him. Something he never thought would happen.

He opened his eyes as she tiptoed by the sofa, trying to avoid drawing attention to herself. He released the girl he was drinking from. She crawled away, and Chelsea moved closer. He leaned back, and his gaze followed Ellie. She stilled and turned toward him.

"I'm sorry for interrupting, Sir."

He bit back the urge to snap at her about not using his name, but the sight of his feeders stopped him. He wanted to talk to her, but what was there to say?

Her eyes still held a lingering disappointment as she glanced at him, her gaze drifting to the line of thralls kneeling before him.

"Please excuse me." Her voice was barely a whisper as she hurried into her room.

Aden growled under his breath as Ellie disappeared behind her door.

"Get out." He'd lost his appetite. The thralls stood and scurried out, all except for Chelsea.

"I said fucking go," he snapped. After an initial look of surprise, she rose and followed the other girls out.

He stomped into his bathroom. With its dark green and white tiles accented with brown, the room had a forest-like winter atmosphere. The water in the shower turned on, set to his desired temperature, and the room filled with steam.

He stripped out of his clothes and stepped into the glass enclosure as the spray hit him from every angle, but even the rhythmic beating against his skin failed to soothe his frustration. Maybe he was losing his mind. There were some pretty crazy vampires in the world, but could a sane one actually go insane?

He couldn't get a grasp on Ellie or her ever-changing moods and attitude toward him. And people accused him of being temperamental. He was at a loss for what to do to help her get over her anger. She could hold a fucking grudge better than his mother.

Aden dropped his head with a sigh, the warmth of the water seeping into his bones. He was still fucking hungry. He drank from his thralls' necks now, and sometimes from their wrists, which he discovered wasn't so bad once he got used to it. But no matter how much he consumed, he was never satisfied. He was starting to think that only Ellie's blood would assuage his relentless desire.

He had already decided that taking her as a pet wouldn't work. Not if there was a chance of her developing feelings for him. The idea obviously appalled her, but if he could just get her in his bed, there's no way she'd be able to resist. How could she deny their growing connection when he was inside her, showing her how he felt about her?

Aden groaned as his groin tightened with need.

Yes! It was the only way. She wouldn't come to him on her own. She might be nervous at first, but she'd give in to it. And it was his decision, not hers.

He'd be gentle. He was capable of it. But he always thought that side of him had died along with Aly. He had lost his desire to be gentle until Ellie came into his life.

He could do this. This would work. It had to. He'd waited long enough, and his patience was at its end.

With his mind made up, Aden exited the shower. After drying off and slipping into a pair of black jeans and a T-shirt, he approached Ellie's door. He heard the rustling of fabric; the door sliding open as she changed into her pajamas. Her shirt was halfway over her head, exposing the faded scars on her back, haunting reminders of the abuse she suffered at Matthais' hands. They weren't as bad as he expected, but fury still consumed Aden at the sight. A low, menacing growl rumbled up from his chest, causing her to startle and whip around to face him.

"Aden." She gasped, clutching her top in front of her, her skin flushing in embarrassment. "What are you doing?"

Planning the various ways he was going to kill Matthais.

"I want to talk to you."

"Okay." Her eyes searched his face. "Can I put my clothes back on first?"

"Yes. Come into my room when you're dressed."

He stepped back, returning to his room. Ellie's door shut behind him, and he let out a breath he wasn't aware he'd been holding. He was still standing in the same spot when her door opened a few seconds later. She walked around him, still appearing embarrassed, although he didn't know why. He'd already seen her bare upper body once. And he was about to see it again. Every inch this time.

"Sit," he said, his voice harsher than he intended.

Ellie sat, looking up at him, her luminous green eyes unable to hide her confusion and hesitancy. Even when she tried, her eyes could hide nothing from him. His chest tightened. All he wanted was for those eyes to shine with happiness and love for him, yet he was losing hope it would ever happen.

"I've made a decision about your living arrangements. You're going to remain with me."

The column of her throat rippled as she swallowed. "Are you taking me as a pet now?"

"Yes." He glimpsed the brief flash of horror and then resignation in her eyes as they dulled. Seeing the light in them fade struck him like a blow.

In an instant, he wanted to take it back because her agonizing surrender made him die a little inside. He said yes because his craving for both her body and blood consumed him. But what he really wanted to say was that he'd give her the world and worship the ground she walked on if she'd let him.

Ellie stood, her body swaying as she took a deep, shuddering breath. She glanced downward before reaching up to unbutton her shirt. A flicker of excitement coursed through him as she released each button, revealing more of her smooth skin to his gaze.

The soft swell of her breasts captivated him, and his mind raced with fantasies of sliding his tongue between them and sinking his fangs into her silken flesh. His eyes followed her fingers as the fabric parted. She shrugged out of it, letting it fall to the floor before reaching up for the front clasp of her bra. He clenched his teeth, trying to suppress a groan as anticipation surged through his body. But it was the sight of her trembling fingers fighting with the hook that sent a shower of ice through his veins, gutting him.

"Stop!" His command was an abrupt, harsh sound in the otherwise silent room.

Ellie's hands stilled. With a surprised blink, she lifted her gaze to meet his.

"Put on your shirt."

She couldn't hide the relief that flooded her body. It was visceral and obvious as her shoulders sagged, and it felt like a kick to his gut. What the fuck was he doing? Forcing her wouldn't make her realize she had feelings for him. It would only make her hate him more.

Confusion stirred behind her eyes, and it robbed him of his breath. But he held firm in his resolve to keep her with him because he couldn't bear the thought of letting her go.

"I'm not taking you as a pet, but you will remain here with me. You don't have to like it, but this is my decision. Now go back to your room."

"Are you sure?" Her eyes scanned his face. Her hands hadn't moved, but the trembling had stopped.

"I said go, Ellie," he barked, shoving his clenched fists in his pockets. "Goodnight."

To his surprise, she frowned. She grabbed her shirt and, clutching it against her chest, did as he instructed.

"Goodnight, Aden."

Ellie

Ellie sat at the console table in the corner of Mistress Keeley's living room. After she fixed a glitch in Sophie's office, Aden's mother asked her to look at Keeley's for the same issue.

With her newfound talent for gardening, Ellie was also assigned to keep the many vases around the compound filled with fresh flowers. It granted her access to the Westcott's private rooms, a privilege reserved for only their most trusted thralls.

Since she was here, she tackled both tasks. She was reading through the code before replacing the living room vases when Aden's sister arrived.

"Hi, Ellie."

"Hi, Mistress Keeley." Ellie shot her a quick smile, then turned back to the table.

Mistress Keeley tossed her jacket over the arm of the sofa and sat down with a flourish. Her suite had a welcoming feel, and her design included mostly sleek, contemporary geometric shapes made of wood, metal, and glass. At first glance, the furniture looked anything but comfortable, but surprisingly, it was in both texture and design.

Her color scheme was bolder than either Aden's or Sophie's, but it was visually and sensually appealing. The colors were a combination of black and white, but her obvious love of purple had the vivid color popping up everywhere throughout the space. The fabrics, rugs, accent pieces, and sculptures in varying shades added warmth and coziness, making the room feel inviting.

Metal-framed mirrors and abstract artwork decorated the walls, creating a sophisticated backdrop that complemented her personality. Although Ellie didn't know her well, it was clear that Mistress Keeley exuded sophistication.

"I think I've got this figured out, so I should be done in a few minutes."

"No hurry." Mistress Keeley toed off her shoes and lifted her feet onto the sofa beside her. "So, how are you?"

Ellie looked up, surprised. Vampires never asked thralls such questions. But the Westcotts weren't like other vampires.

"I'm fine. Thank you." Ellie resumed her work, typing in an alternate code before testing the screen again. "That did it."

Ellie closed the screens and stood. She walked over to the cart and grabbed a vase, swapping it out with the one on the table beside the sofa. She could feel Mistress Keeley's eyes following her around the room.

"Are you enjoying working with my mother?" she asked.

Ellie stopped and gave Mistress Keeley her full attention. "Yes. Very much. Thank you for asking."

"You don't have to thank me for everything, Ellie."

"I'm sorry."

"You don't need to apologize either."

"Yes, ma'am." Ellie wasn't used to being casual around vampires, so she felt uneasy and awkward around the Westcotts, even though she felt somewhat comfortable around Sophie. She moved to the table beneath a giant fish tank in the wall, brimming with vibrant, striped purple fish.

"How are you and Aden getting along?" Mistress Keeley asked. "He isn't being a jerk because you called him on his bullshit, is he?"

Ellie kept her face impassive, not sure how to answer or why she was asking. "No, Aden treats me fine."

That wasn't true, but it wasn't a lie either. He didn't mistreat her, but since she was still his thrall, he would always see her as less.

"Ha!" Mistress Keeley choked out a short laugh. "We're talking about my brother, right?"

Ellie couldn't stop her own chuckle from escaping before she sobered again. She liked Mistress Keeley. The woman had no hesitation about voicing her thoughts, and Ellie respected and envied that about her.

"You know, Ellie, if you ever want to talk to someone, about anything, about my brother, his mood swings, or about the different ways to kill him in his sleep," Mistress Keeley joked, and Ellie couldn't stop her lips from curving upward again. "Or if you have questions about life here, please don't be afraid to ask."

Ellie wondered if Mistress Keeley was aware of Aden's decision to take her as a pet before changing his mind. She would love to ask someone about his unpredictable moods.

"I work a lot right now, but in a couple of months, I'll be around more." Mistress Keeley kept trying to engage her in conversation. "So I hope we can get to know each other better."

"That's very kind, ma'am," Ellie said, surprised but grateful for her words, as she placed the final vase on the coffee table. Mistress Keeley was just as nice as Sophie, and Ellie felt a sudden, unexpected surge of warm affection for the woman. "I'm finished. I'll get out of your way now."

"Don't. Sit with me for a little bit." Keeley motioned to the chair beside the sofa.

Ellie hesitated for a moment but then obeyed.

"It's nice talking to someone who isn't a freaking scientist. They don't know how to communicate like normal people."

Ellie knew from her reading that a scientist was someone who sought knowledge through methodical research and examination. She bit her lip, filled with hesitation but found the courage to voice the question on her mind.

"Why do you always talk to scientists?"

"I run BloodStone. You know that, right?"

"No." Ellie shook her head. No wonder the woman worked all the time. Wait a minute, the Westcotts owned BloodStone?

Almost as if reading her mind, Mistress Keeley said, "My father created it and turned the company over to me a hundred years ago. I forget sometimes you weren't raised here."

"You don't enjoy talking with them?" Ellie felt a little more at ease.

Keeley grabbed a pillow and tucked it against her chest. "I do. I love it and what we do at BloodStone—all the scientific advances we're making. And, technically, I'm a scientist, too. But I know how to carry on a normal conversation. So does Hannah, but she's probably the only other one."

"I don't know who Hannah is."

"You'll meet her eventually. She's my mom's best friend and the head scientist at BloodStone. She's been behind all the groundbreaking scientific advances in the last five hundred years. BloodStone was my dad's idea, but Hannah is the true brain behind it. Don't tell him I said that, though. His nose gets all out of joint."

"Of course." She had never spoken to Master Aurick since the day Aden bit her.

"So, my mom tells me you can read."

Ellie wiped her hands on her pants before glancing away.

"It's okay, Ellie." Mistress Keeley's tone was gentle. "Our family talks about everything, but don't worry about that because we have a tight circle of trust. You never have to be afraid of anything we know about you because no one else ever will."

Ellie was touched by Mistress Keeley's words, but the lasting impact of a lifetime of living in silence and fear still clung to her.

Her gaze shifted towards a violin resting on a stand in the corner. Its curves and polished finish resembled many of the sculptures displayed around the room. Mistress Keeley followed her gaze.

"Have you ever heard a violin?"

"No, ma'am." Ellie shifted in her seat, uneasy, but remembered Mistress Keeley's advice about not being afraid to speak up. "One book your mom recommended was about a woman who dedicated herself to the violin but lost her love because of it. It made me curious about instruments, so I looked them all up in the encyclopedia."

"My mom is a romance junkie, although I admit I like them, too."

"Do you play?" Ellie asked.

"Yes. My parents insisted both Aden and I learn a musical instrument when we were kids. I liked the violin because of its calming, resonant tones."

"What did Aden learn?"

"The drums." Mistress Keeley snorted as she tossed her pillow aside. "He liked how loud and annoying they can be. It drove my parents crazy. We're quite the opposite, he and I."

Vlad came running into the room, meowing, and leaped onto Ellie's lap. Surprised, Ellie scooped him up and gave him a once-over. "How did you get in here?"

"Every door in this compound is programmed to open for him," Keeley said. "The way my mom treats him, you'd think he's a person, but it's always been that way with her Vlads."

Vlad leaped down and then up onto Mistress Keeley's lap. She chuckled and caressed his ears as he nestled beside her. The sight brought a smile to Ellie's face. She sat back, getting more relaxed by the minute.

"Does Aden still play the drums?" Ellie asked, her curiosity piqued by the new information.

"No. He gave it up as soon as they let him. He would play them as loud and obnoxious as he could just to piss them off."

Why didn't that surprise her?

"I could play the violin for you sometime," Mistress Keeley offered.

"I'd like that. I wondered how it sounds."

"My mom said you're a pro at typing on the tablet and computer." Mistress Keeley changed the subject. "But did anyone teach you how to write?"

"No. Writing is as forbidden as reading."

"Not technically."

"Why would a thrall need to know how to write?"

Keeley leaned in and flashed a conspiratorial grin. "I like you. You ask loaded questions."

"Loaded?"

"Yes. That means you pretend to be naïve when asking a question, even though you already know the answer. But you're not ignorant. I think you're quite brilliant."

Ellie hesitated. "I'm not trying to deceive you, but where I come from, smart thralls disappear without explanation."

"Intelligence isn't something to be afraid of. And neither is writing." Mistress Keeley dropped her feet to the floor and stood. "Come over here." She motioned Ellie over to another desk in the corner. "Now that you've learned to read, I think it's time you learned to write."

"Oh, Mistress Keeley, that's alright. I'm sure you have more important things to do." But Ellie couldn't resist following her across the room.

"I don't. I'd like to help you if you'd like that too." She was giving Ellie the choice.

Ellie paused, almost afraid to accept, and then she smiled. "I'd like that very much."

"Good," Mistress Keeley nodded and put her hand on Ellie's arm. "And why don't you call me Keeley when it's just us?"

Ellie couldn't keep the smile off her face as she approached the door to Aden's room after her writing lesson with Keeley. She'd written her name and was so excited that even the thought of returning to Aden's rooms couldn't dampen her mood.

When he told her he was going to take her as a pet, then quickly changed his mind, it left her feeling even more confused and uncertain. She was relieved by his change of heart, but he looked so broken standing there in front of her that night. Ellie struggled to reconcile that image of him with the volatile vampire she had become used to.

She'd started speaking to him again as her fear, anger, and disappointment had dissipated. She hadn't forgotten what he'd done, and nothing would ever bring those poor humans back. Holding on to her anger at him solved nothing, but part of her wondered if she could ever forgive him.

He was so confusing. His personality was erratic, and she never knew what kind of mood he would be in, which kept her on edge.

Some days, he was nice. Others he stormed around, yelling at everyone in sight, including her. She'd learned to avoid his rooms on those days and would hide out in the library with Vlad.

But he would always find her, poking his head in and asking her if she was okay. There was something endearing about it, and she couldn't help but look forward to it. She also often found him looking at her when he didn't think she was paying attention. She could feel his eyes on her and it made her uneasy.

To top it all off, she was dreaming of him again. The dreams had become more frequent, happening almost every night. A pang of longing again washed over her, wishing Carrie was here so she could have someone to talk to.

Her dreams had become more vivid, almost like they were memories. That was impossible. But each time she woke, her chest ached with loneliness, and she wished she could go back to sleep to be with Aden again.

The Aden in her dreams was a different vampire, a different man. He was easy-going, funny, and tender. He made her smile, laugh, and, sometimes, cry. Sometimes he was angry and loud, the way he was in real life. But she didn't fear or dislike that side of him in her dreams.

Except when his eyes turned red. Those times, Ellie would wake up sweating, her cheeks swollen and wet. Those were the times she dreaded going back to sleep, grateful for her chronic insomnia.

In those moments, Ellie wished she would never sleep again.

Aden

Aden found Ellie in her usual spot, sitting in the chair beside the fireplace with both Vlad and her tablet on her lap. She couldn't take her eyes off the late spring snow falling outside the window. With a furrowed brow, she appeared lost in thought. She had that look a lot.

It had been more than a month since he changed his mind about taking her as a pet, but the light leaving her eyes as she'd resigned herself to her fate had been his undoing. If he could go back in time and take it back, he would. But now all he could do was hope she would forgive him for being the dickhead he was.

He cleared his throat, and she looked over at him.

"Hi, Aden."

He walked across the room. "Are you planning to stay here all night again?"

Ellie set the tablet on the table and stretched. With a menacing hiss, his mother's cat made it clear it was not happy about being disturbed. Ellie stroked his fur to calm him.

"I came in here when I finished with Sophie for the night. I didn't realize the time."

He shoved his hands into his pockets because they ached to reach out for her. "You don't sleep enough. Why?"

Ellie shrugged. "Insomnia. I've always had it."

Vampires slept an average of four hours a day, but that's all they needed to rejuvenate their bodies. And now that she mentioned it, he realized Ellie slept less than that.

"Did you eat before you came in here?"

Ellie released an amused chuckle. "Are you still obsessing over my diet?"

Her response made him scowl, his brows furrowing in disapproval. "Well, did you eat?"

Her lips curved, and it caused the corners of her eyes to crinkle. "Not yet."

"Aren't you hungry?"

"Not really. I've never eaten a lot, but thank you for being concerned about my appetite," Ellie said as Vlad stretched and yawned before scratching his claws along the arm of the chair. She pulled him back onto her lap, and Aden watched her, his expression indifferent as she tapped Vlad's nose to show her disapproval.

Aden's eyes met hers as he settled into the chair opposite her, and he couldn't help but soften, completely captivated by her. She looked more beautiful to him every day.

"What are you reading now?"

"Dracula."

Aden had never been one to roll his eyes, but he fought the urge now. "My mother really has a twisted sense of humor. Did she recommend that one?"

"No. I'm at the D's."

"What does that mean?"

"I'm reading the books in alphabetical order."

Of course she was.

"What do you think of it?" He'd read it as a child and found it as ludicrous as the other vampire stories that followed it before humans knew vampires were real.

"It doesn't sound like the writer knew any actual vampires." Her lips quirked. "I didn't know you could turn into a bat."

He chose not to dignify her ridiculous words with a response. "He got a few things right, though."

"Like how vampires are immortal and feed on the blood of humans?"

"Yes, and the stake to the heart or beheading. But that would kill anyone."

Ellie shifted in her seat, and Vlad let out another hiss before settling down and closing his eyes.

"He knew about the sun, too," Ellie said.

"Well, his vampires only lose their supernatural powers in the sun. It doesn't kill them. That came later, as did many other vampire tropes."

"I don't know what that word means."

"It's a stereotype."

The confusion didn't leave her face.

"A cliché?" He tried, and she looked like she might understand. A flicker of recognition crossed her face, her eyes narrowing as she peered at him through her thick lashes.

"Okay, for example, eventually, writers depicted vampires as bursting into flames when exposed to sunlight. Once that idea caught on, everyone imagined their fictional vampires erupting into flames. That's not true. Dying in the sun is a slow and agonizing process."

"I saw it once." Ellie's eyes lost focus as if she were recalling a disturbing scene. "Master Matthais punished a vampire for treason. He was forced to sit on a platform in the city center. The dome was left open all day, and after about five or six hours, the vampire's body burned from the inside out and was just a pile of ash."

"He let you watch that?"

"He made all of us watch, so we knew not even vampires were safe from his wrath." Ellie paused, the silence settling around them like a heavy blanket, before she changed the subject. "Is it weird that your mother names all her cats, Vlad? After Dracula, I mean?"

"No," Aden said, releasing a dark chuckle. "Most people are unaware of how twisted her sense of humor is. She got her first Vlad the year she met Aurick. Sophie is nice and sweet and calm, but she's got a dark side. She's mellowed with age, but from the stories Aurick tells, she was quite a little hellion when she was younger."

Ellie looked intrigued, but Aden didn't elaborate. His mother's past was hers to tell. Ellie shifted to gaze out the window, watching the snow again.

Aden paused before breaking the silence. "Do you like the snow?"

"I used to."

Getting her to open up to him was like fucking pulling teeth.

"Used to?"

Ellie's gaze found Aden's again. "I haven't been in the snow in a long time. Not since before my dad and I were taken from our village. Master Matthais never opened the dome when it snowed. I only remember it open a handful of times."

"We keep the dome closed when it snows, too."

Ellie sighed, glancing back out the window. "There's something so peaceful about it."

The longing in her voice spurred Aden into action, and he shot to his feet. "Come with me."

Ellie lifted Vlad from her lap, setting him on the floor as she stood. He gave one last threatening hiss and ran off.

"Did I say something wrong?"

"No. Just come with me."

Aden walked out of the library, and Ellie hurried behind him. He walked down the long hallway and through the courtyard to his wing.

She kept up with him, but he slowed his pace so she didn't have to run. Aden approached his door, and it opened.

He walked into his closet and grabbed his coat, pulling it on before walking out to find Ellie standing in the middle of his room with a baffled expression.

"Do you have a heavy coat?"

"No."

"Fuck! Why don't you have one?"

"I never leave the compound. Why would I need one?"

"Wardrobe," Aden barked, and a hologram appeared, a young girl's face in the center.

"Yes, Master Aden. How can I help you?"

"I want a women's wool coat brought to the front entrance at once."

"What size, Sir?"

"I have no idea," Aden snapped as he grabbed his boots. "What size are you?"

"Small," Ellie replied, unfazed by his tone.

"This is for Miss Ellie?" the thrall asked.

"Yes."

"I have all of Miss Ellie's sizes, Sir. I will bring boots, gloves, and a wool hat, too."

"Bring a scarf as well. We'll be there in five minutes."

"Yes, Sir."

Aden swiped the hologram closed.

"Aden, what's going on?"

"Go change into something warmer."

Ellie released a long breath and walked into her room as Aden called Kane.

"Have transport bring my car around to the front entrance at street level."

"You got it," Kane replied with a puzzled look.

"And put on two pairs of socks," Aden called to Ellie through the door as he dropped into the chair and changed into his boots.

Aden walked over to Ellie's door, and it opened as she was walking out. "What's taking you so fucking long?"

He scowled when she emerged, wearing the same outfit she had on before entering.

"I thought I told you to change."

"This is my uniform. It's all I have to wear." She looked down at herself, then back up to meet his eyes. "I put on extra socks."

"Fucking hell." He spun around and walked toward the closet. Why was she still wearing that ugly fucking uniform? He would speak to his mother about letting her wear regular clothes.

"Come over here." He rummaged through one of his drawers and found a green wool sweater. He shoved it at her. "Put this on."

Ellie tugged it over her head and pulled her hair out of the collar. Her sweet honeysuckle and jasmine scent wafted outward, and Aden reveled in it.

Ellie looked up at him, eyes wide, though still swirling with uncertainty. His sweater engulfed her slight frame, making her seem smaller, but the color made her eyes stand out even more. He turned and walked away before he could get distracted by how good she looked in it.

"Follow me."

He heard Ellie sigh, but she followed without a word.

Aden attempted to shorten his strides so Ellie could keep up, but he was bursting with excitement. He did his best to hide it, barking commands in his usual way, but he was impatient. There was only a little under an hour before sunrise, and if they didn't get out of the city soon, they would lose the opportunity. Why hadn't they just taken a warp port to the city gates and grabbed a car from there?

He could feel Ellie hurrying behind him, her shorter legs only able to propel her so far with each step. When they entered the foyer, the female thrall stood by the front door, holding the items for Ellie. Before Aden could bark yet another command, Ellie sat on a padded bench beside the door and changed into her boots.

"Will that be all, Master Aden?" the young girl asked, holding the coat out to Ellie.

"Yes. Go away."

Ellie buttoned her coat, wrapped the scarf around her neck, and slipped her gloves on her hands. She tucked her hat into her pocket and raised her eyes to meet Aden's.

"Why aren't you putting on your hat?"

"I don't like hats."

She was so contrary sometimes that it made him grind his teeth. But rather than argue, he led her out the door.

"Are you warm enough?"

"I think I'm a little overdressed. It's not that cold out here."

"It'll be colder where we're going."

Kane stood beside the open door of Aden's SUV. There were two identical vehicles behind it.

Ellie climbed into the passenger seat as Aden walked around and got in the driver's seat. He knew his actions confused her, but she sat back and remained silent. One of the things he liked about her was her quiet nature. It drove him insane when people chattered mindlessly.

"Manual override," Aden said and put his hands on the steering wheel. The wheels remained on the ground. He wanted to drive tonight. He steered the car out of the circular driveway and through the city streets.

"Can I ask where you're taking me?"

He heard a hint of excitement in her tone now, rather than confusion.

"You'll see in a few minutes."

Aden steered the SUV down the main street toward the city's exit. Unlike most of the domed cities around the world, which had only one gate in and out, Aurick insisted all the cities in their region have the entrance on one end and the exit on the other. He believed two points of egress were more secure than one, and Aden agreed.

Not that it would ever happen under Aden's watch, but should the city ever be invaded or have a rebellion within, having more than one way out would be important.

The Westcott's compound was closer to the city exit, so it only took Aden a few minutes to reach the gate. Beside him, Ellie looked around, taking in the sights of the city she now called home, but had never been outside the compound to see.

Aden stopped the car next to two guards at the gate.

"Good evening, Master Aden."

Aden pointed to Kane's SUV behind him. "Keep those two vehicles inside and close the entrance behind me."

"Yes, Sir."

The entrance opened, the tinted steel and glass gate rising to allow Aden's car through. Ellie leaned forward, her eyes widening as she looked through the front window, mesmerized by the sight of large snowflakes falling and evaporating as soon as they touched the surface.

The cars behind them honked. Aden chuckled, pulling away from the city and into the night.

The lights from the city grew dimmer behind them. He was going to catch hell from both Kane and his father when he got back, but at the moment, Aden didn't give a shit. He wanted to be alone with Ellie, and there was no real danger out here. Not for him anyway. With sunrise approaching, they wouldn't have much time. But he had to take her out after hearing the longing in her voice as she talked about the snow.

He drove several miles outside the city, past the training field, and ventured into a peaceful, wintery landscape. The SUV's headlights cut through the darkness, illuminating a path obscured by shadows. With each passing mile, the snow became deeper until he had no choice but to activate the SUV's autopilot and let it hover above the ground. The flat expanse turned into a rolling landscape, forming a picturesque scene with tall trees stretching towards the sky.

Ellie squirmed in her seat, her growing excitement palpable as she took in the sights of the shifting scenery illuminated by the headlights. Aden remained silent, afraid words would break the spell of anticipation surrounding her. He drove through an opening between a cluster of tall pine trees, revealing a vast meadow stretching far into the distance.

The secluded sanctuary was once his refuge when he'd needed to be alone, especially after he'd lost Aly. It was where he'd proposed to her, that one perfect memory making him feel closer to her.

The meadow's isolation and tranquility had provided him with the peace he needed to grieve. Although he no longer came out here, his grief never lessened or left him. The pain lingered, sharp and agonizing, a constant reminder that refused to fade away. Until Ellie came into his life.

Ellie's heart thumped in her chest. Enclosed in the car with her like this, her scent enveloped him, making him dizzy. He had to get out of the car before it overwhelmed him, so he brought the SUV to a stop and let the tires drop into the deep snow.

Ellie turned her head, and her look of wonder was one of the most extraordinary sights he'd ever seen. A slow smile pulled across his lips.

"Go on. Get out."

Ellie grasped the handle and opened the door. Aden watched as she stepped out of the SUV, her boots sinking into the snow. It was at least a foot deep and encased her calves up to her knees, making all but the top of her boots disappear.

Aden exited the car and walked around it. His eyes locked on Ellie as she trudged a few steps through the fluffy snow, careful to keep her balance. She turned around, taking in her surroundings.

The meadow stretched out, covered in a fresh layer of glistening snow that sparkled under the moonlight. Everything was bathed in a silvery glow as shadows danced across the rolling snow drifts. The surrounding trees created an imposing border that hinted at the untamed nature of the dense forest beyond, the faint calls of nocturnal wildlife echoing from deep within the tree line, the only sounds whispering in the silence.

Ellie lifted her face to the sky, watching the falling snow. A giggle escaped her lips as it caressed her skin, and she blinked as the delicate flakes stuck to her eyelashes. Her laughter filled him with warmth, and Aden walked up beside her, watching her.

Ellie turned to him. "Oh, Aden." Her voice was barely a whisper. "It's so beautiful."

Yes, she was. Her joy was infectious, and Aden drank in the sight of her. She must have felt his gaze because she blushed, tilting her head down, and Aden swallowed back a moan as blood colored her cheeks.

"It's just like I remember." Ellie spun around and breathed deeply. "It even smells the same. How is it possible something so beautiful exists?"

"The natural world is a utopia."

The joy slipped off her face as quickly as it came, and her brows furrowed. "I don't think I'd call the world a utopia."

"Do you know what that word means?"

"Yes. I read Thomas Moore's book on my tablet, and I looked up what it meant. But your mom also told me to read Plato's Republic. He didn't call his city a utopia, but our world seems more like his vision because it stripped away everything that gives human life value and makes it worth living." A fleeting look passed between them as her eyes met his. "So maybe that's why you think the world is a utopia."

The sadness in her eyes was haunting. He couldn't blame her for her feelings, particularly about Plato, but the world was a much better place now.

"It is a utopia now, Ellie. Humans were killing the world before we took over. They were raping and pillaging the world's land and resources, all for their own greed. Nearly a million animals were on the verge of extinction. Humans didn't care what it did beyond their lifetime or to those who came after. They were selfish and only cared about their immediate gratification. Fuck the future. We'd all probably be dead by now if vampires hadn't stopped it."

With no knowledge of history, she was clueless about the events that occurred before and after the Great Vampire Wars. And humans weren't without fault. Maybe if Ellie knew the truth, she would understand.

"Humans were killing themselves, too. They covered their food with chemicals that caused incurable diseases. All for convenience. You may not like vampires, Ellie, but we don't poison you. Everything we do is to keep you healthy."

"So you can feed on us."

"It's not quite that simple."

Not that simple at all. But he couldn't deny her words, either. Vampires created a world where humans could thrive. But only for vampires' own ends. While that never bothered him before, Aden recognized what a horrific reality humans lived in.

"Were you alive then? When vampires took over, I mean."

"No. That was hundreds of years before I was born, but my parents told me, and I read about it in books."

"I'd like to read those books sometime."

It would probably be a mistake, but he agreed. "I'll have my mother add them to your tablet."

A brief spark of gratitude flickered in her eyes before she looked away, taking in the vast expanse around them as the pinch between her eyebrows smoothed out. She removed her gloves and held her hands out. Like her face, the snowflakes caressed her palm and evaporated on her skin. Aden brushed several flakes off his face.

"Why doesn't the snow melt on your skin too?"

"You're warmer than I am. My body takes on the temperature of my surroundings."

"It's colder out here than inside the city."

"I told you it would be. The dome insulates the city from extreme heat and cold. It's about twenty degrees warmer inside the city right now."

Ellie reached down and ran her fingers through the snow beside her.

"Oh, it's colder like that." Her breath was visible in the crisp air, her face brightening with delight.

"That's why you have gloves. You should put them back on. Your hat, too."

Ellie let out a weary sigh and tugged her gloves snugly onto her hands. "I know you're a vampire, but have you always been this bossy?"

"Yes."

Her lips curved in a subtle smile, and his mouth mirrored her expression. He found it impossible to tear his eyes from her.

"Are you going to put on your hat?"

She twirled in the snow again, her eyes closing as her head fell back. "No."

Aden's lips twitched, but he let it go. It wasn't worth ruining the moment, especially when she was so captivated by the sight of the snowflakes dancing in the air.

"How long are we staying out here?"

"Do you want to go back? Are you cold?"

"I'm not cold."

Aden glanced around the meadow, an idea forming in his head.

"When we were kids, my parents would take me and Keeley out here every time it snowed. We used to make snow angels."

Ellie's breath caught in her throat, and she sought his eyes again. "Snow angels?"

"Do you know what they are?"

Ellie nodded. "I used to make them with my mom."

A haunting sadness crept into her eyes, and Aden's chest tightened. What had she suffered as a child that left her with such a heavy heart? Aden wanted to hunt down and destroy everything and anyone who hurt her.

"We've got a little time left before sunrise if you want to make a few."

Ellie's cheeks, already flushed from the cold air, grew rosier as she shook her head. "No, that's okay."

"Why not?"

She brushed the snow off her jacket. "Because I'm not a kid anymore."

"Neither am I, but that doesn't stop me."

Aden took five steps away, then fell backward in the snow. He waved his arms up and down, creating a snow angel, before he stood up again and stepped out of it, careful not to disturb it. He shook his head to loosen the snow clinging to his short hair as he threw a daring glance her way.

"Your turn."

Aden

Ellie's expression said that she thought he was crazy. And maybe he was.

She had been so overjoyed when she first stepped out of the car. The way her face lit up in the moonlight took Aden's breath away. Then, with the topics of utopia and the snow angels she made with her mother, her entire demeanor had changed. He would have done anything to take that haunted look out of her eyes, including acting like an idiot and throwing himself into the snow.

"Well?" Aden grinned as he flung his arms out.

"I don't remember how to do it."

"I just showed you. Want me to show you again?"

He took three large strides further away and then flopped back into the snow. Laughter bubbled out of her chest as he flailed his arms and legs. He sat up and cast an expectant look at her.

"Okay, no more excuses. Your turn."

"But I feel foolish." Ellie crinkled her nose, a smile tugging at her lips.

"No more foolish than me," he said. "And I should warn you, calling a vampire foolish isn't a wise thing to do."

"I didn't say you were foolish. I said *I* felt foolish."

"Ellie, if you don't drop and make an angel, I'm going to toss you into the snow myself." There was no heat behind his warning, but he would do it if she didn't drop her ass in the snow.

"Fine." A spark of annoyance ignited in her eyes, but her quirking lips told a different story. "I would have thought a three-hundred-year-old vampire would be more mature."

Unrepentant, he shrugged, and Ellie shook her head in exasperation. But she followed his lead and took several strides in the other direction. Aden watched, rapt, as she took a deep breath and turned to face him. He reached up to brush the snow out of his hair again. "You might want to put that hat on now."

With a snarky arch of her brow, Ellie removed the hat from her pocket and threw it at him before she smiled and fell backward.

He heard her gentle 'oof' as she landed, and he bit back a chuckle. She moved her arms and legs back and forth, and after a minute, she pushed up on her hands. Her smile lit up her face so brightly that it could have illuminated the night sky.

"That was fun."

"Told you." Aden stood and walked over to her, watching her wiggle in the snow as she tried to stand. "What are you doing?"

"Trying not to ruin it."

"You can make another one."

"But I don't want to ruin this one." Her teeth bore into her lower lip as she concentrated on her motions. A laugh rumbled up his chest, and without a second thought, Aden held his hand out to her. "Take my hand, and I'll help you."

He'd never offered his hand to anyone other than Aly, but with Ellie, he didn't even hesitate. He pushed the surprise aside, refusing to think about it.

Ellie's eyes flicked up, surprised, and she shook her head. Aden gritted his teeth. Damn the stupid, ingrained laws about not touching vampires. Not to mention his warning to her when she first arrived.

"Ellie, I said take my hand."

Ellie reached up, and Aden wrapped his large fingers around her smaller ones, pulling her up. Despite the barrier of her gloves, the touch sent a shudder through his body. He took a step closer and looked down at her. Her hair swirled around her face, full of snow.

Without releasing her hand, he lifted his other one, brushing a few strands off her cheek, and her eyes fluttered. Her skin was like a burning flame against his fingertips, the heat spreading up his arm, causing his heart to race in his chest.

Ellie's lips opened with a soft inhale, and her tongue peeked out, licking her full lips. He wanted to kiss her so badly that it was an ache that raged through his entire body. He grasped her elbow and tugged her closer, intending to take her lips and kiss her until she was breathless and weak. But he forgot his own strength, and she lost her balance, tumbling into him.

Aden groaned under his breath when her warm body pressed against his. Ellie jerked as if she had been electrocuted, and she jumped back, losing her balance again and falling into the snow.

"Fucking hell. What's wrong with you?"

Ellie scrambled to her feet, now completely covered with snow.

"I'm so sorry, Aden. I didn't mean to fall into you."

"What have I told you about apologizing all the time? It was my fault. I tugged you too hard. Damn it, Ellie! Stop acting like a skittish kitten every time I'm near you. I told you I wouldn't hurt you. What do I have to do to convince you?"

"That's not it. You told me never to touch you. And it's illegal to touch a vampire."

Aden grasped her arms, stopping her frantic movements as she brushed the snow from her clothes. Her eyes jerked up, and her mouth formed an 'oh' of surprise as her body stiffened and their eyes locked. He tried to keep his grip gentle, but his annoyance surged through him even as he, once again, fought the urge to kiss her.

"I'm so tired of hearing you spout off laws you know nothing about. It doesn't matter what the law is, Ellie. I am the law. And I know what I told you, but you can touch me when we're alone if I give you permission. What happens in private stays private in our world. And stop cringing every time I touch you. Is my touch really that loathsome to you?"

Ellie remained silent, her eyes shifting away. Her arms trembled, and Aden sighed, releasing her. He looked toward the horizon and saw the first hints of the sunrise. The urge to scream consumed him. Everything had been going well, and he had to ruin it. Again.

"Come on, the sun's rising."

Ellie nodded and walked over to pick up the hat she'd tossed at him earlier.

Aden heard the crack of a branch first. He whipped his head to the side, his eyes scanning the darkness. Multiple low growls echoed in the distance and he reached out, grasped Ellie's arm, pushing her behind him.

"What the—" Ellie stumbled, her fingers digging into the fabric of his jacket.

"Be quiet," he snarled, backing them toward the SUV. "Get in the car."

"Aden?" Ellie said his name as she pressed her hand against his back. Aden's body reacted to her touch, and he calmed instantly.

"Get in." He yanked the door open and helped her up into the seat.

"What is it?"

He softened his tone. "I want you to put your hands over your ears, okay? Don't be afraid. You're safe."

Ellie met his eyes, and Aden could have sworn he saw complete trust in them before her lashes swept down and she reached up to cover her ears.

"Stay in the car." Aden closed the door. "Secure vehicle," he commanded, and the SUV's doors locked and metal panels rolled down to cover the glass windows.

"Kane," he barked, and the hologram with his guard's smirking face appeared.

"Snow play over already?"

"I have at least a dozen rogues about two clicks to the west."

"Fuck! This is what you get for going out on your own."

"Tell Roderick to get out here, and I want five hundred soldiers searching five hundred miles in every direction. You need to bring the fleet here and take Ellie back."

"You need to get back here."

The sun peaked over the horizon to his right.

"Just get in the car and drive. We'll handle the rogues," Kane said.

"No," Aden refused as he circled the car to make sure it was secure. "As soon as I try to drive away, they'll jump the car."

"Aden, the sun is about to rise."

The growls grew closer, the silhouettes of the rogues appearing in the distance.

"Kane, don't argue with me. Get out here and take her back to the city."

Aden heard car doors slamming in the background.

"Aden—"

"Kane, you will protect her first! Do what I say, or I'll rip your fucking heart out!"

Aden swiped the hologram away as he saw the first rogue charge him from beyond the trees.

Aden's sharp gaze swept over the scene, assessing the situation and confirming his suspicions. It wasn't just one rogue. There were a dozen.

Fuck! Of all the times he had to be right?

Why the fuck were rogues loose in his region? Again?

Under the silver moonlight, the rogues' eyes glowed with a deranged hunger and madness. Aden could smell their desperation and saw it in their emaciated forms as they rushed towards him.

Aden's muscles tightened, every thought and instinct in his body consumed by one sole purpose: protecting Ellie.

He wasn't armed. Why would he be? Carrying a weapon wasn't necessary in the Vampire Era, and no vampire in their right mind would challenge him, especially in Réimse Shíochánta. But these creatures weren't in their right minds.

Or from his region. He didn't recognize any of them.

A collection of swords and Helios, loaded with UV-infused bullets, were always in the back of all his vehicles for emergencies. But he couldn't access them now that the vehicle was secured. He'd have to rely on brute strength.

Aden worked hard to keep his body fit and in optimal physical shape. Despite vampires' inherent superhuman strength, training was still crucial to maintaining their invincibility. Aden had spent centuries transforming his body into a force of destruction that inspired fear. But a dozen rogues, no matter how weak they were, would be a challenge.

Even inside the SUV, Ellie was vulnerable, and Aden felt her fear as keenly as his own. His fear wasn't of the rogues, regardless of the number. He could take on as many as came at him if it meant keeping her safe. But what if they overwhelmed him? Although a couple of rogues wouldn't be able to penetrate the SUV's defenses, without Aden's protection, a dozen would have no trouble getting to her.

His body rippled with rage as it built within him, a fury born of his growing feelings and protective instincts for the woman behind him. How dare they threaten her? Aden bared his fangs, letting out a roar that echoed across the silent landscape.

Wanting to move the fight as far away from Ellie as possible, Aden charged toward the group of once formidable vampires, now reduced to feral, starving creatures, as they advanced across the meadow. The moonlight reflected off the snow-covered clearing as Aden reached them.

Then all hell broke loose.

Aden threw himself into the group, his movements fluid and precise, unleashing centuries of combat training. Without weapons, Aden's fists become lethal instruments, each blow calculated to inflict maximum harm. They burst forward, connecting with the jaws of the two rogues at the lead of the pack. Sickening crunches echoed through the air as bones shattered and blood spattered across his face.

The strength of the blows sent the rogues flying fifty yards across the meadow, their bodies creating deep divots in the snow. Before Aden could turn, two more rogues lunged at him, clawing as they grabbed for his head. Having sensed their approach, Aden sidestepped them. He kicked to his right, his heel connecting with one rogue's chest, before twisting his body and wrapping his fingers around the neck of the second one. He jerked his fingers and the rogue's neck snapped. With a savage twist of his wrists, Aden tore his head off.

Another rogue grabbed him from behind, lifting him off his feet and flinging him into the line of pine trees on the north side of the meadow. The impact rattled his teeth, stole his breath, and shook loose a cascade of snow that buried him. Aden's veins turned to ice as panic coursed through him, a feeling he was unaccustomed to in a fight.

Until now.

He surged to his feet, shaking off the snow, his eyes scanning the field. The rogues advanced on the SUV. His heart shot into his throat, terror gripping him, and he sprinted after them.

Several rogues to his right lunged, trying to head him off. With a thunderous roar, Aden jerked his body to the side, colliding with them and launching them skyward. One flipped and rolled before pushing to its feet, eyes flashing with fury. But the other sailed through the air, limbs flailing wildly. He slammed down on a massive remnant of a fallen tree limb sticking out of the snow. The pointed end jutted into the sky, like a naturally formed stake.

The sharp, splintered tip punched through the rogue's back and emerged from his chest in a spray of dark blood. His eyes went wide with shock and pain, his mouth agape in a silent scream, his heart skewered on the branch.

Before he could appreciate his stroke of luck, Aden's body was jolted by another powerful collision. With a strong yank, his arm was pulled back, and intense, searing pain shot down his arm as his shoulder dislocated from its socket. He unleashed another deafening roar as pain engulfed his body.

He shook the vampire off, ignoring the agony surging through him. Using his other hand to grip the rogue's neck, Aden snapped it, before plunging his teeth into the rogue's throat, using his fangs to tear through the flesh and cartilage. The vampire's scream was drowned out as Aden divested the vampire of his head, tossing it to the side as he continued to run.

The thought of what they would do to Ellie sent a chill through him, colder than the snow beneath his feet.

Aden propelled his legs forward, the muscles burning from the exertion. With gritted teeth, he gripped his arm, wincing as he popped his shoulder back into its socket.

Two vampires caught up to him. They leaped onto his back, and Aden felt fangs sink into his neck. He bellowed with fury and pain. In a blur of motion, he reached back, peeling them off. He yanked them over his head and slammed their bodies to the ground in front of him with earth-shattering force. He stomped on the throat of one while wrenching the other's head from his body with one twist. Aden dug his foot into the rogue trapped beneath his boot, twisting his heel as he heard bones break. He reached down, tearing the vampire's head from his body before hurling it toward the vampires he was chasing down.

What he wouldn't give for a sword right now.

As they neared the SUV, Aden's heart pounded in his chest. A rush of terror and anger surged through him, pushing him to sprint with an intensity he never knew he possessed.

As he passed the two rogues at the rear, he slashed out with his fingers, his nails digging to the side of their faces. It was enough to stun them, letting him pass as he kept running after the three vampires in the lead.

Just as the first rogue reached the vehicle, Aden threw his body into him. They crashed into the side. The impact dented the metal and sent the SUV skidding sideways. Ellie's scream echoed from inside, its piercing tone striking Aden's chest like a physical blow.

Adrenaline pumping through his veins, Aden seized the rogue by the arm and spun him into the oncoming duo. Their bodies collided with a resounding thud. It sent them crashing on top of the SUV's hood. The entire frame shook, and another one of Ellie's screams reverberated from inside.

Aden gritted his teeth, hating the sound of her terrified cries. But it distracted the vampire, whose arm he held just long enough for Aden to tear it off. He swung the limb, connecting with the rogue's chest, sending him flying in the opposite direction.

Three more vampires closed in. There were too fucking many for him to take on alone. But nothing would stop him from protecting Ellie.

A vampire lunged at his legs, but Aden jumped over him. The rogue skidded across the snowy surface and collided with the front right fender, lifting the SUV's front end off the ground.

Aden's hand shot out, seizing the rogue's his leg, and dragging him back. The rogue clawed at the icy ground, but the snow offered no traction. Aden flipped him onto his back and dug his thumbs into the rogue's eye sockets. The rogue screamed as Aden squeezed, crushing his skull, and his body bucked and writhed.

When all that was left was a gruesome pile of blood, shattered bones, and brains, Aden surged to his feet. A rogue slashed out at him, tearing through the fabric of his leather jacket. The claws dug into the skin along his side. Aden hissed as yet another vampire took advantage of his distraction and landed a sharp kick to his back. Aden heard and felt his ribs crack, and he stumbled into the SUV before righting himself. He let out a frustrated and painful roar. It bounced off the trees and reverberated in the air.

Fuck!

Where the fuck were they all coming from? Hadn't he killed most of them yet?

He'd taken down five of them, but it seemed like they were coming out of nowhere, from every side. Maybe there were more in the trees he didn't sense. But if that was the case, he was fucked because he wasn't sure he could hold them off until Kane and his team got here.

One leaped on top of the SUV, his weight causing the roof to cave in. Once again, Ellie's screams resounded from inside and Aden had to block out the sound so he could concentrate.

The rogue scurried over the roof, no doubt to get to the door on the other side. Aden lunged after him. He grasped the rogue's ankle, crushing the bones with his powerful grip. The vampire screamed and slashed back at Aden. He flung the rogue sideways into a line of trees at the perimeter of the meadow. A different rogue jumped on Aden, and he twisted, kicking out, his foot connecting with the vampire's mouth, shattering his front teeth and sending him hurtling backward.

The eastern sky lightened with the first hints of dawn, and Aden rose to his feet, aware of the approaching sunlight. With his enhanced reflexes, he balanced on the slippery surface as he surveyed the surrounding scene.

Aden's SUV, like all military vehicles, was almost impenetrable when the steel panels were activated. But the weight and violence on it had taken a toll. Aden looked down, and the rogue he'd divested of his arm was using his remaining one to pull on the passenger door, desperate to get to the food source within.

But his weakened state made it a struggle. Aden kicked out, the toe of his boot connecting with the rogue's head. It snapped back, and the rogue snarled up at him. Leveraging his higher position, Aden reached down and grasped the vampire's head in his hands, twisting and wrenching it off. The rogue's body crumpled to the ground in a bloody heap, staining the snow crimson.

Seizing the moment of chaos, Aden jumped off the roof and onto the back of another rogue who was scraping at the metal panels, his claws unable to penetrate the steel. Aden shoved his head into the window panel and he heard glass shatter inside the SUV.

Fuck!

If Ellie ended up injured, it would be his fucking fault.

Aden yanked the rogue away and tossed him face down into the snow. He leaped onto him, firmly pressing his knee against the vampire's back. He gripped the rogue beneath the chin and jerked his head, breaking his neck. Aden used the vampire's shock to his advantage, swiftly ending him by twisting his neck and decapitating him.

The rogue, whose ankle he'd shattered, stumbled over. Aden exploited his handicap and, again, using his teeth and hands, tore the vampire's head from his body.

The last three remaining rogues pressed their advantage, swarming the SUV around two sides. Despite their weakness, they used their combined strength to rock the SUV back and forth until it flipped over. A combination of rage and dread surged through him, overpowering his senses, as another one of Ellie's high-pitched screams rang out from inside.

Where the fuck was Kane?

Aden's body ached, the blood loss weakening him, but he refused to give up. Every second he kept fighting was another second she was protected. In that instant, Aden's survival meant nothing. He would trade his eternal life for hers without hesitation, and his body filled with an immense surge of strength and power.

Aden lunged at them. Using hands, claws, and fangs, he fought like a man possessed—like the monster he was. All pretense of humanity was gone in his desperate battle to keep Ellie safe. He spun, lashing out, a whirlwind of deadly precision with each strike. Blood—his and theirs—stained the SUV and the once-pristine snow around it.

With swift, brutal efficiency, Aden decapitated the first rogue, and then the second. The final remaining rogue stood frozen, his face betraying his shock.

As the first direct rays of sunlight breached the horizon, turning the snow-covered landscape into a glittering expanse of littered body parts, a line of military vehicles sped into the meadow.

"How?" The rogue croaked, and Aden's face contorted with a flicker of smug disdain at the audacity of his question.

"You fucked with the wrong fucking vampire."

Aden thrust his arm forward and shoved his bare hand through the rogue's chest, tearing out his heart.

Aden's head fell back, and he closed his eyes, surrendering to the relief that coursed through his body. His tense muscles loosened, and he dropped the heart into the snow as the banging of doors echoed in the early morning air.

Ellie

Ellie sat frozen as her eyes darted from side to side, her racing heartbeat echoing in her ears.

There was absolute silence outside. She held her breath, her shoulder throbbing from where it had slammed into the steering wheel when the SUV flipped over. The sound of doors slamming reminded Ellie of a night long ago.

"Get her out of here!" Aden roared.

He was alive!

The door locks clicked open, and the sound of metal twisting echoed as someone tore the passenger door off the hinges and filled the tiny space. Ellie scurried away from the awful sound.

Kane poked his head inside. His face mirrored the relief she felt.

"Kane." His name was a croaked whisper.

"Stay where you are, Ellie."

Ellie sat as still as stone. The door behind her gave way, and she tumbled backward. Kane caught her and tugged her to her feet.

"Come with me." Kane led her by the arm toward another black SUV. Ellie's head swiveled, looking for Aden as she forced her starving lungs to draw air.

Blood covered everything she could see. The once-pristine snow was now crimson and littered with what looked like body parts. The sun had risen but still hung low in the sky, bathing the morning in pale pink light.

"Aden!" Ellie called as she struggled in Kane's grip. He couldn't be out here. He was a vampire. "Where is he?"

"Ellie, stop struggling." Kane's voice was close to her ear.

"No!" Ellie twisted toward the direction Aden's roar had come from. "Aden!" she shrieked his name, and then it morphed into a groan as she twisted her injured shoulder.

Before Ellie could make another sound, Aden was beside her, slamming the palm of his hand into Kane's chest, sending the guard flying across the field. The sound of Kane's ribs cracking echoed through the air. She stumbled, reaching out to grasp Aden's forearm. His hands cupped her elbows as she tried to steady herself.

"Did he hurt you?"

Her eyes snapped up, and the air in her lungs evaporated. Blood covered his face, and his eyes were like balls of fire, as red as his skin. More blood and snow dripped from the strands of his hair over his forehead and down his face.

Ellie jerked out of his grasp as images of the same eyes flashed in front of hers. Her legs could no longer support her. She swayed and her knees buckled. As darkness surrounded her, her mind raced with a single thought.

Not again.

Ellie's eyes fluttered as she came awake, her room coming into focus as her vision cleared. It was dark, except for a muted strip of light coming from under the door. Vlad rested against her hip, and she shifted him before sitting up and dropping her feet over the side of the bed. Her shoulder throbbed, and it took a moment for everything to come back.

The blood and the body parts overshadowed the earlier memories of the snow angels with Aden. His blood-soaked face and blazing eyes, looking down at her before the world vanished, were more frightening than her nightmares.

A quick glance at the clock told Ellie it was after five. But was it morning or night? She stumbled into the shower. Her effort to wash away the memories failed. Nothing helped. Several shallow cuts graced her cheek, but someone had removed all the glass. After dressing, she made her way through Aden's sitting room. It was empty, with no sign he'd been there at all.

Call her a coward, but she didn't want to see him right now. She wished he would unseal her hallway door so she could come and go without going through his rooms. It still baffled her that he wanted her in his space all the time.

She found Kane standing in his usual spot in the hallway.

"Oh, Kane, are you alright?" She gave him the once-over, but he showed no signs of injury.

He waved her off with a grin. "I'm fine. That's not the first time he's thrown me across a field."

"But I heard your ribs crack."

Kane smacked his chest with his hand. "All healed. Don't worry about me. I'm pretty tough."

She crossed her arms over her chest. "Why would he do that to you?"

"He thought I manhandled you."

"What? Why would he ever think that?"

"He wasn't in his right mind. He heard you cry out and saw you struggling, and he thought I was hurting you."

Ellie wondered if Aden was ever in his right mind. "I'm sorry he hurt you because of me."

"Don't worry about it, Ellie. I'll get him back the next time we spar."

"What happened out there?"

"You're gonna have to ask him about that."

Ellie scowled. "Thanks a lot."

"Serves him right for locking me in the city. It never would have happened if he followed protocol."

Ellie leaned against the wall and sucked her lower lip between her teeth. "How bad was it? Did he get hurt?"

"He's fine. He needs to get his ass kicked every once in a while."

"Where is he? In his office?" Kane nodded, and she tilted her head, her eyes filled with curiosity. "Why are you here, then?"

"He told me to stay until you woke up."

"You don't have to tell him, do you?"

"Yep. But he probably already knows. The change in your heartbeat would have alerted him."

"That's so creepy."

"That's vampires." He smirked.

She pushed away from the wall. "Well, I've got to go. I'm late as it is. I'm glad you're okay, Kane." She touched his arm, and he smiled at her.

"I'm glad you're okay too, Ellie."

Aden

"Why the fuck were rogues so close to the city?" Aden slammed his fist on his new desk, cracking the wood down the center as he fought the urge to tear the man in front of him apart.

Roderick stood at attention but didn't answer, knowing Aden long enough to recognize he was far from finished with his rant.

"Your only job, your only reason for existence, is to protect this city." Aden strode around the desk and got right into Roderick's face. "If you can't keep a coven of half-starved rogues from getting close to its limits, what good are you?"

Roderick remained silent.

"Do you have any idea of the consequences if she had been hurt?" Aden stepped closer, his nose almost touching Roderick's. "Can you even fathom the destruction I would have wreaked?"

Roderick's stoic facade faltered as he cringed but held his ground. And it was for that reason that Aden let him live. Before Aden, Roderick had been the commander of his father's military and was one of only a handful of inner sanctum half-breeds who survived Aden's dark years. He lived through it once, so if anyone could fathom Aden's destructive power when he went off the rails, it was Roderick.

Aden wanted to rip something, or someone, limb from limb. But not Roderick. He was reaching the end of his useful life and would need to be retired soon, but Roderick's loyalty to Aden was second only to Kane's, and one of the few things Aden respected was loyalty.

He took a deep breath.

"Come here," Aden barked at the four girls kneeling in the corner. He walked to the sofa and sat down as they scurried over to him. "Sit." He waved his hand at Roderick, but the man didn't move.

Aden grasped the first girl's arm and sunk his teeth into her wrist. A residual ache in his back persisted from his confrontation with the rogues.

"I said sit the fuck down," Aden commanded as he released the girl's wrist, and the next one crawled forward.

In the past, Aden would have had all these girls and more beneath him, one at a time, in and out of his bed until he felt completely rejuvenated. How drastically his life had changed in the last five months.

Aden opened his eyes to see Roderick heed his command. After he finished drinking from the fourth girl's wrist, he waved them away, but a slight pang of hunger lingered. "Tell Georgina to send one more girl," he called after the last girl to leave.

He turned his heavy gaze to Roderick again. "You never answered my question."

"Which one?"

"Don't push your luck, Roderick. How did those rogues get close to the city?"

"I don't know."

Aden leaned back in his chair. "That's not what I want to hear. Where were your men? Why weren't they patrolling?"

"You instructed the guards at the gate not to let anyone out of the city."

"They should have been out there long before I was."

"We patrolled earlier in the night," Roderick said. "Nothing was amiss."

"The more important question is why were they that close, coming from the west?"

"Any distance is too close. It doesn't matter what direction they come from."

Aden glanced at the window to see the snow falling again, and he felt a pang of regret, knowing he couldn't risk taking Ellie outside again until he was certain it was safe.

"There's only one village in that direction for over four hundred miles, and the coven we destroyed in December was over five hundred miles beyond that. Their only destination could have been the city limits. What doesn't make sense is why any foreign vampires would congregate in that direction."

"Are you sure they were foreign? There wasn't enough left to identify any of them."

"I know every vampire in this region, and I didn't recognize any of them."

A frown etched the side of Roderick's mouth. "We've never had an issue with unregistered vamps."

"That's why we need to find out where they came from. They were half starved, so it was easy to overpower them." Roderick raised an eyebrow, and Aden's pupils flared, daring Roderick to contradict his words. "But they weren't that weak. They'd eaten in the last few weeks."

"I'll dispatch a team to determine if anything's left of that village. It's possible we missed some last time."

"No, it's not." Aden was sure of that. "And why the fuck haven't you gotten answers out of that rogue yet? Why is he still alive? You've never taken this long to get answers from a prisoner."

Roderick frowned, his displeasure obvious on his face. "His high level of tolerance for torture suggests he was military. None of my methods have worked."

"Well, maybe we should try some of my methods." Aden surged to his feet. "Come with me."

Roderick followed him out of his office and to a warp port that transported them to the dungeons. Two half-breed guards were posted at the entrance to the chamber, and four more stood inside, armed with Helios.

Although they were called dungeons, they weren't anything like the prisons Aden had read about in books and seen in the films his mother hoarded. These cells, designed to imprison vampires, were more like vaults, reflecting the era, equipped with everything needed to keep them confined and in a weakened state.

Like his father's office, the vaults were a fusion of ancient architecture and modern technology. The cells were constructed with twelve-foot-thick stone walls, floors, and ceilings—cold and dank with a faint scent of moss and decay that was inherent to all subterranean chambers.

However, the traditional elements were contrasted by more modern features. The cell's entrances were sleek, lined with tungsten and steel sliding doors with no visible hinges or handles, making the walls look almost seamless when they were closed.

Between the bars were the same shatterproof polycarbonate panels as the dome. The transparent barriers provided a mostly unobstructed view into the cell while preventing any physical contact between the prisoners and guards.

Anchored at strategic points on the ceiling, back and side walls were tungsten chains, infused with the same UV particles as the handcuffs used to transport the rogue here. The shackles could restrain a vampire weakened from the UV fragments and lack of blood. Each set of chains ended in cuffs that could be adjusted to fit wrists or ankles, ensuring that the vampire could be secured in various positions as needed.

Also embedded in the ceiling were grids of UV lights, which could be turned on to weaken a vampire before interrogations and to end them afterward.

The memory of those chains gripping him tightly and the overwhelming glare of the lights came rushing back to Aden as he stepped up to the cell and gazed at the rogue, his fists clenching at his sides. He reminded Aden of the rogues that had gone after Ellie only a few short hours ago. A dark part of him yearned for the chance to kill all of them again as his body pulsed with an uncontrollable rage that threatened to engulf him.

He hadn't taken part in interrogations in over a century, leaving them to Roderick and Drake when necessary. But since they couldn't seem to get the information out of their prisoner and Aden had all this pent-up fury, it was time to show this rogue why Aden was the world's most feared vampire commander.

Roderick stepped up beside him. "We should turn on the lights for a few minutes to weaken him."

"No need. How much blood does he get a day?"

"One pint. Just enough to keep him alive."

Aden waved his hand over the panel on the wall, and the door slid open. The rogue sat on a cot in the corner, staring at Aden with a glare that oozed defiance. His skin was paler than a healthy vampire, his were features gaunt, and his clothes were tattered and bloodstained. Both his feet and hands were chained with barely enough slack to make it to the bathroom in the corner. The prolonged captivity and the effects of the UV-infused restraints had left their mark.

"Do you want me to shorten the chains?" Roderick asked as he stepped in behind Aden.

"No need," Aden said again as he approached the rogue, his boots echoing on the stone floor. His rage simmered beneath his skin as he moved closer, but he couldn't kill the rogue yet. He needed answers. It was too important now. But he hadn't felt this kind of fury in centuries, and the last time he unleashed it, his father was cleaning up the carnage for months.

Aden reached the rogue, the toes of his boots pressed against the toes of the rogue's bare feet. He loomed over him, but the rogue remained unfazed. Only a soldier possessed that kind of bravery, but that knowledge only fueled Aden's anger.

"Who are you?" he asked, his voice low and measured. "And why the fuck have you come to my region?"

The rogue remained silent, his lips pressed into a thin, insolent line.

"I don't know if he speaks English. Sometimes it seems like he has no idea what I'm saying," Roderick said from where he leaned against the opposite wall.

"He understands me." Aden's eyes flicked to Roderick before returning to the rogue. "Your silence won't help you. You know who I am and what I'm capable of."

The rogue's eyes flashed with recognition. Oh, yes, he understood English.

"Roderick's methods are much nicer than mine. The pain you've endured at his hands will pale in comparison if I get involved. It would behoove you to start talking, and I might consider showing you some mercy by killing you quickly."

Still, the rogue said nothing.

"Where are you from?" Aden hissed, baring his fangs. "Who sent you here?"

The rogue just smirked. Aden snarled in frustration, lashing out with inhuman speed to grab this throat. "Answer me!" he roared, his composure slipping. "I took out twelve of you tonight. They wanted something of mine. Something very precious. And now, every one of them is dead."

Aden squeezed his fingers, feeling the bones in the rogue's neck crack. The rogue spit in his face.

Aden hurled the rogue across the room, narrowly missing Roderick, as he collided with the wall.

Aden stalked across the cell and hauled the disoriented vampire to his feet, avoiding contact with the chains. With supernatural speed, his fist connected with the rogue's jaw, the impact sending the weaker vampire reeling, his head snapping back against the wall.

"String him up," he snarled as he pinned the rogue's body against the wall.

Roderick walked out of the cell to a panel on the opposite wall, activating the pulley system that controlled the chains. "Return to your positions. There's nothing to see here," Roderick said to two of the guards who approached.

With his wrists suspended in the air, the rogue stared at Aden as he thrashed, spat, and hissed in resistance. Aden grabbed the rogue's leg, tearing his femur out of the socket. The rogue let out an agonized roar.

"Oh, so he isn't mute after all," Aden sneered as he pummeled the rogue with punishing blow after punishing blow, the sound of breaking bones filling the cell, punctuated by Aden's snarls. "Do you think you can come after what's mine? This is my region. You don't come into my territory and attempt to take what belongs to me. Who the fuck do you think you are to threaten her?"

The 'her' wasn't Réimse Shíochánta. While protecting his family's region had been his top priority since his father had entrusted him with leading his military, there was now someone even more important to protect.

Aden's field of vision narrowed, and the rogue in front of him blurred. All he could see flashing in front of his eyes was Ellie's terrified expression as she looked at him, covered in vampire blood, before fainting in his arms.

Aden gripped the rogue's other leg and jerked his body downwards. Both of the rogue's shoulders popped out of their sockets, and the metal cuff on his left wrist sliced through the skin and bone, severing it. The inhuman sound that burst through the rogue's lips reverberated throughout the dungeons. The chains let out a protesting groan as they surrendered to Aden's strength, snapping and sending the rogue crashing to the ground.

"Shit, Aden," Roderick said as he stepped back into the cell. "You're going to kill him."

Instinct took over, and bound by only the cuffs at his ankles, the rogue lunged forward, aiming for Aden's throat with his fangs. Aden dodged him, kicking him in the stomach, then flipping the rogue around. He pressed him against the wall, pinning one mangled arm behind his back.

"Is that all you've got?" He taunted, increasing the pressure on the rogue's arm, reveling when he felt and heard the bones shattering.

The rogue let out another roar of pain, struggling against Aden's brutal grip before snarling, his accent indistinguishable.

"It's only just beginning."

Aden released the rogue's arm and stepped back. He grabbed him by the back of the neck and flung him across the room again, aiming for the cot, before meeting Roderick's eyes. The omen hung in the air, casting a shadow of unease over them.

"Decrease his blood to half a pint and increase the number of hours the UV lights are on. I want answers, Roderick. I don't care what you have to do. Up the intensity, but keep him alive long enough to get them."

"What about his hand? Should I have medical reattach it?"

"He's not going to need it. But get Zach down here to stop that bleeding. Don't let him die until we have answers."

The faint sound of Ellie's heartbeat speeding up caught Aden's attention. He tilted his head to focus on the soft thumping.

"Everything alright?"

"No. It won't be until you get answers from him." Aden gestured to the rogue, clutching his arm stump to his chest. "And until you figure out where those rogues came from and what they're after."

Aden looked down at himself. He was covered in blood again, and the ache in his back had returned. He needed more blood. And another shower.

He focused on the sound of Ellie's heartbeat again. The comforting, steady, rhythmic sound reassuring him she was safe, soothing his still frayed nerves. His eyes whipped back to Roderick. "Don't make me regret sparing your life tonight."

Roderick gave a clipped nod before he walked out of the cell.

Aden cast one last glance at the rogue as he stepped out of the cell.

"We'll see how long you can keep this up." The door slid shut. "There are worse things than me waiting for you."

Aden hovered in the shadows, his eyes following Ellie as she walked through the courtyard. It was Thursday, so she was heading to meet Sophie in the greenhouse.

Halfway across the open expanse, Ellie stopped, and her head turned toward him. The slight change in her scent and her breathing told him she could feel his gaze. She looked fine, but he had to keep reminding himself of that because the alternative was unfathomable.

If one of those rogues had gotten a hold of her, he would have burned the world to the ground.

"It's rude to spy on people, you know." Her soft voice filled the otherwise silent space.

Aden emerged from the shadows, and the tension melted away from her face as her eyes swept over him.

He'd showered in his office after returning from the vaults, washing away the rogue's blood and his lingering ire. He'd also fed again and was now dressed in his normal attire. His wounds had healed, so he looked nothing like the vicious predator covered in blood she'd last seen. He hated that she'd seen him like that.

He inched his way towards her, his movements deliberate and careful, not wanting to scare her again. "How's your shoulder?"

"Fine." Her eyes met his as he came to a stop a foot in front of her.

"Did Mina get all the glass out of your cheek?"

The cuts were a painful reminder of his mistakes. And the remorse Aden felt was like a persistent gnawing that weighed heavily in his gut.

Ellie winced as she brushed her fingers over the cuts. "Yes. But as usual, I was out cold when it happened."

"You shouldn't have had to see that." His muscles tightened from the remembered fear for her. "And you should have gone with Kane without question."

"Are you kidding me?" Her face contorted in a mix of shock and disbelief. "After everything I heard and being flipped in that car, you expected me to just leave without seeing if you were alright."

He scoffed and crossed his arms over his broad chest. "I'm more than capable of taking care of myself."

"But the sun had already risen." Ellie mimicked his pose, and his lips twitched.

"I told you I don't burst into flames in the sun, Ellie." The half-smile slipped from his lips. "You should have done as you were told. Kane was following my orders, and you should have as well. I won't tolerate you putting yourself in harm's way."

He tried to keep the bite out of his voice. He had to work on being calmer and gentler with her. But the memory of his fear for her was still too fresh.

Ellie stepped closer, unfazed by his biting tone, and gazed up at him through her long lashes. "You didn't have to hurt him. Kane didn't hurt me."

She lifted her hand but pulled back before it reached his arm. An unexpected pang of disappointment filled him as he longed for the warmth of her touch. He held himself back from reaching out and grasping her fingers.

Instead, he shrugged. "I didn't know that."

"What happened out there?"

"Nothing you need to be concerned with."

Ellie's eyes hardened with disappointment. "Of course not. Excuse me."

She turned to walk away but stopped when Aden said her name. "Ellie, I'm sorry you saw me like that."

Apologies weren't in his nature, but the words came surprisingly easily when saying them to her.

She turned to face him. "Why won't you tell me what happened?"

"You don't need to know."

"Maybe not, but I'd like to."

Aden shoved his fingers through his hair as he muttered under his breath. "Why can't I ever fucking say no to you?"

One corner of Ellie's lips inched up. "You do. All the time. But I hope you won't now."

Her patient expression irked him. She had become too good at getting her way with him.

"It was a coven of rogue vampires."

Her eyes widened. "You took on a coven of rogues by yourself?"

Why did she sound so surprised?

"They weren't very strong, and they shouldn't have been that close to the city. If I'd known they were nearby, I never would have taken you out."

"Why would they attack you? Didn't they know who you are?"

"Probably, but they were hungry. Starvation will make a vampire desperate."

"What did they want?"

"You," Aden said without hesitation. They stood looking at one another, neither of them sure what to say. Then Aden's eyes darkened. "Why the fuck are you here?" he barked, startling Ellie with the severity of his tone.

"I was told you wanted to feed, Sir." Chelsea emerged from the shadows, and Aden cursed under his breath.

"Go to my office, and I'll be there in a minute."

Chelsea scurried down the hallway without another word.

"Sophie is expecting me," Ellie said after a moment.

Aden's eyes flickered over her face. He wanted to say more and tell her he was sorry again. But for what, he wasn't sure because there was so much.

Her soft eyes met his. "Thank you for taking me out last night."

"You're welcome."

Ellie's lips curved upward as she turned and headed toward the greenhouse. He saw his mother lurking in the shadows, behind one of the cherry blossom trees, as Ellie disappeared inside. Sophie backed away, giving him a warm smile before disappearing from view.

Of course she'd been fucking spying on them.

He smirked, not caring at all.

Aden

A hologram of his father appeared, an odd expression on his face. Aden glanced up from his relaxed position on the sofa in the plane's main cabin, where he and Kane were engrossed in a game of chess.

"Hey, what's up?" Aden sat up. "I'm on my way back. We should be there in two hours."

"We have a surprise visitor." The hologram expanded to show Matthais sitting across from Aurick in his office.

"Aden," Matthais said.

"Matthais," Aden said, although the word 'fuck' reverberated in his head. "We weren't expecting you."

Matthais' gaze swept over Aden, as if searching for something. "I was returning from Abya Yala, and it was a spur-of-the-moment thing."

Out of view of the hologram, Kane arched an eyebrow in question. Matthais wasn't known for his spontaneity.

"Has something happened?" Aden asked.

"No, but after Aurick submitted his report, I thought it prudent to visit. It was quite astute of you to recommend he initiate an investigation."

Aden glanced at his father before turning his gaze back to Matthais. "I didn't realize the report was finished."

Or that his father had heeded his suggestion and initiated a probe into Paolo.

"I didn't have time to tell you before you left," Aurick said.

Impressed with Aurick's smooth lie, Aden kept his face impassive.

"Changes need to be implemented down there, so it made sense to stop by to discuss next steps. And I'm glad I did. Aurick informed me of the rogue issue you're having."

"Yes, it's unsettling," Aden said. "But I'll find out where they're coming from and why."

"As always, I have the utmost confidence in your ability, Aden," Matthais said. "But it's a shame you're not here. Aurick has also been telling me about your new recruits. It would have been good to see them in action."

Kane stood and walked over to the bar. He held up a glass and Aden nodded.

"Perhaps the next visit," Aden offered, having no interest in showing Matthais anything.

"Well, I can stay an extra day. Perhaps you can show me tomorrow night? That is, if I can rely on your hospitality." Matthais addressed Aurick.

"Of course. I'll have Sophie make the arrangements."

"Wonderful."

Yeah. Fucking wonderful.

"So, how did it go up there?" His father asked, changing the subject.

"No sign of any rogues, but one village had been pillaged."

Kane handed Aden his drink and sat again.

"How many did we lose?"

"A little over seven hundred."

Aden watched Aurick's face fall, his disappointment palpable at the loss of too many human lives.

"There were a few still alive, and we relocated them to a neighboring village, but I don't like the random pattern of it."

Matthais' curious look raised the hairs on the back of Aden's neck.

"Well, I'll see you tomorrow evening, Matthais. I'll take you to the training field after breakfast."

"Of course. I wouldn't dream of interrupting your feeding schedule. I'm also eager to know how you're enjoying your newest pet. Although knowing you, she may no longer be the newest."

Aden stilled the rage coursing through his body. How fucking dare Matthais bring Ellie up after what he'd done to her?

The hologram disappeared, and Aden growled. "Why the fuck didn't I leave you at home?"

"That's not really an option."

Aden leaned forward and called Sophie.

"Hi, Aden. I was waiting for your call," she said as her face appeared.

"Where's Ellie?"

"I sent her back to her room." His mother remained unfazed by his lack of greeting. "I told her I didn't need her tonight and she should go read in her room rather than the library."

"Thank you," Aden said, sinking back into the cushion.

"Of course. Since Kane is with you, I also added a guard outside your room and one outside her hallway door. Matthais shouldn't go into that part of the compound, but it's better to be cautious. You're going to need to speak to her, though. She won't understand why she can't leave."

Kane snorted, and Aden shot him a glare.

"I'll go see her when I get home. Why hadn't Matthais announced his visit? Has he ever done this before?"

"Maybe a handful of times over the last five hundred years. But it's not like him."

Aden sat back, shaking his leg. "Should we read anything into it?"

"Aden, don't worry about Matthais."

Fuck! He was still at least two hours away.

"Ellie will be fine until you get back." His mother assured him, as if she could sense his panic. "I'll take her something to eat so she doesn't get hungry and wander to the kitchen. The guards have instructions not to let her out."

"Thank you, Sophie. I'll see you in a few hours."

He swiped the hologram closed as his eyes met Kane's, who looked as concerned as Aden felt.

Aden walked through his suite and straight to Ellie's room. She looked up, surprise in her eyes. She sat on her bed with her tablet in her lap. An empty plate rested on the mattress beside her, and Vlad curled up against her thigh, sleeping. Her hand stilled on his fur as she set her tablet aside.

"Aden, did you need me for something?"

"No. I wanted to tell you that you're to remain in your room, or mine, until further notice."

"Why?" Her brow furrowed in confusion.

"Because I said so." He turned and walked back into his room. She scurried off the bed to follow him.

He was on edge. He needed to get away from her and feed. She had an uncanny skill for coaxing him into revealing things he hadn't meant to, and he was determined not to let slip that Matthais was there.

"But what about Sophie? She didn't need me tonight, but what about tomorrow night? I'm supposed to help her and Keeley work on the design for the nursery."

"Well, that's canceled. You'll stay in these rooms until I tell you otherwise."

She scowled and folded her arms. He didn't have the patience for this, but he took a deep breath to calm himself. It wasn't her fault Matthais had showed up unannounced.

"Ellie, don't argue with me about this. I need you to trust me. It's in your best interest to stay in here."

Her arms fell, and her scowl morphed into a frown. "Are there other vampires visiting?"

Sometimes she was too fucking smart for her own good.

"Yes. You can't wander around the way you normally do when other vampires are here."

"Well, why didn't you say that? I wouldn't have argued with you if you'd just told me."

A small smile tugged at the corners of his mouth. "At least you admit you're argumentative."

She had the decency to not dispute it.

"How long are they staying?" she asked.

"At least a day."

"Okay. Thank you for telling me the truth."

"I'll let you know as soon as they leave."

She nodded, and he headed to the door.

"Okay." Her voice floated after him. "Goodnight, Aden."

"Where is Matthais now?"

Aden walked into his father's private office, which was a series of connected rooms deep below the compound. The rooms were only accessible through hidden passages in his parent's suite. They weren't exactly a secret, but only he, his parents, and Keeley had access to them, unless the security was overridden.

His father stood behind a climate-controlled glass case to the right of his desk, turning a page of the Book of Kells. As one of its writers, Aurick had received the ancient religious manuscript as part of the distribution of world artifacts among the Ancient Ones after the Great Vampire Wars.

Aurick's private study was the one place that was a genuine reflection of his personality. It felt like being in the ancient Celtic world, or at least how Aden imagined it based on his father's vivid descriptions. The rooms exuded an air of reverence for a time long past, serving not only as a workspace but also as a sanctuary for his most cherished possessions.

On the heavy wood-paneled walls hung tapestries in earthy tones, each one woven with scenes from Celtic mythology and folklore. In between them, ancient ceremonial daggers and swords hung on hand-forged wall mounts, the metal blades meticulously preserved and shining under the subtle glow of ambient lighting.

It was the one space his father seemed most comfortable, much like Aden felt in his studio.

"I believe he's settled in his suite feeding," Aurick said as he glanced over. "Why are you so agitated?"

Aden had a sensation of spiders crawling under his skin, causing him to pace in front of Aurick's desk. "I don't like Matthais showing up here so unexpectedly."

Aurick closed the case and locked it. "He's done this before. He doesn't like complacency."

"I didn't know you took my recommendation about investigating Paolo."

"I always take your recommendations seriously, Aden. I may not have been pleased with your actions, but that doesn't mean I don't trust your instincts."

Aden nodded, glad he and his father were back on even footing.

"Your mom mentioned she has tucked Ellie away for now."

Aden nodded again.

"Good. Since she has such free rein around here most of the time, it's probably best. His inquiry about her was odd."

Sophie walked in before Aden could respond. "Oh, Aden, you're back? Have you seen Ellie yet?"

Aden stopped pacing. "Yes."

"How did she take the news?"

"How do you think?"

A soft chuckle floated from his mother's lips as she stepped up to him. "What did you tell her?"

Aurick moved to the next case containing the Gutenberg Bible and opened it.

"She guessed vampires were visiting, but I didn't tell her it was Matthais."

"She's very intuitive," Sophie said. "You won't be able to keep many secrets from her."

Aden grunted as he turned back to Aurick. "So why do you think he inquired about Ellie?"

"Who? Matthais?" Sophie asked. Off Aden and Aurick's simultaneous nods, she frowned. "Why would he ask about her?"

Aurick closed the case and removed his lint-free cotton gloves. "No idea. He might just be inquiring about her well-being."

"Aurick, don't be ridiculous," Sophie said. "He doesn't give thralls' well-being a second thought. Ever."

"Well, there is an old, obscure law on the books. As far as I know, no one has ever invoked it, but a vampire can request a thrall's return if the thrall is being mistreated, abused, or neglected. Or if a gift goes unused." The distaste in Aurick's voice was obvious. "That's why it's so important to pay for a thrall."

A muscle twitched under Aden's eye. "Why wasn't I told about this law?"

Aurick walked to the sitting area on the left side of the room. Aden and Sophie followed.

"It's expected that you have all our laws committed to memory, Aden." The subtle reprimand in his tone made Aden grind his teeth. "But again, it's an obscure one that's never invoked because there is no need. Remuneration makes it moot unless there is severe abuse."

Fuck!

"What's that look?" Sophie asked as she settled on the sofa beside Aurick.

"Well, I didn't pay for Ellie." Aden dropped into the chair across from them.

"What? Why not?" Aurick asked, his eyebrows raising.

"I tried, but Matthais didn't want payment. He said to consider her a gift."

"Aden, why didn't you tell us?" Sophie asked. "Your father could have gone back to him and insisted."

"If I'd known about the law, I would have. What can I do about it now?"

Aurick glanced at Sophie and then back to Aden. "I loathe to suggest it, but if you could get her scent fresh on you, he'd likely not question anything."

Aden and Sophie understood what he meant right away. "No," they said in unison.

"I'm not suggesting you drink from her." Aurick held up his hands. "But her scent is very faint now because you only drank from her once, and it was months ago."

"I won't drink from her again," Aden said. "Not unless she wants it. And I doubt that will ever happen."

His parents' twin looks of surprise didn't go unnoticed.

"There is no need to drink from her," Aurick said. "Mina can give you some of her blood and, despite how unpalatable I know you find it, you can drink it from a glass."

"I'm sure Mina has a reserve of her blood stored for an emergency."

Sophie stood and walked to the far side of the room, and a small hologram appeared, displaying Mina's face.

Memories of Ellie's taste triggered a surge of venom in Aden's mouth. He stood, too agitated to remain seated.

"You can't give him any reason to want to reclaim her. You haven't been in his presence yet. If you drink a little of her blood, he'll think you're feeding on her like your other thralls."

"Fuck!"

Sophie walked back and sat down. "Aden, your father is right. Matthais needs to detect her scent on you. Ellie doesn't need to know."

"I'm not worried about her knowing. It's just—"

The door opened. "I brought what you asked for," Mina said as she entered, addressing Sophie. "Does someone want to tell me what's going on? Has something happened to Ellie?"

"No. We need her blood for Aden," Sophie said.

"Is this because Matthais is here?" Mina asked.

"Yes," Aurick said.

"Are you sure you can handle this?" Mina asked, narrowing her eyes.

"Does it fucking matter?" He held out his hand. "Give me the blood, Mina."

Mina set the vials in his palm and, despite how small they were, they felt massive in his hand. With one last worried glance at the three of them, she left without another word.

"She's just concerned for you," Sophie murmured.

"She's a busybody," Aden said, but he didn't really mean it. He knew her concern for him was genuine.

"It's a valid question. Are you sure you can handle drinking Ellie's blood?" Aurick asked.

Aden looked down at his hand again and wondered himself.

"I guess we'll find out, won't we?"

Aden stared at the two vials of Ellie's blood on his desk. He'd been sitting in the same spot for over twenty minutes now, debating whether this was the right choice.

His mouth had been watering since Mina gave them to him. He'd excused himself from his parents' company, wanting to do this alone. Despite his hesitation, his only thought was ripping off the tops and guzzling down the liquid, no matter its temperature.

It had been exactly one hundred seventy-seven days since he bit Ellie, since he drank her blood, but he could still taste her as if it were yesterday.

His door whooshed open, and Keeley walked into the room.

"I'm fucking busy."

"Yeah, it looks like it."

"Why are you here, Keeley?" Aden didn't take his eyes off the vials.

"Moral support." He looked up as she approached his desk and dropped into the chair. "I know this can't be easy, Aden."

He paused, unsure if he should ask. "Why am I so hesitant to drink it?"

"Because you want it from her." Leave it to Keeley to state the obvious. "There's nothing wrong with that."

Aden sat forward in his chair and rubbed his hands over his thighs.

"Maybe you should put it in whiskey? Might make it easier to take."

He gave her a horrified look. "And dilute it? Not on your fucking life." Aden continued to eye the vials warily. "Do you think I'm overreacting?"

"It's better to overreact than under in this instance. When do you meet Matthais?"

"Tonight. After sunset."

"Why are you drinking it now? Why don't you wait until right before you meet him?"

Because he was fucking impatient.

"If it's too fresh, it might be suspicious."

"Doesn't he think you're going to have breakfast first?"

"Yeah."

"So fresh would make sense."

Aden shook his head. There was no way he could wait that long. "You should probably go."

"You sure?"

"Yes. I want to be alone."

Keeley stared at him before standing. "I'm going to see Ellie. I bet she's climbing the walls in that small room."

"She's not confined to her room. She can be in my room, too."

"Does she know that?"

"Yes. I don't keep her locked in the fucking closet."

Keeley's mouth twitched as she approached the door. "Let me know how it goes later."

Once he was alone again, Aden cracked his knuckles before picking up the first vial. Anticipation surged through him, causing a lump to form in his throat, his fangs dripping with venom.

Before he could change his mind, he plucked the top off, and the scent of her blood made his eyes cross. Though it had been out of her body for who knows how long, it was still incredibly potent. He inhaled, and the scent filled his lungs, making him feel lightheaded. He'd almost forgotten how it affected him. No wonder he hadn't been able to stop himself that night.

A feral growl rumbled out of his chest, and before he changed his mind, Aden brought the vial to his mouth and gulped it down.

His body reacted instantly, and he was rock hard. The smooth, sweet liquid slid over his tongue and down his throat. It didn't matter that it was cold or wasn't directly from her vein. As his body absorbed it, a tingling sensation surged through him, electrifying his senses.

He grabbed the second vial and gulped it down as ravenously as the first. He tilted his head back, closing his eyes. His heart pounded like a jackhammer, and he could see her face as clearly as if she were in front of him. He resisted the urge to reach down and pull out his cock. He wouldn't debase Ellie like that. But it took all his self-control to resist.

When Aden opened his eyes again, he turned his gaze towards the glass door of his workout room, catching sight of his reflection. His own eyes, piercing and intense, stared back at him.

They were blood red.

Aden

Aden watched Roderick and Drake work the teams when Matthais' caravan pulled up to the training field. He'd left Kane guarding Ellie outside his room.

"Aden," Matthais greeted as he exited his vehicle and walked over. Two thralls, one male and one female, followed him and kneeled on the last vestiges of snow at his feet while Lorcan and three other guards hovered around him. "Good to see you."

"Matthais," Aden said as they shook hands.

"It's too bad Aurick had a meeting at BloodStone and couldn't join us. He's busier than me, it seems."

Aden turned back to watch the soldiers going through their standard drills.

"I was quite disturbed to hear about your encounter with those rogues. Aurick said you were out on your own, and they attacked unprovoked. Any idea why they attacked you like that?"

His father was more skilled at lying than Aden thought.

"They were starving and out of their minds with thirst."

"That's unusual these days. Did you have a thrall with you?"

Matthais was fishing for information, but hell, if Aden would give him any. "Starving vampires have been known to feed on other vampires in dire circumstances."

"Indeed. And you're sure they weren't vampires from your region?"

"They definitely weren't."

Aden motioned to Drake to start the drills again from the beginning.

"Hmmm, I'm happy to send Andrei over to assist."

"That's unnecessary."

Matthais glanced at Aden before looking back at the field. "I would like the two of you to work together to deal with the Abya Yala situation. Your concerns were valid."

Aden shot him a quick glance before turning back to watch.

"I've decided Paolo needs to be removed, and those troops need to be retrained in proper combat. I want you and Andrei to take point on it. A new commander will also need to be assigned, and I want both your input on who you think would be best."

"I don't know if they need to be retrained, because I never saw them in action," Aden said.

"Well, assess them and report back to me and Aurick. Your troops are the best trained in the world, Aden. Dare I say even better than Andrei's?"

Aden smirked knowing how Andrei would react if he heard Matthais say that.

"I'm sure Cecilia won't be happy with this arrangement."

"Yes, she is still quite upset about your last encounter," Matthais said. "You're ruffling feathers everywhere these days. But don't worry about Cecilia. She won't give you any trouble. So, can I count on your assistance, Aden?"

"Of course."

"Good. Good," Matthais said with a satisfied smile. "Only, in your training, let's keep the use of humans as bait to a minimum, shall we?" He chided, and Aden's teeth clenched.

"Can I use Paolo as bait, at least?"

Matthais let out a very rare laugh. "Yes, if you must make a point." He turned back to the soldiers. "So, these are the new troops I've heard so much about?"

"Yes."

"Well, show me what you're doing."

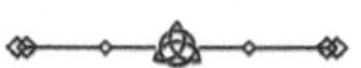

"I'm impressed, Aden. As always, your training and strategy are top-notch," Matthais said as they walked toward Aden's office.

"Thank you."

"You'll have to share those maneuvers with Andrei. Rogues are becoming more of a problem everywhere, so it would be good to have universal training on how to deal with them."

Matthais had been unusually interested in Aden's methods of rogue combat. Aden couldn't recall a time when he had seen him so curious or fascinated.

"I'll send him the details."

As they approached, the door to Aden's office slid open with a quiet hiss. Matthais' thralls followed them in, his guards remaining outside the door.

"So," Matthais said, his eyes drawn to the desk's cracked surface before returning to Aden. "I wanted to inquire. How are you enjoying your pet?"

Every muscle in Aden's body tightened. "She's fine."

"Only fine?" Matthais appeared indifferent, but Aden knew better. "Is she not to your liking?"

Aden motioned for Matthais to have a seat. "She is very much to my liking," he said, cringing at the lecherous undertones in his voice.

Matthais inhaled deeply. "She's fresh on you," he said. "But not as strong as I would expect, considering your reputation for using your toys to excess. In fact, all your pets' scents are quite faint, like you're only feeding traditionally."

How the fuck did Matthais know that? Could he be any more of a creep? For a vampire renowned for sophistication and refinement, asking about another vampire's satisfaction with a pet was far from a suitable topic for polite conversation.

Aden poured two drinks and handed one to Matthais. The male thrall kneeling behind him stood and held his wrist out. Matthais sank his fangs into it before holding it over his glass.

"I go through a rotational purge every decade. I'm in the middle of one at the moment, so I'm spread pretty thin."

"With the number of thralls you have, it's not surprising. As long as Elliana is pleasing you. I would be disappointed to have a gift of mine not live up to expectations."

"I'm very pleased with her," Aden replied.

It was true, though not in the perverse way Matthais meant it or the loathsome way Aden made it sound. But in that moment, Aden realized how truly happy Ellie made him. Despite how uncertain and volatile things were between them at the moment, a flicker of hope filled him after countless centuries of despair. When she wasn't mad at him, at least.

"I always appreciate your gifts," Aden said, realizing this was his chance. "Although I'm aware, I overstepped in January. I would feel better if I paid restitution for insulting you like that."

"Oh, Aden, please. I'm used to your antics after all these years. It was my pleasure to give her to you."

Aden didn't quite believe him.

"Are you staying another day?" Aden took a sip of his drink, wishing Matthais would leave already.

"No. I'll be heading out shortly. I wanted to say goodbye to Aurick if he's back."

"He is," Aurick said from the door. Aden looked over to see both his parents standing there.

"How were your meetings?" Matthais asked.

"Productive."

"Everything on schedule for AEON's release in October?"

"Yes. Keeley has it all in hand."

"Good, well, I'll be on my way. I'll see you at the games then." Matthais said as he turned to address Aden.

Fuck! He forgot the summer games were coming up next month.

"I plan to be there," he replied, struggling to come up with an excuse why he couldn't attend. "But it will depend on what's happening with this rogue problem."

"Keep me posted on that. Of course, Andrei is always at your disposal, should you need him. I'll have him get in touch about the plan for Abya Yala." Matthais turned to Sophie. "Thank you, Sophie, as always for your impeccable hospitality." Matthais reached for her hand and kissed it.

Sophie gave him a smile that even Aden could tell was strained.

"I'll walk you out," Aurick said, and they exited Aden's office.

Aden dropped onto the sofa as soon as Aurick and Matthais exited his office. Sophie sat beside him, wiping her hand on her pants.

"So, how did it go?" She asked.

"He thought the recruits looked good," he replied, knowing that wasn't what she was asking.

"Aden—"

"He commented that Ellie's scent was not as strong as he expected."

"Well, your reputation precedes you, dear."

Aden glared at her but, as usual, it did nothing.

"And?"

"He asked if I was enjoying my pet," Aden said, appalled. "How fucking creepy is that?"

"Matthais' public face is one thing, but he's very different in private. He has a sadistic side to him he only shows to those he trusts."

"How do you know about it?"

"Your father told me about it a long time ago. Despite how it came about, getting Ellie away from him kept her alive. There is nothing you shouldn't be prepared to do to keep her away from him, Aden. Nothing."

Aden's stomach clenched at the implication of her words.

"Thank god you had her blood. How are you doing with that?"

"I've had her blood before, Sophie. I'm not an addict who just fell off the wagon." He felt like he was, but he'd never admit it to her.

With a hushed whoosh of the door, his father re-entered the office. "Did he accept your offer to pay for Ellie?"

"No."

"Damn it." Aurick walked to the window.

"You should have Mina supply you with her blood whenever you expect to see him," Sophie said. "For a little while. At least until he loses interest. I think he will... eventually."

"I don't want her blood that way."

"I know," she said as she rubbed his arm. He shrugged her off.

"I pray she'll someday come to you, but protecting her from him is the most important thing, Aden."

Yes, it was.

His father turned back from the window. "I never thought I'd ever say this, but I'm very glad you bit her that day."

Aden couldn't hide his shock at his father's words. "Why? Because if I hadn't, she'd still be there with him?"

Aurick glanced at Sophie before locking eyes with Aden's. "Or she'd be dead."

His father's words rattled around his brain as Aden walked back to his room. The implications about Matthais, Ellie, and her safety made his insides feel like he was going to burst into flames.

He resisted feeding after he drank Ellie's blood, not wanting to lose the taste of her, but he needed to rid himself of his agitation. Not that it helped. Not even the dozen thralls he drank from in his office could calm him. He almost asked Mina to bring him another vial of Ellie's blood after he was done, but that was a slippery slope he was wise to avoid.

Besides, he didn't want her blood any other way than from her vein and with her consent, and that was something he'd likely never have.

Ellie rushed out of her room to confront him as soon as he entered the suite. "Was Master Matthais the vampire who was here?"

"How did you know that?"

"Was it?"

"Ellie, watch yourself. I gave you permission to ask me anything, but I didn't say you could demand answers from me."

She took a deep breath and looked up, her eyes imploring. "Please answer my question, Aden."

Why couldn't he ever fucking say no to her? It was impossible to hold out when she looked at him that way.

"Yes, it was Matthais." The utter devastation in her eyes hit him like a blow to his chest.

"Aden, was my father here with him?"

"I don't know."

"What do you mean you don't know?"

"I mean, I don't know," he snapped, unable to help himself. "He had several guards with him, but I'm not sure if your father was one of them."

Her struggle to control her emotions was evident as she blinked, hugging herself tightly.

"I'm sorry you're upset, Ellie, but I thought it was best if you were unaware that Matthais was here. I did it to protect you."

"You mean you did it to protect yourself." Her voice was harsh and accusing. "If he had seen me, he would've wondered why I wasn't battered like your other thralls."

"No," he snarled, the intensity of his voice matching the force with which her words hit him. "I was protecting you. Because if he thought I wasn't using you, he could have taken you back. Is that what you want? To be Matthais' thrall again?"

His outburst caught her off guard, and she dropped her arms. "He can take me back?"

"An obscure law would allow it because, technically, you were a gift."

"I thought when you bit me, ownership of me was transferred to you."

"Yes and no, Ellie." He exhaled. "There is no need to be concerned with this because I will never let him take you back."

"I don't understand."

"And you don't need to," he barked, losing his patience. He sighed at her hurt expression. "Ellie, when a vampire bites another vampire's human, yes, ownership changes. But there needs to be payment. I offered to pay for you, but Matthais declined and gifted you to me."

"And that's why it falls under that obscure law?"

"Yes. But I will say it again." He slowly enunciated his next words. "I will never let him take you back."

His growl was fierce, but she didn't flinch.

"I would have liked to see my dad if he was here," she said, her voice broken as she bit her lip.

His aggressive posture eased. "It wouldn't have been safe for you, Ellie. Your safety is the most important thing to me."

She nodded, and he thought he saw tears welling in her eyes.

"Goodnight, Aden," she said as she turned to walk back to her room.

The urge to tear his hair out became unbearable, and he left to go feed in his office again. When he returned a short time later, although he couldn't be sure, he thought he heard soft crying coming from Ellie's room.

It had been almost two weeks since Matthais' visit, and Ellie was avoiding Aden. Again. He barely saw her, even in passing. His schedule was full of working with Roderick, searching for any other rogue vampires, as well as overseeing the additional training of new soldiers whose primary responsibility would be to patrol around the city for at least two hundred miles in every direction. He couldn't allow starving rogues to get near the city again.

He was also working with Andrei to devise an action plan to train Cecilia's military, which would begin after the summer games. Most nights, Aden would leave before Ellie even woke up, and when he came back in the mornings, she would already be in her room.

She was still distraught that she hadn't been able to see if her father was with Matthais. Her disappointment weighed on him, but there was nothing he would have done differently. Protecting her was what mattered most. But not seeing Ellie made him restless and edgy. Didn't she feel the same pull toward him that he felt toward her?

If Ellie wouldn't come to him by choice, he devised a plan to entice her by offering her something he believed she desired, judging by her reaction to their previous outing.

Keeley had given him just the excuse, so he found his way to his mother's office, where he knew he'd find them both. Sophie was busy working at her desk while Ellie concentrated on her hologram table in the corner. Beside her, his mother's cat slept on a chair, its head flipped upside down.

The office, with its main area and cozy seating space to the right, had been recently redecorated. His mother's fixation on changing decor went beyond normal, bordering on obsessive. There was something unnatural about the way she changed things up, as if she couldn't stand anything staying the same for too long. She clearly needed better things to occupy her time.

Ellie's head snapped up when he knocked on the door frame. A satisfied grin spread across Aden's face as her lips curved up into a smile. Maybe she wasn't still upset with him after all.

"Aden, this is a pleasant surprise," his mother said.

"Sophie." Aden tore his eyes away from Ellie and greeted his mother with a cocky grin. His gaze returned to her, but she had gone back to her work, yet her smile persisted.

"Hello, Ellie."

"Hello, Aden," she said without looking up.

He scowled at being denied a chance to see her eyes again, so he turned back to Sophie. "So Keeley hounded me until I agreed to learn about AEON for myself and check in with Hannah."

Sophie looked surprised. "I thought she was going herself tonight."

Aden sat in the chair in front of Sophie's desk. "Something about the incubator. I wasn't listening."

"Aden—"

He waved his hand. "Anyway, she can't go, so she asked me to take her place."

Sophie arched a brow. "BloodStone work? That's not like you."

"I'll admit I'm intrigued by AEON. I want to see it for myself."

"So you thought you'd stop by and let me know?" She asked. "That's considerate of you, Aden, but you stopped reporting your whereabouts to me centuries ago."

His mother's teasing didn't go unnoticed by Ellie, and she snorted, attempting to cover it with a cough.

"Keep your sarcasm to a minimum, please. Or I won't invite you to go with me and, perhaps, spend time at the beach while I'm meeting with Hannah."

Sophie sat forward. "Oh, I'd love that. I haven't been to the beach house in years."

Aden cleared his throat. "I thought maybe you'd like to show Ellie the ocean."

Ellie looked up, unable to hide her surprise.

"That's a wonderful idea," Sophie said. "Ellie, you'll love the beach."

"Me?" Ellie's eyes whipped to Sophie briefly before returning to Aden.

He averted his gaze, afraid that his desire for her to come with him would be too apparent.

"Oh, this is a great idea." With a wide grin on her face, Sophie closed the folder she had been perusing. "When do we leave?"

Aden didn't answer right away. Instead, he chanced a look at Ellie and met her hesitant, questioning, almost disbelieving gaze.

"Would you like to see the beach, Ellie?"

She nodded, looking too choked up to speak. Aden smiled, shifting in his chair and clearing his throat again as he turned back to his mother.

"Well, if you're not too busy now, we can leave in an hour. Rather than take a warp port, we can fly down to the villa. I'll take a car from there."

"Of course, we're not busy."

Sophie pushed out of her chair. Aden stood and shifted to the side so she could pass him.

Ellie looked over at her. "I still have to finish organizing these files."

"Leave it. They'll be there when we get back." Sophie squeezed Aden's arm but pulled back before he could brush her off. "Let me handle a few things and see your father. Then I'll be ready."

Sometimes she was so easy to please. "Relax, Sophie. It's just the beach."

She smiled up at him. "Yes, it is. I'll meet you both on the plane in an hour."

Sophie walked out, and Ellie turned back to her screen.

"What are you doing?" Aden asked from behind her.

"Finishing this."

"My mother said to leave it until you return."

"If we're not leaving for an hour, I can finish it real quick and still be ready on time."

"Okay," Aden said. "Meet me at the entrance to the hangar."

Ellie looked up at him. "I don't know where that is."

"Meet me in the courtyard in one hour, then."

"Okay. Thank you for inviting me." A bright smile spread across her face, confirming he'd made the right decision.

With a crooked grin, Aden couldn't tear his gaze away from her, even after she looked away and resumed her work. At least until it became too creepy, even for him, so he left to go feed.

Ellie

Ellie gazed out the floor-to-ceiling windows with awe. They stretched the entire back of the beach house, offering unobstructed views of the crashing waves on the sand. The sun had risen during the flight, and it reflected off the water, creating multicolored prisms in the early morning light that were visible even through the tinted glass.

The beach house was not just a house. It was a compound in itself—a sprawling contemporary villa with an indoor hangar and direct access to the main house. The color scheme was a soothing blend of cool blues, soft grays, and warm tans. To her surprise, Ellie liked the color palette. She disliked the color gray since it reminded her of Master Matthais' uniforms, but the combination Sophie had used created a warm, inviting atmosphere that mirrored the beach view Ellie gawked at through the glass.

She could hear Sophie speaking to the staff in the other room when she felt Aden walk up behind her.

"What do you think of the view?"

She smiled and met his eyes in the window's reflection. "Breathtaking."

The house sat right on the water's edge. A deck off the foyer hugged the entire back of the house and extended almost to the water, with only a small patch of sand separating it. Ellie's feet tingled with anticipation, eager to experience something she'd never felt before—the sensation of sinking into the silky grains.

"Is this really an island?"

"Yes. It's Oileán Cladaigh Sophie. Or Sophie's seashore island in English."

"Your mom has an island named after her?"

"Aurick gave it to her as a gift after he became Gerent of Réimse Shíochánta."

As she held his gaze in the reflection, a sudden rush of recognition flooded her mind as if she had experienced this moment before. A shiver crawled up her spine, sending a wave of apprehension mixed with an unexpected thrill through her.

She blinked, shaking her head, to refocus on the present.

"What's that language?"

"Gaelic. It was Aurick's native language when he was turned."

"Do you know it, too?"

"Yes." He nodded. "He and Sophie forced Keeley and me to learn it. Just like they made us learn all the Gerents' native languages."

Ellie looked away from his eyes in the reflection and focused on the ocean again, and she sighed.

"When my mother finishes briefing the staff, she'll sleep for a few hours. I'm leaving for the AEON labs in a few minutes."

"Why are you going during the day?"

"It's called a surprise inspection. Many of the support staff are half-breeds, so they work during the day while the vampire scientists work at night."

Ellie nodded, her eyes fixed on him again as he tucked his hands into his pockets. He had developed a habit of fidgeting around her as if he were unsure of what to do with his hands.

"What's AEON?"

"It's BloodStone's new drug."

"What does it do?"

"It replicates a sire's blood, so half-breeds don't need a daily donation to halt aging."

"So that's why most half-breeds don't age? They drink from their sires every day?"

"Yes. Those outside of the breeding program, anyway."

Aden's unusual patience with her questions, never once showing any signs of annoyance, was a pleasant surprise. It was out of character for him. But his attitude towards her had shifted, and he had grown more tolerant and even-tempered. They had grown more tolerant of each other.

"What's the difference?"

"The breeding program only produces soldiers, but all personal half-breed guards are turned. And it's unnecessary to drink. It can be injected, but it has to be pure vampire blood. Doesn't your father receive blood from Matthais?"

"If he does, he never told me," Ellie shrugged. "But he's aged. He's even got some gray hair now. Wait a minute, Kane has gray in his beard? Don't you let him drink from you?"

"Fuck no! Mina draws my blood every month so he can inject it."

"So you have to endure her taking your blood, too?"

"Yes," he said with a sidelong glance. "I have to endure that indignity as well."

"That makes me feel a little better." She tilted her head as she met his eyes in the glass again. "But not for long, I guess."

Aden's intense gaze remained fixed on her, sending a slight shudder across her skin.

"You should try to get some sleep, too. Sophie will wake you up in plenty of time to watch the sunset."

"I wouldn't be able to sleep if I tried. Can I go out and sit in the sun for a while?"

"The villa is secure, and there are plenty of guards, but I don't want you outside without her."

Ellie lifted her eyes to meet his. "Aden, please—"

He shook his head. "No. Wait for Sophie."

"Aden," Ellie pleaded, unable to hide her disappointment.

"Ellie, the sun limits my ability to protect you."

"I know. But there are at least fifty guards I can see just from where I'm standing." Ellie pointed to the dozen speedboats in the water, each filled with armed guards watching the house. "Can't they protect me?"

"Yes, and they will protect you. But no one will protect you better than me and my family. I want you to wait for Sophie. I trust her to keep you safe."

"Fine." With a disappointed sigh, she turned and made her way to a large bronze sculpture across the foyer. It stood next to a wide, wood-and-glass spiral staircase. Vlad dashed over and wound around Ellie's feet, and she reached down, picking him up. He hissed at Aden, but Ellie shushed him.

"Those look like the ones at the compound."

"They're the same artist," Aden said as he moved to stand next to her.

"They're so detailed. Who's the artist?" She asked as she scratched under the cat's chin as he purred.

"My grandmother."

Ellie looked up with surprise.

"Gabby was a legendary artist in her time."

"So that's where you get your talent?"

With a perplexed look in his eyes, Aden replied, "It would seem so."

Ellie hid a smile, her lips curving into a faint grin. He had added a door to his studio, but he had no idea that she had already snooped around before he did.

"That looks like Master Aurick." Ellie pointed to the man sitting on a bench with a little girl on his knee.

"It is. The girl on his lap is Sophie."

Ellie looked closer, and she saw the hint of Sophie's crooked smile. "Oh, I can see it," she said with delight before Aden's previous words registered. "What did you mean by her time?"

"Gabby died two hundred years before I was born."

"Oh." Ellie couldn't resist asking. "She wasn't a half-breed or vampire?"

"No. She was human."

Ellie's next question was on the tip of her tongue, but she held back as Sophie entered the foyer.

"Come on, Ellie. Let's get you set up in the bedroom next to mine, and then we can sleep before we head out to the beach."

"She'll sleep in the room attached to mine like she does at home," Aden said.

"Aden, it's only us here. She'll be safe in her own suite."

"No."

"Aden, I want her to have a view of the ocean." Sophie's tone was firm.

Aden released a harsh growl, and Ellie braced herself, prepared for him to start yelling.

"Go to the labs. And say hi to Hannah for me," Sophie said. "We'll be fine, and we'll see you later, after the sun sets."

Sophie held his gaze, daring him to keep arguing with her before turning to Ellie. "Let me speak to the kitchen staff really quickly so they can have lunch ready when we get up. Meet me at the top of the stairs."

Ellie watched Sophie leave, then looked back at Aden. He was still scowling, and she couldn't stop the chuckle that escaped.

"What?" Aden barked, and Ellie's lips curved into a smile.

"Nothing." She shrugged as she hoisted Vlad over her shoulder, but they both knew he never stood a chance against Sophie.

No one did.

Aden

"Where's Sophie?"

Aden exited the SUV as Hannah's voice echoed from the catwalk above. He glanced up from the hangar's main floor and spotted her leaning on the metal railing, a grin on her face as she peered down at him. The expansive BloodStone foyer was visible through the wall of glass behind her.

As one of only two man-made structures on Sophie's island, the BloodStone laboratory facility was a modern, glass-and-steel monolith. Its blending of sharp angles and smooth curves created a striking contrast to the pristine beauty of the island's otherwise untouched natural landscape. It occupied one-half of the approximately five-hundred-square-mile island. The sprawling, high-tech facility was committed to pushing innovation in various fields, not just pharmaceutical research and development.

"Hannah banana," Aden greeted with a smirk, and she narrowed her eyes at him.

"I hate it when you call me that."

"I know. Why are you here during the day?"

"Keeley warned me about your 'surprise inspection'," Hannah said, using air quotes to emphasize her words.

"Of course she fucking did."

Aden stepped on a warp port and was transported to the catwalk next to her.

"I thought Sophie was coming with you."

"She's here, but she's back at the villa. She wanted to sleep before heading out to watch the sunset."

"I miss that," Hannah said with a wistful sigh.

"What's the big deal? You can see it through the windows. Why do you have to be outside to see it?"

"Oh, come on, Aden. You're not so old that you forget what it was like. Even I'm not that old."

"Wow! And here I thought you were an Ancient One."

"Not quite." She gestured for him to walk through the double glass doors, careful to avoid touching him. "But I am married to one."

They entered the foyer through the sliding glass doors. Aden's gaze drifted upwards, following the smooth curve of the octagonal glass enclosure. The soaring glass walls and curved ceiling bathed the vast lobby in a soft, diffused light, casting a muted glow over the entire space. The UV-filtering polymer, invented by Hannah and her team almost five centuries ago, was incorporated into the transparent panels, allowing the vampire scientists to move throughout the space without fear of the sun's rays.

"Speaking of ancient, you were my grandmother's best friend before you were Sophie's, right?"

"Yes." Hannah smiled. "Gabriella Newman McNamara. I think about her every time I see this sculpture. I still miss her something fierce every damn day."

Casting a shadow over them, in the center of the gleaming white marble floor stood a twenty-foot brushed stainless steel abstract sculpture. Gabby's artistic talent was as extensive and impressive as her collection of works, which included both two-dimensional and three-dimensional, abstract, and abstract-figurative pieces. No wonder he and Keeley had such divergent artistic tastes.

"What was she like?"

"Gorgeous and fierce. And brave and stubborn as all hell." She gave him a sideways glance. "You're a lot like her, actually. She had a temper on her, too."

"I thought I got my temper from Aurick."

"Yeah, you got a double whammy in that department, didn't you? No wonder you're such a hothead."

Aden grunted his disagreement.

"So why are you asking about Gabby?"

Aden followed Hannah up a winding staircase to the second level. He assumed she was taking him to the AEON labs, but he hadn't been here in over a century, so who knew if the labs were in the same location?

"I was looking at one of her sculptures in the foyer before I came over, and it made me realize I don't know much about her other than her art and the few stories Aurick and Sophie told over the years."

"Oh, are you talking about the one of Sophie and Aurick on the bench?"

"Yeah."

They navigated through a maze of hallways, each one leading them deeper into the building. The walls on their left were stark and white, with only periodic doors to break up the monotony of the sterile space. The ones on the right were made of glass and provided a clear view of the bustling labs and workspaces inside.

"I love that one," Hannah said. "Kyle hated it because he was always jealous of how much Sophie adored Aurick when she was a little girl."

"Kyle, my grandfather?"

They reached the end of the hallway and came to a stop. After a series of biometric scans of Hannah's eyes, face, fingertips, and voice, the door opened. They entered the lab and walked towards the opposite end of the room. Counters lined the path, occupied by lab techs busy working.

Hannah looked back at him. "Yeah. He never liked Aurick, but he had valid reasons for it, I guess."

Aden's brow furrowed. Sophie never mentioned that her father didn't like Aurick.

"Anyway, let's get started," she said when they reached a counter along the back wall. She brought up a hologram displaying AEON's chemical composition and molecular structure. One thing Aden appreciated about Hannah was her ability to get straight to the point.

"Yeah. Show me what you've got."

Hannah swiped the hologram closed and turned her gaze toward Aden.

"So, what makes this different from the biologic the half-breeds get now?"

"That's a synthesized version. Yes, vampire blood is the foundation, but not any specific vampire. Like BloodStone, any vampire's blood will work. With AEON, it has to be the sire's blood. It keeps half-breeds from aging without the sire needing to participate beyond the initial donation."

"Can AEON work for all half-breeds then? Get rid of the old drug and replace it with this one?"

"No. There's a difference between sired half-breeds and half-breeds born from the breeding program. Or those from the breeding program who are sired afterward, like you and your dad did to Kane and Horatio. The pellet technology is already part of their program, and it works well for them. There's no need to change it."

Aden glanced at the lab techs working nearby. He never gave much thought to what they did or the commitment they had to their work until now.

"AEON has been our priority for centuries. This is two hundred thirty-six years in the making, Aden. It will sustain a sired half-breed indefinitely. One dose, daily, is the same as drinking from the sire. We're also working on a capsule. Encapsulating it could increase production volume."

"Damn, you're good, Hannah," Aden said, impressed. Yeah, he gave her shit all the time, but she was fucking brilliant.

"A compliment from Aden Westcott? What universe am I living in?"

Aden narrowed his eyes. "I was being nice, and you had to go and fucking ruin it."

With a laugh, she started to bump him with her hip but stopped at the last second. "It happens so rarely, I barely recognize it."

"I really despise you."

"I think you mean you adore me."

Aden grunted, pursing his lips. He'd never admit it out loud because she'd become unbearable if she knew his true feelings.

"So, is there anything else worth seeing while I'm here? I won't return for at least another hundred years, so you might as well give it to me while you've got me."

She tapped her finger on her lips, surveying the lab.

"What?" Aden asked, his eyes tracking hers.

"Keeley told me to show you everything, but," she paused. "It's still a top-secret program. You are an owner of the company, I guess. But the board doesn't even know about it yet."

"You realize you're talking to yourself, right?" He smirked. "If you're not careful, you'll start giving off mad scientist vibes."

She ignored his teasing. "Follow me."

Hannah led him out of the lab and to her private office across the hall. After another biometric authentication, they entered, and she locked the door. He trailed behind her until they reached a wall displaying a large ten-by-ten-foot painting by Gabby. Hannah slid it to the side to reveal a large vaulted door.

"What the fuck, Hannah? Where are you taking me?"

After punching in a code and completing additional biometric scans, the door opened. Inside were two scientists Aden didn't recognize, absorbed in their experiments.

"Shut up and get in here, Aden."

The door closed behind them, and Hannah led him over to another private office in the corner, surrounded by glass. She gestured for him to sit in a chair. She pulled herself up onto her desk and turned to face him.

"Okay, Hannah, now that we've breached Fort Knox, what the hell is this about?"

A smirk spread across her face. "I love it when you reference things you weren't alive for." She crossed her legs and leaned forward. "This is my private lab. Only nine people, including you, know about it. Aurick, Keeley, and I have been working on a special project for a long time. Even before Keeley took over, Aurick and I had been working on it for four centuries."

Now his curiosity was piqued. "Okay, what is it?"

"Have you ever wondered if it was possible for vampires to survive without feeding on humans?"

"No."

"What if vampires didn't have to rely on human blood for sustenance?"

Aden suspected her question was rhetorical, so he waved his hand for her to continue.

"Imagine we could create and manufacture a synthetic blood alternative that eliminated the need for vampires to drink human blood?"

Aden's expression turned serious. "Is that possible?"

"Right now, despite our best efforts, there's no true synthetic substitute for human blood, but there really is no reason we shouldn't be able to develop it." She paused. "They developed substitute blood components over six hundred years ago. Long before I became a scientist, efforts were made to create a safe blood substitute capable of performing all the functions of human blood. We used much of that research as the basis for BloodStone, which eliminated the need for artificial blood for humans' purposes."

She pulled up a hologram that showed him a lot of tables, charts, and blood sequences that made his eyes cross.

"Until now, nothing we've been able to develop can fulfill one hundred percent of vampires' nutritional needs, which are more than just plasma, platelets, and red and white blood cells."

"Until now?" Aden sat forward, intrigued.

"We're not there yet, but we're close. Aden, if it works, we won't have to rely on humans for sustenance and survival."

"What's it called?"

Hannah closed the hologram and dropped her feet to the floor. "ICHOR."

"Isn't that from Greek mythology?"

"Yes. It's the ethereal fluid believed to take the place of blood in the veins of the gods. Your mama would be so proud to know you paid attention to her lessons."

"I don't appreciate your sarcasm, Hannah. I'll have you know I am very well educated."

"That's only because your parents broke the law and taught you all of that in secret."

Aden stood and glanced through the open door at the other scientists in the lab, but they weren't paying attention to their conversation.

"Don't worry. Everyone involved in this is trustworthy."

"I have to admit, I'm not sure how I feel about not feeding on humans. And why, with all our technology and medical advancement, has it taken this long to develop?"

Hannah pushed off her desk and motioned with her hand, signaling for him to step out of the office. They made their way through the lab as the techs ignored them.

"We've had a small team working on this for a long time, but we're missing a component we can't identify to complete the sequence. And AEON was the priority. Now we're turning all our resources to ICHOR. But this is confidential, Aden. Even the board members are unaware of it."

"Why keep it a secret?"

"Let's just say there are vampires who believe that a blood alternative would pose a serious threat to their control over humans."

"That's a valid concern."

"Is it?"

"What would be the need for humans at all if there was a blood substitute?" Aden's jaw dropped in astonishment as the weight of his own words sank in.

Hannah led a slack-jawed Aden back into her outer office, secured the door, and concealed it with a painting before looking at him.

"Humans serve purposes beyond just providing blood. But that's the crux of it, isn't it?"

The potential implications made his gut twist. "If you succeed, do you know what this will do, Hannah?"

Their eyes locked, and a shiver ran down Aden's spine as he knew her answer even before she spoke.

"It will change the world, Aden."

"You've officially blown my mind, Hannah."

Aden and Hannah walked back the way they came, down the same intersecting hallways, as his mind raced with thoughts of ICHOR and its implications.

A knowing smile played on her lips. "Yeah. Now do you see why Keeley wanted you to come?"

"She's been hounding me for decades to be more interested in BloodStone. I hate it when she's right."

"It's about time, Aden. BloodStone is your legacy, too. I know I don't need to say this again, but confidentiality is paramount."

"Of course," he replied in a serious tone, before smirking. "I haven't tattled about what my sister is doing since I was ten."

Turning a corner, they continued down a new hallway that looked identical to the other one.

"So let me ask you something," he said, changing the subject. "You decided to become a half-breed, right?"

"Yes."

"Why?"

A smile tugged at her lips. "I was in love with a vampire."

"How old were you?"

"Don't you know it isn't polite to ask a woman her age?" She narrowed her eyes at him before answering. "I was thirty-nine."

"How long did you stay a half-breed?"

"Fifty-four years."

"Then you chose to become a vampire?"

"Yes."

"Why?"

"Desperately in love with the same vampire. That's what women do. Or did back then. What's with the twenty questions?"

They neared a door Aden didn't remember going through on the way to Hannah's lab. It slid open, and behind it stood Hannah's husband, Nickolas, engrossed in a hologram and narrowly avoiding colliding with his wife.

"Speaking of said vampire." Her tone was warmer.

Nickolas glanced at them over his glasses. "Hello, Aden."

Hannah leaned close to Aden and mock-whispered. "He doesn't have to wear the glasses, of course, but he knows I think they make him look sexy."

Nickolas' lips curved into an indulgent smile, confirming his wife's words.

His dark hair, streaked with gray on the top and around the temples, made him look older than Aurick. Aden was unsure at what age he was turned, but Nickolas was considered an Ancient One. The Ancient Ones were vampires who were turned before the release of BloodStone, which led to vampires being revealed to the world.

Aurick's obsession with finding a cure for cancer, a mostly incurable disease at the time, began after he lost the woman he loved to it. With Aurick's financial support and influence, Nickolas and Hannah developed BloodStone, which was the catalyst for the vampires' rise to power. It also led to Aurick meeting Sophie and her mother, who was among the cured participants in the drug trial.

"So, what did you think?" Nickolas asked as he closed his hologram.

"As much as I loathe saying it, your wife is a genius."

"As she likes to remind me every day."

"Damn straight, I do." Hannah reached up and straightened Nickolas' tie. "I'm walking Aden out, and then I'll join you."

"Okay. I'll get started. See you later, Aden. Say hi to Sophie and Aurick and tell Keeley I'll have those results for her next week."

"What results?"

Hannah urged Aden away and through the door. "Please don't ask. He'll keep you talking about it for hours."

"More experiments?"

"We're scientists, Aden. That's all we do. So, you were asking me about half-breeds and vampires. You don't need me to explain the birds and the bees to you, do you?"

"You're a fucking comedian." They rounded another corner and arrived on the second-level balcony overlooking the foyer.

"I was curious why a woman would choose to become a half-breed or vampire. I mean, I know why she'd want to become a vampire, but why, other than wanting to pop out a couple of brats, would she go the half-breed route first?"

"I knew I wanted to be with Nicky forever and asked him to make me a vampire outright. He refused. Vampire reproduction hadn't been considered yet, so having children wasn't on the table, but he wanted me to be absolutely sure. So, we compromised, and I remained a half-breed for a half-century before he turned me."

They descended the stairs to the foyer and turned toward the doors leading to the hangar.

"I wonder if that's what Aurick and Sophie did."

"That was a completely different scenario. They didn't have a choice. You know your mother's story, right?"

"Yeah. Some vampires attacked her, and Aurick turned her into a half-breed to save her life. I don't know why he didn't just turn her into a vampire from the start."

"Jesus, Aden," Hannah said, exasperated. "She was only eight years old. You don't turn eight-year-old children into vampires."

"I mean after her parents were gone. There was no reason for them to keep their relationship a secret anymore."

They stepped out onto the catwalk.

"It wasn't quite that simple."

"What was it then?"

"Uh uh," Hannah shook her head. "Ask your mother if you want to know."

"Hannah, fucking tell me."

"Nope. Talk to your mother. And don't glare at me like that." She pointed at him. "I brought you into this world and was the first person on the planet to slap your naked little ass, so trying to intimidate me with your growls won't work."

"I really fucking despise you sometimes," he said to her again, but they both knew it was a lie.

"Before you go," she said as he stepped into the warp port. "So, you want to turn Ellie into a half-breed, huh?"

Ellie

Ellie unlocked the sliding glass door in her bedroom, careful not to make a sound. For almost two hours, she sat on a chair in front of it, unable to sleep. Vlad had been sitting beside her at the door, but grew bored and curled up for a nap on the bed. Ellie was dying to go outside, but Aden had insisted she wait for Sophie to wake up.

The guards in the speedboats were still patrolling the waters, but Ellie hoped they wouldn't notice her. She didn't plan to go far. She only wanted to step onto the deck and feel the sun on her face for a few minutes.

Ellie's heart raced as she opened the door, her ears filled with the hushed echo of her own breathing. Vampires had super hearing, but so did half-breeds. She knew that from her father. While she didn't want to disturb Sophie, she couldn't bear to wait any longer. She'd only stay outside for a few minutes. Then she'd try to sleep a little before lunch.

Ellie poked her head out and looked in both directions. No guards were in the immediate vicinity. She stepped through the door and onto the deck. The sight of the water reflecting the sunlight was mesmerizing. The absence of tinted glass made everything brighter and clearer.

She took another two steps, intending to walk to the railing, but the deep voice beside her startled her.

"Hello, Ellie."

Ellie spun around to find Kane sitting on a deck chair, out of sight.

"Jeez, Kane. Are you trying to give me a heart attack?" She did a double take. "Wait a minute." Then the panic set in. "Is Aden back?"

"Nope."

"Then what are you doing here?"

"He figured you'd try something, so he told me to stick around and keep an eye on you."

Ellie scowled. Figures.

Kane laughed out loud. "You're picking up his scowl."

Instead of answering, Ellie growled under her breath and stomped back to her room.

Kane's loud laughter floated through as the door slid closed.

"You're picking up his growls, too."

"It feels so good."

Ellie tilted her head back in a moment of pure bliss as she relished the soothing caress of the sun's warmth on her face, contrasting with the subtle coolness of the air. She and Sophie had removed their shoes early on as they strolled by the water's edge, far from the villa. Their footsteps left gentle imprints in the sand, and Ellie loved the feeling of it squishing between her toes, just like she knew she would. The scent of saltwater and wet sand overwhelmed her senses as she took a deep breath, trying to immerse herself in her surroundings.

Sophie let out a sigh of agreement, nodding beside her. "Sometimes I forget what it's like."

"It's not like the lights in the greenhouse, that's for sure."

Sophie hooked her arm through Ellie's, their steps in sync as they walked side by side. Surprised by the action, Ellie stiffened before relaxing. Kane and two of Sophie's guards followed behind them, their presence almost undetectable, while Vlad ran alongside them, pausing occasionally to sniff and attack anything in his path.

"Are you sure he won't run off?" Ellie asked as Vlad dashed in front of them and pounced on a small, tangled clump of seaweed, rolling on his back as he fought with the knotted strands.

"Yes." Sophie laughed as the cat wrestled with it. "I brought him out here once when he was a kitten, and he loved it. Water doesn't faze him and, besides, where will he go? I'm fast enough to catch him if he tries."

They caught up with Vlad, and Ellie picked up the seaweed and tossed it down the beach. He darted after it.

"I go through phases." Sophie's eyes reflected the often hidden, mischievous nature of her personality. "It usually takes coming here again, but then I'll spend decades with my entire schedule flipped, so I'm awake during the day. I feel one of those phases coming on."

"If it were up to me, I would always be in that phase."

Sophie guided them to a stop and prompted Ellie to look at the water. "No matter how beautiful it is, it gets lonely when the people you love can't enjoy it with you."

Golden sand stretched into the water, disappearing beneath the lapping waves. The coastline, dotted with rocky jetties and jagged rock formations, jutted out, adding a rough beauty to the peaceful, rippling water. The guards in their speedboats continued their patrols, far enough away that it was easy to ignore them.

"Why don't we sit here?" Sophie suggested. "The sun is going to set soon."

Ellie sat beside her on the sand. Sliding the sunglasses Sophie lent her up on top of her head, Ellie looked out over the water, watching the waves, captivated by their foamy crests gliding across the wet sand before retreating. Ellie shivered, clutching her light sweater tighter around her. Both she and Sophie were dressed in light pants and shirts, but the cool weather called for a sweater to ward off a chill.

Vlad ran over with a piece of seaweed in his mouth. He tucked in between them and fell to his side, tearing it with his teeth and claws.

"This is about as warm as it gets now." Sophie stretched her legs, crossing her ankles. "The planet used to be much warmer, but the Antarctic tectonic shift changed everything."

"What's the Antarctic tectonic shift?" Ellie stretched out, mimicking Sophie's pose.

"The end of the world as we knew it."

Ellie's brow furrowed in confusion. End of the world?

"The world was vastly different five hundred years ago, and not just because vampires weren't in power. The geography was different. Earth had more land and less ocean, and the average temperature was almost thirty degrees warmer. Then a comet struck Antarctica, an enormous ice-covered continent that was once at the South Pole. It's gone now. Do you know what a comet is?"

Ellie nodded with wide eyes. There were several books on her tablet about comets or asteroids crashing into the Earth. And the aftermath.

"The comet's impact set off a cataclysmic chain reaction, triggering a dramatic realignment of the earth's tectonic plates, which make up the earth's crust. The force of the impact was so catastrophic that it nearly caused a mass extinction event."

"What happened?" Ellie whispered, twisting her body to face Sophie and crossing her legs. Vlad darted out from between them, leaving the torn seaweed behind.

Sophie's gaze became distant. "It's almost impossible to describe the destruction. The shifting of the Antarctica plate caused all the other plates to collide. The force was so intense that it caused the sea floor to buckle, setting off earthquakes and tsunamis that swept across the entire planet. Cities crumbled. Mountains rose, and valleys plummeted. Coastlines detached from the continents and sank into the oceans. And new land masses like this island rose from their depths. It reshaped the very face of the planet and killed billions."

Ellie's gaze wandered over to the tranquil water beside them, imagining its immense power, capable of engulfing large portions of land and people.

"Even after determining that the impact would occur in Antarctica, most scientists believed that surviving it was impossible. The last time a comet close to that size hit, it caused the extinction of the dinosaurs. If it had landed anywhere else on the planet, all life on Earth would have ceased to exist. There were nine billion people on the planet then, and ninety percent of them died. Mostly humans, but many half-breeds and vampires, too."

The way Sophie looked made Ellie want to comfort her, but despite their growing closeness, Ellie was unsure of how she would respond.

"That sounds like The Conversation of Eiros and Charmion." She frowned, trying to envision the disturbing scene Sophie described.

Sophie smiled at Ellie's words, despite the gravity of their conversation. "I see you've gotten to Edgar Allan Poe on your tablet."

"I'm on the p's now."

Sophie looked at her with a curious gaze. "You weren't kidding when you said you don't sleep."

With a shrug, Ellie pulled her sunglasses back over her eyes and turned to face the water again. Sophie's intense looks sometimes made her feel uneasy as if Ellie was a mystery she was trying to solve. Ellie caught sight of Kane smirking nearby from the corner of her eye. He was obviously listening, and she fought the urge to fling sand at him because he got too much pleasure from teasing her for constantly having her nose buried in her tablet.

"Is that how vampires took over?" Ellie asked.

"No. The vampire wars started a decade earlier. But everything stopped when the comet hit."

"How did you and Master Aurick survive? What happened to the people left on the planet?"

Sophie sat forward and bent her legs, resting her arms on her knees. "We knew it was going to happen. Scientists had long monitored comet and asteroid activity, so they were aware this one was coming for years. But the vampire wars were raging, so the public largely ignored it. Aurick and the other Ancient Ones knew they had to prepare, especially Aurick. They assessed each continent, identified the safest areas, and made preparations to ensure survival. That's how underground and domed cities came to exist. Those underground fortresses served as the initial prototypes. They were built with the sole intention of surviving the impact and ensuring the continuation of life."

Ellie caught sight of Vlad as he swatted at the foamy edges of the waves, his tentative paw reaching out and then retracting, only to repeat the process. She fought a smile, but he was just too cute.

"I'm sorry," Ellie said when she realized Sophie was looking at her. "I didn't mean to let Vlad distract me. I'm genuinely interested in hearing this."

Sophie reached out and gave her a reassuring pat on her leg. "It's okay. Adorable distraction is one of Vlad's superpowers."

Vlad's ears perked up like he heard his name. In a blur of movement, he darted over to Kane, brushing against his legs. Kane glanced down at him with a stoic expression, but Ellie noticed a faint tugging at the corners of his lips. Damn! She couldn't stay mad at him now because, despite being a constant teaser and rotten spy, he was just a big softy at heart.

"So, how do you even prepare for something like that?" Ellie asked.

"We spent nearly a decade planning, constructing, and stockpiling resources and historical and cultural artifacts. Preserving humanity's knowledge and cultural heritage was our priority, second only to human life. What mattered most was that humanity survived. There was no guarantee it would do any good, but we had to try. Building Cathair an Lae Amárach, our capital city, on the border between what was then known as the US and Canada, saved our lives."

"So, the shifting didn't affect you there? You didn't feel it?"

Sophie shuddered. "Oh, no, we felt it. Everything still crashed down around us. It was terrifying. For months, the earth trembled and shifted until the plates settled. We had to stay underground for almost three years until the air was safe to breathe again. Then it took decades to recover and rebuild. It took years for humanity to relearn the basic skills needed for survival and mere existence. You know little about the vampire wars, and I know for a fact that what you've been told isn't the truth, but that comet shifted the balance in the vampires' favor. I don't know if they would have prevailed if that comet hadn't struck, even with the half-breed armies."

Sophie's words left Ellie speechless. She couldn't believe that Sophie was sharing all of this. Vampires kept their secrets hidden from humans.

"Aurick cataloged it all. I have hundreds of journals, too, from that time, but he recorded them for historical accuracy. Remind me when we get back to ask him if he minds if you read his account of it. I'm sure he'll be happy to share it with you. His passion for history extends beyond just learning. He enjoys recounting both its triumphs and tragedies because we learn from both."

"Thank you. I'd like that very much."

"We were fortunate here. Our region remained largely intact, except for the coasts. The ocean swallowed the entire east coast, and this little island paradise popped up out of the water in its place."

"Like Atlantis?"

A chuckle escaped Sophie's lips. "I had a sneaking suspicion you'd latch on to that part of Plato's tale."

"It was disturbingly familiar." Ellie nodded. "But the idea of it fascinated me, so I jumped around in my reading and devoured every book I could find on it. Plenty of writers thought it could one day rise out of the sea again."

"Yes, but most of the theories put it closer to the Mediterranean Sea and Erebu, which was called Europe then, but a few suggested it was closer to our part of the world. So, you never know, we could be sitting on Atlantis right now," Sophie teased.

A brief smile played on Ellie's lips before she sobered again. "I'm sorry you had to go through that, but I'm glad you and Master Aurick survived. And your island is beautiful, Sophie. I am happy and grateful to be here with you right now." A flicker of recognition crossed Sophie's face, causing Ellie's heart to quicken. "What?"

Sophie's eyes softened. "Nothing. Your words just brought up a memory of another young woman saying the same thing."

"Alysia?" Ellie had overheard Sophie and Keeley talking about her one day, which is how she learned her name. Sophie didn't appear surprised that she knew it.

"Yes," Sophie said, her word lingering in the air as Vlad darted closer and pounced on something in front of them. He slid through the sand as his tail twitched and swished. He clawed at the sand, and Sophie reached over and pulled something out from underneath his paws.

"No, Vlad," she scolded, and then held the small shell out to Ellie. "It's a hermit crab."

Ellie held out her hand, and Sophie placed it in her palm. She was startled when the legs came out of the shell and tickled her skin. She let the hermit crab crawl across her palm as Vlad climbed onto Sophie's lap and curled in a circle. Ellie set the hermit crab back on the sand.

"Ellie, can I ask you something?" Sophie asked, stroking Vlad gently.

"Of course."

"I hope by now you're comfortable enough with me to share anything, so I'm just going to come out with this."

As Sophie paused, Ellie tensed, holding her breath in anticipation.

"Surely you know how my son feels about you."

Ellie released the breath she'd been holding. "Honestly, I don't know how Aden feels most of the time."

"We haven't known each other for long, but I know you're full of opinions, Ellie."

"I don't—" Ellie started, not wanting to insult Sophie, but Sophie interrupted her.

"I don't mean that negatively." Sophie's reassuring tone eased Ellie's tension. "But I've seen you and my son interact, and I can see the connection between the two of you. Does anything about Aden or this place seem familiar to you?"

Ellie didn't answer right away because that's what she'd been feeling lately.

Sophie smiled. "It does, doesn't it?"

"I—" Ellie started, but then hesitated, closing her mouth as uncertainty flooded her. It was so hard not having anyone to talk to, and it made her miss Carrie all that much more. During their work on the nursery design, she was tempted to confide in Keeley. Aden's sister made her feel included and comfortable, but Ellie hesitated to open up. This was her chance, and if she didn't take it, she'd kick herself later.

"I know what Keeley told me and what I read, but I still have a hard time wrapping my head around soulmates."

"The idea of it can take time to digest."

"Are you and Master Aurick soulmates?"

"Yes, I believe we are." Sophie's eyes crinkled in the corners as she smiled. "And I believe you and Aden are, too. But what I believe doesn't matter. What matters is what you believe."

"I don't know what to believe." Ellie hesitated again but continued before she could second-guess herself. "I've dreamed of his eyes my whole life. How can I explain that? And sometimes when I dream, it seems so real."

"That's because it is. It's your subconscious mind tapping into those memories, trying to remind you of who you are."

"But how is that possible?" Ellie looked at Sophie, desperate to understand. "I read Freud's The Interpretation of Dreams so I understand what the subconscious is, but what is it trying to tell me? Sometimes the dreams about him are so real, and they really scare me. When I see his eyes turn red, it's like I can't breathe. Even before my mom died, it was why I could never sleep my whole life."

"Some of those memories are frightening, but believe me, the good ones far outnumber the bad."

"All these feelings are so confusing and frightening."

"You shouldn't be afraid of them. They aren't a bad thing."

Ellie pressed her hands into the sand beside her. The coarse grains dug into her palms.

"How are they not a bad thing? I'm a human and he's a vampire. It's not like any of it matters, anyway."

"That's where you're mistaken, Ellie. It's all that matters."

Ellie looked over her shoulder at the sound of wheels touching the ground behind them and saw Aden's vehicle, the black-tinted windows confirming its passenger. She wondered how long he'd been there because the cars were silent.

"He heard all of that, didn't he?" Ellie asked, already knowing the answer. Damn vampires and their super-hearing.

"I'm sure he did," Sophie said. "And I believe my son is probably going a little crazy right now."

"Yes." She could feel Aden's eyes on her, and a tingle ran down her back. "Maybe I should go to him."

"He'll be fine. The sunset is starting, and he wants you to see this even more than I do."

With her toes and fingers buried in the warm sand, Ellie fixed her gaze on the sunset, holding her breath again.

The sky transformed into a symphony of colors that seemed to defy the limits of imagination as it reflected off the water below. The afternoon sky shifted from a vibrant blue to a stunning palette of various shades of yellow with streaks of orange and red, the colors swirling and blending in a hypnotic display. As the minutes passed, the sun sank lower in the sky. The colors grew more intense, and the sky more dazzling. The collage of scarlet hues morphed into a blaze of fiery orange as the sun dipped below the horizon, its last rays illuminating the sky with a brilliant burst of crimson and gold. For a fleeting moment, time stood still, and a warm, otherworldly light bathed everything in a mesmerizing, ethereal glow.

As the last of the sun disappeared, Ellie's eyes shimmered with unshed tears. She was unsure if the moisture was from the breathtaking sight she had just witnessed or from the darkness that now enveloped her. After living most of her life in darkness, losing the light left a sharp ache in her chest.

"Hello, Aden."

Ellie tilted her head back to peek up at him when she heard Sophie's quiet voice beside her.

"Sophie."

His tone was gruff, and the air around him crackled with his crankiness, visible in both his rigid posture and scowling expression.

Sophie tucked Vlad into her arm and stood, brushing the sand from her pants. "Well, I'm heading back to the house. You two come back when you're ready." Sophie looked down at her. "Thank you, Ellie, for an enjoyable afternoon and for watching the sunset with me."

Ellie nodded, her voice catching in her throat. "Thank you so much, Sophie."

"I'll come get you before sunrise, and we'll do this again."

Sophie brushed Aden's arm before she walked away. "Enjoy the moonlight."

Aden

Aden sank down next to Ellie. The beach, once a vibrant canvas of color, was now shrouded in a velvet darkness, broken only by the twinkling stars scattered above and a sliver of the moon. The gentle, hushed sound of the waves lapping at the shore broke the silence.

To Aden's surprise, Ellie shifted closer, so her thigh was touching his. His first instinct was to tense up, but his muscles gradually loosened as her presence soothed him. He could have sworn he sensed her tremble as she leaned back, resting her hands on the sand and gazing up at the sky. The silence between them stretched on for a few minutes before Aden broke it.

"I heard you tried to make a break for it today."

"Kane's a snitch."

Aden snorted a laugh as Kane's insulted scoff echoed from where he stood a few yards down the shore.

"Did you enjoy your day at the beach?"

"Yes, I did." Unmistakable joy filled her voice. "I enjoyed your mother's company very much, too. We had a nice talk." He grunted, and Ellie's lips curved. "Well, I don't know if I would call it nice, but it was enlightening. Thank you for letting me have so much time out here with her."

"Ellie, stop thanking me all the time. I don't want your gratitude. I want you to be happy."

The words came out more harshly than he intended, and Ellie's smile slipped off her face.

"I'm not used to anyone besides my dad caring whether I'm happy, so you'll have to excuse me for wanting to tell you how much it meant to me." She pushed herself to her feet and brushed the sand off her pants. "But I won't bother you with my feelings any longer. I'll just go back to the house."

Aden reached up and grasped her hand. It surprised them both. His flesh came alive at the feel of her soft, warm skin. "No. Stay here with me. I'm not trying to be an ass."

She angled her head to the side as she looked down at him. "Then why are you?"

He tugged on her hand, urging her to sit beside him again. She lowered herself back onto the sand.

"Habit. I've spent too long being one."

He kept her hand in his, threading his fingers between hers. Her eyes dropped to their hands, and he flexed the digits. This wasn't easy for him. He held his breath, expecting no response, until her fingers wrapped around his, and he breathed a sigh of relief.

"I don't like you being able to do something I can't." If he didn't start opening up to her, she would never come to him.

Her gentle scoff didn't surprise him. "Tell me something I don't know."

"I wanted to be out here with you today. I remember the warmth of the sun on my skin, and I miss it. And I hate not having the freedom to do something I want."

"Welcome to my world, Aden."

Aden frowned as Ellie's words hung between them. He'd never given much thought to the restrictions humans were forced to live with. He'd never given them much thought at all in the last three hundred years. They provided blood and sex, and that was the extent to which he thought about them.

How quickly a person's point of view can completely change.

Despite his excitement about AEON and his conversations with Hannah, he resented every second of the afternoon. Unable to help himself, he'd tapped into the surveillance system and pulled up holograms of Ellie a few times, both on his way to and back from the labs. The sight of her, happy as she and his mother enjoyed lunch and strolled on the beach, irritated him. While he was glad she was enjoying herself, he resented being away from her, unable to share it with her.

Sometimes he envied his mother for being a half-breed. Maybe she had the best of both worlds. She could live forever, and she didn't have to fear the sun.

Ellie was waiting for him to respond, but he wasn't sure what to say. "Ellie, I don't know what you want from me. I'm doing everything in my power to bring you into my world, but it seems like that isn't what you want at all."

"I'll never be part of your world, Aden."

Her words were like a slap, and he pulled his hand from hers.

"In your world, I'm nothing. I'm food. I'm inferior to you in every way. You don't even like humans. You use them as bait for rogue vampires."

His eye twitched as she reminded him of his most recent indiscretion.

"What makes me any different?" She asked.

His answer was simple. "Everything."

He caught her eyes, and his own implored her to understand. Why couldn't she see she was everything to him?

Ellie bit her lip, and his eyes dropped as he licked his own. He hadn't wanted to kiss anyone since Aly, but he ached to press his lips to hers. Before he second-guessed himself, Aden leaned toward her. Ellie's eyes widened, and she leaned back. The flicker of hope in him died, and he fisted his hands in frustration.

"I know you hate me, but I'm trying to show you I'm more. I can be more, and I can be better. Do you think this is easy for me?"

"I don't hate you, Aden." He shot her a look of disbelief, and her eyes softened. "I don't think I ever hated you. But I was afraid of you until I believed you wouldn't hurt me."

Her honesty was both refreshing and gutting. "Do you believe it now?"

"Yes."

"Are you unhappy here with me?" Aden asked.

"Why do you care, Aden? Really?"

Was she fucking kidding?

"How can you ask me that after everything I've done for you?"

"You mean biting me? Taking me away from my only family? Terrorizing me?"

Once again, Ellie's words hit him like a sharp slap.

"Vampires don't care about humans. You only care because you think I'm Alysia, your girlfriend who died."

Although Aly's name no longer evoked instant violent reactions, Aden's breath whooshed out of his body.

"I'm not sure what happened. Nobody will tell me. All I know are these images that come to me in my dreams. So, maybe I am her. But what do you expect me to remember? If it's anything like my nightmares, I don't want to."

Aden roared as he stood and yanked Ellie to her feet. With a powerful grip on her arms, he yanked her onto her tiptoes, leaning in to lock eyes with her.

"How dare you speak to me that way? How dare you speak about something you know nothing about?"

Ellie cowered in his grasp, her body trembling with the same fear as the first time, and she quickly averted her gaze, blinking at the moisture that welled up in her eyes. So much for her not being afraid of him anymore. But her words broke him, and the pain came rushing back in a flood of emotions that overwhelmed him.

"Aly was not just my girlfriend who died," he snarled. "She was my wife and the love of my life. Look at me." When she didn't comply right away, Aden shook her. "Look at me," he bellowed even louder, and Ellie's wide eyes snapped to his. "You can't fathom the agony I've lived through."

"Aden, you're hurting me," she croaked, then her lashes fluttered. Her body convulsed in his grip, and her eyes rolled back in her head.

Terror spiked through him. "Ellie!" He called her name as she continued to jerk in his arms. "Ellie, look at me! Ellie!" Aden begged, loosening his grip on her arms, but all he saw were the whites of her eyes.

Drool trickled from the corner of her mouth, and then the unmistakable smell of urine filled Aden's nostrils as she lost control of her bladder.

"NO!!!"

What had he done?

Frantic, Aden lifted her into his arms, and without a second look at Kane or the other guards, Aden sprinted down the beach toward the house.

Aden paced, cursing himself and wearing a rut in the floor. He yanked at the short strands of his hair to distract himself from the sight of Ellie's unconscious body on the bed across the room.

He'd already put his fist through the wall several times, and his mother had threatened to have Kane physically remove him from the room if he didn't calm down. Like Kane could take him.

It had been over two hours since she heard him calling for her as he burst into the house carrying Ellie's jerking body.

"Sophie! Help!" Aden's voice had echoed in the foyer as the glass wall parted and he rushed inside.

Sophie had rushed in and stopped dead in her tracks. "Aden, what did you do?"

"Help her, please," he begged, not caring that his mother's first assumption was that he'd done something to Ellie. He didn't care about anything except her.

"Bring her into her room."

Aden bolted up the stairs, two at a time, as Sophie followed close on his heels, calling to one of her thralls to get the staff nurse.

Aden placed Ellie on the bed, and her body continued to jerk and thrash.

"What's happening? Why is she having a seizure?" Sophie asked.

"I don't know. I was yelling at her, and then she started convulsing."

Sophie sat on the bed and held Ellie down gently. "Why were you yelling at her?"

At that moment, the staff nurse entered the room, interrupting their conversation.

Ellie had been unconscious for two hours now, sedated until Mina and Zach arrived. Her body lay still on the bed. Aden listened to her heartbeat, reassuring himself that she was indeed alive. Sophie had gone to the hangar to meet the plane. The nurse was sitting in a chair beside the bed, monitoring Ellie as Aden watched her like a hawk. Her heart sounded strong, and he focused on it.

Sophie, Mina, and Zach entered the room, a floating medical bay following them. Mina looked at him, and he held her gaze for a moment before she looked away without speaking. Sophie approached him as Zach and Mina spoke to the nurse.

"Come out to the balcony with me. You could use some fresh air."

His feet refused to move as he watched Zach and Mina lift Ellie into the medical pod. It wasn't until he felt his mother tug on his arm that Aden turned to follow. He leaned on the railing, looking out over the water. Sophie stood beside him and rubbed circles on his back, but he barely registered her touch.

"You want to tell me what happened now?"

"No."

"Okay," Sophie said, and Aden glanced over at her in surprise.

"That's all you're going to say?"

"For right now, yes."

"She's going to be alright, isn't she?" He asked, dreading the answer.

"Yes." Sophie looked down at his pants and his shoes and wrinkled her nose. "You probably should go shower and change."

"Why would her bladder let go like that?"

"It often happens with seizures."

The weight of the world seemed to echo in Aden's heavy sigh. "I should have gone to medical school."

"I did when I was in my forties. It was an interesting decade of my life."

"Do you think this could be an aftereffect of deactivating that fucking chip?"

"I doubt it, but Zach will know."

Aden grabbed the railing and clenched his fingers, crushing the metal until it groaned in protest. He rocked back and forth on the balls of his feet.

"I'm going to destroy her, aren't I?"

"You don't have to."

"I don't know how to stop. She hates me."

"She doesn't hate you. She's just confused. Like you are."

"I'm not confused. I know how I feel and what I want, but I'm at a loss for how to convince her I'm telling the truth."

Sophie gave him a rueful smile. "That's your problem. You can't convince her. She needs to realize it on her own. You can't force someone to love you, Aden, but you don't make it easy for them to fall either."

He stood motionless, his eyes locked on the water, his body rigid, on the verge of breaking.

"Aden, I've loved you since the second I felt you move inside my womb. There is no greater love than that of a parent for a child. No matter what you do or don't do, I will *always* love you. But you've made it hard for me to like you for a very long time."

That didn't come as a surprise, but it still stung.

"I've seen this amazing transformation in you since Ellie came into your life. Despite a few lapses in judgment, I've seen glimpses of the man I raised. The man you were before. But you carry too much rage in you all the time. The past doesn't matter anymore, and if you don't let it go, you're going to destroy any chance of a future. You'll never find the happiness you deserve."

"I don't deserve happiness after everything I've done."

She reached up to cup his face in her hands. He flinched and pulled away. She dropped her hands, her hurt at his rejection showing in her eyes. "But you do. And Ellie can give it to you."

"She's the only one." The words spilled out of his lips, hitting Aden with such force that his legs grew weak. "Everything is plunged back into darkness without her."

"Then stop self-sabotaging and let yourself be happy."

"How?"

Before Sophie could reply, Aden heard Ellie's heart rate speed up. He strode back into the room and saw her thrashing inside the medical bay, grasping at her neck. Zach was holding her down as Mina stepped out.

"What's wrong with her?" he demanded before she could utter a word.

"We think she's having a nightmare, but we can't wake her up even though we've removed the sedative. No wonder the girl never sleeps," Mina said as Ellie's body continued to convulse.

"Is this because of that fucking chip?"

"No. The scans show there is nothing wrong with her."

"Then why is she having seizures?" Aden's lips curled into a snarl.

Mina glared at him with her hands on her hips. "Maybe because you won't stop terrorizing her?"

There was that word again, and it made Aden want to rip his hair out. He didn't think he'd been terrorizing Ellie, but maybe he didn't know what that meant.

"Mina, that's enough," Sophie said.

Ellie stopped convulsing, and a wave of relief washed over him.

"Yes, it is enough," Aden said, tired of being at odds with everyone all the time. His mother was right. He had to let this anger go, or he would lose his only chance at happiness. "Will she be alright?"

"She'll be fine if you just leave her alone," Mina said.

"That's not an option." In an instant, his eyes turned a fiery red, reigniting the anger that he had seemingly released just seconds before. "I need to be alone. Call me when she wakes up."

With one last glance at Ellie, Aden left the room. He made his way down the stairs to the deck, where he stood looking out at the water and listening to the comforting sound of the beating heart above.

Ellie

She could barely make out the faint outline of the furniture. Even in the dark, this room was familiar to her, having sneaked into it more times than she could count over the years. But this time was different.

They weren't hurried or rushed, afraid they might get caught by his parents or hers. They were married now.

It was their wedding night, and he was finally going to drink from her, a moment they'd both fantasized about for so long.

His captivating blue eyes, the only things she could see clearly in the dark, bore into hers. They shone with happiness, love, and awe. His eyes were always so intense and full of secrets, but they could never hide his feelings for her.

She moaned, her eyes fluttering closed as they rocked in unison. Every inch of his body covered hers, their synchronized movements sending delicious shivers of pleasure through her body, everywhere their skin touched.

"Look at me, mo ghrá," he whispered, his voice hoarser than she'd ever heard it. "I need to see your eyes."

As she opened them, a radiant smile spread across her face, mirroring the love she saw reflected in his gaze. He loved her eyes as much as she loved his, once telling her they were his true north.

She reached up and traced her fingertips beneath his eyes, which shifted between the intense sapphire blue and the fiery crimson that came out when he was angry or aroused.

"I love you," he said as his body moved over her and inside her. He brushed a wisp of stray hair off her face, his touch soft and tender, before lowering his lips to kiss her.

Her hips arched in response, matching his steady thrusts, their kiss leaving her breathless as she lost herself in the feel and taste of him.

He pulled back, his lips brushing hers with every word. "Are you sure you're ready?"

She nodded.

He opened his mouth, and she knew he was breathing her in, letting the scent of her arousal and blood consume him. His fangs lengthened, and his venom trickled over his bottom lip, before landing on her throat.

"I love you, Aden," she whispered, turning her head, to expose her vulnerable throat to him in absolute trust. He pressed his lips against her neck, taking what she offered as he sank his teeth into her.

Her body froze, paralyzed, as she felt pleasure consume her. She couldn't move and couldn't breathe as he pumped his venom into her bloodstream. All she could do was lay there and feel the rapture coursing through every cell of her body.

When her ability to move returned a few seconds later, her orgasm slammed into her, and she cried out, her entire body convulsing beneath him.

He drank deep, and she let him, feeling her blood leave her body, as she surrendered to the sensation.

Tears prickled her eyes as she was overcome with love for this man, this vampire she had loved for as long as she could remember. When she started to feel lightheaded, she pushed against his shoulders.

"Aden, that's enough."

He pulled his fangs from her neck and licked the deep punctures he'd left in his wake. Her eyes fluttered closed, her head spinning.

"Aly," he choked her name, his voice a mixture of desperation and fear.

Her lashes swept open to meet his eyes again, and she gasped, her breath catching in her throat. His eyes had darkened. They were no longer blue, no longer gentle. The crimson that had overtaken them was fierce, full of bloodlust, and something else she couldn't place.

His penetrating stare never faltered as his eyes bore into hers.

"I need more," he said through clenched teeth.

Locked in his gaze, a prick of icy fear spread through her entire body.

He tore his eyes away from hers and buried his face in her neck. Before she could stop him, he sank his fangs into her again. There was no gentleness this time, just a brutal hunger she felt in every tense muscle pressed against hers, in the searing pain as his fangs sank deeper.

A gasp escaped her lips as the grip of his venom on her body loosened. "No. Aden. Don't do this-"

She pushed against his shoulders, desperate to stop the assault. Pain surged through her body, searing and intense, overwhelming her senses and obliterating any trace of the ecstasy she'd experienced minutes earlier. "Please, come back to me-" She choked, through the blood filling her throat, gagging her, suffocating her, and silencing her plea.

"No," she pleaded again, tears streaming from the corners of her eyes.

His teeth tore at her neck and he growled against her skin as he pumped into her, breaking her body with each ruthless, powerful thrust.

With her vision fading and darkness closing in, she summoned the last remnants of her strength to whisper his name, "Aden," her voice heavy with surrender, as everything in her world faded to black.

Ellie felt Aden's presence beside her. This really was getting ridiculous. For someone who'd never been able to sleep, she spent an awful lot of time unconscious.

She didn't want to open her eyes and see him. Why couldn't he leave her alone for once? Let her absorb and accept what she'd been denying her entire life. It was time to admit that Sophie was right and that her dreams weren't dreams at all.

They were memories.

The images still flashed in front of her eyes, flickering on the back of her eyelids. The emotions were overwhelming her. She wanted to cry, scream, and sob for hours as the reality of her life and death sank in.

She wanted to jump on him and pound until her fists ached, making him hurt like he hurt her. And she wanted him to leave her alone, but he was hovering over her yet again.

Aden was so clingy, and she now understood why. He killed her. In a moment of violent lust, he had drained her, even as she begged him to stop. She'd loved him and trusted him, and he'd killed her.

Ellie knew she felt something when they first met—something beyond the hatred, beyond the fear—but she never understood what it was. Until now.

She heard Aden shift in the chair beside the bed. "I know you're awake."

Damn him and his vampire senses.

Ellie opened her eyes. It hurt to look at him, yet she never wanted to look away. A few minutes ago, she'd wanted him to leave her alone. Now all she wanted was to crawl into his arms, hold him tight, and never let go.

Ellie pushed on her hands, sitting up and against the headboard as Aden watched her. She didn't want to be the first to speak, but Aden clearly didn't either.

"How long?"

"A few hours."

Ellie reached up and rubbed the ache in her biceps. She looked down and saw the bruises on both her arms—bruises in the shape of Aden's fingers. From her peripheral vision, she saw his eyes darken with remorse, so she tugged on her short sleeves, to no avail, before dropping her hands to her lap.

"You scared the hell out of me." His voice was so soft that she barely heard him.

"Aden, I'm fine. I'd really just like to be alone if that's okay."

"No, it's not okay. What the hell happened to you, Ellie?"

"I don't know, you tell me. I was the one unconscious." Ellie sniffed and wrinkled her nose, looking down at the cotton pants she wore. "Why do I smell like I peed myself?"

"You did. But that's me. Mina and Zach cleaned you up."

Ellie's eyes widened in horror. "Aden, I'm so sorry—"

"Stop!" Aden stood, causing the chair to shoot backward and crash to the floor, his fists clenched at his sides. "Don't you fucking apologize to me for this!"

Ellie scrambled to her feet, putting the bed between them. "Stop yelling at me. This isn't my fault."

Aden's shoulders slumped, and he sighed. "No, this is my fault. All of this is my fault." He turned and walked to the window.

Ellie watched him, and she choked back the sob rising in her throat. The hurt radiating off him was agonizing to see, but at the moment she couldn't bring herself to comfort him. She wasn't ready for him to know she remembered.

It was unsettling to have two sets of distinct memories in your head—memories of two different people with completely different lives. Despite the many gaps and missing pieces, the memory of her profound love for the vampire in front of her remained crystal clear. She loved him from the first moment he pushed her down when she was four years old.

But he'd betrayed her trust when he murdered her. Ellie needed time to digest the memories, recognize them as part of her now and not just a nightmare, and mourn for the girl she once was. Mourn for all they'd both lost.

"Aden, please, I need to be alone. I'm begging you to leave me alone for once."

He shook his head but didn't reply.

"I'm fine. You can see I'm fine."

Still no response. Aden kept his gaze fixed out the window, his jaw tight and his fists clenching and releasing at his sides.

Watching him brought back another memory—how he sulked when he was upset, when they would argue. Arguing with her always made him brood until she forgave him. If it wasn't so absurd, Ellie would have laughed. But if she started laughing, it would lead to more, and she would fall to pieces. And that would only shatter them both.

"I'm sor—" Ellie stopped when she saw Aden's back go rigid. "I shouldn't have said those horrible things to you."

She saw his jaw twitch, but he remained silent. She was so conflicted. Her hatred of vampires had consumed her for this entire life. One had murdered her mother, one of her mothers. Now a vampire had also murdered her. A vampire she'd loved and trusted. She'd been fighting her growing feelings for Aden, unable to understand how she could feel something for him after all he'd done to her and his other thralls. Now she knew why. She'd carried it from another life.

"Aden, I know you want more from me, but I don't know how to give it to you. I don't know how to feel safe enough in your world to accept what you're offering."

Aden spun and strode across the room, stopping at the bed across from her. "I will make it my life's mission to keep you safe."

"Aden, please."

"How can you not recognize me?" Aden reached up and tugged on his hair in frustration, his voice rising with each word. "I recognized you the second I looked into your eyes. How can you not see it? Not feel it?"

"I don't know what I feel." Ellie's voice betrayed her as she fought the sob threatening to erupt. "Please, I just need some time and space," she whispered, her voice trembling with emotion.

They stood looking at one another for several minutes, their eyes locked. Neither said a word, breathing in perfect synchrony as they both drew air in and out of their noses. Unable to look away, Ellie feared that if she spoke again, she'd break right in front of him.

Aden's shoulders deflated, and a look of defeat swept across his face.

"My penance will never be enough."

He turned and walked out of the room. Ellie's knees buckled, and she sank to the floor, her entire body shaking. In his presence, she held back her sobs, but now that she was alone, they wouldn't come. She wrapped her arms around herself, rocking gently, feeling drained, empty, and alone.

If he killed her once, even as desperately as he loved her, what would stop him from doing it again?

Aden was right. His penance would never be enough. How could it?

Aden

Aden stood on the deck and watched the plane grow smaller in the distance, taking Ellie away from him. His heart felt like it was being torn from his body and taken along with her.

After he'd left Ellie's room last night, his mother had come to see him.

"I think Ellie and I should head back to the city."

Sophie settled into the chair beside his. She was nothing if not predictable.

"You stay," he'd said. "You shouldn't have to cut your trip short to get away from me."

"I'm not trying to get away from you."

He cast a skeptical glance at her. "No. You're trying to get Ellie away from me."

She didn't reply, and he'd appreciated her lack of a denial.

"I mean it, stay. I'm heading to the capital tomorrow anyway. When you're both ready, I'll have another plane sent down to get you."

"Oh, yes, the summer games," Sophie bristled.

"Sophie, don't start. You know I have to go."

"Yes." She reached for his hand. He yanked it away. She knew of his aversion, but she still always tried. She couldn't help herself. Sophie Westcott was a toucher. "But I think it's best to get Ellie back home. Zach wants to run a few tests on her, so—"

Aden's eyes whipped to her face. "What kinds of tests?"

"Just a few psychological tests. Nothing to be concerned about."

"She's not the psycho one."

Her lips curled into a wry smile. "I think a little space between you would be good. I'd like to move her to the thralls' quarters."

"No!" He grabbed the arms of the chair, and the metal twisted in his tight grasp.

"Aden, I'll have her moved to the private level. She won't be in the communal quarters."

He wouldn't let her take Ellie from him. "I said no."

"Aden, she asked you for space. You need to respect that."

"And you need to stop listening to other people's conversations." He pushed to his feet with a snarl, grabbing the small, round table between them and throwing it over the balcony railing. To her credit, his mother's only reaction was a brief flicker in her eyes.

"I can't turn off my half-breed hearing, dear."

Aden's nostrils flared as he glared down at her. "I won't say it again. She stays where she is."

"Aden—"

"No," he roared before he lowered his voice to only a growl. "If she wants space, I'll give her space."

"And you'll do that by keeping her in your rooms? Brilliant idea."

Aden walked over to the railing and looked down to see the glass table shattered on the deck below. Several thralls frantically cleaned up the broken glass.

"I'll have the hallway door unsealed and the one in my room put on manual override. She can come and go without having to see me."

"Hmm. That's progress, I guess."

"Please, Sophie, contain your praise."

She walked over to him. "Oh, Aden. I don't know how to help either of you."

"There's nothing you can do. She holds all the power here. Ironic, huh?"

"Don't sound so defeated." He hated the sympathy in her eyes. "She'll come around. She's come so far already. I can tell by the things she says she's on the cusp of remembering."

"I don't want her to remember. It's ugly and violent and deserves to be forgotten." Aden turned and leaned against the railing. Did he look as resigned as he felt? "I'm tired of running from the past. I don't care if she's Aly or not." It didn't hurt to say her name now. It just left him with the lingering reminder he was alone. "I just want Ellie."

"You sound like you're giving up."

"Not on her. But I am giving up hope that she'll remember the man I was. I'm not that same man. Fuck, I wasn't even a man then. I was a stupid kid who believed he was invincible, only to have his entire world ripped away because of his arrogance. It doesn't matter. None of it matters anymore. Take her home. I'll give her space. She can come and go through her own door, but she doesn't move to the thrall's quarters."

"I think you're doing the right thing." She grasped his arm, refusing to let him shake her off. She pinned him with her eyes until he met her gaze. "You need to drink some of Ellie's blood again before you see Matthais. Mina probably brought her reserve with her as a precaution."

"She already gave it to me."

His mother nodded and left. Aden had spent the rest of the night staring at the ocean and listening to Ellie's heartbeat.

Was he doing the right thing?

She hadn't said goodbye to him. He'd kept his distance as she'd asked, but she could have at least said goodbye. He felt as if someone had ripped away a part of him, leaving a gaping hole he feared would never be filled again.

At the sound of a heartbeat, Aden turned to find Chelsea standing behind him.

"I was told you were hungry, Sir."

Aden tilted his head and looked at her. She used to be his favorite. Her blood was delectable, and she was always pliable beneath him, but he had no appetite for her or her blood anymore. "Come closer, Chelsea." Her heart sped up as she approached. "Kneel," he said as he sat on the chair. "Give me your wrist."

Chelsea dropped to her knees and crawled closer, lifting her arm. Aden grasped her hand, pressed his nose against her skin, and inhaled.

It had taken time to get used to drinking from his thrall's wrists, but now he didn't think twice about it. He'd missed fucking his thralls while he fed, but the longing lessened over time. Every once in a while, though, the temptation would hit him. Tonight was one of those nights.

It had nothing to do with his feelings for Ellie. It was just a pure desire to fuck. This was the longest he'd been celibate since he was twenty-five, and the itch was building. Aden sank his fangs into Chelsea's wrist, and she whimpered, her body jerking and stiffening. After a few seconds, her body relaxed, and she moaned. Aden took a few more mouthfuls, then removed his fangs.

Yeah, he was done with her blood. And it was for the best. With his urge tonight, if her blood had lit a fire in him, he'd likely have taken her to his bed. And considering his luck, that would be another thing he'd live to regret.

Aden shoved her arm away. "You can go."

Chelsea opened her eyes, shocked. "Sir?"

"I said go."

"Yes, Sir." Confusion flashed in her eyes as she stood up and walked into the house.

The slave auction was in full swing.

His plane landed late, so Aden headed straight to the opening games. He had no desire to play, but he didn't need Andrei or Matthais to question why he didn't attend. Fortunately, they had just ended, so he stayed for the auction. Andrei left to collect his winnings from the first round, and Aden scrolled through the catalog. He had enough thralls but figured he'd see what was available.

He no longer looked at them as thralls to fuck and feed from, so his view of them as he scrolled was different. Maybe he should consider a couple of males. He'd never had male thralls.

Kane stood in his usual spot at the back of the skybox. Matthais walked in with Lorcan behind him.

"Ah, Aden, I was hoping you were still here."

Aden looked over as Matthais sat beside him. A thrall moved into position on her knees at his feet, head down.

"We missed you last night at the welcome party."

Aden looked back at the hologram. "I had some loose ends to tie up before I could get away."

"Hmm. Kira was also curious where you were."

Aden grunted, expressing his indifference without saying a word.

"I couldn't help but notice you didn't use any of your players earlier."

"I arrived late. Besides, I wasn't in the mood. Zurina doesn't exactly make it a fair game anymore."

"My girl is so magnificent, isn't she? Did Andrei tell you I'm thinking of breeding her?"

Aden shook his head. He had no desire to interact with Matthais and wished he'd take the hint and go away.

"I've never seen you back down from a challenge," Matthais said.

"A challenge is one thing. An inevitable slaughter is another."

"You've won for so many years. I think you've become spoiled."

As usual, Matthais was being a condescending fuck. How had he never seen it before?

"A fair fight isn't too much to ask."

A tall, short-haired blonde thrall walked across the stage, piquing Aden's interest. He watched as the auctioneer paraded her around, forcing her to drop the robe she wore to reveal her body to the arena.

For the first time, the display disgusted him. The obnoxious hooting and hollering coming from the levels below churned like acid in his stomach. So he decided to buy the girl to keep her from being harassed and ogled at by a bunch of disgusting vampires. He placed a bid for her.

"I'm calling an emergency meeting tomorrow night before the summer ball," Matthais said.

Aden glanced over, having forgotten he was there, before looking back at the hologram. Another vampire bid higher for the girl.

"Why?" Aden placed another bid.

"It's a strategy session to combat an uprising in Afara."

That got Aden's attention. "Is it more rogues?"

"No, this is a human insurgence."

Aden had been outbid again. He growled and placed another bid, this time doubling it. "What humans would be stupid enough to rebel?"

Matthais' voice, typically level, grew more ominous. "Ones who will swiftly and brutally learn the consequences of their mistake."

"Does Rashidi need ground assistance?"

"That's what we'll determine tomorrow. I spoke to Aurick, and he's going to attend virtually."

Fucking hell! He got outbid once more. This time, he tripled his offer.

"Have you and Andrei decided on a plan for Abya Yala yet?" Matthais asked.

"Yes." Aden leaned forward as he waited to see what the other vampire would do. "Cecilia's lieutenants will come up to my facilities to train for a month, and then Andrei will go to San Allena to work with them in the field."

"Why aren't you going to train down there?"

"Because I have the resources, training fields, and equipment already in place. Fuck!" Aden spat after being outbid yet again. "Vincent!" he barked, and a hologram with the vampire popped up beside him. "Quit fucking outbidding me!"

"Not a chance, Aden," Vincent said with a grin. "I've been waiting for her to become available."

Matthais reached down to his thrall and brought her wrist to his lips, drinking until she collapsed on the ground, unconscious. She was picked up and taken away, as Matthais wiped the corners of his mouth with an air of indifference.

Aden continued his bidding war with Vincent until he finally had enough.

"Fucking take her," Aden snarled, and he swiped the hologram closed.

"You really don't like to lose, do you?" Matthais said, standing. "I'll see you at the meeting."

Aden sat back, seething, his eyes glancing over to where the girl had been. He'd seen enough thralls collapse over the course of his life. There was no coming back from that.

Aden stalked into his guest suite, still fuming about the auction. He needed to shower and feed before he met up with Andrei to iron out the final details for Cecelia's military.

It was the same suite he always stayed in, and he thought nothing of it until he looked over at the bed. He stopped in his tracks, overwhelmed by the emotions rushing through him. Rage was at the forefront, with regret hovering underneath.

Images of Ellie's brutalized body sprawled on the floor in her torn uniform and covered in blood, replayed in his mind on a relentless loop.

Aden called for Kane. "Have four thralls brought to me. I don't care who, just not Chelsea. I want to feed before I meet with Andrei."

Aden took a quick shower, and when he exited the bathroom, the thralls were kneeling on the floor waiting for him. He drank quickly, as was his habit now that feeding no longer held any gratification other than the requisite satisfaction of his hunger. The thralls scurried away when he was done. He sat back, and memories of Ellie flooded his mind as his eyes fixated on that familiar spot on the floor.

Unable to get her out of his mind, he looked for her.

"Find Ellie," Aden said, and she appeared in a hologram. She was in the thralls' kitchen, sitting at a table, talking to a male thrall. She was smiling and laughing with him.

How the fuck could she be smiling and laughing after having a seizure less than forty-eight hours ago? Tracking holograms were silent by default, but had the option for sound. So, even though he knew he shouldn't, he raised the volume.

"Finn!" Ellie gasped through her chuckle. "You did not say that to her?"

"What? What's wrong with it?"

She shook her head in exasperation, taking a bite of her sandwich. "You don't get a girl to like you by telling her that her hair looks like a rat's nest. You really are helpless."

"But it did. Should I have lied to her?"

Ellie arched her eyebrow, an obvious expression of "duh" on her face.

"I blew it, didn't I?"

"Probably. Unless she really likes you."

Pink suffused his cheeks as he dipped his head. "I think she does."

Ellie sat back and tossed her napkin on her plate. "Well, I suggest you tell her she looks nice the next time you see her. It's a good thing you have a cute face. Use that to your advantage."

"You think I'm cute?" he asked with a sly grin.

"Don't let it go to your head."

Finn put his hand on his chest, pretending to be wounded.

"So, what's up with you?" he asked. "You were gone for a couple of days."

Ellie's smile faded, and she fidgeted in her chair. "I accompanied Mistress Sophie on a trip."

"Oh, where?"

"The beach house."

"I've never been there."

"It's beautiful." Ellie's smile returned. "It's right on the ocean. Mistress Sophie let me take a walk with her on the beach."

"Wow. I'm jealous."

Ellie stood, taking both their plates to the counter. When she walked back, he set a slice of pie on the table in front of her. She took a bite, and her eyes closed briefly before she smiled. "You're the best cook I've ever met, Finn."

"Yeah, I know." Ellie's foot connected with Finn's shin with a soft thud under the table, making him chuckle. "So, a couple of us are going to lower level three when we finish today. You should come with us."

"What's lower level three?"

"It's where thralls can go when we're not working. We can relax and visit with other thralls who live outside the compound."

"I can't. I'm not allowed to leave the compound."

"Have you ever asked?"

"No." Ellie sat back and pushed her plate away. "It's still so strange for me to have time off. We didn't get that in Master Matthais' house. Thralls worked every day. They worked, ate, and slept. That's it."

"What were the lower levels like in the capital?"

Ellie shuddered. "They weren't places thralls could go alone."

He reached for her hand. "You gotta come with us. You can meet Lily and tell her what a great guy I am."

Ellie gave him a regretful smile as she pulled her hand away. "Thanks, Finn, but I can't. Master Aden is gone, and I'd rather not ask Mistress Sophie."

"Where did he go?"

"The capital," a female thrall said as she walked into the kitchen. "It's the summer games. He always goes."

Ellie cringed as the girl walked over to the table.

"What are you doing in this kitchen?"

"She's here to see me, Janessa," Finn snapped.

Janessa eyed Ellie up and down. "You look okay."

"What does that mean?" Ellie asked.

"I heard Master Aden hurt you real bad. Chelsea said he rushed in, and you were out cold in his arms, and Mistress Sophie had to call Mina and Dr. Zach to save your life."

"What?" Ellie gaped as she pushed to her feet. "That's not true. I wasn't unconscious because he hurt me."

"So, what happened to you?" Janessa asked.

"That's none of your business." Ellie crossed her arms over her chest. "And you should stop spreading lies about things you know nothing about."

"Ellie's right," Finn said. "Stop being a gossip, Janessa."

"Well, that's the last time I ask you anything." Janessa turned and walked out.

Ellie dropped into the chair, biting her lip as Finn scooted his chair closer. "What happened?"

Ellie looked hesitant before she answered. "I had a seizure when I was out on the beach."

"Are you alright now?"

"Yeah." Ellie reached over and patted his hand. "Dr. Zach ran a bunch of tests when we got back and said I'm fine."

Finn reached out and brushed his fingers over the fading bruises on her arms. "Does Master Aden hurt you?"

"No." Ellie pulled away and stood, her hand moving to cover the bruises on her arms before she tugged her sleeves down, hiding them from view. "He wouldn't hurt me, Finn. At least not on purpose."

He looked like he wasn't sure whether or not to believe her. "I'm sorry Janessa can be such a bitch."

"It's not your fault. Thanks for the sandwich and pie."

"Anytime, Ellie. If you change your mind about coming with us, we're leaving at sunrise."

Ellie grabbed her tablet from the table and left the kitchen.

Aden swiped the hologram closed with a frown.

Who was this Finn that Ellie was being so friendly with? Why didn't Aden know about him? How dare he touch her? And why was that Janessa girl being mean to Ellie?

He hoped seeing her would improve his mood but hearing her talk about how she wasn't able to do anything or go anywhere made it worse. And seeing her enjoying herself with that male thrall—why couldn't she laugh that freely when she was with him?

He wanted to destroy the room, but he sat there, brooding until it was time to meet Andrei.

Aden

Aden entered the skybox to find Andrei already seated.

"There you are. I wondered when you'd get here. We're already into the fourth game."

Aden looked at the hologram above the arena as he took a seat.

"Matthais added your players to the queue again." Andrei handed him a game console, but Aden sat back and tossed it to the side.

"I'm not in the mood to play."

"Again? That's all five nights this week."

"Just not feeling it this trip."

"Your loss." Andrei shrugged. "I dethroned you in January. Don't expect to get it back anytime soon with that attitude."

Aden sat there, feigning interest, his eyes fixed on the game, but his mind was elsewhere. He couldn't stop thinking about Ellie's interactions with the other thralls two nights ago. He was glad she'd looked better because the last time he'd seen her, the haunted look in her eyes had wrecked him.

But even though she was laughing and smiling with that male thrall, Aden saw and heard her loneliness. Until that wicked little Janessa arrived. Keeping Ellie with him isolated her from the other thralls, but she wasn't a thrall to him anymore. She didn't belong with the thralls. She belonged with him and his family.

"Shit!" Andrei shouted at the hologram, drawing Aden's attention back to the games. Zurina was swiping at players, mutilating them in quick succession. "Zurina, what are you doing, girl? You're not supposed to attack our team."

"Damn," Aden said, still impressed with her despite the bloodshed she was causing. "She's vicious."

"I've watched Matthais' daily training sessions, and she's brutal."

"What does he use as bait in the training sessions?"

"Humans, of course."

"Every day?"

"Uh huh."

What the fuck! How many humans was Matthais sacrificing for sport? The man in question appeared in the hologram. "Zurina, my sweet. Leave some for the others."

Zurina howled in response, and Aden glanced over to Matthais' skybox. He narrowed his eyes as Matthais cooed to the human-killing machine below.

"I'll see you later, Andrei. I need to feed," Aden said as he stood.

Andrei looked away from the hologram. "Okay."

Aden walked out of the skybox and toward the warp port that would take him back to his suite. Kane followed behind him. He could feel his eyes drilling a hole into his back, but he was in no mood to engage him.

Once again, Aden found himself repulsed by Matthais. First, there was his brutal whipping of Ellie, then his creepy interest in how she satisfied Aden. And now this. He should have listened to his parents over the years when they warned him not to idolize the ancient vampire.

He should have also listened when they emphasized compassion and kindness, as well as responsibility to those in their care. Why had it taken him so long to see what a sadist Matthais was?

And what did that say about him?

As Aden walked into the suite and again looked at the spot where Ellie had once lain in fear and pain, self-loathing filled him.

The realization hit him like a freight train.

Ellie coming into his life had made him see that his own behavior and callousness were just as abhorrent as Matthais'.

Aden found his father in his office. He was cleaning and polishing one of the swords from his collection of ancient military artifacts that dated back over three thousand years. His father maintained his weapons by cleaning and polishing them monthly, without fail.

"Hey," Aden said as he entered the room.

His father looked up and smiled. "Oh, hi, Son. When did you get back?"

Making his way to the large wooden table, Aden's eyes gravitated towards two of his father's most prized swords surrounded by various cleaning materials. The wall sconces cast a subtle glow, but it didn't affect either of their enhanced vision.

"A few minutes ago."

His father gestured to the sword resting to his left. "You want to help?"

Needing a distraction, Aden nodded. "Sure."

Aden grabbed the hilt of the sword and slid it closer before slipping on a pair of cotton gloves. His skin was impervious to the cleaning chemicals, but the gloves protected the ancient metals from corrosion caused by skin oils and sweat.

He took a lint-free cloth, poured some oil on it, and slid it along one side of the blade.

"I remember the first time you helped me clean these," his father said after a few minutes. "What were you... eight?"

"Yeah. I think so."

"Your mom almost kicked my ass when you nearly severed your thumb."

"She completely lost her shit, didn't she?" Aden laughed at the memory of his calm mother freaking out when his father carried his screaming and crying body, his hand wrapped in a bloody cloth, into their suite.

Vampire children were just as vulnerable as human children until their teenage years when a physiological change turned them into half-breeds. It wasn't until they reached full maturity at approximately twenty-five that they became immortal. But even immortal, losing a limb was permanent, unless it was reattached within a few hours. And there was no guarantee it would be usable.

"It was years before she let you help me again."

Aden turned the blade over in his hands, feeling its weight, and repeated his motions with precise and deliberate strokes.

"That was the first time you told me about Charlemagne the Great giving you Joyeuse." Aden glanced at the sword in his father's hands. "And you wielding it in the crusades before giving it to Phillip the Bold for his coronation."

"You loved my stories of the Crusades."

"That's because you were a badass warrior. I wanted to be just like you."

"Much to your mother's chagrin." His father shot him a meaningful glance, his eyes filled with unspoken wisdom. "But those were my dark years, Aden. I thought what I was fighting for was just. War is rarely righteous, even if fought for noble causes. But sometimes it's all you can do to right a wrong."

"When did Katsumi give you Goujian?" Aden changed the subject as he held up the sword in question.

It was a three-thousand-year-old sword named after one of the last kings of the Yue during the Zhou dynasty in the first millennium BC. Composed primarily of copper and tin, its sharpness and resistance to corrosion and rust made it unique for an artifact that old.

"My thirteen hundred fifty-first birthday. To commemorate the end of the Great Vampire Wars."

Aden coated another cloth with Renaissance wax, and starting at the handle, he ran the material along the blade, applying a thin layer of wax. The familiar, repetitive movements comforted him, calming the anxious and troubled thoughts that lingered from his trip.

"So, what do you think about this insurgence in Afara?" Aden asked. "That's the second one this year."

"People can only tolerate repression and abuse for so long before they rebel, Aden. It's human nature."

"What humans would be foolish enough to rebel?"

"Ones who have nothing to lose."

Aurick's answer was in stark contrast to the response Matthais had given. But it was exactly what Aden had expected his father to say.

His father's calm presence reminded Aden of how much he missed spending time with him. Silence filled the room, punctuated only by the occasional sound of the swords scraping against the wood table and the swish of fabric polishing the metal.

"So, Matthais called me," Aurick said.

"Why?"

"He was concerned about you."

"Again, why?"

"He said he provided you with your usual number of players, but you didn't participate in the games. He also said you didn't buy any thralls at the auction."

"Why is that so fucking newsworthy?" Aden snarled, and the sword slipped and sliced deep into his hand. "Fuck!" Aden sucked his finger, and the wound closed. "I have enough thralls."

"That doesn't explain the games. That's what seemed to concern him the most."

Anger surged through Aden, and he dropped Goujian onto the table with a loud thud.

"I'd just watched Ellie seize until she was unconscious and pissed herself. Excuse me for not being in the fucking mood to play games."

Understanding filled his father's eyes. "Seeing the people we love suffer is soul-crushing."

"You know what—" Aden shoved away from the table, his jaw clenched tight. He couldn't deal with the concept of souls right now. "I need to take care of a few things before I turn in."

"Of course. It was nice having your help again. Maybe we can duel sometime soon. It's been too long."

"Yeah, sure." Aden stormed out of the room.

"I want Chelsea removed from rotation," Aden said as he walked into Sophie's office.

"Yes, Sir," Georgina replied from her chair in front of the desk. "I will only send her once the compulsion has reached its limit."

"Keep her away as long as possible, unless I ask for her," Aden said before looking at his mother. Her expression was one of surprise, though she tried to hide it.

"Yes, Sir. Will that be all?" Georgina asked.

"No. Whose thrall is Janessa?"

"She's one of your office cleaners."

"I want her removed. Reassign her, or better yet, send her back to where she came from."

Georgina made a note on her tablet. "I believe she's from a village in the south. Is there a problem with her, Sir?"

"I just want her removed."

"Yes, Sir. It will be done tonight."

"I think we're through, too, Georgina," Sophie said. "Upload those notes when you have them revised. I appreciate your help this week while Ellie was resting. She should be back to helping me tomorrow."

"Yes, ma'am." Georgina gathered her things and left the room.

Aden dropped into her seat.

"Don't read anything into this." He didn't appreciate his mother's questioning look. "I drop thralls from rotation all the time."

"Did I say anything?"

"You didn't have to. I can see the gears in your head working overtime."

Sophie leaned back in her chair. "When did you get back?"

"A few hours ago. I went to see Aurick before I came here."

"We never talked about your BloodStone visit."

Glad for the change of subject, Aden settled into the chair. "I learned quite a bit about Aurick, Keeley, and Hannah's little, or should I say big projects."

"Yes. We've all been eager to bring you in the loop. We figured Hannah was the best one to do that."

"I wasn't aware Aurick was the primary test subject."

"He always has been going all the way back to BloodStone."

"Can someone say control freak?"

Sophie laughed and stood, walking around the desk and sitting in the chair next to Aden.

"How do you feel about taking AEON instead of feeding from Aurick?"

She looked surprised by his question. "Who said I'm going to do that? I have no reason to stop drinking from my sire, but AEON will be for those who want that."

Aden fidgeted in his chair, his eyes darting towards the empty table where Ellie worked. His curiosity got the better of him, and he asked, "How is she?"

"Better," Sophie replied with a knowing smile.

"Did Zach run his tests?"

"Yes."

Aden ground his teeth in annoyance. "And?"

"She didn't tell them much. She said she remembers nothing of your argument."

"They have no physical or psychological explanation for her seizure?"

Sophie sat back. "No, but Zach confirmed she has an eidetic memory."

His brow furrowed. "I thought that was a myth."

"It's extremely rare, less than one-half of one percent of the human population, and there are no vampires confirmed to have it, to my knowledge."

"So she can remember everything with perfect recall?"

"That's the definition."

"Then why can't she remember her last life?"

"It doesn't work like that, Aden. And it might not have been. Who knows how many lives she's lived in the last two hundred seventy-five years?"

Aden blinked as the significance of her words sank in. How many lives had Ellie lived? Since females were more often accidentally drained by vampires, the average life span was only thirty years. How many chances did he miss finding her because he didn't know to look?

"You realize that's the first time you've admitted you believe she's Alysia."

"She's not Aly."

"No, you're right. She's not." Her smile brightened her whole face. "But she is the same soul."

Aden growled. "You can stop beaming."

Sophie's smile widened.

"You're not very humble when you think you're right. So did Zach say anything else?"

"He also said she's super intelligent. She scored off the charts on every test he gave her. It explains how easily she adapts to new things." Sophie pointed to Ellie's work table. "She figured out how to modify one program on that table, making the entire system more efficient."

"And I called her a stupid little girl."

Sophie's smile faded. "It could also explain Matthais' unusual interest in her. She was likely tested as a child, but then again, it can sometimes take time to manifest."

"Why would her super intelligence interest him?"

"It makes her rare. That's likely why he turned her father. Human males over seven feet are almost as rare. And Matthais covets rare."

That knowledge made the back of Aden's neck prickle.

"Ellie was thrilled to have her door unsealed."

"You don't have to keep rubbing it in."

"I'm not rubbing anything in."

"Yes, you are."

Sophie sat forward and placed her hand on his arm. "No, I'm not, Aden. I simply wanted you to know that you've made her extremely happy."

He shook her off and stood. "Happy to not have to see me."

"Happy to have a little freedom. She's never had that in her life."

"She's human. Humans aren't free."

Sophie stood and walked to the window, taking a moment to adjust the flowers in a vase on the windowsill. "If you want her to come to you, then you can't treat her like she's less than you. You can't keep her enslaved and expect her to want to be with you."

Aden approached Ellie's table and ran his fingers along the edge. "I can't free her, Sophie. No matter how much I may want to."

"Not legally, no. Not at this point. And certainly not publicly, but inside these walls we can live how we want."

He shot her a dubious look. "I'm sorry, but are you advocating I break the law?"

She met his gaze, a defiant spark flickering in her eyes. "I'm advocating bending it a little. It's not like it wouldn't be the first time you've done that."

His look morphed into a teasing smirk. "What would the Gerent say?"

"That sometimes you have to take the law into your own hands to do the right thing."

Ellie

The door slid open and she entered Aden's room. She could hear his voice echo down the hallway leading to his sitting room.

"I said no, Mom. You have no say about this. I know what I'm doing."

For a brief second, she wanted to make a run for it. He'd been fighting with his parents for weeks over their decision about their wedding night.

"That's where you're wrong, Aden. You're being naïve," Sophie said.

Her parents also disapproved of their choice, but as thralls, they had no say. Her mother was Sophie's personal assistant, though, so the two of them had been pleading with her to change her mind.

But once she was Aden's wife, she could share her blood with him and nothing anyone said would change her mind.

Aden was even more stubborn than she was and more vocal.

"Aly and I have made our decision. You have no say over what I do anymore. I'm an adult now."

Her feet felt heavier with every step, her heart racing as she dreaded walking into the ongoing argument. She turned the corner just as Aurick grabbed Aden by the front of the shirt.

"Then act like one. You have no idea how this can go wrong. How easily you could lose control."

"I won't." Aden yanked out of his father's grasp. "This is none of your business."

"Please stop fighting about this." She rushed to stand between them. "The wedding is in two days. Can you please just stop fighting or you're going to ruin it?"

"Alysia, sweetheart, we just want you both to think this through," Sophie said. "Why do you need to rush into this?"

Aden crossed his arms over his chest, his eyes flashing in defiance. "We're not rushing into anything. We've been having sex for years."

"Aden," she gasped and smacked him on the arm. "Shut up."

"What?" He snapped. "It's not like they don't know."

Her cheeks grew hot, and she shook her head.

"We would have done it already if you didn't have this romantic idea about doing it on our wedding night."

With a sharp glare, she locked eyes with him. He shrugged and flashed her the teasing grin he knew was her weakness, before turning his attention back to his father, the smile slipping from his face.

Sophie walked over and grasped both of her hands. "I know you think you want this. And it's a beautiful thing to share with the man you love. But, sweetheart, there's no rush. You're going to have eternity together."

"Aden, you need to give yourself time," Aurick said. "You've only been fully vampire for a couple of months. You can't possibly have that much control over your bloodlust yet."

She pulled her hands away from Sophie's grasp and moved to Aden's side, presenting a united front. His body visibly relaxed as she got closer, as it always did when she was near him.

"Please respect our decision. We know what we're doing," she said to Aurick.

Aurick shook his head, disappointment and resignation shining in his eyes.

"No, you don't, Alysia. But I hope, for your sake, you're right."

Ellie's eyes fluttered open to find Vlad's nose inches from her face, his soft purr vibrating through the pillow beneath her head. Rolling onto her back, she let the memory from her dream integrate into her subconscious and merge with the others that had returned in the last few days.

More of her memories surfaced each night, and trying to keep them straight as they blended with the ones from this life was making her dizzy. Aden was the star of most of them, but she was glad Sophie and Master Aurick were making an appearance. They'd always been the kind, wise and loving people they are now. The deep love she'd felt for this family in her past life made perfect sense and explained her deep connection to them in this one.

Ellie glanced at the clock and saw it was almost time to get up, so she tossed the covers aside and sat up. Vlad stretched and yawned before going back to sleep.

She knew Aden hadn't meant to kill her. He loved her, but his parents were right. She and Aden were arrogant to think they could control the outcome of thousands of years of vampire evolution. They never had a chance. And had they listened to his parents and not shared blood that night, Aden might not have killed her.

No wonder he'd snapped and spent nearly three centuries lashing out at the world, though it didn't justify or excuse the way he treated his thralls. But the idea of him suffering alone, consumed by grief and guilt, was unbearable for her to think about.

At the same time, if he hadn't killed her, she would never have been born again and would never have known her mother, father, and Carrie. And despite everything she'd suffered in this life, Ellie couldn't imagine that.

How twisted was it to feel a small sense of gratitude that your vampire husband killed you on your wedding night, even though it also left both of you shattered?

Ellie walked into the bathroom and turned on the shower. She stripped and stepped under the water, letting the warm water cascade over her as she closed her eyes.

But nothing could wash away the heavy ache in her chest, which was a constant now that more of the memories of her life and death were coming back with a vengeance.

Ellie hadn't seen Aden since the beach house.

Sophie said he'd returned from the capital tonight, but Ellie wasn't sure how she felt about that yet. She spent the last week resting, at Sophie's insistence, spending most of it in the library reading while Vlad slept beside her. He'd taken to following her around the compound so much that she'd started joking that he was her shadow. She looked over to where he snoozed on the chair beside her and smiled.

Sophie hadn't asked too many questions about that night, just if she was alright. When she'd said she was fine, Sophie let it go. Too bad Aden didn't take after his mother in that way.

Ellie was sitting, eating at one of the small bistro tables on the perimeter of the courtyard, when she felt him watching her. The dark hallway leading to Aden's rooms hid him from sight, but when Vlad raised his head, her heart started to race, and she knew she was right.

"I know you're there, Aden," she said, when he failed to make his presence known after several minutes.

"How did you know?" He stepped out of the shadows.

Ellie couldn't help but smile to herself. "You're not exactly stealthy."

He walked closer, looking a little ragged. Actually, a lot ragged.

His hair was tousled as if he had been repeatedly tugging on it. The weariness on his face was impossible to miss, visible in the drawn features and the slight pinch around his eyes. His hands were shoved deep in his pants pockets, and his sagging shoulders were a departure from his usual confident stance.

She'd been upset when she heard he'd gone to the capital for the games, but the more she thought about it, the more she realized he had no choice. Everyone expected him to attend. But it still left a painful knot in her stomach to think about him taking part. She wanted to ask but didn't think she could handle the answer.

"When did you get back?"

"A little while ago. Why do you always eat alone?"

Ellie shrugged. "I don't always, but it's just easier."

"What do you mean easier?"

Aden dropped into the seat across from her. Vlad's reaction was immediate. He sat up and hissed in Aden's direction. Aden's eyes flickered towards the cat before returning to Ellie's face. She reached over and stroked Vlad's ears, and he responded with a lazy stretch and a yawn before curling up once more.

"I don't mean anything by it. I enjoy eating alone, and it also lets me read or practice my writing."

He frowned. "Do the other thralls mistreat you?"

"No." It wasn't exactly a lie.

"I missed you." His expression shifted from surprise to a pained grimace as the words slipped out. The look on his face tugged at Ellie's heartstrings, making her want to both laugh and cry.

"You weren't gone that long."

"It felt like an eternity."

Unsure how he expected her to reply, Ellie pushed her plate away and sat back. "Thank you for unsealing my door. Now I won't get in your way anymore."

When they'd returned to the city a week ago, Ellie had been shocked when Sophie unsealed the door to her room.

"Are you sure this won't make him angry?" Ellie had faced the door as she watched it open for her.

"It was his idea." Sophie had said with a smile. "You can now enter and exit through this door. The one that opens into Aden's rooms will remain accessible as programmed, but it will now only open for you. If Aden wants to enter, he'll have to open it manually, but he promised he won't enter without your permission."

That also surprised her, since Aden usually barged into any room whenever he pleased.

"You were never in my way," Aden said.

"It felt like it."

"Tell me how to fix this, Ellie." Aden leaned forward in his chair.

"There's nothing to fix."

"Yes, there is. You're afraid of me again. I can't stand for you to be afraid of me."

"I'm not afraid of you, Aden."

She wasn't anymore, now that she remembered and recognized the man she loved in him.

"I know I frightened you at the beach. I'm sorry I lost my temper with you. And I'm sorry I left bruises on you. I never should have grabbed you like that. I always seem to lose my temper, and I shouldn't. It's just my feelings for you are—" He stopped, his face contorting in obvious frustration as he struggled to find the right words. "They're so overwhelming and—" Aden stopped again, taking a breath, "I'm at a loss, Ellie. What do you want me to do here?"

She was torn between wanting to comfort him and not knowing how. "I don't know."

"I've done everything you've asked. I gave you space."

"I'm grateful for that."

Although he had little choice since he was at the capital.

"Do you feel anything for me?"

The vulnerable and hopeful look stirring behind his eyes filled her with warmth. She was overcome with an overwhelming urge to give him some kind of reassurance.

"Yes," she replied after a brief pause.

"Have you figured out what it is?"

Ellie closed her eyes and exhaled before opening them again as Vlad jumped down and dashed off. Sure, abandon her now.

"Aden, it's not that simple. I don't know how to be what you want me to be."

Aden scooted his chair closer, and Ellie caught a whiff of his cologne mixed with his distinct scent, sending her heart racing.

"I don't want you to be anything but what you are and who you are."

"You want me to be Alysia."

"That's not true," he snapped, and then exhaled a sharp breath. His propensity to snap and snarl didn't frighten her anymore. That's just who he was and who he'd always been.

Part of her ached to reach out and touch him, to soothe him, but she held back. His aversion to touch had never extended to her, but he didn't know who she was. She didn't know how he would react to her touch or how she would react to touching him, and the uncertainty of it all made her feel like a coward.

Two distinct people battled within her, similar to what she had read about split personalities. And it was so weird to think of herself as Alysia. She had all these memories of a life, people, places, and events with no connection to the last twenty-two years. The only connection was the man, the vampire sitting in front of her, looking as lost and unsure as she felt.

"Isn't it?" She asked, her stomach twisting in anticipation as she waited for his reply.

Aden ran his fingers through his hair in frustration. "No."

His answer was her opportunity to tell him, to admit she remembered. She knew who she was and remembered the love they shared, and she still had for him, despite their differences. But her cowardice silenced her, trapping the words in her throat.

Before she could speak, Aden reached across the table and caressed her cheek. Ellie's eyes fluttered, and she let out a gasp as a rush of heat flooded her face at his touch.

"I want you, Ellie, just you. Exactly as you are."

Unable to form a coherent thought, Ellie opened her eyes. She blinked and jerked her head back, needing space from him.

Aden dropped his hand. "I'll give you the world if you'll let me."

His words tugged at her heart, but she could only offer a sad smile.

"But what kind of world is it?"

Aden

Aden swept the paintbrush over the watercolor canvas, blending and swirling colors as he lost himself in the familiar repetitive motion. It was the first time he'd painted in months. He hadn't picked up a brush since the first painting he did of Ellie after she came home with him. And he'd missed it more than he realized.

The portrait came to life—the image of his mother and Ellie sitting on the beach, watching the sunset. Aden painted it from memory; from one of the half-dozen times he pulled up a hologram when he visited the BloodStone labs.

Ellie hadn't spoken to him again since their conversation in the courtyard almost a week ago. After he told her he'd give her the world, her response hung in the air between them. She could silence him more effectively than even his mother.

He had no response for her, so after several minutes of uncomfortable silence, she'd excused herself.

Aden continued painting, infusing shadows and light into Ellie's long chestnut hair and adding details to her face before moving to the arch of her left brow, a little higher than her right. He grabbed a smaller brush and put the final touches on the small scar below her left eye and the curve of her lips, with the hint of a dimple at the corner, as she smiled at something Sophie must have said to her. But as always, Aden spent the most time on her eyes. Eyes he could paint with his own closed.

Ellie's eyes were wide, expressive, and the focal point of her face. When Aden looked into them, he saw everything he wanted for eternity.

When he'd first seen her, Aden thought she was appealing for a human, but he'd thought her features were relatively plain. And brunette hair had never been a turn-on for him. His obsession with Aly's memory caused him to spend centuries fixated on redheads. But as the weeks and months passed, Aden found Ellie's chestnut hair—the depth, highlights, and color—to be more beautiful than any shade of red. And the more he observed her, studying the features of her face, the more he discovered that not only was she lovely in an understated way, she was alluring and even more beautiful than Aly.

He stood back to examine the painting. He had captured her perfectly—the perfect combination of innocence and beauty.

The sound of Ellie's heart speeding up alerted him that she was waking. He put his brush down before walking out of his studio, hearing the water in Ellie's bathroom turn on as he walked into his own. After a quick shower, Aden dressed and walked back into his sitting room. There was no training tonight. It was the one night the soldiers got a reprieve. He had a pile of work in his office, but he wasn't in the mood. He wanted to see Ellie. This giving her space thing was getting really fucking old, but he forced himself to continue heeding her request.

His head whipped up when he heard the outer door to her room open, wishing for the ability to see through the wall. He listened as her footsteps faded down the hallway.

He only let himself debate for five seconds before he walked over. It was odd to not have a door programmed to admit him automatically. Every door in the city and in the region was programmed to grant him entrance. He knew what he was doing was wrong. He'd promised he would respect her privacy, but her scent that had permeated his room for months was gone now. Whenever she had walked through his rooms, she left her scent behind. But it had faded, and he was desperate for it.

"Enter," he said, and the scent that was Ellie slammed into him. He groaned and stepped into the room, letting it wrap around him. The room appeared tidy, but upon closer inspection, he noticed the wrinkles in the duvet covering the bed, the hairbrush and ties askew on her bureau, and her tablet sitting on the table in the corner.

It surprised him. She was always so neat and organized with his mother's things. It brought a curious smirk to his face as he realized she was a bit of a slob in her own space. Then it faded as he realized this was the first private space she probably had. What was it like for her to live in communal thrall quarters all her life?

A hiss from below and the unmistakable grip of sharp claws digging into his pant leg caught his attention. Aden glanced down and saw Vlad gripping his ankle with his paws while biting at his pants.

"What are you doing?" He lifted his mother's cat by the scruff. He'd been so focused on Ellie's heartbeat earlier that he hadn't registered the cat's presence inside her room.

"I was about to ask you the same thing."

Aden turned to find Ellie standing in her doorway, her face a mixture of confusion, hurt, and irritation all at once.

Remorse settled in his gut as Vlad squirmed in his grasp. Ellie wore a light pair of cotton pants and a short-sleeve shirt. He was glad his mother heeded his request to allow her to wear regular clothes. She looked casual and comfortable, something she'd never looked in her uniforms. She'd pulled her hair up, using one of those many ties on her bureau to keep the long strands off her face.

"Aden?" Ellie walked closer, her eyes questioning.

He wanted to respond, but his words caught in his throat, and all he could do was drink in the sight of her. How was it possible to ache for someone so profoundly?

Ellie stopped in front of him and reached out for Vlad. "Can I have him?"

Aden looked down at the cat as it hissed and squirmed in protest of its current predicament. Aden released the cat's scruff, and Ellie wrapped Vlad in her arms.

"Your mom asked me to look after him while she and your dad were gone. He doesn't like to be alone during the day, so I let him sleep in here with me." Ellie set the cat on the bed, but he jumped down and ran off. She turned back to Aden.

"Why are you in here, Aden? Is there something you wanted?"

"Why did you come back?" he asked, finding his voice.

"I forgot my tablet. Are you alright?"

"No."

Her eyes softened. "Do you need something from me?"

He paused before blurting out the word he'd said that night on the beach. "Everything."

The confusion on her face vanished, and she tucked her bottom lip between her teeth. Before Aden could contemplate his next move, he stepped forward, eliminating the distance between them.

He gave in, unable to deny himself what he'd been dying to do for months.

Ellie

Aden stepped closer to her, and Ellie held her breath. She knew what was coming and saw his intention in his eyes, so she reached up and grasped his wrists as he cupped her face in his hands. She held her body rigid, afraid to move, both fearful and excited.

Finding Aden in her room had surprised and angered her at first. He'd broken his promise, but then again, she'd expected him to. She'd been ready to call him out, but once she saw how unsettled and lost he was, her anger turned to understanding. A rush of memories hit her, each one highlighting Aden's vulnerable side, a stark contrast to the fierce vampire he had become.

With a gentle nudge, Aden tilted her chin up. His eyes swept over her face, meeting hers before they dropped to her lips.

"Aden," she breathed, her voice laced with the longing coursing through her, but his lips capturing hers muffled his name.

She gasped into his mouth, her body tensing, before surrendering to him. She opened her mouth beneath his and felt him moan against her lips. His tongue slipped into her mouth and met hers, caressing more gently than she imagined him capable of. The experience of his lips against hers was completely foreign to her in this lifetime, so she let him lead. But after a few seconds, instinct and memory kicked in as her tongue sought his.

The taste of his lips brought back memories of their first kiss. He smelled like a combination of cinnamon and vanilla, and she loved that he still tasted the same.

Ellie released his wrists and grasped the front of his shirt. She didn't know whether to pull him closer or push him away. All the fear and hesitation left her as Aden groaned her name into her mouth.

His hands traced the contours of her face before slipping into her hair. Ellie felt a gentle tug at the knot on the back of her head, and her hair fell in waves down her back. His fingers tangled in the long strands, and Ellie's body shivered with pleasure, a soft moan escaping her lips.

Aden responded by wrapping one arm around her back and pulling her flush against his hard body. Ellie's head spun, and she whimpered. Aden's other arm came around her, and he deepened the kiss. It was slow, deep, and tender, leaving Ellie breathless. It felt like coming home.

And now her fear crept in again, fear of the intensity of the feelings overwhelming her. She tried to pull back, but he held her captive.

Ellie murmured his name again as his lips released hers and glided down over her chin. She trembled in his arms. As his mouth moved lower, Ellie froze, and she choked back a sob. Fear laced through her at the remembered feel of his lips on her neck.

"No," Ellie gasped, pushing against his chest. It was futile. He didn't budge.

Aden raised his head, his eyes meeting hers. Desire and something else filled them, but it wasn't the beginning of the madness she'd seen before. The rims of his irises were red, but the rest remained deep blue. Ellie pulled out of his arms, surprised that he let her go.

"Ellie." His voice was rough, the column of his throat rippling as he swallowed.

She shook her head and lifted her fingers to her lips, panting.

The defeat flashing in his eyes was more than she could bear, so she turned and ran from the room.

Aden

This was why humans had tracking chips.

Aden stomped through the compound, searching for Ellie. It would have been easy to pull her up on a hologram and find her at once, but he'd needed time to clear his head before finding her.

After he'd kissed her, she'd bolted. It wasn't the reaction he'd been hoping for when he made the split-second decision to press his lips to hers. But he couldn't stop himself. He'd wanted to kiss her for weeks, months if he was being honest. And it had been everything he'd imagined. She tasted soft and sweet as her mouth yielded to his. Aden thought she might push him away. She held her body so rigid that it was almost like kissing a statue, until she shuddered, sighed, and opened her mouth to him.

That one kiss lit Aden on fire, yet it brought him more peace than he'd known in centuries. He hadn't even flinched from the contact. The feel of her beneath his hands and against his body felt right. He could remember everything about Aly—every detail, every touch, and every kiss—but nothing he'd felt with her compared to the way kissing Ellie had felt.

She pushed him away, and her eyes spoke volumes. She had been just as affected as he was. For a split second, hope bloomed inside him, but she shook her head, and that hope died.

Then she ran. Like her ass was on fire.

He focused his hearing, trying to determine her location in the compound. The more he focused, the more he realized he couldn't detect her heartbeat in the vicinity. His immediate instinct was to panic, but Aden forced himself to take a deep breath and focus again. There was still no trace of it.

"Fuck! Track Ellie," Aden said, and a hologram appeared. She was sitting cross-legged on a patch of grass. He blinked, surprised. That's why her heartbeat was undetectable. She wasn't in the compound.

He recognized her location. It was the park along the outer perimeter of the city, just inside the exit gate. How the hell had she gotten there so fast?

Aden checked his watch and cursed himself. It had been almost a half hour since she'd run out of her room. How had she gotten out of the compound?

Aden barked Kane's name, and his image replaced Ellie's in the hologram.

"Yes," Kane answered. Aden ignored his smirk and sarcastic tone.

"Ellie left the compound. You better be with her."

"I've got her in my sights."

Aden exhaled a sigh of relief. He could always count on Kane. He turned and headed toward the front entrance. "Why didn't you call me?"

"It seemed like she needed time to herself."

"Who let her out? And how did you know?"

"I heard her arguing with the guard at the front doors when I returned from dinner. She wanted to go outside, but he refused, and she was getting hysterical. I intervened and told him to let her go."

"Why the fuck would you do that?"

Aden thrust his hands through his hair and tugged hard in frustration. At the rate he was going, he'd be bald in no time.

"You told me she's not a prisoner."

"That doesn't mean she should have free rein to go anywhere unsupervised."

"She's not. I've got two guards shadowing her, and I'm standing about five hundred feet behind her."

"What's she doing?"

"Nothing really. Gazing at the stars and talking to herself."

Aden's steps faltered as he entered the foyer. "Come again?"

"She's debating whether to go back to the compound or try to make a break for it past the gate guards."

Panic slammed into Aden. "I'll be right there."

He bolted for the front door, pushing past the two guards standing in the arched entry before he stopped and turned back.

"Which one of you let Ellie out?"

Both guards looked at each other before the one on the right raised his hand. Aden grabbed him by the neck and lifted him off the ground like he weighed nothing. He snapped the guard's neck with a quick flick of his wrist. He tossed the limp body to the ground and turned to the other with a snarl.

"If she ever leaves this compound again and you don't call me, that will be you."

He turned and headed down the driveway.

"That won't go over well with the Gerent or his wife," Kane said, the hologram following Aden out of the compound.

"I should do the same thing to you," Aden snarled, his pace quickening.

"Dramatic much."

Aden growled. Kane should be more afraid of him. "Shut the fuck up, Kane. She's at the exit gate, right? I'm coming there."

"Is that really a good idea?"

Aden strode through the gate, heading down the street. Why hadn't he just taken a warp port?

"Are you questioning me?"

"Just wondering why she was running from you, and perhaps if there was a good reason, it might be wise to give her space."

"I've been giving her fucking space," he bellowed, and several vampires on the street got out of his way. "And what are you, my shrink, now?"

Kane laughed, but Aden stopped at the street corner, pausing for a moment.

"Is she safe?"

"Yes."

"Kane, are you sure?"

"Yes."

Aden looked toward the city gate, less than a mile away, and then back at the compound. "Don't let her leave your sight. If anyone, human or vampire or half-breed, gets too close to her, I want them torn to shreds."

"Isn't that a little excessive?"

"Kane, I'm in no mood for your sarcasm. Do I need to find someone else to handle this?"

"No. But might I suggest she get her own guard?"

"Don't let her out of your sight." Aden swiped the hologram closed.

Perhaps Kane was right, and it was time to give Ellie her own guard. Aden had never heard of any human in history with a personal guard.

How would he explain that? His family would understand, but no one else would. He didn't owe anyone an explanation, but there would be a lot of questions if anyone found out. Aden didn't want to draw attention to Ellie if he could help it. Not until he knew what would happen between them.

If she rejected him and didn't want to be with him, he would still make sure she was safe. No matter the cost. But he couldn't contemplate her rejecting him. It wasn't an option. His happiness and his very life depended on it. He'd lost her once, and he wouldn't ever live without her again.

So assigning her a personal guard was a given. But who could he trust to protect her? Besides his family, there was no one he trusted more than Kane.

Aden glanced at his watch again. He was impatient and antsy, and not at all in the mood to stand around doing nothing. He'd give her another half hour, and then he was going after her. Screw Kane and his unsolicited advice. Who the fuck was Kane to give him advice anyway?

He needed something to distract him. He called the thralls' quarters as he turned to head back to the compound. Georgina appeared in the hologram. "Yes, Master Aden?"

"Send three girls to my office!"

"Do you have a preference, Sir?"

"No." He reached the front door. The dead guard's body was gone, and a new guard was in his place. He walked through the foyer and toward his office.

"Chelsea is feeling the compulsion. Shall I send her?"

"No. Keep her away as long as she can stand it."

"Yes, Sir. The girls are on their way now."

Georgina's image vanished as Aden walked into his office and to the window behind his desk. He looked out at the night sky, the full moon filling it with silvery light. Aden thought back to that night a few short months ago. Had that much time passed since he took Ellie to see the snow? He could still feel the warmth of her body as she stumbled into him, and the memory made him shiver.

Tonight, the memory of that warmth had become a reality again when he pulled her to him and deepened their kiss. The heat from her body seeped into his bones as she yielded to him, warming him for the first time in centuries.

Aden licked his lips, relishing her unique taste. Part of him didn't want to feed because he would lose it. But being near her when he was hungry wasn't a good thing. Hunger made him edgy, and when he was edgy, he snapped at her. And his hunger made him want to sink his teeth into the softest part of her neck.

She couldn't run from him forever. If that kiss told him anything, it was that Ellie's desire for him ran as deep as his for her.

He would give her space for now, but once he fed and felt steady again, he would go after her.

Aden stood in the shadows, watching Ellie recline on the grass next to a tree. To her right sat a wooden bench and tall stone pots filled with intricately shaped topiaries. Winding granite pathways curled around her on the left, through the neatly manicured landscape. She looked comfortable and relaxed, not like the image Kane painted of a crazy person muttering to herself.

Sunrise was approaching, and the dome was closing as Kane sauntered up beside him.

"She doesn't look like she's talking to herself."

"Yeah, she stopped a while ago after she decided that running from you would be pointless."

"Have you heard her talking to herself before?"

That was a sign of mental illness, wasn't it?

"That was a first," Kane said, to Aden's relief.

"What else did she say?"

"Apparently you're a good kisser," Kane said with a smirk, and Aden narrowed his eyes.

"Does she not realize she's in a public place and that every vampire within a half-mile radius can fucking hear her?"

Kane snorted. "Apparently not."

"I want Drake reassigned to be her guard effective tomorrow. Call Roderick and give him Drake's new orders." Kane nodded, and by the look on his face, he agreed with Aden's choice.

Ellie's stomach growled, and Aden frowned. She likely hadn't eaten all night. She certainly hadn't had time to before she bolted from the compound. Without another word to Kane, Aden walked toward her as she stood up. She turned and came face-to-face with him. The way her eyes widened and then darted toward the gate, Aden knew her first instinct was to flee.

"Running from me is futile."

Instead, she sighed. "I know."

"Ellie, we have to talk about this." Aden motioned for her to walk with a wave of his hand. "Come, let's take one of the warp ports back to the compound."

"Can we please walk? It's not that far."

"Okay." He conceded more easily than either of them expected, and a small smile curved her lips.

"Thank you. Will Kane and the others follow us?" She gave him a knowing look that told him she was aware of Kane's secret surveillance operation.

"I've sent them all back, except Kane. And you should be more mindful that both vampires and half-breeds can hear you if you talk to yourself out loud."

She bit her lower lip, and an eruption of pink bloomed on her cheeks, causing him to stifle a groan.

They walked down the sidewalk. Glossy glass-and-steel buildings lined the street. Thriving foliage spilled over their exteriors, framing the illuminated windows and offering a glimpse of the world inside, broken up by fluttering holographic displays across the building's facades. The city's ambient soundscape created a low hum in the background as they turned onto the main street.

Ellie walked a few paces behind him, as all humans were required. It made Aden's teeth clench. He wanted her beside him, but it was probably best. Inside his family's compound, they didn't follow these rules, but it was necessary in public.

"You haven't eaten tonight." It was a statement and not a question.

"No. That's why I was heading back home."

As they turned the corner, he wondered if she realized she called the compound home.

"Why did you run from me, Ellie?"

Ellie's hesitation was palpable. "It's too much."

"What's too much?"

"These feelings."

Aden stopped and turned back to her. "You can't say something like that and keep running from me."

"What do you want from me?"

"I want you to love me, damn it!" Aden's thunderous voice was so loud that several vampires walking with their pets on leashes across the street stopped and gaped in shock.

Ellie's eyes widened, and she looked around them. Aden turned his head and snarled. "What the fuck are you looking at?"

The onlookers scurried away. Aden motioned to Kane with his head in an unspoken instruction to handle the situation. Kane nodded and followed the vampires.

Aden turned back to Ellie, his face still blazing with anger. She looked at him, her eyes reflecting her disappointment.

"We can't have this fucking conversation out here." He grasped Ellie's arm and led her down an empty side street.

"Aden, what is Kane going to do to those vampires and their pets?"

"Don't worry about that."

Ellie tugged her arm, and Aden stopped. "What is Kane going to do?" She crossed her arms over her chest.

"Ellie, don't push me on this. They're just vampires. What do you care what I do to them?"

"I've learned that not all vampires are evil. They did nothing wrong."

"They heard what I said to you."

"Why do you care?"

"Ellie—" he growled, but she held up a hand.

"If you want me to love you, Aden, this isn't the way to do it."

"I'm trying to protect you."

"I don't want that kind of protection. Or love. Not at the expense of someone else's life."

"Fuck." Aden put his fist through the wall of the building beside them, resulting in a shower of broken glass.

Though she was far enough away to avoid the debris, Ellie flinched but held her ground. "Aden, please."

"Kane," he barked, flexing his fingers as blood dripped onto the ground. Kane's hologram appeared beside him. "Stand down."

"Are you sure? Drake and his team are already on the way."

"I said stand down. But I suggest having a conversation with them, stressing the need for discretion and the consequences of failing to comply."

"I'll take care of it." Kane looked over at Ellie and smiled before his image faded.

Though it was unnecessary, Aden took several deep breaths. "Are you happy now?"

"Yes, thank you." She smiled, and when she looked at him like that, hope bloomed in his chest again. But her moods were giving him whiplash.

"Sometimes I think you're more mercurial than I am."

A laugh escaped her lips. "Sorry." She chuckled at his confused expression.

Aden turned, and they continued down the street. "Why are you laughing? Do you even know what that word means?"

"Yes, I do, actually. I have a dictionary on my tablet." When he didn't respond, she tapped her temple. "Eidetic memory."

"Did Sophie tell you that?"

"No. Master Matthais tested me when I was a child. I didn't know what they were doing, but my dad told me later. The tests when we got back from the beach were the same."

"Wait, you read the entire dictionary?"

"Not yet. I'm on the r's right now."

"Why would you do that?"

"Because I can."

Aden walked up to the warp port that was at the corner. "I think we've walked enough tonight. Get in."

Ellie followed him into the booth. He swiped his hand over the hologram that appeared and typed in the coordinates of the compound. Less than a minute later, they appeared beside the front door. He guided her inside the foyer, where another warp port dropped them in the hallway outside his door.

"Whoa," Ellie said, shaking her head.

Aden grasped her elbow to steady her.

"Thank you," she whispered.

They walked down the hallway and into his sitting room.

"Call for food, and then we're going to finish our talk, Ellie."

As she called the kitchens and ordered dinner, Aden went into the bathroom to wash his hands, both dreading and anticipating the conversation.

Aden stepped out of the closet to find Ellie sitting on the sofa with her head resting in her hands. "Did you order something to eat?"

Ellie looked up. "Yes. If you need to feed before we talk, I can go to my room while you do."

Aden poured himself a drink and then sat down in the chair next to the sofa. "No, I fed earlier, during your excursion to the park."

"Oh, okay."

"Does my feeding make you that uncomfortable?"

Ellie shrugged.

"I've tried to keep it out of your sight, but everyone needs to eat, Ellie."

"I know that."

"If I had the choice, I would choose food over blood, but I don't. I can't help who I am."

Aden thought he saw a flicker of understanding in her eyes, but it vanished so quickly that he thought he'd imagined it.

Ellie leaned back against the cushion. "I thought all vampires enjoyed drinking blood."

"I'm sure they do."

"Do you?"

"Yes. But I enjoyed eating food too, when I was able."

"Do you remember what it tastes like?"

"Some of it. I remember chocolate. I liked chocolate."

A subtle smile tugged at the corner of her lips, but she remained silent. He gulped back the last of his drink as the door buzzed.

"Enter," Aden called, and a thrall entered with a tray of food. "Put it on the table," he said in his usual no-nonsense tone.

"Thank you, Finn," Ellie said.

Finn looked down, nodding his head, a small grin on his lips.

"Get out," Aden snapped as he recognized him.

"Yes, Sir," Finn said as he exited.

"How do you know him?" Aden asked, curious to see what Ellie would say.

She leaned forward to smell the steam over her soup. "I work with him in the kitchens sometimes."

"There's no need for you to work in the kitchens anymore."

Ellie glared at him over the spoon she was lifting to her mouth. "Why not?"

"Because you don't need to do that kind of work."

"I enjoy cooking sometimes, Aden."

"Ellie, second-level thralls don't do manual labor." Ellie choked on her soup, and Aden realized his mistake. "What I mean is that you're not a thrall to me, and I don't want you working like one."

Ellie put her soup back on the table.

"Why aren't you still eating?"

"I've lost my appetite."

"Ellie—"

"Aden, you need to stop obsessing about my diet. It drives me crazy. I'm a grown woman, and I can decide when I want to eat and when I don't."

Aden gritted his teeth. "I don't want to argue with you."

Ellie leaned back again, studying him with a mix of anticipation and wariness. Her stomach growled again.

"Ellie, just fucking eat already."

For a moment, she just stared at him before she reached for her soup again. Aden waited several minutes, allowing her to finish her food. When she set her empty bowl on the table and sat back, Aden leaned forward.

"I need you to tell me what you meant when you said your feelings were too much."

"I think that's pretty self-explanatory."

"Not even close."

She held his gaze as a myriad of emotions crossed her face. "I'm trying to wrap my head around what this is between us, Aden, but I—"

"Then let's figure it out together." He reached out and brushed the backs of his fingers down her neck and over her scar. Ellie bolted off the sofa and around the table.

"You're asking me to rethink everything I've ever known."

He dug his fingernails into his palms. "And you think I'm not? This isn't easy for me either, Ellie. You think I wanted to fall in love with a human again?" Ellie blinked, and she looked like he'd slapped her. "That didn't come out right." Aden stood. "Fuck!"

"No, this is a mistake. There's no way this can ever work."

In three strides, he stood in front of her, taking her face between his hands. For the second time that evening, the touch didn't make him flinch, and he welcomed the feeling of her warm, silky skin beneath his fingertips.

"I refuse to accept that," he said, not caring how desperate he sounded. "I haven't waited almost three hundred years for you to just lose you because I'm a vampire and you're a human. That doesn't fucking matter."

Ellie stepped back. "Please, I can't think when you're touching me like that."

Aden frowned as she retreated, but he didn't stop her. His hands fell to his sides, and he clenched them to stop himself from reaching for her again.

He debated his next words, almost feeling as if he was betraying Aly. Until he realized he wasn't.

"You think I'm still in love with a memory, but I'm not. I don't care if you're Aly's soul or not. None of it matters anymore. And I'm not saying that to manipulate you. I loved Aly. I wanted her for eternity." He reached out and grabbed her hand, unable to bear the distance between them anymore. "But what I feel for you here and now, Ellie, eclipses anything I've ever felt in my life."

Ellie looked down at their joined hands and then back up at his face. "Aden, this is crazy. Do you hear yourself?"

He smiled and loosened his grip a little. It had to be her choice. She had to come to him, or it meant nothing.

"Ellie, you don't have to believe. I'll believe for both of us."

Ellie

Aden gazed at her with such intensity that Ellie could feel the heat of it fill her body. Those eyes. She could see the truth in his eyes, and she believed. She believed he would do anything. And if he was brave enough to take the chance, why shouldn't she?

She pulled her hand from his and saw the brief flash of hurt in his eyes before she stepped closer and held it up.

"Can I touch you?"

He gulped and nodded.

Ellie pressed her hand to his chest. She felt him shudder and then still, but he didn't look away from her. His chest rose and fell with shallow breaths until, all at once, everything in him relaxed. He gripped her hips in his hands and a sigh escaped his lips as his eyes slipped closed.

She lifted her other hand and rested it beside the first before her fingers traced a slow path up his chest. She felt him tremble, and a surge of triumph washed over her. Ellie remembered the first time they'd done this. They'd been in their teens, and it took him several minutes to get used to her touch. But once he did, he'd begged her to never stop.

His eyes opened, darkened with need.

"Can I touch your face?" She reached his neck.

"You don't have to fucking ask," he growled, and she arched her eyebrow at him. His tone softened. "You don't have to ask anymore. Please."

That one broken plea was her undoing.

Ellie's hands glided up his neck to his face. His eyes fluttered as her fingers brushed over the skin of his jaw, feeling the faint stubble of his barely visible five-o'clock shadow under her fingertips. Her fingers traced a path up his face, relearning it as his body shuddered again beneath her touch. She brushed the pads of her thumbs underneath his eyes, and they briefly flashed red before returning to their familiar sapphire blue.

Her fingers continued their gentle exploration and climbed over his temples, sliding into his hair and entwining with the soft, short strands as she pulled his face towards hers. Aden groaned as she fused her mouth to his, and he pulled her flush against his body as his arms came around her. She grasped his hair, tugging gently as the kiss deepened. Aden reached down, lifting her up, and she wrapped herself around him.

Ellie let out a soft whimper, her lips parting to allow his tongue to explore. The kiss deepened as their tongues intertwined, dancing in a sensual rhythm, gently stroking, caressing, and tasting. Aden slipped his hands down her back and hiked her up higher, pulling her legs tighter around his waist.

Ellie lost herself in the feel and taste of him. She remembered how cool his body would feel against hers at first—until her body heat warmed him. But he always kept his rooms warm for her now. So, while he wasn't as hot as she was, she could feel his body warming against her as, once again, her body heated him.

Ellie pulled away, gasping for air, struggling to catch her breath. Her tongue and lips tingled from his venom and the hunger of his kiss. Soft pants slipped past her lips as Aden traced a warm, wet path down her neck to the base of her throat.

Ellie's body froze. She held her breath, opening her eyes, as images of her death flashed. "Aden," she choked his name and pushed at him. He lifted his head. His eyes were dark, but still all blue. No sign of red anywhere. Ellie leaned in and captured his lips again, sliding her tongue along the seam, silently asking for permission. He allowed her entry, and the moment their tongues met, a fiery longing consumed them both.

Before Ellie realized what was happening, Aden walked across the room and laid her on his bed. Without breaking the kiss, he bowed over her, crawling on his knees as he shifted them up onto the mattress. His hands traveled up her sides, and a shiver rippled through her as he pushed her shirt up, exposing her abdomen.

Ellie pulled her lips away from his and gasped. "Aden, wait."

Aden groaned and leaned back on his heels. Ellie sat up and pushed her shirt down before reaching up to touch her still-tingling lips.

"Fuck!" Aden swung his legs over the side of the bed and dropped his head in his hands.

"I think I should go to my room." Ellie shifted toward the edge of the bed, but Aden's hand shot out and grabbed her arm.

"I don't mean to push you."

"You didn't, but I'm not—I mean, I don't—It's just—"

Aden caressed her cheek. "Not until you're ready."

Ellie tried to hide her surprise. She was five years over the legal age to be taken as a pet. He had every right to take her, with or without her consent. But as she looked into his eyes, she remembered that wasn't what this was. She may be human, but she wasn't his pet.

Aden leaned in and pressed a tender kiss to her lips, causing a flutter in her heart. "I love you, Ellie."

Ellie blinked and opened her mouth to reply, but no words came out, his declaration making it almost impossible to breathe. To the depths of her soul, she knew it, but to hear him say the words out loud left her speechless.

"You don't have to say it back, but I needed to say it. You needed to know."

Ellie's brain and body were overloaded, and though she longed to say it back, the words caught in her throat. She got to her knees and leaned closer to him. His eyes followed her movements, almost wary of them. She braced her hands on his arms as she kissed the corner of his mouth.

"Goodnight, Aden."

Ellie kept her eyes open and watched his eyes flutter as her lips brushed his. She slipped off the bed and padded to her room, glancing at Aden one last time to find him sitting in the same spot, watching her.

When the door closed, Ellie's knees gave out, and she hit the floor with a gentle thud. She half expected Aden to call through the door, asking if she was okay. But he didn't.

Vlad padded over and climbed into her lap, nudging her hand so she would pet him. Ellie remained in that spot all day, reliving every moment over and over again.

Aden

"This whole thing was a huge mistake."

Aden eyed his sister as Keeley sat, seething, on the chair in front of his desk. When she was in this kind of mood, it was always best to let her get it out, but he couldn't help asking.

"Keel, don't you think you're overreacting just a little?"

"Who's side are you on?" Without waiting for his response, she continued ranting. "I have no idea what I was thinking. Surrogates aren't the answer."

"They're the only answer for vampires who want kids."

Keeley stood, pacing the length of his office. Aden rocked back and forth in his chair as his eyes followed her.

"Why did I think you'd possibly understand? When the time comes, you'll make Ellie a half-breed, and you'll have your own children."

Aden wasn't touching that with a ten-foot pole. Ellie barely loved him at this point. At least he thought she loved him, though she hadn't said it back to him yet. And she despised vampires, so he couldn't fathom her ever wanting children with him. Not that it bothered him. Kids weren't his thing.

"At least it's only a couple more months before the baby is born. Then you can ditch the incubator, and all will be well."

"Don't be an ass. I should have asked Mom to do it for us."

"Why didn't you?"

Keeley dropped onto the sofa and tucked her feet beneath her. "It just felt weird."

"You can always ask her now. Get rid of this one and have Sophie do it." Aden grinned as he walked over to sit beside her, careful not to sit too close, lest she touch him. "Keep it in the family."

"You're still being an ass."

He shrugged.

"No," Keeley said with a sigh. "I've started down this road now. I have to follow it to the end."

"Whatever you say." He didn't believe her, but his sister was incredibly stubborn.

"Anyway," Keeley said, leaning toward him. "Enough about me. How are things going with Ellie?"

Aden couldn't keep the goofy grin from tugging at his lips. "Perfect," he said, and then realized how he sounded, so he cleared his throat and tried to look serious again. "She's stopped running from me, at least. That's a start."

Keeley looked at him, amused. "Seriously though. You listen to me go on and on about what's up with me, but you never tell me anything anymore."

"There's nothing to tell." Aden trusted Keeley, but he wasn't ready to share yet. It was too new and too fragile, and he didn't want to jinx it.

"Come on, you've got to give me something. Otherwise, I'll have to ask her."

"Don't you dare, Keeley!" Aden snarled. "I mean it. Leave her alone, or you'll fucking piss me off."

"Mom says she's been nonstop smiles for days now. Kinda like that." Keeley poked him in the cheek. He swatted her hand away as he stood, walking over to his desk and leaning against the front of it.

"You're too cute, baby brother."

Aden folded his arms across his chest. "Enough, Keeley."

"I'm thrilled for you, you know."

"Well, I'm terrified." Keeley was probably the only person he would admit it to. "What if I hurt her?"

"You won't."

"I did once."

"That was a long time ago."

Aden remained unconvinced.

"You won't."

"But what if I do? I'm aware of how fragile she is, but I can't bear to keep my hands off her."

"She was always the only one you could stand to let touch you."

"It's only ever been her. That's why I'm terrified of touching her."

"You know how to control your bloodlust and your strength now, Aden. You didn't then."

"I'm not just talking about physically. I don't want to rush her or crowd her or spook her, but I feel like I'm crawling out of my skin with wanting her."

Before Keeley could reply, the door to his office opened.

He programmed it to admit Ellie a week earlier, but this was the first time she came to see him. Aden couldn't contain the grin that curled his lips, but his smile faltered when he saw her face. She was glaring daggers at him.

"How dare you?" She growled, crossing her arms.

Keeley snickered under her breath. "Hey, Ellie."

Ellie looked over, surprised, and her entire demeanor changed. "Oh hi, Keeley. I'm sorry to interrupt."

"It's okay. I was just leaving. I'll talk to you later," Keeley said to Aden as she headed toward the door.

Aden tore his eyes away from Ellie's face and glanced at his sister. From behind Ellie, she smirked and mouthed, 'Someone's in trouble.'

Her amusement about his life wasn't fucking appreciated at all.

"Why is Drake following me everywhere?" Ellie jumped right in as soon as the door closed.

"He's your new guard."

"Why do I have a guard?"

"Because you need one."

She looked furious enough to spit. "I don't need a guard, Aden."

"I think you do."

"I'm human. No one gives me a second thought."

Aden crossed his arms, mimicking her posture. He wasn't used to people questioning him, especially not a human.

"Don't fucking say that. You need protection because of who you are to me."

"No one knows that but us."

"They will. I won't hide you like a dirty little secret."

"But it's dangerous for anyone to know about us." Her tone softened as she dropped her arms.

"It is, right now, for anyone outside this compound anyway. Our thralls and guards won't reveal anything, but we have to be cautious in public. Besides, you can't tell me you never had a guard accompany you outside of Matthais' compound."

"Of course I did," she replied, exasperated. "When I went to the market, but that was so I wouldn't try to escape."

"Then why would anyone think it's any different now?"

She shot him a pointed look. "Aden, I don't want to be shadowed everywhere."

She could be so infuriating sometimes.

"I don't care. Everything is different now."

"But I never leave the compound. What do I have to fear here? Even Kane doesn't follow you around the compound."

"You have a propensity for taking off unaccompanied."

"I did that once." She scowled.

Unable to resist any longer, Aden reached for her, grasping her hand and pulling her toward him with a gentle tug. He reached up and brushed a few strands of her hair behind her ear, letting his fingers linger.

The scowl melted off Ellie's face, and she closed her eyes, leaning into his touch. "Aden," she said, her voice a breathy whisper.

Since he started touching her, he couldn't help but be amazed and awed by the way her breath shuddered and her blood rushed through her veins underneath her skin whenever he did. After going so long without touch, he was desperate and insatiable for hers.

Aden pulled her closer and leaned down to press his lips against her ear. "Don't fight me on this, Ellie."

She turned her face toward his. Her eyelashes fluttered against his cheek like butterfly wings, and she inhaled deeply.

"Aren't you going to kiss me?" She breathed against his skin.

Aden released a low groan and captured her lips. The dam broke again. Like the other night and every night since, when their lips touched.

Ellie wrapped her arms around his neck and pressed against him as the kiss deepened. With a gentle tug on his hair, she moved her mouth against his and he reveled in the warmth and softness of her lips. Everything around him faded away, leaving only the feel and taste of her.

Ellie tore her lips away from his when her need to breathe became necessary. She gasped for breath, her head falling backward. Aden trailed his lips down her jaw to her neck, his tongue swirling on her skin, and she stiffened in his arms.

Aden lifted his head and looked at her, his brow furrowing. "What's the matter?"

She shook her head and pressed her lips to his again. She was trying to distract him, and he leaned back out of the kiss.

"No, Ellie. Why do you always stiffen when I kiss your neck? Are you afraid I'm going to bite you?"

She stepped out of his arms. "Isn't it inevitable?"

"What's that supposed to mean?"

"It means eventually you're going to want to bite me, right?"

Aden looked away, and he knew his face was a mask of irritation and guilt. She reached out and touched his chest.

"Aden, I know you won't hurt me."

His eyes whipped back to hers. "I will never bite you again without your permission, Ellie. Never again." He said the words with such conviction that it startled them both. "Never."

Ellie's eyes softened, and she pressed herself against him, pulling his face to her throat. Her head fell back again, and she offered her neck to him.

"I trust you, Aden."

She wasn't inviting him to bite her, but she was showing him just how much she trusted him. Unable to resist, he took what she offered. He brushed his nose under her jaw, and his breath caressed her throat. His tongue again swirled over her skin. This time, when she trembled, it wasn't from fear.

When a breathy moan escaped her lips, Aden closed his and pressed them to her skin, against the scar he left. It was his turn to tremble as he held her, matching his breathing to hers.

They stood in each other's arms for a long time, until Ellie lifted her head and met his gaze.

"I love you, Ellie." Aden's words were soft and sincere.

Disappointment flooded him when she didn't say them back. Not that he expected it. She still needed time, and he'd give her as long as she needed. He just hoped the waiting wouldn't kill him in the meantime.

She leaned forward and kissed the base of his throat. "Thank you."

He gave her a confused look. "What for?"

"For getting Drake off my back when I'm in the compound."

"I don't remember agreeing to that."

She massaged the back of his neck with her fingertips, and a sweet smile played on her lips. "But you're going to."

He agreed, unable to deny her anything anymore. "He goes with you any time you leave the compound."

Her lips curved in triumph. And, in that instant, Aden decided he would always let her win as long as she smiled.

Just like that.

Ellie

"I thought I might find you here."

Ellie turned from the hologram she was looking at over Sophie's conference table to find the woman standing behind her. "Did you need something?" She swiped her finger over the image to close it. "I finished updating those files we talked about earlier."

Sophie's smile was unnerving, and Ellie squirmed in her seat.

"Was there something you needed?"

"I just wanted to see how you were."

"I'm fine. Wait a minute. Aden didn't send you to check on me, did he?"

"No. Believe it or not, he didn't." Ellie narrowed her eyes, and Sophie laughed. "Honestly. I know it's been an eventful couple of weeks for both of you, and I wanted to make sure you knew that if you need or want to talk about anything, you can come to me."

Ellie chewed on her bottom lip, tempted by Sophie's offer.

"Aden is my son, and maybe you feel odd talking to me about him, but I know he can be intense sometimes and not always easy to deal with."

"You think?" Ellie slapped her hand over her mouth. "Oh, I shouldn't have said that."

"It's okay. I won't tell him." Sophie walked to her sitting area, settling in a chair as Ellie shifted to face her.

"Thank you, Sophie, but I'm okay. We're taking it slow, but..." Ellie's words trailed off.

"But what?"

"I'm still a little unsure how to act around everyone."

"Being with Aden means changes in every aspect of your life. You're no longer a thrall, Ellie. You need to get used to that."

Ellie rose and moved to the sofa. "But doesn't being a human automatically make me a thrall? I have no idea what it means to not be one."

"It'll take time. Just like it took time for you to learn how we live here. So, how are you handling everything? I worry my son is too impatient for his own good. Not that I blame him. He waited a long time for you."

"It's all so—" Ellie struggled to find the right word. "Surreal, I guess."

Sophie raised an eyebrow, and it made Ellie laugh. "I just finished the s's in the dictionary."

"I'm impressed. I've never read the dictionary cover to cover."

Ellie leaned back and settled into the cushions. "What else do I have to do? Aden won't let me do anything anymore. I had to really fight him to keep working with you."

"Yes, I had the same argument. It makes me happy that you wanted to, even if you weren't required to any longer."

"I like it. It makes me feel useful and relevant. And I enjoy spending time with you."

"I like it too." Sophie reached out and rubbed Ellie's arm gently. "So, getting back to the surreal?"

"When anyone looks at me, all they see is a human. But what does that mean? I'm not sure anymore."

"Being with Aden changes all of that," Sophie repeated. "Everyone who knows who you are to him will view you differently, especially after you decide what to do."

Ellie looked at her, confused.

"You can't stay human forever, Ellie. Legal issues aside, and you have a few years before you need to decide, but you'll have to make a choice, half-breed or vampire."

Ellie looked toward the window and bit her lip again. She could see the sun rising in the distance.

"You don't want to be either, do you?"

Ellie met Sophie's eyes and saw nothing but understanding. "I've lived my whole life as one thing, viewed as nothing—abused, and fearing for my life every day. And it's hard to reconcile all of that being gone now, just because Aden loves me. What makes me any different, really, than I was yesterday, last week, or last year? Or from the millions of other thralls, who are slaves just because they're human?"

"It doesn't."

"Why would I ever want to be the one thing that kept me and my father and Carrie enslaved?"

"Slavery is a blight on the soul of humankind."

"I remember that word from the dictionary."

"I imagine your memory is both a gift and a curse."

"Sometimes." Ellie thought of the memories of her past life that would randomly resurface. "You're not like all the other vampires and half-breeds I've ever known. None of you are. You treat your thralls kindly. Your thralls know they're protected, and it makes them feel safe. Safe isn't something I ever felt before coming here, though my dad tried. The things he had to do to prove his loyalty to Master Matthais to keep me safe, I know they still haunt him. Especially since it was all an illusion. No matter what my dad did, we both knew, deep down, that Master Matthais could and would end my life at any time."

"I'm so sorry he hurt you the way he did."

Ellie shrugged. "A lot of thralls had it worse."

"This is never what we wanted..." Sophie's voice faded as she fell silent.

Ellie waited to see if she would say more, but when she didn't, Ellie continued. "I guess to answer your question, I don't know if I want to become either. I know that means I'll die someday, and I don't know how I feel about that now that Aden and I found each other again, but—"

Sophie's eyes widened. "What do you mean you and Aden found each other again?"

Ellie realized her slip and cringed. She looked away but could feel Sophie's eyes on her, curious and intent. The sofa dipped as Sophie moved from the chair to sit beside her.

"You remember."

Ellie pinched her lips together, unable to look at her. Sophie's hand covered hers, and before Ellie could process the gentle touch, she felt herself pulled into Sophie's arms. Her body froze. The older woman didn't speak. There was no need.

A moment later, Ellie sagged in her arms, sobbing.

Ellie entered Aden's room to find him sprawled on his sofa, his bare feet resting on the arm. A hologram of the latest Rogue Vampire Extermination virtual reality game hovered above him.

She did a double-take, her eyes widening in surprise. Had she walked into the wrong room or somehow entered an alternate universe? Seeing him look so casual and relaxed was unusual.

Another memory rushed back to her—one of the two of them sitting in this very room. It looked different, but it was familiar all the same. They were again in their teens, and he was trying to teach her to play his latest game, but she was more interested in trying to distract him by kissing his neck. But very little could distract Aden from a new video game. Ellie felt her cheeks flush at the memory of her brazen behavior, especially when he gave in, pinning her to the sofa, as he removed her clothes.

She shook her head, letting that memory join all the others that had come back in recent weeks, becoming a part of her as they fused with her memories of this life. It was still unsettling at times, but she felt as if missing pieces of herself were returning from the dark.

Ellie had checked her face in the mirror to make sure her eyes were no longer puffy and red from crying. If he saw her like that, he'd drive her nuts all night, wanting to know what was wrong. She felt better and more clear-headed after her breakdown with Sophie, and now it was time to tell Aden. But the thought of how he might react terrified her.

Not of him.

But of what it would do to him.

Aden

Aden tilted his head back to see Ellie standing above him. "I knew I heard your heartbeat."

Her eyes crinkled at the corners as she smiled at him. "What are you doing?"

"Killing rogue vampires." He grinned, closing the hologram as he sat up.

Ellie plopped onto the sofa beside him, tucking one foot beneath her. "Who are you, and what have you done with serious and cranky Aden Westcott?"

"Don't tell anyone. It will ruin my reputation as a no-nonsense, badass vampire."

A quick laugh burst through her lips, and Aden leaned forward to kiss her. She smiled against his lips, and he felt her sigh into his mouth. He breathed her in and urged her to lay back, moving with her as he deepened the kiss.

"I can't believe I'm saying this, but I love the way your venom makes my tongue tingle when we kiss." She licked her lips when they both came up for air.

He nibbled at her chin and then trailed kisses down her throat, unable to resist the allure of her skin. "Venom is an aphrodisiac and paralytic when it's released into the bloodstream," he said between gentle nips. "But it also has analgesic properties. That's why when a vampire licks a puncture wound, not only does the blood stop flowing, it soothes the bite mark." He licked the one he'd left on her to prove his point, though hers was long healed and no longer painful.

Ellie nodded, her body arching against his as he pulled her closer, their lips meeting once more.

Her fingers tangled in his hair, tugging gently as she let out a soft moan. A low growl rumbled in his chest as she scratched his scalp, the feel of her fingernails sending delightful shivers down his spine. He loved it when she did that. He shifted his body over hers, settling his hips between her thighs and pressing her deeper into the cushion.

Ellie broke the kiss, pulling her mouth away from his, gasping for air.

"Aden."

The erotic way she said his name traveled through his entire body and straight to his cock. Every day, it became harder to keep his hands off her. He wasn't trying to pressure her, letting her set the pace, but he always wanted her. Every second. Of every minute. Of every day.

"Wrap your legs around me," Aden murmured against the skin behind her ear as he gently tugged them around his body. He sat up, pulling her with him, before he lay back, bringing Ellie over him. He groaned as she settled on top of him, pressing the length of her body against him. Trembling, she kissed him again, rolling her hips against his. Aden's hips jerked in response. He was hard and thick between her thighs and if she kept it up, he was going to come in his pants, but there was no way in hell he was going to stop her.

After several long minutes of slow, deep kissing, Ellie pulled back. She pushed on his chest and sat up. He grunted as the movement pressed her down on him. His already aching cock throbbed even more painfully.

She looked down at him, her breath ragged, her cheeks flushed, and her heart hammering in her chest. He had never seen her look as beautiful as she did in that moment.

Aden reached for her, but she grasped his hand in hers and pressed it to his abdomen to keep him from touching her. His brow furrowed, and he pushed up on his elbow.

"What's the matter?"

"Nothing. I just need to catch my breath a minute."

A rakish smile tugged at his lips, and he let his eyes drop to her breasts, watching them rise and fall. She flicked his nose, and he looked up at her, shocked.

"What was that for?"

"My eyes are up here."

Aden blinked as the memory of those familiar words sliced through him. Once upon a time, Aly had spoken those exact words. But with the woman on top of him, most of those memories were no longer painful. He sat up, shifting and leaning back against the arm of the sofa. "Your eyes are my lifeline. I see them all the time, even when mine are closed." He flexed his fingers on her hips and grinned. "But you can't blame me for being distracted by such an incredible alternate view."

She caressed his cheek. "Aden, we need to talk."

"Now?"

"Yes. I need to tell you something before this," Ellie gestured between them, "goes any further."

Aden frowned as the delicious tension in his groin deflated. "Ellie, I told you this doesn't have to go any further than you're comfortable with."

"I want this to go further. But you need to know something before it does."

"Okay," Aden said, his unease clear in his voice as he contemplated the implications of her words and the desire that stirred within him and his traitorous body.

He shifted and watched her as Ellie opened her mouth once and then a second time before closing it again. She chewed on her bottom lip.

"What is it, mo ghrá?" he asked, the endearment slipping from his lips before he realized it. Ellie's eyes whipped up to meet his.

"I remember."

"Remember what?"

"Aden, I remember," she said again, her voice barely a whisper.

Realization dawned, and his eyes widened. His hands dropped from her hips as her meaning sank in. For the longest time, all he wanted was for her to remember him and them. But he resigned himself to the fact that she never would. She was with him now, and that was all that mattered. Those memories, it seemed, were best left buried, but evidently, they were not.

"When?" he asked over the lump in his throat.

"My seizure at the beach. That was my memory coming back."

"How much of it?" Aden was almost afraid to ask.

"Only bits and pieces so far. More come back every day, but it's usually triggered by something."

"Ellie." His voice broke as he said her name.

"I had dreams of us for months, but they were just flashes. But while I was having my seizure, I remembered that night."

Aden's voice lodged in his throat, at a loss for words. What could he possibly say? Sorry, I killed you. My bad.

Ellie wrung her fingers together, unable to meet his gaze. He wanted to lift her chin so he could see her eyes, but he feared what he'd see there might break him.

"I remember being with you. I remember the pleasure. And I remember the pain and the fear I was going to die. I remember giving up and letting the darkness take me."

She could never fathom the depth of the darkness that consumed him that night, too.

"I'm sorry I didn't tell you sooner," Ellie said.

He reached up and gripped her hips again, relieved that she didn't flinch or pull away. "No, Ellie, I'm sorry. So incredibly sorry." The weight of his gut-wrenching remorse for what he'd done to her was so heavy that Aden felt like he was being crushed. "Why didn't you tell me?"

"I needed time to process it without you hovering." Her honesty, as it often did, struck him like a blow. "Can you imagine what it's like to die, Aden? To remember your death? To relive the memory?"

He didn't need to imagine it because he had been reliving every moment for centuries. Or at least he had until she came back into his life. He'd never know it from her perspective, but he would trade places with her in a heartbeat if it would take away her pain.

"Are you afraid of me? Afraid I'll hurt you like that again?"

She lifted her eyes, and he rushed on before she could answer.

"I didn't know how intense drinking from you like that would be. My parents warned us, but I was arrogant. I wanted you so badly, and I thought I could control it."

She pressed her hand against his heart, and he could have sworn it jerked against her fingertips. "I know, Aden. I wanted it too. We both thought you'd be able to control it."

"You trusted me."

"Yes."

"And I betrayed you."

"No." Ellie shook her head. "It's taken me a while to work through this, and that's part of why I didn't tell you right away. I needed to come to terms with it. I needed to figure out how I felt about it and you before I told you." She cupped his face in her hands, and Aden felt weak from her touch. "You didn't betray my trust. It was an accident. You loved me beyond reason—"

"Love you," Aden interrupted, gripping her wrists the way she always gripped his when he kissed her. "Love you beyond reason, Ellie. Present tense, not past."

"I know." Her gaze softened as a gentle warmth filled her eyes. "I think I've always known."

"Are you afraid of me?" He needed to know.

"No."

He searched her eyes for any hint of dishonesty and saw nothing but truth.

"And I forgive you, Aden."

Aden felt the weight of almost three hundred years of pain, grief, and guilt finally lift. He tugged her in his arms, pulling her against his chest and burying his face in her neck.

"Thank you," he whispered.

He never expected to find absolution for what he'd done because he believed he had lost her forever. With her pressed against him and her heartbeat thumping in a comforting rhythm against his chest, he thanked a deity he never believed in for being given a second chance.

Aden raised his head, his eyes meeting hers before he leaned toward her. Her warm breath fluttered against his skin as Ellie pressed closer, her lips meeting his in a soft, tender kiss, letting the forgiveness she offered—forgiveness he wasn't sure he deserved—wash away the past.

Aden turned and dropped his feet to the floor. With one arm, he scooped Ellie up and held her pressed against him as he stood, carrying her across the room. With each step towards the bed, her playful nibbles on his lips grew bolder, sending the blood rushing to his cock again. He gently placed her on the soft mattress, his body hovering over her.

Ellie kicked off her shoes and gazed up at him as she lay in the center of his bed, her skin flushed, her chest heaving, and her eyes shining with love and anticipation. She, quite simply, took his breath away.

Aden straddled her hips. He leaned down, his lips grazing her clavicle, feeling the warmth of her skin beneath them, tracing a path along her delicate flesh.

"I'm only going to ask this one time, Ellie," he murmured against her skin. "If you're at all unsure, you need to tell me now."

She arched her back and stretched her arms over her head, turning her face and brushing her lips against the shell of his ear.

"I'm sure," she breathed.

Aden groaned in response, turning his head and kissing her. He sat back on his heels, pulling her with him. He released her lips, leaving her panting and breathless, savoring the lingering taste of her on his lips.

Ellie's eyes fluttered open. Her bright green irises were dark, and it sent a shot of need straight through him. Aden yanked his shirt over his head and tossed it aside. Unable to resist, he leaned forward and took Ellie's lips again.

He reached for the hem of her shirt, pushing it up, his thumbs brushing against the silky skin of her stomach, then against the underside of her breasts. He felt her muscles quiver, and he smiled against her lips.

Aden pulled back and pushed her shirt higher, urging her arms up, and removed the fabric, leaving her in only her simple white bra. Ellie froze.

"Ellie," he said, his voice laced with concern.

She closed her eyes, grabbed her shirt from him, and held it in front of her.

"Ellie. What is it? I thought you said you wanted this?"

"I do." She pushed back, leaning against the headboard.

Aden crawled closer. "But?"

"It's stupid." She looked away, embarrassed.

Aden grasped her chin and turned her head to face him. "Tell me."

"I know you've already seen them, but my scars…" Her voice trailed off.

Aden shifted to sit beside her. He pulled her into his arms before she could protest and pressed his chest against her back as she squirmed.

"Ellie, stop," he said, and she stilled. He pressed his lips against her ear. "Listen to me. There is nothing about you that is anything less than beautiful. I'd take your scars away if I could, but they don't make you any less lovely, and you have nothing to be ashamed of."

As he spoke, Ellie melted into his embrace, her initial stiffness dissipating.

"They're so ugly."

"There's nothing about you that could ever be ugly." Aden tightened his arms around her. "I'm going to worship every inch of your body tonight. I want to kill Matthais for what he did to you, but please don't hide from me. Trust in my love for you, mo ghrá."

Ellie rested her head against his shoulder. "I remember you used to call me that. I don't remember what it means, but I remember you saying it."

"My love," Aden whispered as he tilted her face toward his and kissed her. She melted into him. He reveled in the feel of her in his arms, and their kisses grew deeper as Ellie straddled him.

Ellie

Ellie sat astride Aden, resting on his thighs as she kissed him, her body trembling with desire. She believed him. She'd never be able to forget the angry scars or how she got them, but she believed in Aden's love for her.

Aden's large hands gripped her bottom, and he pulled her closer, pressing her down on him. He was hard beneath her, and she moved her hips in a slow, circular motion, eliciting an almost agonized groan from him.

She trusted him. She wasn't afraid of him, but she was nervous. Ellie remembered their time together now, so she knew they'd been intimate before he became fully vampire, before they tried to share blood. Control and tempering his strength hadn't been an issue in the beginning. Just the end.

As she kissed him, memories flooded back of their first time—how awkward, clumsy, nervous, and tender he was—and she smiled against his lips. She knew he was nervous again, and his hesitation was endearing. And she knew he would be tender, at least as tender as he was capable.

"Ellie," Aden whispered, his breath mingling with hers as their lips moved in sync. The kiss deepened, their tongues swirling together in a languid dance that left her breathless, dizzy with desire, and craving more of him.

The pain of losing her virginity wasn't a vivid memory, but she knew there was going to be pain because her body, in this life, was a virgin again. And Aden was a vampire—one who had spent centuries using sex as a weapon rather than an expression of love. Her memories of their intimacy were some of the first to resurface after her death—the overwhelming love and profound physical connection they had. She craved that closeness to him again.

Almost as if he could read her mind, Aden tore his lips away from hers, brushing them along her cheek to her ear. "I don't want to hurt you. You have to tell me if I do."

He clutched her to him, his body trembling. She pulled back so she could look at him and found his eyes were dark and full of fear. She'd expected desire, but the fear caught her off guard. Gone was the cocky, arrogant vampire, and before her sat a man full of terror, afraid that he would hurt the woman he loved.

"You won't hurt me, Aden."

"You don't know what I'm capable of."

She blinked at the fierce tone of his voice. She knew what he was capable of, more than anyone, but she couldn't think about that now.

"I know you *can* hurt me, but I believe you won't." Caressing his cheek, she watched as his eyes closed and a pained expression flickered across his face.

"But I did once, and I won't survive it again. I won't survive it, Ellie. Promise to tell me if I'm hurting you. Do whatever you have to do. Hit me, kick me, bite me, yell and scream, and don't stop until I do." He kept his eyes closed, almost as if he couldn't bear to look at her. "I have more control now, but if I hurt you again, I'll never recover."

In that moment, Ellie knew she would have to take control. Blood sharing wasn't on the table, so Ellie wasn't afraid of him losing control, but her powerful vampire needed her to reassure and guide him, and his trust in her to protect them both was humbling.

"I will."

His eyes snapped open, and he held her gaze, searching for and finding what he needed, before he relaxed, his trust reflected in both his eyes and body.

Ellie reached behind her back and released the clasp on her bra. She tossed it aside and bared herself to him. An almost strangled groan escaped Aden's lips, and a rush of pride flooded her.

He cupped both of her breasts. "So beautiful," he murmured with a mixture of awe and reverence.

Ellie let her head fall back in surrender as he massaged the soft flesh, his fingers flexing as his thumbs brushed over the hard tips of her nipples. Her entire body trembled as the sensation traveled down her body and settled between her thighs, pulsing and throbbing with every heartbeat.

His lips brushed her collarbone as he leaned forward and tasted her skin. She grasped his biceps as she moaned long and low. Aden's lips moved lower and ghosted over the swell of her left breast. He stopped, and she felt his lips press a gentle kiss against where her heart lay beneath.

Ellie wrapped her arms around him as Aden's hands released her, and he pulled her against him. She felt him shudder in her arms.

"You feel so fucking good," he choked as his lips glided over her skin again.

His aversion to touch had always been a part of him. She was the only one he could bear to let touch him, and even now, it made her feel just as privileged as it had before.

"Kiss me," Ellie breathed against his cheek.

A low growl rumbled in his chest as he lifted his head and took her lips again. She surrendered to the kiss, savoring the exquisite dance of their tongues. The sharp flavor of his venom as it dripped from his retracted fangs tingled on her tongue.

The man knew how to kiss, his lips soft and gentle against hers, and her mind was flooded with a barrage of memories, each one showcasing his remarkable oral skills. Her body trembled, overcome by a powerful wave of desire.

His eyes opened and locked with hers. They were dark and intense, but there was still no sign of red. A tenderness tempered the heat in them. It left her breathless, and any last vestiges of hesitation or shyness left her. With a gentle smile, Ellie pushed up on her knees and scooted back.

"Down on your back," she commanded, and he complied without a word.

She moved off his lap and sat on the bed beside him. His eyes followed her every move as she unbuttoned her pants and pushed them, along with her panties, down her legs before tossing them to the floor beside her shoes.

She rose to her knees again and turned to him. His heated gaze made her feel like she could burst into flames. She took a shuddering breath as she slipped her fingertips into the waist of his jeans and tugged. "Lose the pants."

He moved so fast that her eyes blinked twice, and then he was lying on the bed in all his glory. He was fully erect, thick and hard, eagerly twitching as she took in every inch of him with her eyes. Her tongue slipped between her lips, moistening them. The muscles of his stomach rippled as a low growl rumbled throughout his entire body.

"Ellie."

His hoarse voice reverberated through the room, sending another rush of arousal between her thighs.

She straddled him again, resting on his thighs. He sat up and reached for her. She stopped him with her hand on his chest. "No. Down."

She relished the sensation of being in control. Aden's eyes narrowed, and he looked at her for a long minute before he complied.

Ellie's lips curved as she gazed at him. His eyes roamed her body, devouring every inch of her with hunger. Gone was the hesitant man from a few minutes ago. His anxiety and fear were gone. All that remained was the self-confident vampire she loved. The man who wanted, desired, and loved her beyond all reason. He looked at her like she was a goddess, and she felt powerful and beautiful under his gaze.

Aden shifted and his breath hitched as she glided back and forth, her arousal bathing his thigh, teasing him. The scent of her arousal permeated the air, and a sultry smile played on her lips as his nose twitched. She reached out and wrapped her fingers around him, and his hard flesh twitched in her hand. His skin was silky and warm. This part of his body had always been warm, and a tiny moan slipped from her lips as she squeezed, feeling him pulse and throb beneath her fingers.

"Fuck, Ellie," he choked out, a sound that Ellie could only describe as raw agony, and he grasped her wrist. She met his gaze, and she saw it was too much, so she released him. He released an audible sigh that sounded both like relief and regret.

He reached for her hand, tugging her down to lay on top of him, trapping his erection between them.

His arms surrounded her, and before she could react, he had flipped them and settled between her thighs.

Aden pushed up on his hands and sat back on his heels. Ellie watched him with a gentle smile as he caught his breath.

"I've waited almost three hundred years to touch you again," he whispered, gazing down at her.

A soft snort escaped her. "Do you realize how weird that sounds?"

"Not to a vampire." Aden grinned as he brushed his fingertips up and down the outside of her thighs as they draped over his.

"You're not in bed with a vampire," she reminded him as her entire body quivered, his gentle caresses leaving a trail of electrifying tingles across her skin.

"No, I'm not. I'm in bed with a fucking beautiful twenty-three-year-old woman."

"That makes you sound like a creepy old lech," Ellie teased, but it morphed into a moan as his fingertip circled her belly button.

Aden's voice dropped several octaves. "I don't give a fuck."

He leaned down and brushed his lips over her abdomen. Ellie slipped her fingers into his hair, sighing and arching her back as Aden swirled his tongue over her, tasting the thin sheen of sweat forming on her skin. He traced a slow, meandering trail up Ellie's body until he reached the soft underside of her breast. A shaky moan escaped her lips as Aden twirled warm, wet circles over her breast until he reached the bud in the middle. He wrapped his lips around it, and Ellie's back arched deeper. She whimpered his name as he flicked his tongue against her nipple. The feel of his venom sent a rush of desire between her thighs, the muscles in her core clenching as images of his head buried between her thighs flooded her mind. He didn't stay long and moved to her other breast, fulfilling his promise to worship her as she moaned, mewled, and writhed beneath him.

With a soft growl, Ellie clenched her fingers and tugged on his hair. "Stop teasing me."

He pulled back and looked at her again, his eyes darkening before they slipped closed as he breathed through his nose. She pushed up on her elbows. "Are you okay?"

Aden opened his eyes again, and his throat bobbed as he swallowed.

"You're trying not to bite, aren't you?" she asked, and guilt filled his eyes. He was fighting the urge to lean down and plunge his fangs into her neck, but the expected rush of fear never came. Instead, she felt a strange sense of comfort and reassurance.

"It's okay, Aden."

His eyes filled with gratitude, and in that moment, Ellie knew they were going to be fine. Someday, she might let him bite her again, but she knew with absolute certainty that he wouldn't hurt her.

His fingers caressed the curls between her thighs. Ellie gasped as her elbows gave out and she dropped back on the mattress. She released a shuddering breath as her thighs trembled.

Aden's fingertips dipped lower, and Ellie jerked her hips when they glided over her swollen flesh. Her body was ready for him, vibrating with anticipation. Her lips parted and a low moan slipped past her lips, echoing through the room.

"You feel so good." He groaned and pulled his hand away, lowering his body onto hers, settling between her thighs. "I won't hurt you. I swear on my life."

She reached up and cradled his face in her hands. "I know you won't."

"I love you," he breathed into her mouth as he pushed inside her.

The momentary pain was sharp. Ellie's breath hitched, her eyes watering as Aden entered her. But he was quick, and her body flooded with gratitude, both for his speed and that she was so aroused because the man was not small.

"Are you alright?"

His voice came out as a strangled groan. Ellie nodded as she gripped his shoulders, dug her short nails into his skin, and buried her face in his neck.

Aden braced himself on one hand, and the other gripped her hip, holding her in place. His breath was rapid and strained, whistling between his clenched teeth. His warm breath fluttered over her skin until he finally pulled his head out of her neck. She knew the scent of her blood overwhelmed him, so she held still and waited for them to adjust.

She relaxed into the mattress and opened her eyes, watching the myriad of emotions flash over his face until he exhaled a long breath. He pulled his hips back and then pushed forward again, this time slower, and his body vibrated with the control he exerted. His eyes were shut tight, his face contorting in agony.

"Aden."

His eyes flew open. They were dark, and she could see once again the familiar tinges of red around his irises. She reached up and brushed her fingers below his eye. His face relaxed, and his eyes slipped closed. Ellie braced her feet on the mattress, tilting her hips and angling against him as he slipped deeper. Ellie's thighs trembled around his hips. Aden groaned and pulled back once more before driving forward, filling her completely.

Ellie drew in a sharp breath, and Aden's eyes whipped open as his body stilled.

"Am I hurting you?"

Ellie shook her head and offered him a reassuring smile, hoping to ease his worry. Her body was throbbing around him, but the discomfort was lessening. She pulled his face down to hers. "Kiss me," she breathed against his lips, and he released a strangled moan before complying. He sank his body onto her, shuddering, and Ellie wrapped her arms and legs around him.

Aden pumped his hips in gentle, shallow strokes, allowing her body to adjust to the feel of him. His movements were jerky at first, but after a bit of stumbling, accompanied by a combination of groans and chuckles, they found their stride and settled into a rhythm. His body took over as his erratic plunges turned into long, smooth, deep thrusts.

This was nothing like her memories. Their past youthful experiences felt nothing like this. Aden had hundreds of years of practice now, but Ellie forced that out of her mind. This was not the time to think about that. Instead, she let him lead, trusting her instincts, and once the initial discomfort of the intrusion passed, the pain gave way to an exhilarating ache that transformed into pure pleasure.

Ellie clung to him, holding tight as tears pricked her eyes. She wanted this more than anything, craved it, and yearned for it. For him. She rocked her hips, using her legs to pull him deeper. She knew how to move beneath him, even though this was her first time in this body.

If someone had told her six months ago that she would ever love a vampire—love him—Ellie would have told them they were crazy. But that was before she'd remembered her past life, before she'd remembered Aden and the love she had for him. And despite his past, despite his faults, she loved this man, this vampire, in her arms more than she ever thought possible.

He made love to her, unhurried and with reverence, just as he promised. Their lips parted, and he buried his face in the curve of her neck. She licked her lips, savoring the lingering taste of him. He trailed his lips across her neck and shoulders, igniting a surge of warmth beneath her flesh. She no longer feared he would bite her. A small part of her wished he would. Waves of breathtaking ecstasy crashed through her, rendering her incapable of coherent thought or speech.

Ellie released her tight grasp on his back, and her hands found their way to the back of his head, tangling in his hair. She tugged on the short strands and bucked under him. Every powerful thrust of his hips made her feel like she would break apart, and the only thing holding her together was his arms around her.

Aden

The way Ellie had tormented him, stripping, straddling him, then wrapping her warm, soft hand around him, had been Aden's undoing. He'd intended to let her set the pace, but, by god, how was he supposed to endure that without losing his mind? No one could withstand that and survive. Not even a vampire.

Like their bodies, vampires' hearts were alive. They still beat, just slower than a human's. But the moment he first slid into Ellie and felt her warm, silky flesh wrap around him, Aden was sure his heart stopped.

It took every ounce of self-control he possessed to hold still and let her adjust. Then the scent of her virgin blood slammed into him, and he was sure he would lose it. She held still underneath him as if knowing he needed her to, and he willed his body into submission, the thought of hurting her terrifying him. He'd begun thrusting slowly, but the sensations were too much, and he could feel his self-control faltering. But the madness receded when his name slipped past her lips and his eyes met hers.

She moved with him, and instinct took over. Her scent and her softness surrounded him, and he lost himself in the sensations. Now that he was inside her, everything in his life fell into place. It had been so long since he last experienced the sensation of a body against him like this.

Aden had no idea how he had survived so long without it—without her—because her touch was the only thing that made him feel truly alive.

Aden brushed his lips in soft whispers along her neck and up over her face. She chanted his name as she clung to him with her entire body. His fangs dripped, but he swallowed the venom back, determined to ignore the instinct to sink them into her neck and drink from her until his eyes rolled back in his head.

It had to be her choice. He'd never take from her without her consent again.

"You feel so fucking good," he whispered against her lips.

Ellie whimpered into his mouth and fluttered her fingers up and down his back. Her touch sent a cascade of shivers down his spine, and he knew he'd never be able to live without it again. If he had his way, he'd spend the rest of eternity exactly where he was, with her hands on him and his on her. He wanted her body wrapped around him for eternity as she chanted his name, and he lost himself inside her.

With each thrust, Aden's hands roamed her silky skin, memorizing it. They found their way under her body, cupping her ass, and pulling her tighter against him. With a firm grip, his right hand slid down her thigh. His fingers pressed into her soft flesh, and he ground his hips, slipping deeper into her. He could feel every inch of her around him.

He'd fucked thousands of humans, but none of them had felt like this. Not even Aly. Aden's thrusts faltered and for one fleeting moment, a wave of guilt washed over him, as if he was betraying her memory by making love with another woman. But then Ellie pressed her soft lips against his ear.

"Aden," she whispered.

Her voice was throaty and erotic, and he felt it all the way to his toes. Just like that, she brought him back to her. This *was* Aly beneath him. It was the soul of this woman he loved. No matter what body her soul inhabited.

Fuck! There was that word again. But for the first time in his life, Aden understood his parents and their beliefs. There was something after death. Souls did exist and went somewhere after the life faded from a vampire or human. And some souls were drawn back to each other, like magnets.

This was the only woman he was meant to worship in this life, or any other, for the rest of his existence. Aden knew it with such certainty and conviction that it burrowed into the center of his being and took root. Fate brought her soul back to him, and he would never doubt again.

Ellie writhed faster beneath him, and her soft gasping cries increased in volume. Her scent deepened as her orgasm approached. Aden clenched his teeth, refusing to even entertain the thought of biting her. He took a long, deep breath, letting her scent surround him and ground him. Relaxing his jaw, he captured her lips again, slipping a hand between them. He rubbed his fingertips against her, giving her the friction she needed to reach completion.

Ellie whimpered as her body responded. She clamped down on him and her orgasm pulsed around him. He kept thrusting, prolonging her pleasure. Her body convulsed beneath him, her hips jerking as she came in long, deep waves, gasping and crying out into his mouth. Aden never wanted it to end, but after several more thrusts, he felt the familiar sensation rush up his spine. Ellie tore her lips away from his and pressed them against his ear. "I love you, Aden."

Her quiet words set him off.

Now his eyes did roll back in his head, and he growled low and deep. Her words healed him, offering him the absolution he'd needed for centuries. Aden pumped his hips once, twice, and then three times before holding them steady as he erupted inside her. With a shudder, his body collapsed onto hers, and her name escaped his lips in a reverent whisper.

Aden trembled, and Ellie tightened her arms, clinging to him. Her insides clenched around him as they both struggled to catch their breath.

She arched her back, and the movement pulled a groan from deep within Aden's chest. She released a low, sultry laugh, and he buried his face in her neck. The soft honeysuckle and jasmine scent of her, combined with the subtle scent of sex, enveloped him.

"Say it again." Aden's gruff command vibrated against her throat.

Ellie's delighted laugh tickled his ear. "I love you, Aden," she breathed, and he choked against her neck.

She caressed his back, her fingers trailing along his spine and through the damp sweat on his skin, before entangling with the short strands of his hair at the nape of his neck. She leaned in close, brushing her lips beneath his ear, before whispering her love a third time.

He convinced himself the words didn't matter, but he hadn't realized how much he needed her to say them. When he lifted his face from her neck and looked at her, all doubt disappeared. The depth of her love for him was reflected in her eyes, mirroring his own, but they also swirled with something else. They danced with the familiar need, and he knew she wanted him again. She didn't have to say it. She just pulled his lips back to hers.

Aden walked into Aurick's office to find him speaking to Indira in Hindi over a hologram.

"Thank you for taking the time to listen, Indira."

"Of course, Aurick. I appreciate you keeping me informed."

Aurick waved him in. "We'll see you at the Council meetings in January."

"Tell Sophie to call me when she gets a chance. I'd like to get her thoughts on this."

"Of course," Aurick replied.

They said their goodbyes, and Aurick swiped the hologram away, turning to look at Aden.

"What was that about?"

"It's not important. Politics is a constant dance."

"Better you than me."

"So, what did you want to talk about?" Aurick asked.

"Roderick has completed his interrogation of the rogue."

"Did his methods work?"

"It took some extra special cajoling, but in the end, yes."

"And? What did he say?"

"They came from Sever Sib-Ir."

Aurick stood and walked around the desk to lean against it. "Why would Sever Sib-Irian vampires be in our region without registering?"

"That's the question, isn't it? Have you had any friction with Yuri lately?" Aden thought he glimpsed something in Aurick's eyes, but it disappeared too fast to be certain.

"Well, you know Yuri and I don't see eye to eye on many things, but nothing in particular lately."

"They must have come down over the ice."

Aurick pushed off the desk and walked to the window. He pressed an electronic pad beside it, and the opaque glass cleared to reveal the view of the mountains in the distance. "But that means they might have decimated villages farther north than we realize."

"Roderick is putting together a team to go to the continent's edges. If there are any others hiding out or any villages that have been attacked, we'll find out." His father looked pensive. Aden stood and walked over beside him. "Is there something you aren't telling me, Aurick?"

"I'll reach out to Yuri and inquire if he's aware some of his vampires are entering other regions without approval. So, anything else?"

His father didn't answer his direct question, which was unusual.

"Not at the moment."

"Did Roderick manage to extract any more information from the rogue regarding his cryptic 'It's only just beginning' comment?"

"No." Aden eyed Aurick as he walked to the bar. "But his ability to speak was greatly diminished by the end."

"What are you going to do with him now?"

"Incinerate him."

"He's dead?"

"Yes. He served his purpose."

His father's narrowed gaze conveyed his disapproval, yet he chose not to reprimand him. Aurick understood that prisoners of war were sometimes casualties. And there was a war coming. Aden could feel it.

"Do you want a drink?" Aurick asked as he poured himself one.

"No. I'm heading to free Ellie from Sophie's clutches in a few minutes, and she dislikes the taste of whiskey." His father gave him a curious look as he sat behind his desk. Aden dropped into the chair across from him. "She duly warned me to stay away from it if I want to kiss her."

"Well, she's definitely not Irish, is she?" Aden simply shrugged, grinning, while his father regarded him with a pleased expression. "I haven't seen you this relaxed in centuries. I'm happy for you, Son. Truly."

"It's all Ellie. She's brought a light to my life, even the darkest recesses of my soul." Fuck! There was that word again. "I don't deserve her."

"That's not true, but I'm glad things are going well with the two of you. Your mother was certain about her right from the beginning. I had my reservations, but as usual, she was right. You'd think I'd stop doubting her after five hundred-plus years."

"You had your doubts about Ellie being Aly's soul or about my ability to control my blood lust and not kill her again?"

Aden shifted in his chair as he waited for his father's response.

"Both."

"Well, at least you're honest. We haven't shared blood again yet, though, so don't—"

"I know you'll prevail this time," his father interrupted. "You're the strongest man I know."

Aden noticed he used the word "man" instead of "vampire." Turned against his will, his father had never wanted to become a vampire, so he always strove to preserve his humanity. It wasn't until recently that Aden understood the importance of aspiring to be better than his worst impulses.

"But?"

"But you've hated yourself for a very long time. That kind of self-loathing is a powerful thing. You gave into it long ago, and coming out of darkness like that isn't easy. Believe me, I know. The darkness that stains my past is beyond anything you could imagine."

"I doubt that." His father was better off not knowing that part of his life.

"Your mother and sister adore her. That's half the battle in this family."

"And what do *you* think of her?"

"I don't know her well yet, but she's lovely and, according to your mom, very much like Alysia. She has a good heart, and despite what she's suffered in this life, she has a kind and forgiving nature. She brings out the best in you. For that, I'm eternally grateful."

Aden swallowed back the lump in his throat that his father's words provoked. He sometimes forgot how much Aurick's opinion of him mattered, especially when they were all lost in the day-to-day chaos of life.

And now, his father's opinion of Ellie had become just as, if not more, important to him.

Ellie

"Hey, Ellie."

Her lips pulled up on one side in response to Horatio's slanted grin as she approached the door to Sophie and Master Aurick's suite.

"Hi, Horatio." She stopped in front of him. "Did Aden come through here?"

"Yes. He and Aurick are sparring, I believe."

"Oh, I guess I'll leave them alone then."

Just then, Sophie's voice came through the speaker. "Ellie, come on in."

Ellie looked at Horatio. "Half-breed hearing," he said, gesturing to his ear.

Ellie laughed as she walked into the suite. She found Sophie sitting on the sofa with her feet tucked under her, writing in her journal. She introduced Ellie to journaling several weeks earlier, after Keeley had taught her to write, and Ellie had admitted she remembered her past life. Ellie started doing it right away, and it helped her sort through not only her feelings about her previous life and death but also her newfound relationship with Aden and his questionable past. She hadn't found the courage to ask him about it, but part of her didn't think she wanted to. His reputation spoke for itself, and there was nothing he could do to change what he'd done. But they would need to talk about it at some point, and she wasn't looking forward to that day.

"I didn't mean to interrupt," Ellie said.

"You didn't. I'm just finishing up." Sophie set her journal aside. "I think they're probably finishing up down there, too. Do you want to go down with me?"

"I don't want to bother them."

Sophie stood. "You won't. Aden will want to see you. Do you remember how to get to the salle?"

"That's the sparring room, right?"

Sophie nodded.

"Kinda."

"We'll have to get these doors reprogrammed for you so you can get around easier. You should be able to get to Aden from anywhere."

They entered a warp port at the far end of the living room, which only went to rooms within their private quarters. A few seconds later, Ellie and Sophie arrived in the salle to the sounds of metal clanging and the sight of two bodies, clad in all white, feinting and parrying around the room, their sabers clashing.

Aden and Master Aurick wore the standard white fencing uniform, their faces hidden by black fencing masks, which was odd because the sabers they used were too dull to inflict any harm on either of them.

"I never tire of watching them do this," Sophie murmured.

"It's like they're dancing," Ellie whispered as they circled each other, their movements synchronized, one lunging while the other retreated, almost in perfect unison.

The faint scent of sweat was familiar, as was the resounding clash of steel echoing through the air, blending with the rhythm of their measured breaths and the steady sound of their footsteps on the wood floor. She'd done this before, many times. Stood here, in this very room, unable to tear her eyes away from the intense and graceful movements of father and son engaging in their deadly duels.

When Aden turned his head and pinned her with his gaze, Master Aurick took advantage of his distraction and struck him in the face, scoring the final point.

"Fuck!" Aden stepped back, reaching behind his head to release his mask. "That doesn't count."

Aurick laughed as he removed his own. "Sure it does. You can't get distracted in a duel, or you're dead."

Aden tucked his mask under his arm as he walked over to Ellie and leaned down so he could kiss her. "You got me killed."

"Sorry," she murmured, but she didn't feel any remorse.

"Well, I thank you, Ellie," Master Aurick said. "I was on the verge of losing until he realized you were here."

"I want a rematch," Aden said as he started tugging on his lamé and jacket.

"Sure. But only if Ellie comes to watch again. I need an advantage against you. You've become too good."

"Next time, I want to use swords. It's about time Joyeuse and Goujian came down off the walls for a good workout."

"You don't stand a chance against me with actual swords."

"Try me, old man."

"Would you like to try, Ellie?" Aurick asked, and Ellie's eyes widened. She wasn't used to him addressing her. She'd only been in his presence a few times since she arrived almost nine months ago.

"Aden and I were just teaching you when—uh, well, just before—" He looked back and forth between Aden and Sophie for help. "You might, uh, remember..." he trailed off, and Aden scowled at him.

"Aurick, you're making it weird."

"What? I'm not sure how to refer to—" He paused again. "Before."

"Then don't! Ignore it. That's what we do."

"What kind of logic is that?" Ellie poked Aden in the side as she laughed before turning to his father. "I remember, Master Aurick."

"You can call him Aurick when it's only us," Aden said.

"No, I can't."

"Sure, you can. You used to—well, you had started to—" Aden shot his father an annoyed glare, as if blaming him for his own stumbling.

"Not gonna happen." Ellie shook her head.

"Alysia called him Aurick," Sophie said.

"Okay, now you're making it weird, too." Aden shot at his mother before he walked into a side room to change out of the rest of his outfit.

"Everything about this life is different from that one. I'm not comfortable doing that," Ellie said.

"You'll get there." Sophie reached for Ellie and squeezed her arm.

"Well, if you ever decide you want to try fencing, come find me," Master Aurick said. "It would be interesting to see how much of it you remember."

Aden came back out as he shoved the hem of his shirt into his pants. "You ready?"

Ellie nodded.

"What are you two up to today?" Sophie asked.

"Do you really want to hear about all the indecent things I intend to do to her, Sophie?"

"Aden!" An embarrassed flush rose to Ellie's cheeks. He had no filter whatsoever.

"It's not like they don't know how we spend our days now." Aden grabbed her hand and tugged her toward the door. "Bye."

Sophie and Master Aurick's goodbyes echoed behind them as Ellie smiled and waved.

"I can't believe you said that to your parents."

Ellie pulled her hand away from his as they stepped out of the warp port in his parent's sitting room.

"What? It's no secret we're having sex, Ellie. We've hardly seen them for the last month. They know we have better things to do than chit-chat with them."

"I enjoy talking to your mom."

He grasped her hand again and led her toward the door. "But wouldn't you prefer to spend your time letting me give you multiple orgasms? I know I would."

"If you think I'm having sex with you after you said that to them, you're mistaken."

He stopped and turned his intense gaze on her. "I don't think so."

Her body's reaction was immediate. She couldn't control it. When he looked at her like that, her knees turned to jelly. He stooped and lifted her off her feet, tossing her over his shoulder.

"We are most definitely having sex."

"Aden, put me down." Ellie squirmed in his grasp as they exited the room. She tugged on the belt loop of Aden's pants as he strode right by Horatio without a word. The guard tilted his head towards her, a slight smirk playing on his lips, but he didn't say a word.

"Aden, let me down. What's wrong with you? You're acting like a crazy—"

"Quiet!" Aden slapped her on the bottom as they entered the courtyard. It didn't hurt, but it was hard enough to startle her and rob her of her words.

She was about to retaliate when the thralls who cleaned the courtyard scurried out of Aden's way. Most thralls knew of their relationship, but they shouldn't see her hitting him. What kind of rumors would that start?

She responded with a submissive "Yes, master," fully aware that it would serve as the expected reply in the presence of the other thralls and, as a bonus, irk him.

He came to an abrupt halt and stood motionless, with her hanging over his shoulder. She could feel the thralls' eyes on them, and she held her breath, unsure of what he'd do.

"You're going to be punished for that." He resumed his lengthy strides, slapping her again, this time a little harder. Ellie heard at least one thrall gasp. Given his reputation, they most likely thought he planned to hurt her.

Keeley and Ryan entered the courtyard just as Aden's hand connected with her butt.

Keeley's voice was casual. "You okay, Ellie?"

"She's fucking fine!" Aden walked past them without even a glance.

"It's fifty-fifty," Ellie said, and Aden slapped her again for her impertinence.

"I'll take those odds," Keeley said, and Ellie heard them chuckle as they headed in the other direction.

"Aden," Ellie said once they were out of earshot of the other thralls. "You're being a brute." He grunted, his hand rubbing gently over her backside in silent apology.

"Get the fuck out of here." Aden jerked his thumb at Kane as they passed him in the hallway. Similar to Horatio, Keeley, and Ryan, he simply smirked, appearing entirely unconcerned.

Despite Aden's overbearing behavior at the moment, Ellie couldn't help but feel overjoyed at how effortlessly their relationship had evolved once she remembered her past life and they admitted their feelings. Their defenses melted away, and they were swept up in a profound sense of familiarity that made them feel secure and loved—akin to being embraced by a comforting blanket.

Yes, he was intense. But when he focused that intensity solely on her, which he did often now, everything else in the world fell away and ceased to exist. All that mattered was the two of them and that they'd found each other again.

"I'm getting a head rush hanging like this."

"I'm about to give you another one," he said before barking at the black cat, who had taken to snoozing on his bed now that Ellie slept there every day. "Get lost, you mangy furball."

Ellie squeaked as Aden flipped her onto her back. "Sorry, Vlad," she called after the traumatized cat as he jumped out of the way, hissing and scurrying toward her room. Aden crawled over her as she scooted up the mattress. "Don't let your mother hear you call him that."

He gazed down at her, the intensity in his eyes softening, before laying his body on hers and burying his face in her neck. She wrapped her arms around him as he kissed her scar and breathed her in.

"Are you okay?" she asked when he still hadn't moved after almost a minute.

"Yeah. I love the feel of you under me."

"Me too." She pressed a kiss on his ear.

"More," he whispered. She curled her legs around the back of his thighs and tightened her arms around him. His entire body shuddered with pleasure.

His aversion to touch was nonexistent now, at least with her. He didn't flinch or still or pull away. And he craved having her hands on him as much, if not more, than his on her. And that was saying something because the man always seemed to want his hands, his lips and his body on her. Sometimes, after they made love, he would stay on top of her, inside her, with no attempt to arouse either of them again. He'd revel in the feel of her and would only move when she told him she couldn't breathe.

He desired her constantly, and she lost herself with him and in him, losing track of time and even forgetting to eat. She suspected she was going to miss dinner again today.

"You aren't really going to punish me, are you?" He couldn't see her smile, but she was sure he felt it.

"I should." He lifted his head and arched a teasing brow. "You're not really going to withhold sex, are you?"

"I should," she mimicked, and he lowered his mouth to hers. One hand slipped under her shirt, his fingers seeking and finding the soft underside of her breast, caressing and teasing her warm skin. After a few minutes, he softened his kiss to let her breathe, releasing her lips and lifting his head so he could look at her.

"I didn't mean to embarrass you in front of my parents."

Her eyes fluttered open, and it took a few seconds for them to clear. "You didn't really. It was just weird."

"I know. Aurick made it completely weird."

"No, I mean, it's strange being around him when I now remember so much about him. He's such a noble figure in the world, but in private, he's just your dad. The man who always treated me like a daughter, even though I was human."

"He loved you. My whole family did. They still do. Not the same way I do."

"I hope not. Otherwise, every day would be one big incestuous orgy."

A sour look crossed his face as he pushed up on his hands. "What the fuck, Ellie! There goes my hard-on. I knew Sophie giving you that dictionary was a mistake."

She laughed and brushed her fingers over his frown. "Even though you swear way too much, I love how you make me laugh."

"I'm more interested in making you moan."

She pulled him back down to her, lifting and rolling her hips as she rubbed against him. He hardened against her again with a groan.

"Then why don't you get to it, brute?"

"Fuck, yes," he growled, capturing her lips again.

Aden

Aden heard the outer door to Ellie's room open. He looked up from reading the training report Andrei had sent. He glanced at the clock and it was a little after three. His lips curved. His mother must have finished with her early. That left more time for them to do what they'd been doing in almost all their free time lately.

When she left his bed that evening, it had taken all of his willpower not to drag her back. In the weeks since they became lovers, he couldn't get enough of her. She seemed to feel the same way, but he had to remind himself that she was not a vampire and, therefore, her body needed more time to recover.

Aden waited for the door behind him to open, announcing her entrance, but it remained closed. He scowled as one minute turned to two, then to five. After ten minutes, his agitation and impatience were on the verge of boiling over. What the fuck was she doing?

Her heartbeat was steady and slow. Aden let it wrap around him, hoping it would calm him, but it didn't. He stood up and paced, looking up when she entered his room seven minutes later. His face morphed from a scowl to a boyish grin, and his entire demeanor softened at the sight of her. He walked over to her, cupped her face in his hands, and lowered his mouth to hers.

Ellie reached up and wrapped her fingers around his wrists, smiling against his lips. He kissed her deeply, inhaling her breath and surrounding him with the scent and taste of her. She pulled on his wrists, and he softened his lips against hers, allowing her to pull away and take a breath. Sometimes he forgot that she needed more oxygen than he did. But she always made it clear to him when she wanted him to stop and he was grateful she didn't hesitate to express her need for relief.

He leaned his forehead against hers, and Ellie smiled as she opened her eyes. Aden stepped back but reached for her hand.

"I was going crazy, knowing you were in there."

"I know. I was practicing my writing."

He pulled her down on the sofa beside him. "I hate when that door is closed."

"I know," she said again.

Aden tugged her closer. "I want you to move in here with me."

She pulled out of his arms. "What?"

"There's no reason for you to keep staying in that room, Ellie. Everything is different now."

"No, Aden."

Aden's scowl returned. It was still unfamiliar for both of them for her to tell him no. "Why not?"

"I like having my own space."

"Why?"

"You're very intense, and sometimes I need space to myself." The pain from her words was swift, and she must have seen it because she reached up and touched his face. "Aden, this is all still so new to me. Give me time to get used to this."

"Patience isn't one of my virtues, Ellie."

"I know." She knew him better than almost anyone, despite her only being back in his life for less than a year.

"You sleep in here every day, so what's the problem?"

Ellie dropped her hand and wrapped her fingers around his. "I like having a room that's just mine, where I can be alone to think."

"Why can't you think in here?"

"Because when I'm around you, I have a hard time thinking about anything but you."

His lips curved into a cocky grin. "I don't see a problem with that."

"Don't you ever want space from me?"

"No."

Ellie eyed him skeptically.

"I lived without you for almost three hundred years. If it were my choice, I'd never let you out of this room, or my bed, for the next three hundred," he said with a scowl, because they both knew she held all the control now, and neither of them was used to the power shift yet.

Her eyes softened. "How am I supposed to resist when you say things like that?"

"You aren't. That's the point." He tugged her against his chest, pinning her arm behind her back. "Don't deny me, mo ghrá."

He called her that all the time, and it softened her toward him. He was sure she was yielding, but then she shook her head and pulled her wrist out of his grasp. She stood, looking down at him. "No, Aden. I want to keep my room."

"Fine," he barked, and he shot to his feet to glower down at her. "We'll have these rooms reconfigured, then. We'll demolish the concubine suite."

Surprise bloomed across her face.

"What? It's never going to be used again, so we might as well use the space to give you a proper place to escape from me."

"Aden, that isn't what I said."

"But it's what you meant." He couldn't hide his annoyance. "But there will be no fucking bed in there. You will sleep with me every day."

He held her gaze, daring her to defy him. She looked like she was about to, but when she didn't, his scowl slowly faded and his gaze heated.

"I want to kiss you again."

Her body reacted instantly to his words, her scent deepening as she walked backward towards his bed. "Then why aren't you?"

He followed her as she lifted her shirt over her head. A blush crept up her chest under his heated gaze. The back of her legs hit the mattress, and in an instant, he was standing in front of her.

"Turn around."

Ellie's breath hitched, and she did as he instructed, crawling to the middle of the bed. He climbed behind her and pressed his fully clothed body against her partially clothed one. His arms encircled her waist, and he leaned down to plant a tender kiss on the middle of her spine.

By the time he finished making her convulse with pleasure, he was confident that all thoughts of separate rooms were long gone.

Ellie

"So what you're saying is that you'll always feel compelled to be with them?" The horror in Ellie's voice matched the look on her face as they sat on his bed, still naked and sweaty from their lovemaking. But Ellie pushed away from him when their conversation turned to compulsion.

"I'll always feel compelled to drink from them, but I don't need to fuck them. Drinking without sex isn't as strong of a pull."

"Why don't I remember this?"

Aden shook his head. "It wasn't an issue before. I hadn't compelled anyone then."

"I don't understand. What does having sex with them have to do with it?"

"It's the act of sharing blood and sex. It's not only on the vampire's side. The human craves the same thing."

"So you'll always want them?"

"No, I don't want any of them. I only want you."

She shifted away from him. "But you still crave their blood."

"Yes, but only their blood, Ellie." Aden's restless fingers, clenching and releasing, betrayed his intense desire to touch her, but she wasn't in a state to handle it at the moment. "I have no desire to fuck and drink from any of them anymore."

Ellie cringed. Sometimes he could be so vulgar. "But you want to drink from me when we have sex." After what happened, she wasn't sure if she would ever want that again, but the possibility of him not wanting it bothered her.

"Yes. I'd be lying if I said I didn't, but only if that's what you want, sweetheart." Aden reached out and caressed her cheek. "I want everything from you, Ellie, not just your body and blood. And that's all it's ever been with all of them."

Ellie scrambled out of bed and reached for her clothes.

Aden got to his feet. "Where are you going?"

"I need some air." Ellie pulled her pants up. "I'm leaving the compound. I'm going to take a walk while the dome is still open, and I don't want you or Drake following me."

"No."

He was so frustrating, she wanted to scream. Ellie yanked her shirt over her head, opting to go braless. "I'm not a child, Aden. I survived for almost twenty-three years before we met."

He tugged on his boxer briefs. "I'm amazed you did."

Ellie's glare intensified as she reached for her shoes.

"I can't allow that, Ellie. I'm sorry. We made an agreement about Drake. I won't follow you, but Drake has to if you leave the compound."

"Fine, but I want to be alone."

"Ellie, we need to talk about this. You can't run every time you find out something you don't like about me. It's gonna happen a lot. You'll be running forever."

"I need time to think about this, Aden. I didn't know—" The weight of Aden's impending answer pressed down on her before she gathered the courage to ask. "How many of them are there?"

He winced, and a pained expression crossed his face. "Ellie—"

"You have a lot of thralls, Aden. More than any vampire I've ever known. Have you been with all of them that way?"

"Ellie, I haven't been with any of them since right after I brought you back with me."

More like a couple of months after, but that was semantics. His confirmation that he'd stopped long before they got together filled her with relief, but she still dreaded his answer. Aden had hundreds of personal thralls.

"That isn't what I asked you." Ellie crossed her arms across her chest as she braced herself for his reply. "Have you been with all your thralls that way?"

"Ellie, I can't change what I've done."

"Please answer my question."

She noticed his body tense. "All of my feeders, yes."

All the air rushed out of Ellie's lungs, and she grabbed onto the back of the chair to steady herself. Aden reached for her, but she pulled away from his grasp.

"Don't, Aden. Just don't."

He pulled his hand back and dropped it to his side. He was struggling to keep his temper in check, but she didn't have it in her to appreciate his effort at the moment.

"Don't you dare follow me. And tell Drake to keep his distance." Ellie walked away and down the hallway to the door. "Don't you dare call Kane to come after me, either."

She didn't wait for his response. She exited his room and hurried down the hallway, breaking into a run.

Ellie never made it out of the compound. After a series of confrontations with the guards at the front door, then Drake and Kane, who Aden sent after her despite her objections, Ellie sought refuge in the greenhouse. She turned on all the daylight bulbs. They wouldn't keep half-breeds like Drake and Kane out, but they would keep Aden away, giving her the space she needed to process her newfound understanding of compulsion.

Ellie found herself at the Koi Pond, letting the sound of the waterfall soothe her. The greenhouse was open to the night air, so it was like being outside. Almost. Ellie could pretend that she escaped her life in the vampire city, at least for a little while.

Lost in her thoughts, she didn't hear Sophie approaching until she sat beside her on the grass.

"He always finds a way." Ellie shook her head with a frown.

"Finds a way for what?"

"To follow me even when I've asked him not to. I have a tracking chip in me, and it's not like he isn't watching my every move."

"He worries about you," Sophie said.

"He's a vampire. He can find and reach me almost instantly if he wants. Why can't he give me space when I ask for it?"

"That's not in his nature. It was very hard on him last time."

Ellie felt bad for being so resentful. She knew it was hard on him, but didn't he realize his smothering was hard on her?

"Did he ask you to come talk to me?"

"He may have mentioned that you might need someone to talk to."

Ellie sighed.

"Don't be angry with him, Ellie. He told me you don't remember about compulsion. It wasn't an issue because Aden and Alysia were mated, and he never would have been with anyone but her. He thought I could help you understand it because I've lived with it almost all my life."

Despite her irritation, Ellie fixed Sophie with a curious look.

"I never told you about Aurick's and my history. I was born over five hundred years ago. Aurick met my mother first. He was our neighbor. He lived in the house next to ours. That was back before BloodStone, when vampires were in the shadows and humans could own property."

"So, those weren't just stories, huh?"

"No. Most of what you've read is based on reality. I was only eight when we moved in next door to him. My mother and Aurick became lovers. He drank from her while they were intimate, and the compulsion enslaved them. It almost destroyed my family. It almost killed them both."

That wasn't what Ellie expected Sophie to say. She bit her tongue, wanting to ask for more details, but Sophie just kept going.

"Aurick made me a half-breed. I think I told you that, but it was a long time ago, and I don't have your eidetic memory. It was a necessity of circumstances to save my life. I was attacked by a group of vampires when I was a child and I would have died if he hadn't turned me into a half-breed."

"Oh my god," Ellie gasped. "I haven't recovered that memory yet."

"You were still young. I don't remember if I told you the details. Anyway, that's a story for another time. Unlike the sex compulsion between a vampire and a human, the desire to share blood is deeper between a half-breed and a sire. Though not always sexual. After Aurick turned me, I didn't drink from him again for almost thirty years. Not until he told me he wanted me with him for eternity. I wanted him for eternity, as well, but I didn't want to become a vampire, so this was our compromise. Our relationship had turned sexual, and the compulsion took over, but our bond is much stronger because he was the one who made me what I am."

Unable to stop herself, Ellie asked, "What about your mother?"

Sophie's mouth curved into a bittersweet smile. "That's also a story for another time. I'm surprised you didn't learn about compulsion when you came of age."

"I know the basics of it. My dad asked Master Matthais not to make me a pet when I turned eighteen. For whatever reason, for which I am eternally grateful now, he agreed. Most pets just disappeared after a while. None of them were around long enough for any of us to realize the unbreakable nature of compulsion." Ellie pursed her lips. "Besides, my father kept me pretty isolated and ignorant about the reality of things."

"It's remarkable Matthais approved your father's request. That's completely out of character for him." Sophie furrowed her brows. "I'm sorry that you have to learn about this now, given the circumstances. I wish things were different with my son, but they're not. What I'm trying to help you understand by sharing my story is that compulsion doesn't need love. It only needs sex and blood, and once it starts, nothing can break it but death."

Ellie blanched, understanding her implication.

"So he'll need all those girls until they die. Even his feelings for me won't stop it."

"Only death will break the compulsion."

"He's been with so many. Where are they? What happened to them?" Ellie was almost afraid to ask. Sophie's eyes echoed remorse. It made Ellie's stomach ache because she was sure she knew the answer. "Once he tires of them, they're euthanized, aren't they?"

Matthais euthanized his humans all the time. When humans grew too old and lost their usefulness, he would euthanize them. Memories of Rodney flashed in Ellie's mind. She had seen older humans around since she'd been here, so she thought the Westcotts were different. Apparently, she was wrong.

"Ellie, I know this is hard for you to understand. I don't blame you for being shocked and horrified. There is more to all of this than you can understand right now, but someday I hope you'll see that certain things are a kindness, even though they seem brutal and cold."

"How can killing someone be a kindness?"

"Compulsion is a strong physical and emotional pull that will drive both the vampire and human mad if it's not fulfilled. The pain is excruciating, and the only relief is sharing blood or death.

Ellie wrapped her arms around herself.

"I'm not sure how much Aden told you about what his life was like or the things he did after he lost you. It destroyed him, and he descended into what I can only describe as hell on earth. But underneath his still sometimes callous and arrogant exterior, he is a good man with a good heart who regrets the pain and destruction he left in his wake. And there was a lot of carnage, Ellie. Carnage that needed to be cleaned up, and we did it in the most humane way possible."

"What did he do?" Ellie's heart thudded in her chest with both anticipation and fear.

"Oh, Ellie," Sophie said, the sorrow clear in her voice. "That's something he needs to tell you. It's not my place."

Ellie bowed and covered her face with her hands, sure that even her worst imaginings couldn't touch the reality of it.

"I feel like I'm going to throw up." She covered her mouth with her hands, her stomach churning as she processed both what Sophie said and what she hadn't. "So you still euthanize his girls now, when he's grown tired of them?"

"I try to find other ways to keep them useful for as long as I can. If a vampire stops having sex with a human and feeds on new ones, the compulsion for past ones is not as intense. Proximity is also a factor. The farther away a vampire is, the less the pull of compulsion is, but it will still grow in intensity until it becomes overwhelming. Aden can go quite a while. The girls become desperate long before he senses even a twinge. And he'll feed from them when it does, and it satisfies the compulsion until the next time it becomes too much. But eventually, it has to end. It's impossible to tolerate that level of desperation and pain for long before it becomes unbearable. Most of the girls beg for it by the end."

Ellie swallowed. "It's only Aden who has this problem because he's always shared blood and sex?"

"No, he's not the only one, but most civilized vampires don't mix the two. Blood sharing during sex is a practice reserved for mates and pets."

"So he doesn't have to have sex with them to satisfy the compulsion?" Though Aden already told her and she believed him, she needed additional confirmation.

"Technically, no," Sophie said carefully. "Just drinking helps ease it, but it's not the same. That's why he gets very edgy sometimes. It requires more blood to satisfy a vampire's hunger when not fulfilling the compulsion with sex."

"If he was drinking my blood, how would that affect the compulsion with his thralls?"

"If you and Aden were sharing blood, because you're his mate and the only one he's intimate with, the sex aspect of the compulsion would transfer to you." Sophie's words shouldn't have relieved her, but they did. "He would still feel a pull to drink from them, and if he didn't, it would eventually become uncomfortable. However, it would eliminate the compulsion for sex. For him. But it doesn't eliminate the compulsion on the human's side."

"So unless he drinks from me during sex, there's no compulsion between us?"

Sophie shook her head. "No. If you ever let him drink from you, it will start. And if he turns you into a half-breed and you drink from him, it will increase tenfold. It's why there are very few vampire-half-breed couples. The half-breed usually gets turned because the intensity of mutual blood sharing takes it to another level. There have been many times over the years that Aurick almost turned me."

"Is not fulfilling it really that painful?"

"When it's not fulfilled, it's agonizing. But, Ellie, we don't allow indiscriminate euthanasia of humans here. Aurick is very strict about that."

"Unless it comes to cleaning up after his son?"

"We've never condoned Aden's behavior, but what would you have us do?"

"How many of them have there been?"

"Ellie—" Sophie began.

"Please tell me how many. I need to know. Hundreds? Thousands?"

"He told me to be honest with you, but I'm having a hard time not feeling like I'm betraying my son."

"Please."

"Over the course of his life, there have been over eighty thousand."

Ellie felt lightheaded, and she choked over her next words. "And now?"

"There are about two thousand girls right now."

"Oh, my god." Ellie jerked as far from Sophie as she could before she heaved and vomited onto the concrete beside her.

"I want all of them gone!"

Aden's raised voice drifted out the open door of Sophie's office as Ellie turned the corner the next evening. She hadn't seen Aden since yesterday, avoiding him since her talk with Sophie.

"Aden, you can't be serious." Sophie's gasp was barely a whisper, but Ellie heard it as clearly as if she'd yelled.

"I don't want Ellie to have to be reminded of their existence."

Ellie pressed herself against the wall, holding her breath, hoping that Aden wouldn't detect the slightest trace of her scent or the sound of her heartbeat. He'd sense her presence soon enough, but she wanted to know where the conversation was going before she interrupted.

"What do you want me to do with them?" Sophie asked.

Aden was silent. Ellie swallowed back the bile that crept into the back of her throat.

"Aden, I won't do that. How can you ask me that?"

"Then send them all away."

Instant relief washed over Ellie, flooding her body and leaving her feeling so weak that she could barely stand.

"Send them to the other cities. I never go there. I just don't want to see any of them ever again."

"Aden, be reasonable. What about the compulsion?"

"It won't bother me if they're that far away."

"But what about them? You'll be able to endure it, but they won't. I explained this all to Ellie last night, and she seemed to understand—"

"I don't care how it affects them." Aden cut her off. "All I care about is how it affects Ellie and it upsets her. She's pulling away from me, and I won't let that happen."

"But, Aden—"

Having heard enough, Ellie pushed herself away from the wall and hurried down the hallway.

Aden

Aden heard her heartbeat first, thumping in her chest, then her footsteps. Desperate to see her, he poked his head out of the office. His hesitant smile faltered when he saw the fire in her eyes. She walked into the room, shuffling around him, and exchanged a quick glance with his mother. Unable to stop himself, he reached for her, slipping his hand behind her neck and attempting to tilt her face up as he lowered his to kiss her.

Ellie jerked out of his grasp. "No!"

His eyes narrowed. "How much did you hear?"

"Enough." She crossed her arms, holding herself back from him. "You can't do this, Aden."

"I won't keep them here if it upsets you."

"This upsets me."

Sophie stood. "I'll let the two of you talk." She walked by Ellie and squeezed her hand before she shot Aden a disappointed look.

Aden stepped closer, but Ellie moved back, keeping distance between them. "Aden, I mean it. I don't want you to touch me right now."

Aden clenched his fists as both rage and panic rose in his chest. "Ellie, listen to me—"

"How can you be so cruel?"

"How am I being cruel?"

"Aden, you know what this will do to them. Even if it won't affect you as much, it will torment them."

"Fuck!" he roared and slammed his fist down on her worktable, shattering the glass top and sending everything crashing to the floor. Ellie jumped back out of the path of the flying debris.

"Fuck, I'm sorry. Did any of that hit you?"

She shook her head and walked around him to the window.

"What do you want from me, Ellie?" he asked, calmer now, as he stepped toward her. Her back was rigid, and she wrung her hands as she looked out at the setting sun. "I'll do whatever you want."

"I want you to think about how this will hurt others, Aden. Sometimes you don't care if your decisions hurt anyone else."

"I only care if my decisions hurt you."

His words might have been selfish and insensitive, but they were the truth.

"That's not enough, Aden. You need to think beyond me."

Aden shifted where he stood, aching to be closer to her. "But it disgusts you, and you can't tell me that seeing all those girls I was with doesn't bother you."

She turned to face him, her expressive green eyes almost unreadable, and that alarmed him.

"Aden, I know you have to drink blood, and I know how you used to drink it. I don't like how you used to feed. I hate it, in fact, but I accept who you are and that you need to continue to drink from all of them."

"I can start fresh with all new feeders."

"No."

He fought the urge to yank his hair out. "Why not?"

"Because you're not cruel, Aden. There was a time I believed you were, but you aren't." Ellie stepped closer to him, and his body relaxed a little. "You're callous and self-centered, and selfish."

Aden scowled. Why did everyone always say that to him?

"But you're not cruel. Not really, deep down in here." Ellie reached up and pressed her hand against his chest, over his heart. It throbbed in response. "You can't send them away without condemning them to a painful death."

She was right, and he looked away, his lips pressed into a thin line.

"You ran from me again last night."

"I needed time to think."

With a hint of trepidation, he met her eyes, hesitating before voicing the question. "What did you decide?"

"I want to be with you, Aden."

A wave of relief surged through him, easing the tension in his body. He took a chance and gripped her hips in his hands, tugging her closer. She didn't pull away this time.

"I don't like everything that comes with you. We're going to sit down and talk about that someday. But not today. And I'm sure you're not fond of everything that comes with me, either, but I know you love me. I love you, too."

Every time she said those words to him, it felt like a gift.

"But as much as I love you, I can't be with you if your first instinct to protect me is to hurt someone else."

One hand released her hip and reached up to press hers tighter to his chest. "Ellie, just tell me what you want from me. I'll do it, whatever it is."

"Drink from your thralls when they need it and when you do. You have to fulfill the compulsion. I don't want to see it." She touched his face. "But I don't want you to suffer either."

Aden let the warmth from her hand seep into him. "I only suffer when you're hurt—when I hurt you—and I can't seem to stop."

"Did you really think this would be easy for us?"

"I want it to be."

Ellie ducked her head, tilting it forward and lifting her eyes to look up at him. "Me too. But you're a vampire, and I'm a human."

Aden grasped her hand and lowered it to rest on his chest again. "What are you saying?"

"Just that we're not the same. But if this is going to work, we have to accept each other for who we are. And that's more me than you, but, let's be honest, you come with a lot of baggage." He grunted but didn't contradict her because, as usual, she was fucking right. "And I love you, baggage and all, but Aden when you hurt someone else because of me, it hurts me too."

"Fine. But you have to stop running from me, Ellie. That's your fucking baggage."

Her eyes crinkled in the corners as her lips curved upward. "Deal." She pressed against him. "Now, I missed you today, so shut up and kiss me."

Grateful and relieved, Aden did as she commanded.

Once again, Aden heard her heartbeat first. Then her scent wrapped around him before she was standing behind him. It was the first time she ventured into his studio.

It took a few days, but Ellie moved past the shock of her discovery of compulsion. True to her word, she left whenever his thralls came around for dinner. He'd done everything he could to make her feel more comfortable, even avoiding feeding in his rooms and only having his thralls brought to his office. He still wanted to start over with all new feeders, but he'd adhered to her wishes.

Regardless, he was still in the best mood he'd been in for almost three centuries, and painting had always been his sanctuary. Several weeks earlier, he removed all the portraits from his studio, and after Ellie visited his office, he removed Aly's portrait from his wall. It had taken him almost a week to accept the loss because it had been such a part of him. But he was planning to replace it with one of Ellie's as soon as he could convince her to pose for him.

"Hello, beautiful." He turned from the canvas, setting his paintbrush on the table beside his easel.

Ellie wore jeans and a blue cotton shirt that showed more of her cleavage than he thought it should, considering she just returned from being out and about the compound. But at least she wore a light sweater over it, which she removed as she walked closer. As she often wore it now, her hair was in a messy knot, with wisps falling out around her face. He preferred it down, but no matter how she wore it, she took his breath away.

Unless there were visitors in the compound, she wore regular clothing now instead of her thrall uniform. But she still kept out of sight when other vampires came around, to not raise any suspicions because of her constant proximity to Aden.

He much preferred her in normal clothes, as they showed off her curves. He most preferred her in nothing at all.

"Hi," she smiled as she tossed her sweater on the back of a chair. "I hope it's okay I came in here to see you."

"It's always okay." Aden wiped his paint-covered hands on his jeans before reaching for her.

"Don't get paint on me." Ellie held her hands up and stepped back out of his reach. "Keeley bought this outfit for me."

Aden scowled. Of course, his sister bought Ellie the revealing shirt.

"My hands are dry." He insisted as he grasped Ellie's elbow and brought her closer so he could kiss her.

"Mmmm," she murmured against his lips. "You're back early." She took his hands in hers, inspecting them to make sure they were dry.

"I left the training to Roderick because I wanted to finish this painting."

Ellie released his hands and walked around him to look at the canvas behind him. She let out a soft gasp at the sight. He'd told her he was painting a portrait of her, but this was her first time seeing it.

She was in profile. One leg was kneeling on the bed, the other foot resting on the floor. The disheveled sheets mirrored the state of her sheer robe. It was open in the front, revealing her bare skin. The material draped over one breast, contrasting with the exposed skin of the other. Her stomach curved, dipping down towards her thighs, which were parted, hinting at the secrets hidden in the shadows.

Her hair was down and tousled, loose and curling around her face as she looked down. One hand rested on the curve of her throat, and the other was on the arch of her hip, above her ass, leaving her body open. The sun from a window behind her streamed across her body, the highlights and shadows on her skin, and the bed, creating an alluring and sensual picture of a woman who had been well and thoroughly ravished. Despite not being concealed, it was the first portrait he'd ever done that didn't prominently feature her eyes.

"It looks like me."

"Yes."

"I look so beautiful," she whispered in awe.

"It's how I see you."

Ellie turned to him, her eyes glassy. Before he could ask her what was wrong, she launched herself at him, fusing her lips to his as he caught her in his arms.

"Fuck, Ellie." Aden grunted against her mouth as he stumbled backward, hitting the chair and tumbling over it before landing on his back on the floor. His body broke their fall, but she was oblivious as she sank her teeth into his bottom lip.

Aden gripped her ass and squeezed as the kiss grew more frantic. She ground against him, and he could feel the heat of her through her jeans. He was hard in an instant. With a moan, she ran her hand down, exploring the contours of his stomach. Aden tore his mouth away and reached for her fingers. As much as he wanted to do this, he would not fuck her on the cold marble floor.

"Ellie," he groaned her name again before he sat them up and tore his mouth from hers.

She sat back on his thighs, breathing heavily. Her skin was flushed, and he heard the whooshing of her blood beneath her skin as it coursed through her veins. The green of her eyes was the darkest he had ever seen.

"Wow," Ellie said breathlessly. "Where did that come from?"

Aden chuckled and urged her to rise. "Just for the record, you can do that anytime you want."

He stood and picked up the chair as she laughed with him.

"Did I hurt you?" she asked, and then snorted, obviously realizing the absurdity of her question.

He lifted her hand to his lips and kissed her fingertips. "Can I assume you like the painting?" If Aden ever needed confirmation about a painting in his life, it was now.

"Did my reaction leave any doubt?"

A surge of satisfaction filled him.

"No one else is going to see it, though, right?" She asked, walking over to the painting again. "I don't really want anyone else to see me naked."

He growled behind her as a rush of jealousy surged through him. "This painting is just for me."

She looked at him over her shoulder. "Don't you mean us?"

"No, I mean me." He didn't give a fuck if that sounded selfish, but she was gracious enough to ignore it.

"Where are you going to hang it?"

"Right above our bed."

"How is that not letting anyone else see it?"

"Ellie, we don't have visitors in our bedroom."

Her lips quirked. "The sitting room and the bedroom are the same room."

"Not once the renovations are done. Until then, we'll have to turn it around before anyone arrives and turn it back after they leave."

She laughed at him. "Now you're being ridiculous." He crossed his arms. There was nothing ridiculous about what he said, but perhaps he needed to rethink this. She patted him on the arm and turned to walk away. "I'll let you finish."

He whipped around to face her. "Where are you going?"

"To read."

"But I'm done for the night."

"Oh, okay." She turned back to face him.

"What is that supposed to mean? Doesn't it look finished to you?" His eyes darted to the canvas, analyzing each detail with a critical eye. Yeah. It was definitely done. "Well, it's finished. And I haven't seen you all night."

"Okay, I can read later. What do you want to do?"

Aden's eyes swept up and down her body as his lips curved upward. Maybe he still had more painting to do for the night.

Aden

Aden grabbed the chair and dragged it in front of the canvas, turning it sideways so it faced the table. She watched him with a curious expression on her face. His eyes roamed over her, tracing every curve, once again struck by her understated beauty. Her breath hitched, and her skin flushed under his intense gaze.

"Come here." He held out his hand.

"Why?" she asked breathlessly.

He pointed to the painting. "Because I am going to put that look on your face."

She swallowed hard and walked toward him, almost as if in a trance. Aden grabbed his paintbrush and held it up so she could see his intention. Ellie stopped in her tracks and eyed him warily.

"Uh, what are you doing?" She asked.

"I just told you what I'm gonna do."

She quirked one eyebrow. "When you said you were going to put that look on my face, I didn't think you planned to paint it on."

"I have no intention of painting your face, Ellie. The rest of your body, however, is fair game."

"And here I thought you wanted to ravage me in your studio. Color me disappointed."

"Oh, I'm going to ravage you, alright." He dipped his brush in the paint and twirled it to sharpen the tips of the bristles. "But first, I want to paint on the most exquisite canvas I've ever seen."

Realization spread across her face. "You wouldn't dare." She backed away from him. "Aden Westcott, if you even think about doing this—"

"Too late." He stalked toward her, his smile feral, as she continued to back up. "You can't run from me, Ellie."

He realized how that sounded, but he didn't care. He grabbed her wrist and yanked her against him. She expelled a sharp breath as their bodies collided. Once she was against him, he softened his grip and gazed down at her. Despite his intention, he would never force her, but he wasn't above begging.

"Please," he asked with a playful tilt of the brush in his hand, his eyes twinkling as droplets of paint splashed onto the floor.

Her face softened, and he could see the subtle surrender in her eyes. "You're going to regret it if you ruin my clothes," she warned as she pointed at him.

"Then, let's get you out of them, shall we?"

He led her over to the chair and set the brush down before turning back to her. Her eyes had darkened again, and he cradled her face in his hands. She gripped his wrists and released a low moan as his lips descended to hers, as she always did just before he kissed her. Her body swayed against him as he kissed her breathless.

He needed to slow this down. The last thing he wanted was for this to be chaotic and rushed. He wanted to savor every moment and worship her slowly.

Aden grasped the front of her shirt and tugged it out of her jeans. He broke the kiss and tugged it up over her head. When her hands were free, she started unbuttoning the front of his shirt, and he reached around and released her bra.

Ellie shook it off as Aden did the same with his shirt. He pulled her naked torso against him again, groaning at the warmth and softness of her skin.

"You feel so fucking good," he murmured, looking down at her. From the look in her eyes, he could tell that his irises were turning red. She reached up and ran her thumb across his bottom lip.

"You look hungry."

"Only for you," he assured her.

She smiled and pulled his lips down to hers. Her warm breath filled his mouth. "I love you," she whispered.

"Come," he said as he pulled his lips away, walked around, and sat on the chair, pulling her to stand in front of him. Her bare breasts teased him, and he leaned forward and brushed his nose along the inside swell and up over her nipple before he wrapped his lips around it. As her fingers found their way into his hair, she arched her back, letting her head fall back in surrender.

"Aden." His name slipped past her lips in a breathy moan.

He fucking loved her breasts. They were firm and lush. Not what one would consider well endowed, but a generous handful. They fit perfectly in his hands, as though they were custom-made for him.

He'd spent hours worshiping her breasts, exploring their softness, shape, and texture, lavishing them with his undivided attention, just as he did with every inch of her as he learned her body. After nearly three centuries of using a woman's breasts, not to give pleasure but solely as a means to feed, Aden decided they were his second favorite female body part. And Ellie's enthusiastic response to his attentions revealed she derived equal enjoyment from the time and attention he devoted to them.

Together, they had quickly learned that there was a direct connection between Ellie's nipples and her clit. Sometimes a simple touch to her nipples was all it took to ignite her like a firecracker. Aden couldn't wait for the day she'd let him sink his fangs into them.

He used his tongue to tease and flick her hardened nipple, his fingers delicately rolling the other one as her fingers tightened in his hair.

With a gentle tug, he pulled her between his legs, his lips leaving her nipple to trail down her abdomen, exploring the softness of her skin. Wasting no time, he tugged at the snap on her jeans, unzipping them and pushing them and her panties down her legs. Ellie kicked off her shoes and stepped out of her jeans, leaving her completely bare.

Damn, he loved how quickly she let him get her naked.

As his tongue swirled around her belly button, she scratched his scalp with her fingernails, eliciting a deep rumble in his chest. Aden reached between her thighs and brushed his fingertips against her. He groaned against her skin. Her arousal, warm and wet, bathed his fingers. He resisted the urge to lift her by her thighs and bring her to his mouth.

He'd yet to bury his face between her thighs, but it wasn't from a lack of wanting. Just the opposite. He didn't trust his mouth and fangs that close to her femoral artery.

Aden let his eyes sweep up the length of her body. She shivered under his heated gaze as she reached up and released her hair, letting it fall in silky waves over her shoulders.

"You're so fucking beautiful, Ellie," he breathed.

She released a soft, gentle laugh as he pulled her down to straddle his lap. "You just have to curse, don't you?"

A smirk played across his lips. She didn't like that he cursed so much, but he'd been doing it for hundreds of years. She would just have to get used to it.

He felt the heat of her through his jeans and groaned as she wriggled on his lap, grinding herself against his zipper.

"Fuck! You need to stop that or this will be over before it starts. Lean back and brace your arms on the table." He reached for his brush again. "I've got you," he murmured as she did as he asked, without question.

"This paint better come off." Her words trailed off into a moan as he began swirling the brush over the skin of her stomach.

"It's watercolor. It'll wash off," he murmured, his eyes fixated on the intricate patterns he created on her skin as he made lazy circles around her belly button. The paint dripped down her abdomen and disappeared between her thighs, pooling on his jeans beneath her. Aden licked his lips, his mouth again watering at the thought of tasting her.

Ellie's breath hitched, her eyes darkening as she watched him. A smirk curved his lip as he took his time, sweeping the bristles over her thighs, creating soft, looping shapes. He dipped the brush back into the paint and then moved up her torso, painting swirls up and over the curves of her breasts, making smaller and smaller circles until he reached her nipples.

Ellie's arms trembled on the table behind her as her thighs quivered around his. Her head dropped back in surrender, a symphony of soft moans escaping her lips, each one growing a little louder and longer with each sweep of the bristles against her skin. He brushed her hair off her shoulder, and then he painted long sweeps along her neck and clavicle. As much as he wanted her and longed to be buried inside her, he could do this all day. Venom pooled in his mouth as he watched and felt her writhe and wriggle under his touch. He wasn't lying. She truly was the most exquisite canvas he'd ever had.

"Aden, please," she begged, and he chuckled at the desperation in her voice. "I need you."

He only granted her mercy because he was as desperate for her. Tossing the paintbrush on the table, he grasped her thighs, pushing them apart before tearing the front of his jeans open.

Her eyes met his, and her yearning for him was palpable. He was one of the strongest and most disciplined vampires in the world, but her desperate pleas were too much for him to resist.

"Brace yourself on your feet," he commanded as he urged her to lift up. Her legs shook, and he kept one hand on her ass to steady her as he lifted his hips, shoving his jeans and his boxers down, getting them only halfway down his thighs before his patience gave out. He gripped her hips and pulled her down as he thrust up inside her. She cried out, the sound a sultry gasp before it morphed into a groan. Her body was ready for him, but she always groaned when he pushed inside her. Her silken flesh wrapped around him, hot and wet and tight, and he clenched his teeth to keep from erupting.

She called out his name and eagerly pressed her body against his as their lips met. The paint smeared between them as they moved in unison. Aden chanted her name softly, his voice blending with the rhythmic sounds of their bodies moving together. She panted into his mouth, and they fell into the familiar rhythm of push and pull.

The kiss deepened as he felt the hard tips of her nipples brushing against him, painting his bare chest and leaving a scorching imprint on his skin. How had he ever lived without the feel of her skin on his? His hands slid around and gripped her ass, tugging her impossibly closer. He pressed his fingers into her soft flesh as he guided her movements, their bodies moving in sync. His lips swallowed her imperceptible sobs as he pushed her to the brink of ecstasy again and again.

Aden tore his lips away with a groan. "Lay back," he urged as she panted, trying to catch her breath. He let his eyes roam over her. Paint smeared her skin, and her labored breaths caused her chest to rise and fall. He rubbed his hands over her breasts and up her neck, creating new shapes on her skin with his fingers.

"Who knew finger painting was so much fun?" He drawled with a sexy grin.

Ellie released a breathy laugh as she watched him from beneath heavy-lidded eyes. He worshiped her body with his hands, his large fingers caressing every inch of her he could reach. Her head fell back and to the side, and her eyes fluttered. She was looking at the painting beside them, and he tore his eyes from her. Although the painting was a hyper-realistic representation of her, nothing could compare to the real woman in his arms.

Ellie moaned and writhed, and he could feel she was getting close. She never lasted long, but he benefited from her body's multi-orgasmic capacity. Again, his thoughts drifted to his anticipation of biting her and what would happen when his venom ratcheted her ecstasy into the stratosphere. He hoped they'd both survive it.

He thrust his hips in a slow, steady rhythm, enjoying the sight and feel of her as she met each of his thrusts with enthusiasm. Her eyes held him captive and the desire and love he saw there stole his breath.

"Fuck, Ellie," he groaned as he watched her. She was stunning in her abandon, moving with a grace and confidence that was impossible to look away from.

He reached between them and rubbed her clit, manipulating the little bud, knowing exactly how to drive her wild. Her body bucked and her shaky breath quickened.

Much too soon, her back arched, and she cried out, her orgasm slamming into her. Her thighs trembled around him as her body jerked. He felt her clamp down on him, and he grunted as the tight, pulsing sensation tore his orgasm from him before he could stop it. He pulled her up against his chest, and she embraced him as her body continued to convulse.

Aden captured her lips, kissing her long and soft and deep before burying his face in the curve of her throat.

"Goddess."

Aden

"Why are you out here?" Aden asked when he found Ellie sitting on the balcony in a pair of pajama pants and a tank top. The sun was rising, and the dome was almost closed.

They showered after their painting escapade in his studio. The messy affair left them both covered in paint, but it was well worth it. While most of it came off their skin, they couldn't get all of it out of their hair. Only the ends of Ellie's hair were affected, so she trimmed them after she got out of the shower. She offered to cut the paint out of his hair too, but as short as it was, it would have likely left him with bald spots. So he decided, fuck it. He'd wear it like a badge of honor and just let someone fucking ask him about it.

"Hi." She looked up from her spot on the sofa, her lips spreading into a smile. The hologram she was looking at disappeared. "I wanted to get some fresh air before the dome closed."

Aden dropped onto the sofa beside her. "Aren't you cold?"

"The weather hasn't turned too cool yet."

"What were you doing?"

"Reading a book Keeley recommended."

He gave her a sour look. "It isn't one of those stupid romance novels of hers, is it?"

She arched one eyebrow at him. "You think romance is stupid?"

He had the decency to look sheepish. "I walked right into that one, didn't I?"

"Yup." She reached over and picked at the paint in his hair.

"What were you reading?"

Her eyes lit up at his question. "A book on regenerative and stem cell biology."

"Come again?"

Ellie turned to look at him. "Keeley recommended a list of science books a few weeks ago. I'm almost done with the last one."

"What would possess you to want to read those?"

"Aden, it's fascinating. I haven't been able to put them down. I had no idea something like this existed."

The excitement in her eyes and voice brought a smile to his face. It reminded him of Keeley when she first discovered her love for science. But it always made his eyes cross, even after his last visit with Hannah.

"And that really doesn't bore you to tears?" He asked, his tone oozing with skepticism.

"No." She grasped the front of his t-shirt and tucked in closer to him. "Aden, I never considered who created BloodStone, or what led to its discovery, or how it works to replenish human blood," she said. "I mean, I know it only exists so vampires can continuously feed on humans, which kind of sucks, but the fact it exists at all is only because of science. She told me more about AEON. Who would have imagined they could create a drug that eliminates the need for vampires to sustain half-breeds?"

As she rattled on, he couldn't help the indulgent smile that tugged at his lips at her enthusiasm.

"Does that mean it's possible to create an alternative to human blood for vampires?"

Keeley hadn't told her about ICHOR, but he wasn't at all surprised that her brain had already thought of it. Of course, his super-intelligent goddess would find her way there.

"Keeley told me when I'm done with these books, she has a whole other list, but she needs to check with your dad before adding them to my tablet."

"It seems like all you do is read."

"I love to read. There are so many things I don't know, and I feel like my world is being opened up." She shrugged. "Besides, it's better than not having anything to do."

Aden reached up and brushed a lock of wet hair behind her ear. "Are you getting stir crazy, always being stuck inside?"

"I've always lived that way. I don't know anything different."

"Would you like to get out of the city for a while?"

Ellie's eyes lit up again. "And go where?"

"I have to check on a few of the outlying villages in the east."

"What are you checking on?"

"Just doing the recurrent evaluation, making sure there are no issues. All our villages are on a rotational schedule. Aurick handled it personally, but when he decided it was my time to take the reins, I passed it off to my generals. Drake used to handle these kinds of visits, but since he has new responsibilities..." Aden trailed off at her narrow look. "Anyway, there are five villages to eval, so I'll be gone for almost a week. That's too long to be away from you."

Ellie tilted her head, and his gaze followed the curve of her neck. The sight of the long column of unblemished flesh, except for his bite mark, always made him want to bury his face there.

"What are your country thralls like?"

He lifted his eyes back to her face. "What do you mean?"

"All the country thralls who came into Master Matthais' city were starving. Their clothes were always dirty and ripped, and they never had coats to protect them against the cold."

"Ellie, we don't starve our thralls. You know we don't treat our thralls the way Matthais does."

"I know." She bit her bottom lip and looked up before she met his eyes again. "Except for the two times you took me out, in the snow and to the beach, I haven't been out of a domed city since I was five. I'm a little hesitant about what it's going to be like."

Aden brushed his fingertip over the shell of her ear, and she shivered. "What was the village you lived in like?"

"It was nice, I guess. I don't remember being hungry or dirty or cold. At least until the night Master Matthais took us."

"Your father must be an anomaly. It's rare for humans to grow to a size suitable for a guard. And most are sired before they have families."

"Yeah," Ellie said, her expression suddenly haunted.

"What is it?"

She shook her head and averted her eyes. The sadness that filled them made his chest constrict. He gently tilted her chin back to face him, his voice firm as he demanded, "Tell me."

"I just miss him and worry about him. And my best friend, Carrie."

"He's an elite guard. They're the most powerful of all the security teams. You don't have to worry about him."

"Master Matthais used to use me as leverage to keep him in line. Now that I'm not there, I worry..."

She didn't finish her sentence, but Aden could see the turmoil reflected in her eyes.

"I'm sure he's fine," he said, attempting to comfort her, but reassurance didn't come naturally to him.

So he redirected the conversation back to their upcoming trip.

"Well, our villages are primitive, but they're safe, and all our thralls have adequate shelter and resources. You'll see."

She nodded, and he thought he saw a glimpse of relief in her eyes at the change of subject.

"So, you'll come with me?" Aden tugged her closer and brushed his nose over her bare shoulder.

"Do I have a choice?"

"Not really," he murmured as he gave into temptation and pressed a kiss to her throat.

She grabbed his head and pushed it away from her. "Then why bother asking me?"

"It seemed like the polite thing to do." He moved to kiss her neck again, but she leaned back, out of his reach. He growled under his breath and looked back up at her.

"When do we leave?"

"Tomorrow night."

"Where will we stay during the day?"

"All our villages have a home for our use when we're there."

"So when you're not doing your evaluation, we'll be in your houses?"

"When we're not traveling, yes." He nudged her tank top strap off her shoulder. "What ever will we do with all that time?"

"You're insatiable." Her eyes crinkled as she smiled.

Aden grinned. "Have I told you I changed my mind, and I'm glad you read the dictionary?"

She wriggled away from him, and he growled. "Don't tease me, Ellie."

She laughed, and the soft tinkle made him smile as she stood and pulled him off the sofa. "Come. I'm hungry."

"Are you kidding me?" He scowled this time.

"And so are you. I can tell because you're getting cranky."

"Ellie, I'm not hungry for blood."

"But you need it." She tugged him forward and led him back into his room. He followed, grumbling under his breath.

She released his hand. "I'm going to the kitchen. I'll be back in a little while."

He reached out and tucked his fingertip underneath the strap of her tank top. "No."

She looked back at him, and her breath hitched before she swallowed. "I guess food can wait."

"Sophie, I will not yield on this!"

Aden exploded as he stared down at his mother in his parent's living room.

"Aden, your mom is right," Ellie said from where she sat next to Sophie, presenting a united front against his tantrum.

"I can't believe you're going along with this," he snarled, his eyes blazing.

"Aden, following protocol makes sense," Ellie said. "We shouldn't draw any attention to me."

"How the fuck is wearing a different color uniform not drawing attention to you?"

"Aden, pets don't wear the same color as the other thralls," Sophie said.

"Ellie is not a pet!" Aden stomped over to the bar to pour himself a drink. Too fucking bad she didn't like the taste of whiskey.

"As far as the rest of the world knows, I am," Ellie said in the calm, even tone she'd learned soothed him. But Aden was having none of it as he gulped down the strong liquid.

"Your scent is obvious on her now that you're intimate," Sophie said.

"I'm not discussing this with you," he cut her off.

"You're carrying more of her scent, too. The village stewards will notice her on you."

"Half-breed's sense of smell isn't that sensitive."

"Wanna bet?"

Ellie stood up and walked over to him. "Aden—"

"What?" he snarled again as he spun around to face her. "Should I put you on a fucking leash, too? If we're going to do this, Ellie, we might as well go all out. Why don't I drag you around on a leash and make you kneel in front of me for all to see, too?"

"Are you done?" she asked, crossing her arms.

"Not even close," he spat. She didn't cower from him anymore, and while that made him happy, at times it was inconvenient. Like now, when he wanted his way.

"Aden, keeping the reality of our relationship a secret is the only thing that can protect me."

Of course she would use his obsession with keeping her safe against him.

"Everyone believed you took me as a pet when you brought me here, so this will just confirm it."

"I said no," Aden roared as Keeley walked around the corner.

"What the heck is going on in here? Even with the soundproof walls, I could hear you in the courtyard."

"We're talking about Ellie wearing a pet uniform on their trip," Sophie said.

"Oh." Keeley looked between Aden and his mother and then to Ellie. "That's a bad idea."

"Exactly!" Aden loved his sister so much in that moment.

"You really don't want to single her out like that, do you?" Keeley looked at him for confirmation, and he shook his head.

"His scent is obvious on her now, Keeley. There's no hiding it."

With a dismissive wave of her hand, Keeley took a seat. "They've only been having sex for what, two months? His scent is not that heavy on her yet."

"Is it really that noticeable?" Ellie asked. "What do I smell like?"

"Aden," both Keeley and Sophie said before Sophie continued. "It's not bad, Ellie, but vampires and half-breeds have more sensitive olfactory senses."

"That means Drake and Kane can smell me?" She asked, horrified. "If I shower more, will it help?"

"Nope," Keeley quipped, and Aden thought she was enjoying this a little too much. "It's not only on your skin. His scent is in all your cells now. But not as much as it will be when you let him—"

Aden's lips twisted into a snarl. "Shut the fuck up, Keeley!" He didn't want his sister to bring up blood sharing and compulsion. Ellie was just getting over it.

"Aden," Sophie said. "It's not only your scent on her. It's her scent on you, too. Before, it was obvious you were having sex with all your thralls. Now, it's obvious you're intimate only with Ellie."

"I said no," Aden barked as Ellie and Sophie exchanged a frustrated look. "I'm not drinking from her, so it's not that strong."

"Why is there a separate uniform, anyway?" Keeley asked, looking at Sophie. "It's like the Scarlet Letter. Why do we even do that here?"

"Technically, it's the law," Sophie answered as Aurick walked around the corner and into the living room.

"I would say what a delightful surprise it is to have my family here when I come home," he said, glancing around warily. "But I'm not sure delightful is how I would describe this room."

"We're talking about Aden and Ellie's sex lives," Keeley said with a grin that Aden thought was far too gleeful.

"Oh." Aurick looked visibly disturbed, his brows furrowing and his lips pressing tightly together.

The twin look of mortification that twisted Ellie's face at the mention of their sex life to Aurick would have been comical under any other circumstances. It served her right—for breaking ranks with him. But Aden would protect her. Even from his own family.

"This conversation is fucking over."

"Ellie agrees she should wear the pet uniform on the trip, and Aden is not on board," Sophie said to Aurick as he came to sit beside her.

"Why can't she just wear a collar?" Keeley asked.

"Oh, that could work," Sophie said as she sat forward.

"What the fuck, Sophie?" Aden hissed as he glowered at her.

"I don't mean a real collar. She can borrow one of my necklaces with the family crest. As long as she has something with the family crest around her neck, the stewards and guards won't give her a second look. They'll just assume it's a collar."

"She'll still have to wear proper colors," his father said. "Matthais wants pets clearly identified."

"Ellie is not a fucking pet!" Aden felt like his head was about to explode.

"It's probably the safest idea, even though there won't be any other vampires present." Aurick ignored Aden's outburst. "But it's the first time you are leaving the city together, and the stewards are going to know as soon as they smell her."

"Who the fuck cares? Our half-breeds are loyal to us."

"Yes, but that doesn't mean they don't talk," Aurick said. "It's human nature. And when there's talk, it can spread like wildfire."

"Yes, I'm well aware that thralls' gossip." Aden's words were tinged with distaste. "And I've made sure they pay the price when they do."

"What is that supposed to mean?" Keeley asked.

"Nothing."

"Are you talking about that thrall you had me send away?" Sophie asked. "What was her name, Janessa?"

"You sent Janessa away?" Ellie looked over at him, surprised. "Is that why she's not here anymore?"

"Yes, I sent that bitchy girl away. She was mean to you, spreading rumors I abused you at the beach house."

Keeley exchanged glances with their parents as Ellie's eyes widened.

"I told her that wasn't true and to stop spreading lies. I took care of it. You didn't have to send her away. Wait a minute. How did you know that? You were at the summer games when that happened."

"I saw it on the hologram," Aden replied before he realized the implication of his answer.

"You were watching me on the hologram?" The edge to Ellie's voice set off warning bells, but before Aden could deflect her ire, Keeley interrupted as she sat forward in her chair.

"Whoa! Whoa! Whoa! Just whoa! Back it up a minute. Let me make sure I've got this right." She looked at Ellie. "So this thrall, Janessa, was going around saying Aden abused you so badly he knocked you out." She turned to look at Aden. "And you heard this because you were spying on her through a hologram. Creep!" Keeley shot him a glare before looking back at Ellie and continuing. "And you told her off and to stop telling lies about big, bad Aden." And back to Aden. "And then when you got back, you had her banished to the boonies because she was mean to your girlfriend, who, by the way, wasn't your girlfriend yet."

"She wasn't banished, Keeley," Sophie said. "She was returned to the village where she was born."

Keeley sat back with a chuckle. "If this wasn't so twisted, I might just actually admire how protective the two of you were of each other before you even got together."

"I wasn't spying on her!"

"What you did is the exact definition of spying," Keeley shot back.

It's a good thing none of them, especially Ellie, knew how often he checked on her via hologram.

"For fuck's sake, Keeley. She'd just had a seizure. Sophie took her away from me, and she didn't want to see me. I was fucking worried, okay."

"Aden." Ellie's voice was quiet as she said his name to get his attention.

"What?" he snapped, turning his anger on her again.

"You and I are going to talk about this when we're alone later, but in the meantime, I've made my decision."

"Ellie." He exhaled a harsh breath, and she shook her head.

"If you want me to go with you, I'm wearing the uniform." He ground his teeth tighter with each word. "But—" Her lips quirked, and he knew she was trying to soften him. "I'll agree. No leash. We can skip that one if that's okay."

"What's this about a leash?" Keeley asked no one in particular.

The fight drained out of Aden. "You won't give in to me on this, will you?"

"No." Ellie stood her ground, and, as aggravated as he was, he couldn't have been prouder of her resolve.

"Fine," he snarled once again, ensuring his tone communicated his displeasure.

"Thank you," Ellie said as she tilted her face up and kissed the corner of his mouth.

"Wow! Did you guys see that?" He heard Keeley's teasing voice. "She's the Aden whisperer."

Ellie

"Keeley, wait up," Ellie called after Aden's sister as she exited their parent's suite and headed down the corridor toward the courtyard.

Keeley slowed as Ellie caught up to her. "Where's Mr. Cranky Pants?"

"He and your dad had a few things to go over for the trip. Do you have a minute for me to ask you a couple of questions?"

Keeley looked over at her. "Sure, but you have to walk with me. I'm already late, and Ryan is going to be Mr. Cranky Pants number two if we don't get out of here on time. We're meeting friends at Club V."

"That's the club downtown you used to go to all the time, right? The place where vampires can bring humans?"

"Yeah. It's probably the last time we'll be able to go before the baby's born. It's too bad you and Aden can't come with us."

Ellie's lips twitched. "Aden isn't really the dance club type."

Keeley let out a laugh that was far from ladylike. "No. But I bet you would be if I got a little alcohol in you. It would be so worth it to see how awkward and uncomfortable Aden would be, just to make you happy."

"Keeley, it isn't very nice to torment him."

But what was nice was how comfortable Ellie felt with Keeley now. Now that she remembered how much like a sister, Keeley was to her in her last life. She'd been an only child in that life, too. In this one, at least she'd had Carrie. For a little while.

Keeley reached around Ellie's neck and pulled her closer as they walked. "It's so weird to say this, but I missed you."

"I know. Me too."

"Though your tendency to always defend my baby brother can be annoying."

"Says his indulgent, overprotective older sister."

Keeley hip-checked Ellie as she released her. "Touché. So what do you want to ask?"

"I want to know more about what makes pets so different from what Aden did with all his thralls."

A sour look crossed Keeley's face. "Your insatiable curiosity was always a little creepy."

Her curiosity, it seemed, was deeply rooted in her soul and followed her from one life to another.

"I know what a pet is. I didn't live under a rock in either of my lives, but I don't understand why it is so much stronger on me than all the other thralls he had sex with."

"Aden had sex with a lot of girls."

Ellie gave Keeley a withering look. "Yes, I know."

"So he spread his scent around a lot," Keeley said as they crossed the courtyard to Keeley and Ryan's wing. "Now you're the only one who carries his scent like that. It's not as big a deal as my parents made it out to be. Vampires are used to humans always smelling like them, but when one human carries such a concentrated scent, it's noticeable. That's the way it is with pets. Most vampires don't feed on their pets. Yeah, they bite them to increase arousal, but they don't feed on them as much, so they're not pumping a ton of venom into them."

"Okay. But that's my point. He doesn't bite me or drink from me. We're only having sex."

"But you let him violate you six ways to Sunday, every freaking day, Ellie."

Ellie crossed her arms. "Not every day." At Keeley's skeptical look, she conceded. "Okay, most days, but I'm still human with normal female bodily functions, so there are certain days of the month we don't."

"Good thing vampires are sterile unless they take LIBER. Otherwise, you'd already be knocked up by now, considering how often you let my brother defile you."

As more of Ellie's memories returned, she recalled Aden telling her that male vampires could only impregnate half-breed females by taking LIBER, a drug developed as part of the vampire procreation program. The drug made vampire sperm viable, but the law only allowed half-breeds to conceive because humans couldn't survive carrying or giving birth to vampire offspring.

"Can we get back on topic, please?" Ellie asked as they entered Keeley's suite. The sounds of soft music playing in the living area greeted them. "I could understand if Aden was drinking from me. But isn't my scent less than the thralls he drank from and had sex with?"

"No." Keeley shook her head. "Under normal circumstances, you'd be right. But you have to remember, he bit you, and you drank his blood. That makes the scent more potent. And yeah, you're only having sex, but there's venom in his semen, and he's pumping that into your body every time you let him come inside you."

"What the—" Ryan stopped in his tracks and slapped his hands over his ears as he walked out of the bedroom. "Why is this conversation taking place when I am anywhere within earshot?"

Ellie felt heat rush to her face, and Keeley laughed at both her and Ryan's matching horrified looks.

"She's the one who started it. And, before you say anything else, I know. I'll be ready in ten minutes." She looked over at Ellie. "If you want to finish this, you're gonna have to come with me so I can change."

Ellie followed Keeley into the bedroom. She sat on the bed as Keeley walked into the closet. She ran her hands over the duvet as she looked around the room. It was no surprise that the color purple was everywhere—from the duvet to the pillows, to the abstract artwork on the walls.

"So, what you're telling me is that his venom has overwhelmed my entire body because we have sex?"

"Not overwhelmed yet, but it's pretty strong." Keeley's voice was muffled as she changed. "Like I said, I think my parents are overreacting. It's only the half-breed stewards and guards at the villages you'll see on this trip. Now, if you were going to be around other vampires, I'd say, hell yes, you need to wear teal."

Keeley poked her head out of the closet. "And when you let Aden bite you, you'll have to wear it anytime other vampires are around because it will be more than obvious."

"After what happened, I don't know if I want him to bite me, Keeley."

Keeley's lips curved into a sultry smile. "Oh, you will. Trust me. It's inevitable when you're mated with a vampire. Sex is so much better with a little biting."

"For the love of God, I can still hear you," Ryan yelled from the other room.

Keeley snorted, and Ellie shook her head and let out an uncomfortable chuckle.

"It'll be different this time. He knows how to control it now."

"Is that why Aden snapped at you to stop talking earlier?"

"Yeah," Keeley said as she ducked back into the closet. "That, and because any discussion of him biting you would automatically turn to the topic of compulsion. Considering your last reaction, he probably thought you'd bolt for the nearest city gate."

"I only did that once." Ellie sounded petulant as Keeley's laugh floated out of the closet.

"I hear it would have been twice if Drake hadn't caught you. Anyway, Aden's over-protectiveness is kind of cute, but I hope you're gonna give him hell about spying on you. It's one thing for him to check up on you or try to find out where you are, but watching and listening to you is just being an invasive, creepy stalker."

"Keeley, I'm under no illusions that was the only time he's done it, but he's going to stop now if I have anything to say about it."

Keeley hopped back into the room as she slipped on her heels, and Ellie slipped off the bed as Keeley headed into her bathroom.

"I'll get out of your way. Thanks for explaining that. Have fun tonight."

"Give him hell," Keeley called after her. "Withhold sex. That will get him to do anything."

Ellie walked out of the bedroom, and Aden was there, talking to Ryan, his eyes fixed on the doorway as she joined them.

"You better not have been listening."

His guilty expression gave him away. She grabbed him by the front of his shirt and tugged him toward the door. "You and I need to talk. Night, Ryan."

"Bye, Ellie."

As they exited the room, Ellie heard Ryan say, "I think your brother's in trouble."

Ellie followed Aden to the transport vehicle.

"Watch your step." He motioned with his hand to the shallow hole in the street in front of them. Ellie sidestepped the hole as Aden turned to Kane. "Tell Tobias that if he doesn't repair those holes by tomorrow, I will bury him in them."

"It's being handled as soon as the sun rises."

"Make sure it fucking happens."

Ellie climbed into the backseat, and Aden settled in beside her. "One more village, and then we can go home."

Ellie sighed. "Yeah."

"You don't sound like you want to go back," Aden asked with a frown as the vehicle lifted off the ground, settling at its normal hover height before speeding away.

"There's something about being outside in the open air. I guess because I was born in a village." Ellie fiddled with Aden's fingers. "And I enjoy being in the sun for a little while every day."

"After we get back and I give Aurick the eval reports, why don't we go to the beach house again? Just the two of us this time."

She quirked an eyebrow.

"Okay, it didn't go so well last time. Do over?" He grinned, his sexy, boyish smile making her laugh, and she was glad he wasn't still brooding over what happened there.

"Will you let me on the deck by myself this time?"

"Maybe, but I'm not making any promises."

"Aden," she warned in a low tone.

"Ellie," he mimicked, and she scowled until he leaned down and brushed his nose against the skin of her neck. She pinched him gently, and he grunted, trying to get his hands under her top. "You smell so good."

"Not according to everyone else."

He lifted his head. "They never said you smelled bad. Just that you smell like me. Don't you like how I smell?"

"Mmmm... most of the time. At least you smell like me too." She nuzzled his cheek.

"Yes," he growled as he buried his face in her neck again.

"That doesn't bother you?"

"Fuck no."

"Really?" she asked, delighted.

He raised his head again. "Yes. It's not as strong as mine on you, but anyone who knows you will recognize it. And it will get stronger the longer we're together and if I ever drink from you again."

It surprised her that he brought it up. They hadn't talked about it, even after her chat with Keeley, but it was always there under the surface. He vowed to never drink from her again without her permission. She believed him, but she knew he struggled with it because she often felt him grinding his teeth when they were intimate.

"You really want to drink from me, don't you?"

"Yes," he said after a brief pause, and she loved him for his honesty.

"How is the sex different? I mean, I remember what it felt like that night, but it's hard to separate those feelings from what happened after." His lips turned into a frown as his eyes darkened. She cupped his cheek and tilted his face to look at her. "Hey, we have to talk about this if we're ever going to try it again. So what's so different about the sex?"

His intense gaze softened like he was assessing whether to be honest.

"Being inside you is like nothing I can describe. The feel of you is the closest thing to perfection I could imagine."

Ellie felt her body respond to his words, and she inhaled a shallow breath.

"But drinking blood during sex is more intense. The taste of blood and the sensation of my body absorbing it make everything more pleasurable. And the feeling of my venom in your bloodstream would increase your arousal and make your orgasms ten times more intense."

"I don't think my body can take any more pleasure." She smiled to let him know she was teasing.

"Oh, it definitely can," he said, the naughty twinkle in his eyes fading as he furrowed his brow.

She brushed her fingertips between his brows. "Aden, I'm not afraid of what happened before. I know you can control it now, and I want to share every part of me with you, but—" She wasn't sure how to explain her hesitation.

"Ellie, I told you, only if you want it. I want it, but I don't need it. And I swear on my life, I won't hurt you again. But there's no going back, so you have to be absolutely sure."

"Can I think about it?"

"As long as you want."

"Thank you." Ellie fluttered her fingers over his lips before kissing him. When their lips parted, he pressed his face against her neck again and resumed his attempts to get under her shirt.

"So are you satisfied that the humans in our villages aren't being mistreated?" He scowled at her buttons. "I told you they had enough food and shelter and weren't afraid of the guards."

Ellie laughed at his attempt before helping him. "Yes, but all of them seem terrified of you." He grunted. "It's obvious the well-being of your humans is important, but why are they only allowed five hours of electricity a night?"

With her shirt now fully open, Aden pushed it off her shoulder and leaned down to bury his face between her breasts. "Why would they need more than that? They sleep at night." His voice was muffled against her skin.

"They've all been awake at night this week." Ellie sighed and gently scratched his scalp the way he liked.

"That's because of the evals." Aden traced his tongue along the swell of her breast. "Normally, they're on opposite schedules as vampires. They work during the day and sleep at night. Now, will you shut up and let me concentrate?"

Ellie pushed his head away and sat up, pulling her shirt closed. He tried to kiss her, but she leaned away. "Still, it doesn't seem fair. It's not like electricity is scarce."

"The solar panels only have so many hours of battery life this time of year. You're ruining the mood."

Before she had time to respond, they arrived at the last village. Aden growled in disappointment as Ellie set her shirt to rights. The sun hovered below the horizon, ready to burst free for the day. Villagers filled the lit center square, awaiting Aden's arrival. The village looked identical to the last one, but that was intentional. Each of the Westcott's villages had an identical footprint and design.

Ellie and Aden exited the car, and the villagers greeted them with cheers, like in all the other villages. The three vehicles behind them came to a stop, and Kane, Drake, and the rest of Aden's guards poured out of one while Aden's thralls exited the others.

Ellie stood behind and to the right of Aden, her eyes lowered. Kane flanked his right, and Drake stood beside her left. To anyone who didn't know better, it looked like Aden had two personal guards.

The half-breed village steward, a tall, burly man with gray hair and beard, walked over to greet Aden. "Master Aden, welcome. We are so honored for you to visit us."

"Malachai, I'm in no mood for niceties. I expect you to be waiting for me the moment the sun sets. I will give you two hours to show me you deserve this position. Otherwise, I will have you replaced. Is that understood?"

Ellie's lips quirked. Aden had spoken to each steward the same way, and like the previous ones, this one sputtered obediently.

"Of course, Master Aden. I'm confident that the condition of the village will please you."

Aden turned to walk into the villa without so much as a farewell. Ellie followed behind him. Several male and female thralls were waiting in the foyer for them.

"Get out," Aden barked, and they scurried away like the rats Ellie used to see in the lower levels of Master Matthais' city. He enjoyed making his thralls nervous too much sometimes.

As soon as the door closed behind them, Aden turned to her, his mouth descending on hers as he backed her up against the polished wood. He reached down and grasped her thighs, lifting her and wrapping her legs around him.

Aden did this at all the other villages, too. They always arrived before sunrise, and he knew she would want to go out into the sun for a short time before she settled down for the day to sleep. He hated letting her go, but he didn't stop her. And she loved him for it. But he had to have her first.

So once again, Ellie moaned into his mouth as he pulled away from the wall and carried her down the hallway to his bedroom.

Ellie

It took Ellie four hours before she made it outside, with Drake at her side and two other guards walking a short distance behind them. She strolled around the large lake behind the villa, enjoying the crisp air.

The weather had turned cooler, so she dressed in jeans and a teal sweater similar to the green one Aden gave her the night he took her in the snow. Over it, she wore a teal jacket, leaving no doubt that she was Aden's pet.

All the villagers, both human and half-breed, were sleeping or sent to the opposite end of the village by Drake. Despite the chilly weather, the warmth of the sunshine on her face felt glorious and made her wish she never had to go back inside.

The grass was turning brown. Leaves crunched under her feet and created a colorful blanket around the base of the trees. The few remaining leaves on the bare branches were crimson, gold, and amber. Now and then, she came across a scattered patch of snow, remnants of recent light snowfall.

Drake strolled beside her, measuring his steps to match her slower pace. Their relationship had developed a somewhat hesitant yet comfortable rapport as they both realized the other wasn't so bad. Guarding her was not what either of them wanted, but Ellie knew he would protect her with his life. There was a noticeable shift in his attitude, and she mirrored his change by softening her own grumpiness. So their once contentious relationship had thawed a little, characterized by gentle teasing and a growing sense of trust.

The winding path around the lake was lined with boulders large enough to sit on, their weathered surfaces offering a comfortable spot to take a break. A few scattered ice patches floated on the water, suggesting the imminent arrival of winter. But despite the chill and the signs of impending winter, the lake remained unfrozen, its rippling waters responding to the occasional breeze that rustled through the trees.

It was peaceful, and Ellie let her mind wander. Until, as he had three times already, Aden appeared in a hologram in front of Drake.

"Where are you?"

"Two clicks from the villa."

Ellie wasn't sure what a "click" was, but Aden seemed pacified by his response. "Aden, will you please stop?"

The hologram appeared in front of her.

"When are you coming back?"

"We're only halfway around the lake. Now stop calling. I'll be back when I'm back." She swiped the hologram closed and pulled a face as she looked over at Drake. "I probably shouldn't have done that."

Drake murmured his agreement through a short laugh. "No one has ever done that to him and lived."

He checked on her because he was terrified that something might happen to her. Aden was fierce and fearless in every aspect of his life, except her. He'd gone almost three hundred years thinking he lost her forever, and as much as she wanted to tell him to chill out, she had to let him work through the need to smother her. But if he didn't do it quickly, she was going to lose her mind.

Ellie stopped and sat on a boulder. Resting on her hands, she leaned back and tilted her head, letting the sun warm her face before looking out over the lake again.

"This place is so pretty."

"I guess," Drake said.

"It seems so familiar."

"It looks like the last one."

"I know all the village streets and neighborhoods look the same, but I can't explain it. Maybe everything is just blurring together for me."

Aden's face appeared again. "Why are you sitting? Are you tired? Drake will bring you back—"

She threw her arms up in the air in frustration. "Aden, stop. I wanted to sit for a minute. Drake is not bringing me back."

Aden scowled. "You've been gone for a half hour already."

"I told you, we're not even halfway around the lake. Why don't you take time while I'm gone to feed?" She suggested as she leaned over to pick up a rock.

"I already did."

"Did you feed enough?" She worried that since he now only fed from his thrall's wrists, he wasn't getting enough.

"Will you stop obsessing over my diet?" He threw her words back at her.

Ellie's lips curved upward, and she felt a sudden rush of love for him. She wished he could be out here with her.

"Aden, I know you have plenty to do. You're neglecting it because you're obsessing over me. Now let me finish my walk, and I'll see you in a little while. And stop calling Drake every five minutes."

Aden grunted before his face disappeared.

"I can't believe he lets you talk to him that way."

With a flick of her wrist, Ellie threw the rock in her hand over the water and watched it skim the surface. Her father had taught her how to do that when she was four, and she blinked as a sense of déjà vu came over her. She gave her head a quick shake to clear it before resuming her walk.

"I'm going to pay for it when I get back."

Ellie was sure of that. But the shiver that spread through her body at the thought wasn't one of fear.

Ellie exited the villa, behind Aden. The sun had set, and Malachai and four other half-breed guards were waiting to show them the village. Pets wouldn't go with a vampire on a tour, but Aden insisted, so she could see that the villagers were well.

"Good evening, Master Aden."

"What did I say about the niceties, Malachai? Let's get on with this."

His gruff response had the steward sputtering like he'd done earlier. "Yes, of course, Sir. Shall I have your pet escorted inside to wait for you?"

Aden clenched his teeth so loudly that Ellie was sure everyone could hear it. She shifted closer and grazed his lower back with her fingers, hoping her touch would calm him.

"No, she will accompany me on this tour."

"Yes, Sir," Malachai said before glancing at Ellie. She looked up and smiled at him.

"Oh my," he said, blinking.

"Is there a problem?" Aden growled as he stepped in front of her.

"No, Sir. No." Malachai recovered and plastered what Ellie thought was an overly fake smile on his face. "Follow me."

Aden glanced at her, and she shrugged before following behind him. The crowd parted to make way for Aden and Malachai as they entered the village square, where the residents had gathered once again. They cheered at the sight of him, but then an eerie silence overtook the crowd. Many of the older villagers stared at her with wide eyes, making her feel uneasy, and she averted her gaze.

Drake leaned toward her and whispered. "Why are they all staring at you?"

"How the heck should I know?" She said as Aden's head whipped around to look, first at her, then at the crowd.

"Send these people home," Aden barked, and Malachai instructed his guards to disperse the group. Drake moved closer, blocking her from the view of the crowd as it scattered.

Once the crowd was gone, Ellie felt less self-conscious.

She looked around at the cottages that lined the main street. Just like the other villages, it blended rustic charm with thoughtfully incorporated modern touches. The homes were modest, sturdy, and well-maintained.

Each was equipped with essential amenities, including running water and solar-powered electricity. Inside, most cottages were identical, with comfortable furniture, well-equipped kitchens, stone fireplaces, and attached greenhouses that housed thriving gardens. Once again, the Westcott's kind treatment of their thralls filled Ellie with a sense of relief and gratitude.

During the tours of the previous villages, the villagers treated her with the same respect as Aden, assuming she was his preferred pet. Their fear of him was unmistakable, and he derived entirely too much pleasure from it, in Ellie's opinion.

Aden was listening to Malachai provide his report on the status of the village. Hololamps floated around them, lighting up their way as they walked. They took a turn at the end of the street, and the cottages here appeared abandoned and dilapidated.

"Why are these cottages boarded up?" Aden asked, and Ellie shifted her eyes to where he was pointing. "This is an eyesore."

"There were problems in this part of the village seventeen years ago. The cottages were closed off to maintain their integrity and security since no one is comfortable living here anymore."

"What problems?"

"There was violence inside one of them."

Ellie couldn't take her eyes off the cottage in front of her. It held her spellbound like time had frozen in that moment. As if in a trance, she stepped off the street and approached the small building.

"Ellie?" She heard Aden's voice, but she didn't stop. "Drake, what the fuck? Go get her."

Ellie felt Drake's large hand on her elbow, attempting to stop her, but she jerked her arm out of his grasp and continued walking. He grabbed her arm again, tugging harder.

"Ow, Drake, let me go."

Aden was beside her in an instant, shoving Drake aside. He grasped her arm more gently than Drake. "Ellie, what are you doing?"

"I have to go in here."

"No, absolutely not."

"Aden, please." Ellie's chest tightened as she stared at the door, unable to look away.

"No one has been in that cottage for seventeen years, Ellie. It's probably not structurally sound."

Ellie tore her eyes away from the door and looked up at him, her eyes imploring him. His face shifted from annoyance to worry as his eyes met hers.

"You're as white as a ghost. What is it?"

"Please, Aden, I have to know."

Aden cursed under his breath. "Malachai, get the fuck over here."

Malachai rushed over. "Yes, Master Aden?"

"Is this structure sound?"

"It should be. But you don't want to go in there. No one's gone in there since that night."

Ellie swallowed back the bile in her throat. She reached for the doorknob and turned it, only to find it locked.

"Aden, please." Her eyes met his.

Malachai gasped beside them, no doubt because she had used Aden's name. Aden shoved his hand out and pushed the door off the hinges, sending it flying inside the house. Ellie stepped inside before Aden could stop her.

"Fuck!" she heard him say from behind her. "She needs a hololamp to see in there."

It was dark and dank, and a hololamp appeared next to her as she moved deeper into the cottage. Broken furniture cluttered the area, and Ellie sidestepped a large piece that looked like a wooden table as she moved to her right. She approached a splintered door, and it felt harder to breathe with each step she took.

Ellie crossed the threshold and gasped. Her world crashed down around her as she dropped to her knees next to a child's bed.

Nowhere is safe.

Not even nestled under the covers of her bed, in her tiny bedroom, in her parents' small house.

In the darkness, unable to sleep, she clung to a worn-out doll, its tattered fabric offering some solace as she sang a soft lullaby. It was because of the eyes. For as long as she could remember, Ellie had been dreaming about those eyes. They didn't frighten her, but there was something about the blue eyes that made her not want to close hers, so as usual, she lay awake, waiting for morning to come.

Ellie lifted her head off the pillow, and her eyes followed the reflection of the headlights dancing along the window before they went dark. Then the sound of multiple doors slamming outside made Ellie hold her breath. Cars didn't come into her village very often, so their arrival only meant one thing.

Vampires.

They already visited the village once this week. Why were they back?

The muted sounds of her parents' voices beyond her bedroom door faded into the background as the thumping of her small heart echoed in her ears. Trembling, Ellie grasped Gladys closer to her chest, promising to find the doll's eye tomorrow. There was a moment of strained silence before Ellie jerked at the sound of wood splintering, followed by her parents' screams. She skittered across the bed, pressing her back against the wall.

More banging and screaming echoed outside her door before it burst open, the doorknob embedding into the wall. A tall giant, who now filled her doorway, threw her mother and father to the floor beside her bed.

Ellie's mother scrambled to her and clutched her against her chest. Bruised and bloody, Ellie's father, just as tall as the giant, leaped to his feet in front of them.

Another man, this one slightly smaller and clearly a vampire, glided into the room. His pale skin and silver hair shone in the moonlight as he passed in front of the window. He looked around the small room.

"It smells like a barn in here. Lorcan, open that window."

Ellie's eyes followed the giant as he walked to the window and thrust his fist through it, shattering the glass. His skin was as dark as the night outside, and his eyes were like two full moons with blood-red rings in the center. Ellie shivered.

The vampire turned his penetrating gaze toward her, and she heard her father growl. "What do you want here?"

The vampire's eyes flashed red for a moment, then he bared his teeth.

"Show some respect, human." His arm shot forward and grabbed Ellie's father by the throat, lifting him into the air.

"What is your name?" When her father didn't answer, the vampire's fingers tightened around his neck. "I said, what is your name?"

"Myles," her father choked.

"Well, Myles, today is your lucky day," the vampire chuckled. "I'm going to give you something humans don't have anymore. A choice." Ellie continued to tremble in her mother's arms as the sound of the vampire's voice sent chills up her spine. "You can join my guard willingly, and I'll allow you to bring your family with you into my city." The vampire's eyes glowed red again, and his fangs lengthened as he yanked her father closer. "Or you join, unwillingly, after I drain them both before your eyes."

"Drinking from children is illegal." Her father gasped.

The vampire's thin lips curled into a sneer. "That's the beauty of being the man who made the law. I can break it."

"You're not a man. You're a monster."

Unaffected by her father's words, the vampire dropped him to the floor. In a move almost too fast for her young human eyes, Ellie watched as the vampire grasped her mother by the neck and jerked her off the bed, tossing Ellie to the floor. Gladys fell out of Ellie's arms.

"Mama!" Ellie's frightened scream echoed through the room as the vampire sunk his fangs into Ellie's mother's neck.

"No!" her father roared, jumping to his feet before the giant grasped him from behind and yanked his arms back so far that Ellie heard his bones break.

"No! Please!" Ellie's mother's pleading cries trailed off as the vampire drained her. He threw her limp body to the floor with a thud and licked his lips as his fangs retracted.

Before her father could react any further, the vampire reached out and grabbed Ellie off the floor, jerking her against him.

"Daddy!"

The vampire's eyes flashed red a third time as his fangs lengthened again.

"Make your choice, Myles."

"Ellie, what the fuck are you doing?" Aden burst into the room. He reached down to pull her to her feet, but she struggled, thrashing against him. "Ellie, stop! You're going to hurt yourself."

Aden released her, and Ellie dropped to her knees again, not caring about the throbbing ache in her knees as she hit the hardwood. She saw something under the bed.

"Gladys," she choked as she reached under and pulled the old, tattered doll out from beneath it. With a gentle touch, Aden grasped both her arms, lifting her to her feet. He held her steady as she swayed on her feet. He turned her to face him, his eyes searching her face.

"Ellie." She didn't look up at him. "Ellie, look at me."

When her eyes met his, she knew horror and pain reflected in them.

"Ellie, what is this place?"

Her throat tightened with agony, rendering her speechless as she looked down at the doll in her hands, tears welling up in her eyes.

"Ellie." Aden's gentle whisper shook her from her nightmare.

She raised her eyes to his as her tears escaped past her lashes and slipped down her cheeks. Her knees gave out and Aden caught her in his powerful arms as her broken words slipped past her lips.

"This was my home."

Please Leave a Review

I hope you enjoyed the beginning of Aden & Ellie's journey. There is more to come in Atonement.

Reviews are like crack to writers. It helps our books get exposure and new readers. So, if you enjoyed The BloodStone Legacy, please consider leaving an honest review on Amazon, Goodreads, BookBub, or any other platform you leave reviews.

Below are easy links for you to use:

Amazon

Goodreads

BookBub

Coming Soon - Atonement

ADEN AND ELLIE'S STORY CONTINUES
IN THE DARKLY SENSUAL BOOK TWO OF
THE BLOODSTONE LEGACY SERIES

ATONEMENT

Coming Spring 2025

Read a preview here:
https://dl.bookfunnel.com/8lps35jhr5
Pre-Order Here: https://mybook.to/90nm

For more previews, deleted scenes and goodies, sign up for my newsletter:
Sign Up Here: https://vehuntley.com
Connect with V.E:
https://www.facebook.com/v.e.huntley.author
https://www.instagram.com/vehuntley/
https://x.com/vehuntleywriter
https://www.tiktok.com/@vehuntley

About the author

V.E. Huntley is a retired producer who has spent her life telling stories in one way or another. Just ask her cats. They had to endure a lifetime of her endlessly reciting entire dialogue scenes to them, even though all they desperately wanted to do was nap.

Her childhood fear of Dracula was so intense that she couldn't sleep without the lights on and her mother guarding her bedroom door. Over time, this fear evolved into a lifelong obsession with the dark and sensual world of vampires. So, after more than two decades in the film and television industry, she finally decided to follow her heart and pursue her true passion—writing dark and sexy paranormal romance.

Besides writing, her hobbies include watching movies, reading, traveling, and keeping her husband busy with an endless honey-do list. You can find out more about V.E. on her website, www.vehuntley.com.